D1647728

PASSAGE AT DELPHI
A Novel

BOOK ONE OF THE APOLLO SERIES

BY A.K. PATCH

To Gail,

You're a great friend!

Enjoy the ride!

Best Wishes,

A.K. Patch

3/31/14

AKP Publishing

Copyright 2013 A.K. Patch

ISBN-13: 978-0615917023 (AKP Publishing)
ISBN-10: 061591702X
Digital ISBN: 978-1310443503

Visit the author at: www.akpatchauthor.com

Cover Design: Lisa Maine, GreetScape Inc., in association with Word Journeys, Inc.

Printed in the United States of America. Worldwide Electronic and Digital Rights. 1st North America, Australian and UK Print Rights.

To my wife and children—Nancy, Alexander, and Lauren.

You are my inspiration.

Acknowledgements

I am thankful for so many talented people who contributed to this novel.

Editors, consultants, and readers
Michael and Enriqueta Sullivan, Dr. Tony and Bobbie Marciante, Laura Taylor, Michael Thompkins, David and Betty Feldman, Professor Lisa Hemminger, Pat LoBrutto, Wendy Graham, Jeanette Rigopoulos, George and Mary Koulaxes. Shirley Bening, Susan Taylor, Ellen Citrano, Marsi Bowers, Linda Sommers, James and Deborah Dugan, Jean and Larry Patch, Joyce and Erica Pallasigue, Dr. Gregory Morando, Carol Tohsaku, Dr. Peter Toyias, Janice Abbasov, Diane Buska, and Joe Vecchio

Publishing professionals
Robert Yehling, Lisa Maine, Mitch Gandy and Jesse Doubek

Staff members
Patty Habercom, Indira Barragan, Cynthia Upchurch, and Jamie Garrison

The most beautiful thing we can experience is the mysterious.

It is the source of all true art and science.

— Albert Einstein

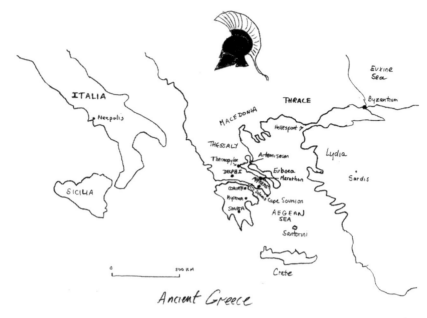

ITALIA

Neapolis

SICILIA

MACEDONIA

THRACE

Evxine
Sea

Byzantium

THESSALY

Hellespont

Lydia

Thermopylae

Artemiseum

DELPHI

Euboea

Sardis

CORINTH

Marathon

Mycenae

Cape Sounion

SPARTA

AEGEAN
SEA

Santorini

Crete

0   300 KM

Ancient Greece

DELPHI, GREECE

There were many oracles in ancient Greece but none more famous and trusted than Apollo's sanctuary high in the mountains west of Athens. For almost two thousand years, pilgrims traveled from near and far to reach Delphi, at the time considered the center of the Earth and a place of divine inspiration.

The trance-induced ranting of the Pythia, a chaste holy woman, converted into versed prophecies by temple priests, was considered to be the divine will of the god Apollo. This foretelling of the future influenced decisions of everyday life, but also the prospects of colonies and the fate of kingdoms.

Unforgettable are the simple virtues carved into the forecourt of Apollo's temple: *Know Thyself* and *Nothing In Excess*. These proverbs, so replete with human truth, demonstrate how the triumphs and tragedies of ancient peoples can serve to guide our lives in the modern day.

PART ONE

CHAPTER 1
DELPHI, GREECE
MAY 2011

FAR-SEEING

A sudden tempest arose, assaulting night-shrouded Mount Parnassus. Amid groaning rocks and searing flashes, an aperture opened on a slope below its hallowed twin peaks. An entryway lost to the ages revealed itself.

Following an effortless ascent on a long stairway, a perfect male figure emerged.

Apollo, the god of order, spiritual light, and far-seeing prophecy, concentrated his thoughts upon endless blue skies, and lives brightened with choruses and dance.

However, no amount of meditation could truly distract him from the images of destruction that plagued him. He remembered a day in 1687 A.D. when a Venetian cannonade rocked Athens, blasting precious Pentelic marble from the heights of the Acropolis. The jagged stone and splintered columns of the Parthenon, ancient wonder and venerated symbol of western culture, rich with the worshipped memories of an age like no other, lay scattered upon the sacred hill.

His insides quaked with the memory of this desecration. Architectural genius violated. Ageless cultural brilliance shattered.

This disaster happened so long ago, and still he could not bear to dwell upon it because he accepted the vow not to interfere.

Regret can be an ugly companion in eternity.

Now, in the modern age, a new threat emerged, not limited to the Parthenon.

The future of free societies hung on a knife's edge. More disturbing visions assaulted him. He gripped his forehead with his fingertips because only he knew how, and when, America would fall.

With his fist, he slammed the stone wall surrounding the stairway landing. Shards of rock flew. Was it guilt, indecision, or abject fear that caused him to lose control of his emotions?

He decided this was no way for a God to act. Order must be maintained. He shut his eyes and slowed his breathing, in and out, until the throbbing in his temples subsided.

It was time to carry out the plan.

Apollo vaulted to the surface, past a fractured column of dark marble. A transparent dome of swirling blue light encased him. Torrential rain pelted this protective sheath, but shot away in brilliant yellow ricochets, unable to penetrate it.

Tightening a golden band around his head, Apollo ensured that waves of lustrous blond hair were in place, except for one long curl purposely falling across the right side of his forehead. Twin bronze medallions, a third the size of a man's hand, lay on his chest, suspended by leather cords tied loosely around his neck. The figure of a kneeling archer was embossed crudely on both surfaces. Rays of a sun spread out from its center.

Apollo waved a medallion over the opening. The ground filled in from the sides of the sloping hollow, leaving the fractured marble column slightly exposed. He bounded down the steeply terraced hillside in a white tunic, silver bow slung across his torso, quiver of arrows rattling over his back. The sight of fallen temples, along a serpentine path, the renowned Sacred Way, filled him with both pride and regret.

Descending to a paved roadway beside a museum, he turned to face the storm-blurred ruins. Golden streaks, radiating from the center of his jade-colored pupils, cast beams of illumination upon the silent sentinels of an era thought long gone.

Now, that was no longer true. He would bring Delphi back to life. However, mysterious Pythia would have to wait for her restoration over the heady vapors seeping from a crack in the rock.

Apollo decided to find his way to the Americas. He would seek out allies to train, allies chosen from the *Book of Histories*, to see if they could pass his crucible of survival. After all, heroes do the work of the gods. "Gods and goddesses of love and war, of wisdom, the limitless heavens, the sea, rich Earth, of lifeless shadows, now that you are gone, I will take no more vows to leave history untouched!" he cried out.

Apollo turned off his protective blue dome. Rain drenched his pristine tunic, leaving his long curl limp and dripping. "Only your spirit survives with mine, sister Tyche, you troublesome goddess of the unpredictable."

With arms raised, he accepted the vigor of the storm, absorbing nature's onslaught as an initiation into the realm where mortals dwelled, and in which he must now inconveniently operate. "Tyche," he shouted, "leave me alone to bring order back to these mortals. Must I battle you, too?"

Lightning cracked. A see-through image of the goddess appeared. Apollo drew an arrow from his quiver and notched it while staring at her dour expression. "You threaten everything I love with blind fortune, with your simple throws of the dice," he cried out. Her figure, distorted by wind, did not respond. Vexed, Apollo shot an arrow straight at the goddess' heart. The projectile sailed through her without effect, struck a stone embankment, and clattered onto the ground. "I alone must defeat you and all your uncertainty," he declared as the goddess disappeared. "I must succeed for hope, at last, to have a home."

Visions of destruction took hold again. He saw eyes- eyes of the vanquished, of the traumatized fleeing the cities, of the desperate hoping to survive in the wilderness, eyes of the multitudes endlessly enslaved and those whose eyes only bore vacancy. Apollo locked his lips together as if to seal the agony amassed inside him. He could rant, shake his fist at the injustice, even slay all his enemies in a moment, but the certainty of what would occur in the near future overwhelmed him.

He wailed aloud, drowning out the tempest. Even gods have tears.

No more promises, he told himself. No more sentiment. Now I must act before history becomes… reality.

Wavy blue filaments sprouted from the twin medallions. The dome re-formed and enclosed him. It levitated briefly before gaining altitude, reaching the heavens, and then rocketing, like a shooting star, westward.

CHAPTER 2
SAN DIEGO
MAY 2011

SUBSTITUTE

As she neared the end of a PowerPoint presentation on the Greco-Persian Wars in a San Diego State University lecture hall, Professor Lauren Fletcher concluded that none of the young men in her audience heard a word she said.

Tired of turning back and forth toward the screen, Lauren walked out from behind the podium. Her light olive skin blended her mother's Greek heritage and her father's blond Irish stock. Full lips, alluring curves, and a nose that hinted at her Mediterranean ancestry tipped the genetic balance to the warmer south. She swept aside a tumble of honey-colored hair while pacing just before the front row. Digging into the muscles of her neck with her fingers, she continued lecturing, providing background on the main city-states of Athens and Sparta and their impossible stand against the vast slave empire of the Persian King Xerxes. Her husband, Classics Professor Zackary Fletcher, should be giving the lecture. She hoped against hope any of the students would care enough to listen.

Then she wondered how she let Zack talk her into this.

Pointing at a map depicting the mountainous terrain of the Greek homeland, Lauren heard snickering and turned quickly. She realized that fraternity brothers filled the five rows closest to her.

From the corner of her eye, Lauren saw the men leaning in, poking each other with their elbows, a kind of slack-jawed awe on their faces that she'd seen before. Several snapped photos of her on their cell phones.

This can't be. In a university classroom?

How she suddenly wished she'd made the trip to the dry cleaners a few days ago, so she wouldn't be stuck wearing this tight-fitting, light blue business suit! Her cream-colored Steven Madden shoes matched the outfit, but even with low heels, the garment accentuated her long athletic lines and well-developed calves. Worse still, she had dabbed on *Jadour,* her favorite perfume, a little too liberally.

Silently cursing the frat brothers' lack of respect, Lauren decided to change tactics. After all, she was no rookie lecturer. Still, it had also been a long time since she left her senior and graduate students in ancient languages to teach freshman history.

"Now, I'd like you all to pay strict attention, since I'm sure Dr. Fletcher will include this on your final next week," she said, her tone authoritative. "I would appreciate you turning off your cell phones."

Retreating to the podium, she switched to what she hoped would be more distracting material. "Who can tell me about the differences between how the Persians and Greek formations armed themselves, and the effect that had on the war?"

"The Greeks fought with bronze armor and shields in compact formations," a female student said, "while the Persians were more light infantry and horsemen, shooting arrows."

"That's right. The Greeks mostly fought each other in small pitched battles. Their armored spearmen, called *hoplite* in ancient Greek, concentrated themselves into dense rows to create the *phalanx,* developed over generations of warfare between isolated city-states."

Meanwhile, the frat brothers sitting up front had created their own phalanx of voyeurs. She kept her body camouflaged by the podium, like one of the Greek bowl-shaped *hoplon* shields displayed on the screen.

She moved on. "So, from 490 to 479 BCE, the Greeks that didn't surrender decided to put away their unending differences to make a stand for their independence." Another woman in the back row raised her hand. "The Greeks fought to keep themselves from being enslaved, yet they had their own slaves. Isn't that hypocritical?"

Lauren grinned. She succeeded in reeling the students back into the lecture, most of them anyway. Sitting just aside from the others, a fresh-faced frat brother with a cleft chin and highlighted brown hair, still damp from a morning of surfing, made eye contact with her. Then he pursed his lips. She avoided his unyielding stare.

"You're right," Lauren said. "It is a bit of a paradox, but many ancient Greeks thought that if a man couldn't maintain his freedom, he didn't deserve it. Let's not forget the status of women then, either. Even an enlightened city-state like Athens kept their women behind closed doors, in back rooms, relegating them to caring for children and overseeing the household slaves. Quite different from opportunities in the U.S. today. Think for a moment how life would be for those women. What were their dreams? What would they talk about?"

The surfer blurted out in a feigned female voice, "I'm tired of milking the goats. I'm going to join a Dionysian cult and do the wild thing."

Laughter erupted. Even Lauren joined in. She couldn't resist.

"Okay, you get the point though." Lauren stopped laughing, but her smile remained. "Our culture owes a lot to those ancient Greeks for preserving freedom in its infancy, for beginning the conversion of a world of mysticism and magic into one that studied nature with a logical mind. Think about it. In about 200 BCE, the Greek mathematician Eratosthenes figured out the circumference of the Earth by comparing elevation angles of the sun in two different cities."

The surfer couldn't hold himself back. "Still, Professor Fletcher, women say they want these great careers, but don't they have trouble balancing professional lives and their prime motivation? What they *want* is to have children and take care of them. Maybe the Greeks had it right in that respect, also."

"That comment is just too simplistic, even Paleolithic," Lauren countered. Shouts of support came from the female students. "All people should have the right to decide their own destinies. The Greeks gave us that idea of self-determination, free thought, and speech."

She paused, but not enough to let the surfer interrupt her. "I submit to you that free societies are held together best by a populace that voluntarily restrains those freedoms for the good of all. That's where civility and manners come in."

She looked directly at the surfer, but the young man didn't waver. "Come on, Professor, you can't change biology. That's a kind of destiny all by itself. A chick can carry a career for so long, but inside she just wants to nest. In other cultures, that's still the way it is."

The frat brothers pumped their fists and cheered. One asked another where this guy was all semester and if they could get him to join their house. Arguments started between different rows of students.

"That's enough," Laura said, the pitch and tone of her voice rising. "Let's get back on track. It's a good discussion for another day. Now, can someone tell me what happened to the Athenians and their concept of democracy? Consider the beacon of enlightenment that ancient Athens and the Greeks presented to their world and ours, the energy, valor, and devotion to personal independence. The Golden Age."

She braved another foray before the podium. "The tragedy that haunts many of us still is that their society fell apart so fast. Why did their Golden Age fail? Think of the violence, arrogance, corruption, wars, loss of democratic ideals to feed the power of a few … a cautionary tale for all civilizations, when you think about it." She turned her palms upright. "Why do you think it failed?"

Just when a student raised her hand to answer, her classmates stood and headed for the doors. Time was up.

"The material you still need to cover for the final concerns the Persian Wars, the other Professor Fletcher's absolute favorite subject, by the way. His lecture on Monday will be about the Battle of Thermopylae."

The men shouted their approval.

"Concentrate on King Xerxes, pronounced 'Khshayarsha' in ancient Persian, along with his top general, Mardonius, and King Leonidas from the city-state of Sparta." She paused. "Let me give you a little hint: focus on their different approaches to the Persian Wars, how their troops felt about their about leadership skills."

"Cool," the surfer boy said as he milled with the students on the way out. "And didn't those Spartan babes run around naked? For the taking?"

More hooting followed. The surfer stayed behind.

Lauren's laptop shut down slowly. She bent over to check the DVD drive. "Anything I can help you with?"

The surfer stood behind her. She smelled the brine of dried saltwater on him. Lauren stood up, reset her skirt, and turned her head to see an ever-growing smile. "I'm good, thanks."

"Were you ever a model?" He dropped his voice to a more mature tone. "The pictures on the backs of your book do you no justice."

The DVD finally popped out. She nervously reached for it, grazing his thigh with her hand inadvertently. "Oh, sorry. I have to be going."

Lauren grabbed her purse, slung it over her shoulder, and pressed the laptop and attaché over her chest like a shield. The student blocked her way. She altered course, accidentally bumping him with her shoulder. Again, he tried to block her exit.

A full-toothed grin emerged on his face. "You know, professor, I'm not buying your notion about women wanting a career over family," he said, following her closely.

"Well, that's pure ignorance on your part. A simple look before Greek history, smart a—" she stopped herself, realizing he was a student "—and you'll find women have always been capable of so much more. They ruled in goddess societies that existed for thousands of years. Even in Greece, they had their goddesses, women whose powers were celebrated – Athena. Hera. Artemis. Persephone. That's what frightens boys like you, that we carry that power inside us. The power to rule by love." She clenched her fists. "And might, when necessary."

She delivered her comments with the bite of a rising anger, hoping he would back down. She looked in his eyes. The words didn't faze either his thoughts or apparent intent.

"Writing those books isn't really all that satisfying, is it?" he asked, winking.

Lauren reached to push the door open, but he grasped the handle. "Maybe you could use a massage to help ease the tension in your neck." His smile clenched into a sneer. "And I'd be surprised if that laid-back professor husband of yours is really ringing your bell like he should."

Rage reddened her face. "I've had enough of you!"

"Thought we were having an intellectual discussion here, professor? You know; free speech and all. Women's rights." He snickered. "The power of a goddess."

Lauren groaned and pushed him backwards. "Get out of my way! What's your name? Dr. Fletcher is going to know about this."

She tried to squeeze through the barely open door. *Why is this happening to me?*

"Let me carry the laptop for you." He yanked the edge of the computer down, grinning again, shocking her.

"Get your hands off that!"

"Not really interested in the computer," he shot back, releasing the laptop and reaching for Lauren's lapel. "You just don't get it, do you? The purpose of life isn't achievement, or even survival. That's secondary."

"Son of a bitch... let me go!"

"As I see it, professor, the purpose of life is to pro-generate the species." He held her tight, his face nuzzling hers. "You're not doing your part, and your time is running out."

Lauren gulped.

The surfer locked his eyes on hers. "I can help you."

The lecture room door jolted open. A clean-cut frat brother barged in and saw the professor and student embrace. "Oh, sorry man... I just left my notebook..."

"Get this bastard away from me!" Lauren cried out.

He didn't hesitate. He reached for the surfer's t-shirt. The surfer boy released Lauren and drew his fist back, aiming for her protector's jaw. He ducked just as the surfer's fist flew past him, hard and fast ... and crashed into the door.

He yelped and shook his hand.

Lauren twisted and lurched through the doorway, dropping her attaché case. She saved her laptop, but smacked a wall with her shoulder.

The frat boy got his hands on the wiry, full-chested surfer and grappled with him. Lauren's would-be assailant raised his arms and dropped to the floor, breaking the frat brother's hold.

"What the hell's wrong with you!" the frat boy shouted.

The tormentor rolled, jumped up and bolted for the stairwell. The frat brother raced out the door and yelled to students mingling down the hallway, "Someone, go find a campus cop."

After asking Lauren if she was okay, the frat brother blurted out, "I'm going after him."

Despite her rage, her desire to ring the surfer's neck, her rescuer's action concerned her. "I don't know if you should, he might be…"

He took off after the tormentor anyway. Lauren hyperventilated.

A minute later, a heavy-set campus policeman bounded towards her, talking into his hand radio. She let out a long breath and told him what happened.

"Sometimes, Professor Fletcher, we get kids on campus that aren't students. You ever see this guy before?"

"I don't know. This is my husband's class and I was subbing. If you'll excuse me, I'm late for a meeting."

"I'm glad you're alright. I was here earlier and saw a man with a weird-looking curl on one side of his head watching your class. He held some sort of big coin and waved it in front of the door window, but he left when I walked over to check him out. Let me know where you're lecturing, and I'll stick around your class for a few weeks."

"Thanks. I'll get you a list of times and locations."

After reaching her red, second-generation Prius, Lauren glanced around for the surfer before putting her lecture materials onto the back seat. She drove the mile to D.Z. Akins Restaurant and circled the tiny parking lot until a space opened up.

Twenty minutes late, she dropped into the booth where a friend waited. "Sorry, Roberta. I got held up by trouble in my classroom." She shared the details.

Roberta James, a diminutive, wiry professor of African-American studies, gave her an incredulous look. "I would've smacked him on the head with my laptop. I have basketball stars and rap queens in my classes, and I tolerate nothing less than total cooperation. Even the big ones know I'll kick their butts into little pieces if they give me any disrespect."

"The police didn't think he was a student. Maybe if I knew that I would have reacted differently. I did my best to talk him down, but... Do I need a bodyguard just to go to my lectures?"

"Oh, girl, you need a harder edge to survive in this world. Someday, there might not be anyone around to help you. I've never heard about attacks on staff before, but I suppose anything can happen."

"I've been thinking about getting back into self-defense courses." Lauren withdrew a dill pickle from the appetizer jar and took a bite. The sour taste made her face scrunch. "Love these things."

"Well, I'm glad you're okay," Roberta said as a waitress delivered menus.

Lauren wasted no time ordering. "Turkey Reuben with a bowl of mushroom barley soup."

Roberta pursed her lips. "Hmmm, I'll have the same. How's Zack?"

"He's pretty much over the surgery."

"Never got his wisdom teeth out when he was a kid, huh?"

"No. One started swelling. Then the socket bled for a while after it was out and got infected. He fell behind on his work and asked me to sub."

"Any luck with the… getting pregnant?"

Lauren sighed. "Not yet. My fertility specialist said to give it a little more time. Then there's the fact that Zack isn't up for being a father yet."

"You'd really have some beautiful children. When is that man going to realize what *you* want?"

Lauren blinked. "I'm starting to wonder where I fit in the pecking order." She stared at her half-eaten pickle. "He promised to skip the digs and stay home this summer. If I don't get pregnant, we'll start with the in-vitro staff at the UC San Diego Clinic." She bit into the pickle. Roberta's cellphone drowned out the crunch. "Lord in Heaven," she said. "Thought I put that thing on vibrate."

Lauren listened to Roberta's one-sided conversation. It was clear that lunch was over.

"I'm sorry, Lauren. Eldred didn't tell me there's a parent-teacher conference today. Since the divorce, I don't know how I teach and get everything done."

Lauren's stomach squirmed. *Divorce, children, harried schedules, this morning's lecture; maybe I just picked out too big a pickle.* "You're incredible," she said, struggling to ignore her discomfort. "I can't imagine how you make it all work. Let me know if I can take Eldred to the beach this summer."

"Thanks." Roberta stood up. "I'll call to reschedule. See you." She dashed away, punching keys on her phone with her thumbs.

The waitress slid lunch in front of her. Lauren stared at it, thinking of how she might graft some of Roberta's toughness onto herself, and be more persuasive with Zack. She wasn't hungry anymore. "Could I get this to go also, with a chicken soup?"

"You too?"

"Wait, one of those giant éclairs as well. I'll devour it on the way home."

"Comfort food, I take it?"

"That obvious?"

"Sweetie, sometimes I need two of 'em."

The waitress left for the kitchen and Lauren closed the pickle jar. Her insides ached. The éclair might have to wait.

God, I wish I could start this day all over again.

.

Zack knew he was in Greece at a black-tie function. How he arrived there was another matter entirely.

He made his way to a platter of stuffed grape leaves, and was just starting to munch on one when photoflashes startled him. A short, portly man dashed out of a crowded room and knocked into a reproduction of the Parthenon, dropping his wine onto a marble floor. Zack watched the moment play out, as in slow motion, but then he lunged to save the toppling artwork. Half a grape leaf, along with its lamb and rice filling, vaulted out of his mouth.

A blurry moment later, he found himself in a city of monuments, in Athens he thought. Fear shone in everyone's eyes. People ran in the streets, propelling him along, as if caught in a "B" movie- *Invasion of the Body Snatchers* or something. He searched for Lauren. *Why isn't she here?*

He saw a bird in the sky, a big one, a Blue Jay maybe, soaring ever higher as if in a rush, but it was on fire suddenly, and it shuttered and went into a death spin.

Then an explosion and massive cloud raged above the Acropolis. The maelstrom sucked Zack in, but he could also see from the outside, as if watching from afar through a fisheye lens. The Parthenon –much as he could tell, because his distorted view of it kept toggling back and forth between a temple on a hill and one on flat ground. The real Parthenon, not some sculpted reproduction – erupted and burned.

Zack jerked awake, glazed in perspiration. He wiped his brown hair off his forehead and swallowed. His mouth was dry. He lifted his six-foot-two frame from the beige leather sectional, and meandered to the kitchen, still groggy. In the refrigerator, he spied a lone beer, opened it and chugged. The bad dream must have been from the medication they gave him for the infected socket; one beer wouldn't hurt. He poured the rest into a glass while walking back to the couch. He lay down and put on his Chicago Cubs baseball cap.

He never took another drink. In a few moments, he was back in dreamland.

CHAPTER 3
SAN DIEGO
MAY 2011

NO TIME TO WAIT

Apollo entered the Fletcher's home through an open patio door. The ocean breeze carried a jasmine fragrance, welcoming him inside. He floated with the aroma down a hallway, past a glass case stocked with artistry and pictures of a woman. She captured the eyes. His eyes. He stared at Lauren, contemplating how the woman he called "Golden Hair" might be coerced to join his plans.

He left her photos to check the rest of the dwelling. One small room held an infant's crib, but it was empty, as if awaiting its occupant.

Apollo smiled. *Golden Hair has a deep-held dream, one I must conquer to carry out my mission.*

He entered the kitchen and paused, listening for his quarry. From another room, he heard labored snoring, cut with wheezes and gasps. On soft soles, he glided over the travertine tile floor. The hands of a clock moved silently on the wall. Peering into the living room from behind a door jamb, Apollo saw Zack sleeping on the couch with his unsettled face turned towards him. *"Traveler."* A muted television returned the intruder's gaze.

Among the disarray of medicines and food on the tabletop, Apollo selected a conduit: cold beer in a glass. He took a metallic flask from his pocket and dripped thick dark syrup into the beer, watched the liquid churn, change hues, and calm until the original color returned. "You need this, Traveler, and I will apologize for the level of irrationality that will come upon you," he whispered.

Zack's eyelids fluttered. He stirred and murmured, as if dreaming.

"Neither of you realize the depth of your involvement. Your world is about to be upended," Apollo continued. "Enjoy the dream, Traveler. Sleep well, for it will be your last good rest."

He withdrew towards his entry point, but stopped under the kitchen clock to weigh its quiet work, wondering if the occupants understood that when time no longer favors you, never should it be allowed to pass so silently. He passed through the patio door, shutting it behind him.

Zack sat up fast, pulse pounding, startled for a second time by the same dream. He walked into the kitchen, searched the bedrooms, and locked the patio door. Finding nothing, he returned to the couch. Suddenly, he felt exposed, vulnerable. He drained half the beer in one gulp, sloshing the foam around the still-open wound in his mouth, enjoying the palliative effect of the bubbles.

He stared at the froth as it fell away from the glass's rim, trying to shake off the unsettled feeling left by the dream. He began contemplating the phone call earlier that morning from their graduate school professor in Athens. Professor Papandreou, whom he and Lauren knew affectionately as "Professor P", bore exciting news of a new project on Santorini. He said there might be great discoveries unearthed there, remains of the ancient civilization of Thera, destroyed by a volcano long ago. The career-building work would be the talk of the archaeological world. Just what Zack wanted – and needed – to help ensure his tenure at San Diego State's Classics

Department. He needed that kind of breakthrough… except he'd already promised Lauren they would spend the summer at home.

He took a second swig and turned on the television before preparing a snack, dismissing the sound of a car in the driveway.

Lauren stumbled through the doorway, juggling a plastic takeout bag and an unmanageable heap of mail. She kicked the door closed with her foot, dropped the letters on the floor, and spotted Zack. "If you're going to let the couch swallow you 'live,'" she joked, "at least take those candy wrappers with you."

She saw the man she fell in love with, those heavy-lidded, hazel eyes that first drew her to him. His lashes were the thickest and longest she'd ever seen on a man. He used to laugh when she amused their friends by placing paper matchsticks on his lashes. They stayed in place until he blinked. His rugged handsomeness, his jaw line just a few degrees below square caused many women to give him a second look. Strands of brown hair lay beneath the edge of his ball cap.

Zack adjusted his six-foot-two frame along their leather sectional, the knuckles of one hand hitting the carpet. Lauren saw the beer and stack of chocolate- dipped biscotti.

Right now, she could roast him on a spit. "You look more like an overindulged gorilla than a professor with work to finish," she said.

With a look that approached pity, she swept the wrappers into a wastebasket. "And *why* did you need to stay home today?" She held up his beer-dipped biscotto. "You have no idea what I put up with in your class today."

He stared past Lauren into the kitchen. "Zack? Hello?"

"Huh?"

"What are you doing?"

He set his beer on the table. "I woke up and thought someone was in the house. It scared the hell out of me. I looked around and didn't find anything. Still, I had a dream about an attack on... it's just too horrible to think about."

Lauren chewed on her lip for a moment. "Enough of the beer when you're taking pain meds."

"Hey, it was the only thing in the fridge. It felt good when I swirled it around where they took the tooth out. Didn't they clean wounds with alcohol before they had antibiotics?"

"I don't think it's a good idea to drink while your mouth is healing."

Zack clicked off the television. "I did get a lot of work done earlier."

Lauren rolled her eyes. "I wouldn't tell the oral surgeon in your follow-up that you're sucking down beers."

"Not to worry." He snagged her hand and kissed it. 'You've been a great help, honey."

"I'm raising my substitute fees, especially if I have to teach your classes and clean up your mess every day."

"Sorry." He paused for a moment. "How were my students? I'm sure all the boys were thrilled to see my sub."

He hoisted Lauren atop him and laced his fingers through hers. "I'm not doing that ever again," she said, immediately lifting herself away from him.

"Was it that bad?"

"You'd better take attendance. Someone crashed your class today. I had to fight him off and call a security guard."

"You're kidding? Are you okay?"

She glared at him. "Just fine."

"That's never happened in my classroom... I'll look into it Monday."

"I brought you lunch," she said, sifting through the mail. "Chicken soup from D. Z. Akins; it's more likely to help you than the beer."

"My favorite deli. Thanks!"

As he sat up, Zack noticed the distinctive letterhead of his brokerage house on one of the envelopes. "Any mail for me?"

Lauren swiveled her head, the look in her eyes pinning him to the couch. Must've been bad with that student, he thought. "Are these confirmations from your broker? I can't believe you were buying stocks while taking narcotics. Your brain must have more leaks than a showerhead."

"Hey, as long as I'm supporting the pharmaceutical companies..." He knew he was so busted.

"You never learn."

"Sometimes, you have to take a chance. The market is going up. Across the board."

"Some people take too many of them." Lauren thrust out a hip and continued flipping junk mail like Frisbees into the trashcan. "It's time for us to start a new set of priorities. I'm pulling in the reins on you."

Remembering what triggered his anxious wake-up, he scanned the front yard through their bay window, assuring himself his earlier concerns of a break-in were groundless. "You already know I'll always have to do field work."

"The only field work I want you to do this summer, sweetheart, is on me." Lauren lifted her chin. "I'm tired of absorbing all your delays, for whatever reason. You promised we were going to concentrate on starting a family… *this* summer."

"It's time for me to produce something big." He hesitated for a moment. "If you're going to get pregnant, why does it matter if we're here or someplace else, honey? I have a great idea for summer vacation, if you'll just listen to me."

"No." She said it with hands on hips. "I want a child. It's time. I need you with me on this."

"That's a lot of pressure."

Zack gazed outside the window. He rolled his tongue inside his mouth, exploring the cavern left by the extraction. "Other guys have told me it's not so easy to deliver on command," he said. "Shouldn't baby-making be something that's done, you know, in a more relaxed state?"

Her eyebrows elevated into her forehead. "It's not a job."

"I'm only saying that we can still go somewhere and just let things happen naturally. If you get pregnant, we can fly back. I'll arrange to have the ice cream truck stop by here every day."

"This isn't funny. I'm serious. I want *us* to get pregnant, not just me."

Zack's shoulders slumped. He closed his eyes. Silence began to stretch between them.

Lauren folded her arms. "Are you listening?"

He covered his eyes with his hands. Their ongoing arguments about having children sucked the life out of him. How could he get Lauren onboard for Greece? Whatever happened to their marriage being a democracy, two people choosing their future together? More and more, as she intensified the pressure to have children, their household democracy seemed to be as endangered as it was nationwide – with all hell about to break loose, an anarchy and chaos within their walls that would rip the fabric of their love apart. Just as, on a larger scale, once great civilizations tumbled. Like Ancient Greece.

The whole thing wound him up. He pulled Lauren back into his arms. "Maybe it wouldn't be a bad idea to go away, just for a month or so, like a second honeymoon." He practically sang the words into her ear, his voice tender, melodious.

She blinked rapidly. "Where to, exactly?"

"Greece…Santorini."

"If we go there, I know where all your attentions will be, and they won't be on me." Her voice was measured.

"You told me once it's the place you felt the most at ease in the whole world. Who knows? Maybe we'll discover temples devoted to fertility goddesses?"

Zack gently massaged her neck. He forged ahead, probing her defenses. "We could visit Professor P in Athens. Thank him in person for arranging our positions at State; two unknowns from Northwestern."

She shifted to back out of his embrace, but it felt good to be held. "You're not making me feel guilty."

"I guarantee that whenever your little calculations tell you the time is right, I'll be ready."

"You'd really like to go, wouldn't you?" She kissed his cheek, a light little peck that barely made contact.

Zack grinned, victory at hand. "Grilled octopus, Mavrotragano red wine, sunsets…"

She abruptly braced her lower belly with her hand and jolted to the bathroom. After fifteen minutes, she returned and leaned against the door jamb. "Your face looks white," he said, concerned.

"I'm not pregnant."

"I'm sorry, honey." He stood up and wrapped her in his arms. "I'm sorry."

Lauren looked away. "It's just not working. Now we have to wait another month. We have to think seriously about what's important here, Zack."

She headed for their master bedroom.

Zack stared blankly at his beer, as if it could somehow conjure up a ruse to convince Lauren to go. Opportunities like the dig in Santorini were rare, and his clock was ticking in the Classics Department. But for now, he had to stop thinking about the whole mess. He picked up the mornings' edition of the San Diego Union. The front page reported bitter partisan gridlock, the country sprinting down the road to destruction. With an entire angry world ready to jump right in and grovel for the pieces.

Democracy's on the run, everywhere.

He took another sip and let the foam run over the back of his mouth. Amazement blossomed on his face. The hole had completely healed.

CHAPTER 4

SAN DIEGO, CALIFORNIA

MAY 2011

DROPPING SHOES

"Zack, you ready?"

Lauren opened the front door and headed toward the Prius.

"I'm not sure my eyes are open yet." Zack trudged down the walkway, his arms folded against an early morning chill. "Who scheduled this doctor's appointment at the crack of dawn?"

"You did, so hurry."

He dropped himself into the passenger seat. "Little misty today."

She didn't respond as she drove onto Madras Street. Their house sat at the heights of Del Cerro, a few minutes from San Diego State University. "I can hear the mourning doves all the way down the canyon," Zack said, changing the subject.

A hundred yards down the road, a retired couple backed their silver Cadillac out of the driveway. "Hey, Mr. and Mrs. Freeman are up early, too. Looks like a long day ahead at the casino," he said.

Zack struggled between telling Lauren the truth about Professor P.'s message and getting his way. He wanted to tell her, but … "Honey, I'm sorry about yesterday…"

The sound of a roaring car interrupted any chance of candor. The screech of tires and unmistakable crunch of car metal and broken glass followed. "What the hell?"

Zack turned in time to see a dark sedan fly across the street into a line of shrubs. Lauren pulled over to the sidewalk and jumped out. A big man with a shaved head and graying beard stormed out of the black sedan. Screaming at the old couple, he marched up to the Cadillac and drove his elbow through the driver's window. Mrs. Freeman screamed.

"Hey, I'm calling the cops!" Lauren warned.

Zack ran next to her. When the man heard Lauren, he halted his assault and peered at her. He rubbed his eyes with balled fists and then took a step backwards. Jabbing his finger at her, he threw his head back and emitted a shriek that startled her. "*Ja- doo-gar! Ja-doo-gar!*" he howled.

He bolted to his car, backed the sedan away from the bushes and headed straight for them.

Lauren sprinted for the Prius. "Oh my God, he's crazy!" Her hands fidgeted with the steering wheel. "Should we call the police?"

Zack checked his pants pocket. "I left my cell in the house. Give me yours and let's lose him on the streets."

He turned to see the sedan speed towards them, swerving around cars parked along the sidewalk. "Drive, Lauren!"

She floored the gas pedal and headed down Madras Street.

"Who the hell is he?" Zack asked, keeping his eyes on the sedan while he searched Lauren's purse for the cell phone.

"Don't know. Where do we go?"

She ran the words together as she took serpentine turns in the road, driving entirely too fast. Two neighbors holding their morning papers hopped back from the curb.

"Anywhere there're people. The supermarket near College Avenue." She glanced in her rearview mirror. "Damn, he's still behind us!"

The dark sedan propelled itself over the height of the hill, wheels in the air, smacking its front end upon landing. "First that weird dream at the house, and now this?" Zack found the phone, but fumbled it and watched it fall under the seat. "Crap! I dropped the phone."

"What? Look, there's traffic at College." Lauren sped through the 25 mph zone, ignoring a stop sign and nearly sideswiping a double-parked truck.

"He's shaking his fist out the window. Go faster." Zack put both hands on the dashboard. "No, pull into the gas station. I'll never get the phone now."

She looked at him with wild eyes.

"Forget it, Lauren – keep going. His front end is crunched and smoking. Maybe he'll break down."

"This isn't a freaking Mustang. Let's get help or we're going to kill someone – and us."

The signal turned yellow, then red. Morning commuters raced across the intersection.

The sedan was gaining. In front of them, a row of pine trees divided the curving roadway. Lauren gripped the wheel. Her knuckles whitened.

"Run the light. Do it. Go faster," Zack pleaded.

"Faster? This car's for doing errands."

"He's closing in."

"We're gonna crash."

She streaked towards the red light like a bullet in flight. With only the sound of the blood rushing in her ears, she held down the horn and hurtled through the intersection, then jerked the wheel to make the ninety-degree turn onto College Avenue.

Commuters veered to avoid colliding with the two streaking cars. The Prius threaded between two pickups and bounced back from the curb. The pursuer's sedan missed a minivan – only to be broadsided by an oversized SUV. The sedan spun off the road and slammed into a bus bench.

Horns and screams filled the intersection. Drivers sat in their cars, stunned.

A gas station mechanic ran to the scene. The dark sedan blew steam from its radiator and the driver remained motionless, his head awash in blood.

Lauren strangled the steering wheel. Zack held onto the dashboard. "Honey, are you okay?" he asked.

She didn't answer. He touched her arm. "Lauren?"

"That son of a bitch. Let's go see who he is."

She sprinted to the scene. "It was like he knew us," she said, craning her neck to get a better view while listening to his deep-toned groans. "I want to see his face."

The mechanic blocked Lauren's path. "Ma'am, stay back."

"But this guy chased us. He attacked an old couple up on Madras."

"We called 911," the mechanic said. As the driver stirred inside the car, the mechanic cringed at the sight of his injuries. "Sir, sit still and put your hand over the cuts."

The driver didn't move. The mechanic pressed his left hand over the stream of red coursing from the driver's forehead and face. The injured man bellowed, seized the mechanic's wrist, and tried to jerk him into the car.

"Hey, asshole!" The mechanic strained to pull away. The injured driver spit up blood but didn't let go. The mechanic drew a wrench from his belt and smacked the driver's wrist. Only a second, much harder prompted his release.

Revived and enraged, the driver pounded the fractured windshield with his fist and sent shards of glass flying. A growing crowd gasped. Then he revved the engine. Wheels spun. Witnesses scattered as the dark sedan lurched forward. With his face a collage of splattered blood and snarl, the driver searched the crowd. His eyes lit up when he recognized his targets.

Lauren and Zack.

Other drivers scattered out of his way, sending their cars to all points of the compass. An onlooker across the road, a tall, blonde-haired man, with wind blowing a long curl across his face, boomed out, "Traveler, beware!"

Zack turned to the voice and saw the man briefly. Then he caught sight of death hurtling towards them, and seized Lauren's hand. "Jump! Jump!"

They leapt over the sidewalk, onto a raised knoll of grass. The driver crashed into the rear end of a green Camry cutting into its way. The front end of the sedan spewed smoke.

The enraged driver shook the steering wheel as if to rip it off. Fire engines approached from College Avenue. He struggled unsuccessfully to open his mangled car door. The wail of police sirens stopped him. Another commuter lost control of his car and smashed into the sedan, shoving it free of the tangle of vehicles. The injured driver hesitated, as if weighing his chances of escape. Crazed and frustrated, he jabbed a bloody, dripping index finger at Lauren, coughing out a garbled *'Jadoogar.'* He repeated the word mantra-like until he saw the blue police lights in his side view mirror. He took off for the nearby Highway 8 on-ramp, leaving a trail of black smoke in his wake.

A fire engine and police cruiser arrived, splitting the air with sirens. The police, finding College Avenue blocked by vehicles, took directions from the witnesses. They tried to thread the menagerie of obstacles to pursue the suspect, but could not do so quickly enough. The deranged man got away.

Lauren and Zack held each other on the knoll. "Honey, are you okay?" He stroked her back.

"I can barely breathe. He pointed at us, at *me*, like he wanted nothing more in the world than to splatter us." Her voice trembled. "Did you hear what he called me?"

"No ... he was screaming some kind of crap."

"That wasn't crap. That was ancient Persian, Zack. He was calling me a witch."

"What? You probably heard it wrong with the ruckus."

She pulled away from him. "I don't think so."

After making a report to the highway patrol, Lauren drove to the oral surgeon's parking lot.

Zack kissed her cheek. "We're safe now, don't worry. Come on, we're late. We can talk later."

"We still don't know what he really looks like."

"He's big and ugly."

Lauren mustered a smile.

"They're going to catch him. They have helicopters for these kinds of chases," he pointed out.

Lauren paused, pensive. "Zack, that guy is crazy. What if he comes back after us?"

"He's going to jail."

Lauren exhaled a long breath of assent. "Maybe I didn't hear him correctly. You know, when you're a hammer, everything looks like a nail."

Zack checked his watch. "I'll only be a couple of minutes late."

"The last day has been out of control. First, that kid at the college, now this? I wonder if there's another shoe to drop."

That night, floodlights illuminated the outside perimeter of their house. Zack's baseball bat leaned against the couch where he and Lauren sat. He checked the door and window locks twice. Lauren mashed her lips together. Quiet ensued. They listened for breaking glass. "I've always felt safe here. Now I'm not so sure," Lauren said.

She pushed her gym bag aside and covertly slid the bat closer with her foot. "You thought someone was in the house yesterday?"

"I had a bad nightmare. Besides, if it was him, why didn't he just rob us then?" Zack could see from Lauren's expression that his reasoning did little to allay her concern. The creases on her brow deepened. "Maybe we should get a gun," he said.

"My dad offered you one. You wouldn't allow it. You detest violence, remember?"

"Right, how 'bout pepper spray?"

"Zack," Lauren said, rolling her eyes. "Guys like that use it for breath freshener. That's not going to stop someone like him."

"We're probably overreacting. Still, a guard dog could be a good idea."

"Yeah, a three-headed dog like Cerberus might be enough," she said, referring to the mythological monster that guarded the entrance to Hades. She wrapped her toes over the bat. Her stomach grumbled. "I have to eat something. You wanna split some of the soup from yesterday?" She took the bat to the kitchen, put the soup in a bowl, and punched the keys on the microwave.

"You can have it. I had a big lunch. It's a lot easier to eat without that cavern in my gum."

"Your doctor said he's never seen an extraction site heal so quickly."

"I've got amazing powers of healing. Maybe I'm part Planarian." Zack thumbed through a book on Santorini and the Greek islands.

"Do you think that guy knows our address?"

"He was after the Freemans." Zack put the Santorini book on the table, closer to Lauren.

"Just because he crashed into their car doesn't mean he was after them." She concentrated on the soup, taking a big spoonful. "Boy, that's good."

"Don't worry. The police promised to call us when they get him."

Lauren finished the soup. "Zack, we need to talk, different subject."

She was dead serious. His stomach grumbled for a different reason.

"Something's wrong." She kept her eyes locked on his. "A lot of things aren't right."

"I'll change my ways. I promise."

Lauren picked up the book, veins popping on her strained hands. On the cover, a famous wall painting from ancient Thera caught her eye: a young man holding up fish in each hand, an idyllic scene from long ago. "Maybe we do need to get out of town for a while," she said, the book shielding her face.

Zack neared his own successful catch. He silently vowed to thank the fisherman by painting his likeness on the living room wall if its subliminal suggestion worked. He tiptoed into the subject, wondering if he was walking into another trap. "You mean, go on our second honeymoon?"

"Look, we have our issues right now. But, we could go to Greece for the summer and relax there." She shook her hands vigorously, a surrender of sorts. "Maybe I've been trying too hard in a lot of ways. I'm just obsessed with getting pregnant. Are you going to gloat over your victory?"

"I know I should feel like celebrating, but I don't."

Zack bit his lip. Revealing the news about Thera might spoil it all.

"I haven't felt this vulnerable in a long time," she said softly. "That guy today pushed me over the edge. I have bad feelings about him and I want to get as far away from here as possible…until he's caught."

She reached for the bat and took a practice swing, measuring the distance so she wouldn't take out the antique lampshade Grandma Asimos had given her for their wedding.

"Whoa!" Zack shouted, dodging the bat. "We're going to be just fine, honey. I know it. Let's start packing and stop worrying. We can advance our careers and have kids. We *can* have it all."

"I just need something to take my mind off all this."

"Well, if you really want distraction…"

"Are you kidding?" What about my ticking biological clock? And the fact I almost died today? Not distracting enough?

She cocked the bat for another swing. "Okay. Meet you in the bedroom. Let's see if you get to home plate."

"Put down the bat first."

CHAPTER 5
ATHENS
JUNE 2011

DESIDAEMONEIA

"There she is."

Zack peered out the window of their British Airways jet. Darker cotton-wool clouds yielded to reveal a faraway view of Athens. The urban sprawl along the hills and valleys seemed an artistic violation of the beauty of a countryside punctuated by distant mountains, sharp-tipped peaks, rocky peninsulas, sea, and shoreline. Despite this breach of esthetics, a 190-foot limestone rock dominated the center of the city. Atop it stood the skeletal remains of one of the eight wonders of the ancient world, the Parthenon, the majestic temple to the goddess Athena. The late morning sun cast an alabaster patina upon the building and ruins.

"As magnificent as when we saw her the first time," he said. "A testament to the ideals of a culture long gone."

The flight attendant announced final preparations to land at Athens International, about twenty miles from the city.

"Lean back so I can see," Lauren said. "Returned to your element, Dr. Fletcher?"

"Immeasurably so. Twelve years to build her the first time. It'll take decades to complete the restorations."

"Well, it won't be long before we can walk up the Acropolis and see her close up. You said you wanted to see Professor P right away?"

"Yeah, I guess," answered Zack uneasily, the nagging nightmare and his unannounced plans seeping into his thoughts.

She smiled. "I thought you'd want to. Then we can start our second honeymoon."

Zack nodded pensively.

Less than an hour later, they stood in line at the airport taxi stand. A stocky cab driver snatched their suitcases and stuffed them into the trunk, taking three slams to close it. "Pray we don't have to hoof it," Zack said.

They both grimaced as the engine coughed like it had consumption. "I don't know if we should stay in this relic," Lauren complained, finding no seat belts.

"Lady, you'll be lucky to get another. Look at the line of people waiting," the cab driver said in raspy English, scratching a couple days' growth of whiskers on his chin.

Lauren and Zack locked arms. "Never accuse me of depriving you of first-class treatment," he said, settling into the green vinyl back seat, reinforced with strips of black electrician's tape.

"Where to?" the driver asked brusquely.

"Sofetel, by the National Archaeological Museum," Zack answered in Greek.

The bushy eyebrows of the driver lurched in the rearview mirror before he pulled away from the curb, cutting off other cabs trying to slide in. As the cab wove through the streets, Lauren and Zack noticed a proliferation of protesters. "Not been easy around here, lately," Zack said to the driver again in Greek.

"Are you American?" The driver seemed to draw a week's worth of mucous from his sinuses.

Lauren smiled. "We are."

"Then you should know why this country is in shambles."

The driver spit out the window and stepped on the gas pedal. Zack and Lauren lurched backwards against their seats.

"Wait just a…" Lauren began.

"Honey, don't bother," Zack whispered, "not worth it."

She gave him a scornful look. No one said another word.

Finally, the cab screeched to a halt. Lauren slammed the door shut and stormed into the hotel. Zack slapped thirty euros in the cabbie's hand and joined her at check-in, noticing her hands balled into fists beneath the countertop. "Are you all right?"

"I'm just overtired. A hot shower will do me good. After a full day of flying and that ride from hell, I'm ready to collapse or explode; I'm not sure which."

"You might want to opt for that shower," Zack mumbled as they got into the elevator.

Lauren opened her suitcase. Something didn't look right. "Zack, you snuck in a cocktail dress after I packed in San Diego?"

"Well, you can't exactly wear Capri pants and a tee-shirt to the fundraiser."

"A fundraiser?"

"It's for Professor P's new project. There will be a lot of influential and wealthy people: socialites, financiers."

"You knew about the fundraiser and didn't tell me? After flying for a night and most of a day, you expect me to go to a party?" She shook her head in disbelief. "What shoes am I supposed to wear with this little slip of a dress?"

"Your high-heeled pumps; they're also in there."

"Oh my God, you've become quite the underhanded sneak."

"That's why I didn't tell you. We'll just go see the professor and give him our support. It's really important to him."

Lauren blinked her eyes rapidly. "What am I going to do with you?"

Her heels clicked a staccato beat on the pavement. Her dress swirled. She was a vision – still angry with Zack, two steps behind her – but a vision nonetheless. Once inside the large doors of the National Archaeological Museum, she stopped to check her hair.

Professor Nikolas Papandreou halted a conversation with several donors and, wine glass in hand, smiled at the pair, motioning them over. Amidst a sea of tuxedos and fine tailored suits, Zack tightened his necktie and fastened the top button of his Navy blazer, only to discover he was missing a gold button on one sleeve. No one was looking at him anyway, most likely, not with Lauren on his arm.

He squeezed her hand. She looked at him, confused. He smiled and brought his lips to her ear. "We can really raise a lot of money tonight for Professor P. Work the room with me."

"I don't understand why this is so important to you, Zack. I mean it's not like we're a part of this excavation. We could have easily seen him tomorrow."

Professor Papandreou's voice boomed, "My dear friends, right on time. How I've waited for your return."

He extended both his arms. Lauren reached him first, catapulting herself into his embrace. He kissed her on both cheeks and then held her at arm's length.

"Let me look at you. Lauren, you are still the same magnificent beauty I remember, such sparkling eyes and the face of a goddess. Even at my age, you cause a man's heart to beat too fast." He embraced her again, squeezing his eyes shut. "How I have missed you."

He turned to Zack. "And oh, you're here also?" The professor threw his head back and laughed. "Come here, my good friend."

"How've you been feeling, Professor?"

Zack gave him a hammerlock hug but thought better of it and loosened his hold. Their mentor was no longer the robust archaeologist who drove much younger graduate students up and down mountain ranges and into the countryside in search of obscure ruins. Now he had hunched shoulders and wisps of thinning hair.

"A few more gray hairs, brought on by two erratic interns I trained a few years back. Ha, ha!" He motioned them towards a group. "Come. Join us. Everyone is eager to meet you."

Introductions followed. Zack scanned the crowd: mostly men, and a few elegantly gowned and bejeweled women, probably the wives of wealthy donors, gathered by the bar, resigned to yet another fundraiser, and digressing to subjects more to their liking. A gray-suited man, with short clipped hair parted on one side, extended a hand beyond a sleeve secured with black onyx inlaid cufflinks. He flashed a toothy smile. "Bartholomew Parsons, attaché to the U.S. Embassy, Welcome to Greece." He bowed to Lauren. "Professor Fletcher, a pleasure. Your work on the language of the Persian Achaemenid kings was a delight, even for us laymen."

She blushed. "Thank you. I wasn't sure it made a single sale past university bookstores."

"Well it did, and I'm sure it will be an exciting project on Santorini. Please let me know if I can be of assistance."

"How long have you been stationed in Athens?" Zack asked, trying to head off the Santorini reference.

"Five years now."

"That would be a dream for someone like me."

Professor Papandreou beamed. "It will be a joy to have them along."

Zack glanced quickly at Lauren, who was checking out the array of cocktail dresses and didn't seem to hear the professor. His eyes darted to an adjoining exhibit room. "Excuse me a sec?"

Lauren shook her head and turned to the professor. "Do you see what I'm up against?"

"Do not trouble yourself, my dear. He is driven, I admit, but a far more balanced man than I was at his age. I'm married to my profession. He has you to ground him and make him whole."

Zack reached a glass case that held the famous funeral mask of a long-forgotten king buried at Mycenae. He put his hands on the glass as if to bond with what lay inside.

Lauren let out a long breath, watching him from a distance. "It's a full-time job keeping his attention."

"He loves you, Lauren. Don't forget that. Anyone could see it the first summer that you were my students. Remember how he strove to impress you by running the original marathon course to Athens."

She nodded and approached Zack, whose face seemed stuck to the glass. "Laid him up for a week."

"But I always bounce back." He didn't turn. The death mask of the long-gone king peered back at him across the ages.

"Three years ago, Professor P, he nearly drowned body-surfing in Hawaii. I told him he had to hang up his fins. Last year he broke his arm rock-climbing. I finally convinced him to take a nice safe cruise through the Panama Canal. How do I keep him at full strength?"

"The same Zack I've always known," the professor said, sticking close to Lauren.

She bent to look at several pieces of jewelry beside the mask. "Such a talented goldsmith, whoever he was. Look at the paper-thin leaf and the lions running along that dagger."

"For sure, but I'm impressed by the architects who built the walls and Lion Gate at Mycenae," Zack said. "With those huge blocks of stone, I always wondered what it would have been like to try to attack the defenses and take the city."

"Leave it to you to find a military angle. I find it a captivating citadel. When I stand on that hilltop, with the ruins all around me, I can look out over the landscape below, feel time flow past me, and imagine I'm a lady of the court of Mycenae."

"The souls of the ancient artisans still live in their work. Don't you think so, Professor?"

"I've often wondered the same, Zack," the professor said. He removed his glasses to reveal dark rings under his eyes, just above equally noticeable deep creases in his face. "The ancients hoped for a peaceful existence, as we do, but rarely found it." He sighed. "This is the struggle that is the human condition, mournful at times, but nevertheless, it is our nature. Come now, follow me."

Zack halted again before a display of ancient swords, spearheads, and armor, made of bronze and iron, darkened and pitted by time. "Hoplite weaponry," he declared, almost standing at attention before them. "They would have to be strong to carry seventy or so pounds of armor into battle. Those Spartans must have been men of steel."

Lauren wandered around the perimeter of the case. "You know, I'd be surprised if Spartan warriors were as stoically cold as history suggests."

"Well my dear," the professor answered, "war by nature is brutal. The barbarians were all savages to the Greeks. Yet the Spartans would have had to be as barbaric in war as the Persians. We also know that Greeks imposed atrocities on other Greeks during the many conflicts that marked their history." The professor looked around the room, but seemed to be peering beyond its confines.

Zack looked at the professor with surprise. "Still, I've always felt that the culture the Greeks built, despite their failings, far excelled those of the despots in Asia."

"Easily argued, Zack," Lauren interjected. "But you're not giving the Persians any credit. How did they rule an empire of such dimensions? They devised a postal service, trade routes, and beautiful gardens out of the hot desert. How about the dualism of the Zoroastrian religion? Good god, Ahura Mazda; bad god, Angra Mainyu. Interesting parallels to Christianity, you have to admit."

She gesticulated, waving her hand. "For crying aloud, Cyrus the Great came up with a charter for human rights way back in 539 BCE. They have their own accomplishments, and Western prejudice should not brush them aside. Even today, they are some of the most wonderful people you'll ever know."

Zack directed them towards the buffet table, not about to give in. "Still, in ancient times, I would rather have lived in Greek communities than barbarian or Persian."

He looked over his shoulder, awaiting her reaction. She wrapped her arms around him from behind. "You know what? I could use a barbarian for once, and the only one I want tonight is you ... got it?"

Her sudden transformation surprised him. "Grrr… barbarian man-slave girl; sounds good to me."

"Come on, sweetheart," she said louder. "Let's leave the past behind, for the moment." She grabbed a stuffed grape leaf and took a bite. "Yum…"

While they feasted, the professor pulled out his kompoli, a string of amber worry beads. He massaged the balls between his fingers, clacking them together, almost unconsciously. Recognizing his habitual nervousness, Lauren said, "I remember those."

The professor nodded slowly. "A man of my age begins to look deeply into the chapters of his life. I wonder if I accomplished all that I could have. Did I assist those in need and give back more than I received? Doubts and fears consume me. Years ago, I would attack problems head-on; now I hope everything will sort itself out if I just… wait."

She moved to his side. "Is something bothering you?"

He took a deep breath and looked around the room. "I don't know what it is. I have this feeling of dread, a *deisidaemoneia,* despite the excitement of the discovery." He massaged the muscles on the back of his neck. "I hope this mood will be fleeting. This new discovery may rival what we uncovered in Akrotiri in the 60's. How I miss my old friend Spyridon."

"Professor Marinatos was a giant. I wish we had known him," Zack replied quickly.

"If only he were here to assist us on this dig," the professor said. "I need a trusted, experienced staff, and both of you will be an enormous help."

Zack sucked in his breath, waiting for the tornado to hit.

"Us, at the new dig you're talking about?" Lauren asked, narrowing her eyes, rotating her head towards Zack.

A look of confusion spread over Papandreou's face. "I called Zack and gave him the information a couple of...Oh my." He put away his worn beads, picked up a napkin, and scrubbed his glasses clean.

"You know we'll do anything for you," Zack said, not looking at Lauren.

"Thank you. You're the son and daughter I never had, but I don't understand what's going on here, Zack."

Lauren wagged her finger in Zack's face. "You knew about this and volunteered the both of us without telling me?" She slapped her hands on her hips. "And you with your promise to stay home this summer? I should have known."

"You wouldn't have agreed to come here."

The professor buried his face in his hands.

"No kidding, Zack, but you should have been honest with me." Tears crept into the corners of her eyes.

"There was another reason we decided to come here. Both of us wanted to get out of town. Remember the accident?"

"That happened *after*. This kind of deceit is inexcusable." Lauren threw her head back in defiance.

"Honey, can't you see this will all work out?"

The professor groaned.

She paused a moment, eyes disengaged from Zack's, until she cocked her head up. She couldn't make a scene because they were in a room full of people. "You know what? I'm sorry, Professor. I know we're like family, but I don't think I can do this. I'm flying home and leaving this man-boy to himself."

The professor moved to block her. "Lauren, dear girl, think on it a little while, not when you are exhausted. Please. " He patted her hand. "Let's sit and discuss how you and I will both carve Zack up and feed him to the anarchists protesting in the streets for pulling this on you."

"Professor?"

"You deserve it, Zack," he said with a little venom of his own. "Apologize this instant and hope she doesn't turn you in for some playboy with a yacht down in Mikrolimano Harbor."

"That's sounding pretty good right now," Lauren said, smiling as she awaited Zack's response.

"I'm sorry Lauren… I was going to tell you…"

She turned to Zack and the professor, "If you'll excuse me, I'm going to the powder room."

"Dammit."

Professor Papandreou shook his head. "You should have told her."

A man standing nearby with dyed, thinning black hair and a salt-and-pepper moustache coughed. He withdrew a handkerchief from his coat pocket and covered his mouth, but this was not a choking cough, more the chronic ministrations of a smoker. "Pardon me," he muttered.

Next to him, an older police officer in dress uniform said, "This is Inspector Trokalitis from Livadia. I am Commissioner Darzenta. When he finishes clearing his lungs, I'm sure he will tell you he is well-schooled in archaeology himself."

"Everyone here is excited about the possibilities," Professor P. said.

Trokalitis sipped from a plastic cup, alternately gazing up and down Lauren's figure as she sauntered towards the ladies room. The conversation meandered between what fundraising would be required and the length of the project. A photographer requested poses and snapped pictures of the attendees.

Zack listened to the tennis match of predictions about the successful excavation of the site, but found his attention wandering to a miniature marble sculpture of the Parthenon atop a chest-high white stand. Waiters with small trays of hors d'oeuvres negotiated the dense packing of patrons swilling their second glass of wine. He excused himself and zigzagged through the crowd to the sculpture. Off to the side, in a darkened corner, a short man barked into his wireless. Zack could not make out the language. Finishing his call, the man waddled over to the reproduction of the Parthenon.

"The column drums had to be raised and set atop one another with enormous pulleys. What a marvel," Zack said.

"Pentelic marble dragged sixteen rugged kilometers to the Acropolis. The greatest symbol of Western culture…all in the end all for noth…" The man clipped his words short.

Zack scrunched his eyes and looked at the man, puzzled. A waiter offered glasses of red wine to both men. Zack swallowed half his glass. The man took one, but didn't drink from it. "How are you connected here?" Zack asked, still wondering if he had heard the man correctly.

"I own Limmasol Antiquities. I'm Saabir Hasan; pleased to meet you." He extended a business card. "We've a number of very wealthy collectors obsessed with the past."

Zack took the card, viewed it superficially, and then pocketed it. As Saabir turned to leave, Zack said, "Well, Mr. Hasan, I don't know much about your business, but…"

He looked around. Suddenly, the room seemed oddly familiar. An electric shock ran the length of his body. A photographer scanned the crowd, archiving participants as they meandered through the exhibits. Another platter of olives and stuffed grape leaves arrived. Zack handed his wine glass to the waiter and bit into a grape leaf. "Everything I've ever dug up went to museu…."

Photoflashes exploded. Saabir ducked and twisted in an apparent attempt to escape the incessant snapping of the photographer lenses, but he collided with the waiter, who dropped his tray onto the marble floor. Heads turned as Saabir fell backwards in slow motion, smacking the column stand with his elbow. He reached out to support himself, only to hit the sculpture with his hand. His wine glass shattered on the floor with a spray of red.

This is my nightmare. It's real…

The Parthenon sculpture toppled. As Zack lunged for the artwork, half a grape leaf and its mixed lamb and rice filling exploded out of his mouth, spraying Saabir's white shirt and silk tie. The photographer snapped a picture of Zack saving the sculpture.

He struggled with the tumbling art piece. Saabir moved aside for others to assist. Zack dropped to his knees, cradling the Parthenon in his arms.

A dark-haired man in a suit emerged from the shadows and raced for the front entrance to open the doors. Saabir, hunching his shoulders as if to protect his face from more pictures, met him on the outside staircase. They spoke, gesticulating intensely, and stormed down the steps.

Zack sat dumbfounded on the floor. *What just happened?* Others ran over to help him lift the Parthenon model back atop the pedestal.

Lauren returned from the restroom to a scene of the patrons congregating around Zack, congratulating him profusely. She weaved her way through the circle of smiling faces until she reached her husband and the professor. "What's going on?"

Zack brushed his hair back into place with his fingers, while waiters on their knees cleaned up broken glass and spilled wine. "Our dear Zack here just saved our oldest and grandest symbol of Western culture and architecture from destruction," Professor Papandreou joked, pointing at the repositioned statue. Uproarious laughter followed. "Unfortunately though, we may have lost a wealthy patron."

Zack grabbed Lauren. "This is my nightmare."

"No, Zack, this is *my* nightmare," she whispered.

"Who was that gentleman?" Professor Papandreou asked.

"An art dealer," Zack said as Commissioner Darzenta patted his shoulder.

The professor asked for quiet. "Before anyone else befalls an accident, allow me to thank you all for attending. The work we will perform in Santorini is sure to yield astounding results. As we all are aware, budget problems have severely limited the funds available to pay staff, properly guard the site, and to purchase supplies. We deeply appreciate the donations of individuals to support our work."

While the professor continued about previous projects on Santorini and Crete, Lauren pulled Zack to the outer ring of the attendees. "I want to leave," she said in hushed tones.

"We just got here."

"I don't care. You lied to me. Don't you have anything to say?"

"I want to tell you about my dream."

"I think I already know what it is, and guess what? I don't care."

"Lauren, you don't understand."

"No, Zack, I understand all too well. I know it's your dream to be here. It's just that I'm never a part of that dream. I'm getting a cab. I'll see you back at the hotel."

"But you've barely visited with Professor P."

"Make a lunch date for tomorrow. Don't wake me when you come in."

After sleeping late, they scurried for their lunch date. The taxi dropped them off in the Plaka, one of the oldest and most beautiful neighborhoods in central Athens, just beneath the Acropolis. The Plaka bristled with tourist shops amid quaint homes, overstuffed kiosks, restaurants, flower stands, street vendors, and musicians.

"Feeling better?" Zack asked.

She forced a smile. "Better rested, but you're not off the hook."

"Please just think about the opportunity before us."

"Why should I, when that's about all *you* think about."

"I admit that I shouldn't have done it this way. I'm sorry."

Narrow streets led them to the Byzantino Taverna, an indoor/outdoor restaurant nestled among others on Plaka's Kidathineon Street. Professor P. awaited them, fingering his worry beads. "I wonder what's eating at him." Zack said.

"Maybe he's worried that I'm going to kill you."

Zack grinned sheepishly. "What concerns me is he's had premonitions before and they've been reliable. How many times did he pull us into port early to beat sudden squalls, or off a mountain before bad weather hit? Or when he had us dig in spots where there seemed like we had no chance at all of finding artifacts, only to hit pay dirt? He only takes out those beads when he thinks things might get really bad."

"Well, I can tell you one person I know things are going to be really bad for," she snapped. She stopped to breathe in the fragrance of potted basil near the entrance.

The taverna greeters, strategically positioned to lure tourists, bowed and stepped aside for the professor to approach his customary table reserved for each Friday afternoon, an inside window seat shielded by a wide canopy. "Truly, this is my favorite *taverna*; lunch is my treat," the professor said, watching Zack scan a list of *mezedes,* plates of appetizers, posted on a chalkboard. " I assume your legendary appetite has not diminished these past few years?"

A tall waiter, the top two buttons of his white long-sleeve shirt left unfastened, seated them. Sporting a clipped goatee and dark hair tied into a ponytail, he greeted them with a hurried '*kalimera.*' While delivering menus, he revealed a tanned neck beneath gold chains and leather strings tucked under his shirt. A strange-looking curl escaped the stretched ponytail. He quickly stuffed it back in place. As he announced the specialties in Greek, his German accent brought a giggle from Lauren. The waiter raised an eyebrow.

"Good day to you also," the professor returned, furrowing his brow. "Might we speak English in honor of our guests?"

"Easily done," the waiter answered in English, but with the same German accent. Lauren bit her cheeks to keep from laughing.

"A sense of humor. Refreshing. You will need all you have, believe me," the waiter said.

"Oh, I'm sorry. I just wasn't expecting a German accent from a waiter in a Plaka *taverna*." She ran her finger over the list of entrees. "Here's what I want: a chicken Greek salad and iced tea.

"I may order three dishes," Zack said, nibbling his lower lip. "I'll take the lamb with lemon you suggested, pork in sauce, a salad and an Olympia beer." He handed the menu back to the waiter without looking at him.

After placing his order, the professor asked, "How was your flight from San Diego?"

The waiter slowly collected the menus, beaming. "Americans… How wonderful. Are you on holiday?"

"They are colleagues and dear friends. Professor Fletcher of the Classics Department, San Diego State University, and his wife, Professor Lauren, herself a published professor of ancient languages. May we also have a liter bottle of mineral water?"

"Right away, Professor…?"

"Papandreou, Nikolas Papandreou of the National Archaeological Museum." The professor set a white napkin over his lap.

"Then I am in esteemed company," the waiter said, clicking his heels together. "It will be a pleasure to serve you all."

"You must be new," remarked the professor.

"The owner just hired me for the summer season, but I am also a student of the Classics."

The waiter excused himself, promising to return with bread and salads.

"He looks like a body builder, or maybe a male model," Lauren said.

"Lucky too," Zack pointed out. "How does a foreigner get a summer job in Athens? We could never find work here."

He scanned the street scene, full of tourists in summer wear. "I can close my eyes and imagine I'm in the ancient city of Athens, strolling within the marketplace, listening to the men argue politics."

"The conversation now is not always so stimulating," Professor P said. "Instead, stray dogs and cats vie for control of the forum at night. How comforting to see you are still quite the dreamer, my dear Zack."

"Tell me about it," Lauren said, resetting her eyes on the waiter, who returned with warm sesame seed bread in a wire basket and a bowl of olives. Leaning in closely, he overpowered the aroma of the bread with a lemon-scented aftershave.

She brushed her eyebrow-length bangs to the side of her forehead.

"If you would humor me, could we catch up before dealing with our miscommunication," the professor asked. "It's better for digestion."

While receiving affirming nods, he speared several Kalamata olives with his fork and set them in a neat row across his plate. "Five years is such a long time to be away. What do you miss the most?"

"There're so many beautiful places I would return to: Cape Sounion, The Mani Peninsula, Corfu, and The Cyclades. We never set an itinerary; now I know why." Lauren flicked her head in Zack's direction. "Visiting my Grandma Asimos's people in Amfissa or a drive around the Peloponnese would be nice, but I'm not committing to anything."

Zack, unable to speak with a mouth full of bread and Tzatziki sauce, chewed furiously, holding up his hand to hold a spot in the conversation.

The waiter dallied. "If I may be so bold," he interjected, "I once spent almost a month wandering around Delphi. The mountains sing of the past in that place, if you listen well." He rearranged the tabletop to allow for more plates.

"Is this one of those restaurants where the waiters not only sing, but offer philosophy and travel planning too?" Lauren asked while fingering the fasteners of her blue sapphire earrings.

"You are very gracious, Lady Professor, to be so warm, and to me, a humble waiter. And if I may add, your beauty truly adds elegance to our café." The waiter bowed, locking his jade-colored eyes on her.

She thanked him for the compliment, and then hid her face by sipping on her iced tea.

Zack, suddenly attentive, eyed the waiter. "Must have been a sad day when they closed the Oracle down in A.D. 393," he said smugly.

"Yes, yes," the professor said, playing along. "One day you can converse with the gods, then the next, Emperor Theodosius disconnects their phones."

They broke into deep laughter, but not the waiter. "It remains a most holy place," he said.

"Times change, gods change." Zack spat an olive pit into his partially closed palm.

"Of that I am not so sure." The waiter closed his eyes for a moment. "I've heard even now, a god resides there and can be sought after for answers, for those who believe." He set his gaze on Zack. "For myself, I find solace under those twin peaks, *Hyambeia* and *Nafplia*."

Hiding his surprise at the waiter's knowledge of the ancient names, Zack said, "It appears that in the great-dreamer category, I have found my match."

"So Zack, you admit your head is permanently seated in the clouds?" Lauren twirled her hand in the air as if it were floating off.

"I love history too much and you all are on to me, including our friend here, who may have an irate employer if he allows our meals to go cold in the kitchen." Zack motioned with his eyes for the waiter to get to business.

"I shall return promptly."

The waiter walked smartly to the kitchen, and then waltzed back with five plates stacked along his arm. He delivered them, starting with Lauren.

Zack winked at the professor; time to bait the waiter for more conversation. "In the end, the Oracle was not holy at all," he declared. "The Oracle needed priests to interpret the Pythia's wailings; priests who were corruptible and therefore not at all divine."

The waiter moved around the table, refilling the glasses with water and iced tea.

"The gods are gone. In the end, the people knew they couldn't answer their prayers. So they've been replaced, forever," Zack said, punctuating 'forever.'

"Zack," Lauren said. "Aren't you being a little...?"

The waiter reached to top off Zack's glass but instead tipped it over, along with his half-full beer bottle, sending a deluge running onto his lap.

Zack leaped off his chair, red-faced.

"Pardon me. I'm so sorry," the waiter muttered. He extracted white table napkins from his pocket and touched Zack's shoulder, just for a moment. The flash of anger instantly disappeared, replaced with his customary grin. They all laughed except the waiter, who swabbed the puddle on the table.

"You are quite the philosopher, my friend, but you need practice at your job," the professor said.

The waiter joined in the laughter this time, displaying white even teeth.

"Perhaps the gods could return and send a blast of hot air through here to dry the tablecloth," Zack said, not letting the moment go.

"Once again, my most profound apologies." The waiter left for the kitchen.

The professor raised his glass. "Ah me, it's good to be with the both of you again." They toasted. "Now, what is this about the car accident?"

Lauren stopped chewing. The waiter set another foamy glass of beer in front of Zack.

"Lauren saved our lives," Zack replied. "That guy I told you about, he got away, although I don't know how. He was pretty smashed up. We still can't figure out who he was or why he was after us." He lifted his glass of beer and took a long sip. He stopped, looked at the beer queerly, and drank again. "This beer just keeps getting better-tasting." By the end of lunch, he drank enough beer to satisfy the Greek custom of leaving your glass neither completely full nor empty.

The waiter interjected. "Beauty *and* courage. I applaud you, Lady Professor." Her gaze followed the waiter while he went to a corner and pulled a stool towards the center of the room.

"Scared the hell out of me," she said, returning her attention to the professor. "We have our neighbors watching our house while we're gone."

"Needless to say, your invitation came at a perfect time. We needed a road trip," Zack said.

Diners turned their attention to the tall waiter, now strumming a guitar. All conversation ceased for a moment.

"Versatile man, but a bit too full of himself for my taste." Zack returned to his beer, his eyes rose in surprise. "That song's from *Abbey Road*, though his voice seems a couple octaves too high for a man his size … Never imagined hearing 'Here Comes the Sun King' in Athens."

Lauren swayed in her seat. "Actually, he's got a pretty good voice. Music has been my solace, lately."

She glanced at Zack to see if her silent dig registered. If so, he didn't show it.

The waiter finished to the applause of the patrons. He placed the guitar on a stand, disappeared into the kitchen, and returned with a bronze-colored bowl and pita bread. He leaned over Lauren, placed the bowl on their table and, upon withdrawing, slowly breathed in her scent as he passed by her ear. Curious of the bowl's contents and surprised by its weight, Zack picked it up with two hands.

"I had the chef make you special hummus for the pita. It is our apology for the mishap." The waiter bowed at the waist behind Lauren, drawing in her bouquet once more before slowly rising.

"Apology accepted," Zack said. He took a triangle of pita and dipped it in the humus. "Not bad."

Lauren smacked her lips after trying it. "Very sweet and nutty." She offered a piece to the professor.

He pushed it away, glancing at the waiter with an annoyed look. "Oh, thank you, no. My diet is quite strict these days."

Lauren looked at the waiter. "So, you are a singing waiter, after all?"

"Music lifts the spirits and can carry a person through difficult times."

"How prophetic. What's your name?" She brushed back her hair.

"Calchas Der Shooten. I am able to deliver even your smallest desire."

Zack pursed his lips, weighing the waiter's continued fawning over his wife.

"So, you are German, with a Greek first name?" she asked.

"I am from the Black Forest, but spent many summers on the isle of Crete as a youth. You will have to excuse me; my other orders are ready."

Zack rubbed his stomach. He reached for the bottle of water, refilled his own glass, and then Lauren's.

"I am so full. Let's go walk it off after I visit the restroom." She walked to the bathroom, drawing the glances of the other patrons.

The professor pressed his hands together as if in prayer. He leaned towards Zack. " You are truly a lucky man to have the love of such a woman. There once was a woman whom I considered for my wife." He briefly closed his eyes, the corners of his lips turned downwards. "But, I would not change my ways for her. There was always another ruin to uncover. If there would have been someone to sit me down, counsel me, I might have seen my obsession. She left me and I could not get her back. Now, I regret the decision I made because, in the end Zack, life is about the people you love."

They exchanged glances. Zack knew exactly what the professor was referring to, but diverted his gaze to a nearby painting of snow–capped Mt. Olympus instead. "There is so much I want to do," he said defensively, since he knew where the conversation would lead.

"Someday, you will have to give up the appetites of youth, settle down, and attend to her needs instead of yours. Don't wait too long."

"I'm not worried about Lauren. That day will come, I promise you. I'll buy a minivan and make her happy; it's just not right now." Zack stood up from the table, watching the bathroom door. He didn't need her to drop into this discussion. "You know, all that talk of Delphi has me yearning for the aroma of mountain pine and cypress trees."

As Zack kept a close eye on her whereabouts, Lauren left the bathroom and bumped into Calchas in front of the kitchen. They exchanged quick pardons, some laughter, but spoke together long enough to make Zack uncomfortable.

With narrowed eyes, the professor said, "I'm not sure I've gotten through to you."

"Calchas, Calchas..." Zack said, squinting. "That was the Greek prophet who knew the present, future, and past."

Lauren returned before they could finish talking. "Let me have a last drink of water." She wiped her forehead with a cold hand towel from the bathroom. "I don't know if it's the heat or the meal, but I feel really warm. I have to move around, Zack. I'd like to see the Parthenon before I fly back home."

Professor Popandreou clasped both of Lauren's hands in his. "Dear Lauren, despite this barbarian here and his rude behavior, please consider staying and joining me in Santorini. You'll not regret it."

The waiter cleared a table next to theirs, keeping his head down, but tipping his ear towards their conversation.

"I can't keep giving in to him. I have not made my mind up about staying for the summer. Maybe I will return to the States and go visit Grandma Asimos in New Hampshire. Zack can stay here if he wants."

Zack bristled. "Please, Lauren. I want you to stay. Let's go to the Acropolis and talk about it. Professor, join us?"

Looking past his mentor, Zack watched the waiter bend over to pick up a white napkin he'd dropped on the floor. When the waiter arose, Zack noticed a long lock of curly hair falling free from the tight gathering of hair. He did a double take.

The professor shook his head. "I've so much to finish before I head to Santorini. Stay away from the protests near Monasteriki and Syntagma Squares. Legions of people are very upset about the failing economy."

"Got it," Zack said.

"We're all meeting in a few days down near Pylos. Here are the directions to my beach house." He handed them a computer printout. "There you'll be greeted by nightmares from the past, some of your former friends."

Lauren pointed her finger at Zack. "This just gets worse. Drunken beach parties till dawn."

"We'll keep the Retsina and the cigarette smokers away from you," he said.

The professor and Zack burst into laughter, remembering Lauren's tortured grimaces as a student when she was unable to develop a taste for Greece's resin-flavored wine. Lauren stuck her finger down her throat to feign vomiting.

"Please, Lauren," the professor said. "Please stay."

She blinked and threw a long sigh. "We'll see."

Before leaving, the professor whispered in Zack's ear, "I'm going to go talk to the owner about this new waiter, and Zack, I beg you, don't be like me. Think about what I said."

Zack cooled his sweaty forehead with a wet cloth and stared at the waiter, who was again sliding his long curl back into place. Lauren waved goodbye. Calchas smiled broadly and threw her a kiss. Grimacing, Zack led her to the doorway. His stomach did slow cartwheels.

Apollo walked outside the restaurant. He studied Zack and Lauren while they climbed steep steps towards the tiny cottages of Anafiotika, leading to the Acropolis. Marching back inside, he saw the professor talking to the owner of the café. Both were pointing at him.

He walked through the restaurant past their astonished faces, slung his apron across the counter, and strolled out the rear door. Outside, he shut his eyes, raised a medallion from beneath his shirt, and directed his will upon a servant waiting nearby. He then took a shortcut to put himself ahead of the young couple.

The heat of summer sun radiated off the walkway. Parents held their children's hands while ascending the steep stone stairway to the Propylaia, the remains of an elaborate entranceway constructed in the Classical era. Beyond this grand entrance rested the three main buildings of the Golden Age: the Erechtheum, Temple of Nike, and Parthenon, all built on the ruins of previous temples. Tourists and nationals alike approached the heights with reverence and awe.

"I can shut my eyes and imagine the statue of Athena standing majestically in the back of the Parthenon." Zack said, putting on his sunglasses. "I wish we could have seen her …the gold and ivory."

Lauren's hair blew across her face from the stiff wind, which bore the salty Aegean air. "If only the Golden Age could have survived," she said.

"There wasn't just one cause, honey. They were fighting the elite military-state of Sparta. The Sicilian expedition during the Peloponnesian War ended in disaster. They abused their strength in foreign invasions, and emptied their treasury. They lost their leader, Pericles, to that devastating plague."

"All of that is true. In the end, they betrayed the attributes that forged their greatness. You remember how Edith Hamilton suggested that the Athenians, in their glory, found excess distasteful, sought excellence, dissected and yet respected the laws of nature, and by choice were self-reliant, putting limits on their own personal freedom? They displayed what free men working together could achieve."

"They lost themselves?"

"They succumbed to gluttony; for power over others, greed for riches, and for luxuries," Lauren continued. "Where before, they devoted themselves to the good of the state, in decline they expected the state to take care of them. They plummeted to barbarity and lawlessness during the Peloponnesian War." She raised her voice over the growing crowd of tourists. "They were arrogant. Their arrogance overcame restraint. They violated the wisdom of '*Nothing In Excess*' and left the door open for domination by others."

"You're depressing me."

"All right, I'll change the subject. This is probably a good time for us to talk anyway." She paused, and clenched her eyes. "No, wait. I'll talk and you listen."

"I should have been more upfront with you..."

She stopped and grabbed his arm. "Look, I'm doing my best to figure out what the hell you really want. I know we've enjoyed academic successes: two professorships at SDSU, a house in Del Cerro. We've come a long way... *together*." She searched his face for confirmation, wondering if he loved his work more than her. So far, the trip had confirmed her fears.

"We *have* come a long way," he replied. "And now we're back in the country where it all began for us." He searched her eyes. He saw hurt. He wounded her.

"I feel like I'm doing all the work in this marriage and this is supposed to be our romantic getaway, remember?" she murmured.

Zack raised his eyebrows. "Yeah, I remember. I will refocus…on you. If we go to Santorini, we could redo our vows." He slanted his eyes, awaiting Lauren's answer.

"You're not playing fair," Lauren answered, relenting a little. "You mean down to the last detail, even the donkey ride up the trail?"

"You got it."

"And the same sunset supper with a bottle of Mavrotragano red wine, sitting in that *taverna* overlooking the caldera?"

"Only place in the world they grow that grape. I'm already there."

"Unless of course I'm pregnant by then…"

"And if you're not, we'll leave after a couple of months and go back to start in-vitro."

"No more lies, Zack. No more manipulations so you can get what you want. Just be honest with me."

He smiled. "I'm sorry. Maybe I've been freaking out about my tenure. I won't do it again."

Lauren brushed his cheek with her fingertips. "I'll never forget what you said to me that night you proposed," she said, her eyes luminous. "You said you'd always been captivated by the lives of the people who had lived there so long ago; that you wished you could live among the ancients and be one of them."

Zack sighed.

"During the excavations on Thera, you said that you sensed the presence of their souls; that their existence transcended time. Then you told me that your love for me would be timeless too, and that our souls would always be inseparable."

"Did I say all that? Back then, my knees didn't crack when I knelt down to propose. This time…"

From the bottom of the stairway, they heard shouts, followed by a rush of movement that rippled through the crowd. A girl screamed. Deeper voices sounded and threats were hurled between men. Visitors scattered, tripping on the stone steps. They peeled away to safety, as though clearing a path through Pamplona for the running of the bulls. Lauren saw his wicked eyes first … the shaved head. The graying beard. The man that chased them in San Diego.

She reached for Zack's elbow, but weakly. She couldn't speak.

"Jadoogaaaar," the giant roared, his finger pointed at her.

"It's… him." The words croaked out. She set her foot on the next highest step. Zack now saw the giant, twenty feet below them. "That's … impossible." He turned left, then right, indecisively.

"What's he doing here?" Lauren shouted, frantically.

She pulled Zack up the last steps, through the final gate of the Propylaia and towards the Parthenon, fifty yards away, over column drums scattered on the ground. "I told you he called me a witch."

The brute had just reached the same entryway by the time they made the corner of the seventeen Doric columns of the Parthenon's long south side. "*Jadoogaaaar!*"

"Where to now?" Zack's breathing heaved. "How could he know we're here?" He turned his ankle on the rocky surface pockmarked with holes and cracks. He let Lauren's hand go. She caught a foot on a sharp edge, spun, fell, and cracked her knee. "God damn it!" she cried out.

Zack hoisted her up, the maniac in close pursuit, maybe ten yards away. Museum attendants shouted at the madman to stop. Fathers shielded their children with their bodies.

"Run!" he pleaded, favoring his ankle.

Lauren grimaced, rubbed her knee and followed him past the trailers of the restoration crews and piles of marble roof shingles. "Head around the temple." To bystanders, she pleaded, "Call the police!"

"Shit, he's close," Zack warned.

Their pursuer puffed and strained. They turned the corner for the shorter eight-column east side of the Parthenon. Workers yelled at the lunatic to leave the couple alone. Undaunted, the brute stumbled over the uneven ground, dodging an obstacle course of fragments blown apart from the Parthenon during the sixteenth-century Venetian cannonade. Almost within grasp, his prey turned the corner for another long side of columns.

Their pain subsiding from a rush of adrenalin, they ran faster and made ground. "Back to the entrance," Zack strained to say.

They heard the wail of police sirens on the streets below the forum. Zack glanced backwards and saw the pursuer and his canine-bared sneer.

"Down the steps," Lauren coughed out. "Towards Monas...tiraki."

Leaping down the steps three at a time, they scrambled towards the pedestrian walkway that circumnavigated the Acropolis. They heard the steady clomp of the man's boots. Drums from a street musician and crowd noise seemed to build together. Coursing the walkway beneath the sheer rocky heights, with the remains of the Roman forum and Hadrian's library in sight, Zack pointed to where they should head.

More tourists moved out of the way, but a crowd gathered before the street musician. His attention diverted from the road for a moment, Zack banged into a man listening to the performance. Both fell in a heap. Lauren stopped and whirled, wheezing, her face streaming with sweat. The madman ran up to Zack and drew a curved knife from his belt. Zack rolled towards the grass beside the road, hoping to scamper behind a tree. The crowd scattered, leaving the guitar player and a taller man in a floppy hat and baggy clothing.

Sunlight glinted off the blade. The madman seized Zack by the collar, immobilizing him with a stamp of his foot. "Mumbler," he blared in ancient Persian. Zack raised his arm, feebly, knowing the game was up.

Suddenly, the tall man ripped the guitar from the astonished musician. Swinging it backhand, he slammed it over the madman's head. Fractured pieces of the guitar flew off. The giant groaned, stumbled, and dropped his knife. Zack kicked out with his sneaker, and Lauren grabbed his arm, freeing him. An eruption of loudspeakers, horns and the chanting of thousands of protestors hit their ears from the northeast.

The madman spewed unintelligible words at the tall man holding the broken guitar. A slight grin emerged on the tall man's camouflaged face. Zack and Lauren scrambled away from the Acropolis, down Panos Street. The madman regained his footing, retrieved his weapon and ran after them. They hooked a right past the ancient Tower of the Winds, heading towards the crowds near Syntagma Square.

"The bastard damn near got me," Zack gasped.

Lauren noticed something different in his eyes. Even during the car chase in San Diego, he didn't look so rattled. He was panicking. "Faster!" she ordered, sprinting, fueled with adrenalin, looking back to determine the space between them and the brute. The maniac was closing in again, steadily.

Weaving through side streets, with the cacophony of the demonstration growing, they hit dense lines of protesters. Fighting broke out among police and young men in front of a government building. They extended their arms and met a wall of bodies. The madman made more ground. They pushed through the first rows and immersed themselves in the sea of protesters who were voicing their outrage.

Still on their trail, the lunatic jumped high to keep them in view. He drew his knife again. Protestors backed away from him, sending waves of chaos into their ranks. Zack and Lauren broke free of the mob and took another side street, screaming for people to get out of their way. Taxi drivers stood outside their cars, watching the anarchists battle the police. They picked a cab on the far end and shouted in Greek for a driver to get ready to take off. They aimed for opposite doors. The madman sprinted towards them, his head pulled back, chin raised, eyes barely open as he made an all-out effort to catch them.

"Wait till we get in!" Zack yelled at the driver, bending to jump inside.

Their attacker drew his arm back and hurled his knife. Zack dropped his hip onto the seat, not seeing the blade pinwheeling towards him. He was not fully inside when the knife struck his outstretched thigh. It was half a rotation short. The rounded pommel end bounced off him, clanging when it hit the pavement.

Zack swore as he pulled his leg into the cab. "Now!" Lauren screamed at the cabbie.

She took one look back. The attacker was throwing onlookers out of the way, searching for his knife.

"Omonia Square, the Novotel." Zack garbled the words, staring straight ahead, scrunching his long legs towards his body, fetal-like. He clasped his hands over his forehead. "What the hell is going on?"

"He obviously followed us from San Diego. Maybe he found out from the university that we're here? Did you see the scars on his face? His skin looked like it had been burned, too."

Zack rubbed his leg. "The police have to hear about this guy. We're locking the door to our room. I'll have the rental car delivered in the morning. We're high-tailing it out of town, early as possible."

Lauren bumped against Zack as the cabbie took a quick turn down a side street. "Mountains sound good to you?" he whispered. "He can't find us in Delphi. He can't possibly know we're going there."

CHAPTER 6
ATHENS
JUNE 2011

DELPHI

Zack awoke before dawn to the sight of Lauren's nearly naked body highlighted by light coming through the window. He imagined her swollen with their child, a vision that both terrified and fascinated him. He wondered what their child would look like, but shook the notion away before it could take hold. A baby would change his life, permanently. He wasn't ready. This was no time to slow down. His career wouldn't allow it. He heard the infinitesimal beating of her clock and escaped to the bathroom to get ready.

"How 'bout we get our early start out of the city?" he asked, returning to bed, leaving the bathroom light on.

She stirred. "We may need a crane. I tossed and turned for hours last night. I just got to sleep."

He smiled and wrapped her in his arms. "I didn't sleep well either. I considered offering you a different kind of sleeping pill, but I figured with everything that's happened, you wouldn't be too crazy about the idea."

Lauren looked up at him. "So much isn't making sense right now. That guy's tried to kill us twice now, and we don't know why. This is just freaking me out."

"I left a text message on Professor P's phone. Told him this was the same guy. Maybe he can get one of his police friends to help. I said we'd call from Delphi."

She ran her fingers over Zack's chest. "It really throws you. I mean when you're not safe. We're so used to everything being stable and dependable."

She looked at her watch and rose – suddenly. Throwing the sheet back, and wearing only blue panties, she rushed to her purse lying on a desk. After flipping through the pages of a small calendar book, she stopped. She whacked the book. "Oh Zaa...aack, you just got lucky." She turned, straightened her shoulders, clasped her hands behind her back, accentuating her breasts, and smiled demurely.

"But we have a car being delivered," he stammered. "I had to pay a fortune to have someone bring it over early. Are you really in the mood after everything that's happened?"

"You know what?" she cooed, crawling towards him on the bed. "The hell with him; even he's not messing up my schedule." She ran her fingers through his hair and kissed the tip of his nose. "You made me a promise, remember? I'll be out of the bathroom in a minute."

"I'm screwed," Zack said, but not quietly enough.

Her muffled voice came through the door. "Exactly what I had in mind."

Yellow hues of light stretched from the horizon to the distant hills as they connected with E-75 northbound. Within an hour, the sun's rays illuminated the rolling hills of countryside replete with the resonating echoes of history. They traveled into the highlands past the ancient city of

Thebes. Their steady climb into the mountainous areas beyond Athens ultimately ended in the area of Mount Parnassus and Delphi.

"How would you like to do this on foot, like the ancients? They walked everywhere," Zack said.

"But if they believed that this spot was where heaven and earth met, they probably considered it a small price to pay if Apollo could help them decide what to do."

"I wish he could give us some guidance right now. I have a question for him: why does that guy want to kill us?"

Lauren shook her head. "I can't figure it out, but we're going to be fine now. Professor P is the only one who knows we headed this way."

Less than an hour from Delphi, they passed the spot outside the Livadia where Lauren's bike had broken down years earlier. "Really lousy luck to get a broken bike chain," Zack said, his memory kicking in.

"Yeah, told everyone I could make it up the hill in two days. How many people did I have to pay out on that bet?"

The car engine made its own protest. Zack downshifted. In the distance, a blanket of olive, pine, and almond trees crowned the highlands. After passing the cliff-side village of Arachova, Zack and Lauren saw Mount Parnassus, the bold twin peaks guarding Delphi. The much-photographed remains of the round "tholos" sanctuary of Athena Pronaia signaled their arrival. Rounding a last corner, they rolled into the street-side parking spaces outside the museum.

"Let's stretch our legs for a while," Lauren said. "Maybe we can go up in the heights, camp a few nights in the wild if we want to. We can revisit the Kouroi twins and the Sphinx in the museum later."

They changed from their sandals into hiking boots. Lauren donned a large straw hat to complement her white button-down blouse and khaki shorts. Zack put on his Cubs baseball cap. He loaded their backpacks with the necessary items for a brief field trip: a digital camera and hand-held Sony video camera, freezer bags and tweezers, digging tools, reading glasses, flashlights, and an acid-free paper notebook. He admired his multi-faceted Swiss army knife, a gift from his grandfather for making Second Class in Boy Scouts.

"Hey, could you fit this into your backpack?" Lauren handed him a plastic baggie of toiletries, antibiotics and pain medications they always took on trips abroad. She dangled Zack's money belt at arm's length after strapping on her own. "You weren't going to forget this, were you? I might have to leave you in Greece if you lose your passport."

"You'd take off on me?" He faked an incredulous look. "After our little soiree, I'd wager you're hooked, forever."

Lauren smiled. "So proud."

After paying the admission, he led her up the Sacred Way, the main pathway of the temple complex that switch-backed uphill. Pedestals that once held elaborate statues of gods now stood empty. The broken columns, stone terraces, walls, and buildings spoke of past grandeur that now lay in ruins, sacked by invaders, pilfered by Romans, nature, a religious purge of pagan ways, and by the passage of time itself.

They approached the remains of the Temple of Apollo, rebuilt in 330 BCE upon the ruins of temples destroyed by fire and earthquakes. It missed most of its structure and roof. Only a few columns and a substantial foundation remained intact, supported by an elaborately latticed stonewall. They stood silently, reaching back into the hopes and dreams of past millennia. Fallen monuments cluttered Delphi, but its former glory did not seem diminished in aura. For them, Delphi lived.

"We all look for answers, but there are always more questions than answers," Lauren said. She placed her palm on a truncated column, waiting to sense the pulse of time locked within.

"Did the ancients receive the answers they desired, or the ones they dreaded?" Zack asked.

She withdrew her hand from the column and ran her thumb over the tips of her fingers, as if to see whether the past had somehow transferred to her. "What about the questions they were afraid to ask?"

"In its present state, it's hard to imagine the impact these tumbled remains had on the people of the ancient world..." Zack ducked his head suddenly. "Oh no, don't turn around." He covered his face with his hand. "It's that waiter from the *taverna*; he's coming up the Sacred Way."

"What? That's odd, isn't it?"

Lauren turned to say hello. Zack grabbed her arm. "Why were you flirting with him?"

"That was flirting? It's sweet of you to be jealous of a student waiter." She tugged Zack closer to her. "You were condescending."

"Are you kidding? Guys have been hitting on you ever since I've known you."

"I don't think he saw us. If we head up that ridge, we'll have a better view of the whole site from the Sikelanos Mansion. He bothers me, but I don't know why." She stepped onto rocky ground. "You know, when I was leaving the bathroom, he asked if we have children. Told him I was having trouble. I'm tired of people asking me about that."

"I think the guy's kind of creepy. You know, like too perfect."

"Get over it, sweetheart. I would take him anytime over that big bastard that chased us. Wow, what an incline. I'm glad we're wearing boots."

He led the way over steeply terraced walls carved into the mountainside. Tall pine trees reached for the heavens beside a cemetery and the Sikelanos Mansion, built by an extraordinary couple that strived to recreate the Delphic Festivals in 1927. A panorama of the Corinthian Gulf, rugged Peloponnesian highlands, scenic village of Delphi on the downward slope from the mansion, spread out before them.

"Come on, let's head up there and earn our lunch," Lauren said.

After struggling uphill another fifty yards, Zack stopped suddenly. Lauren ran into him, knocking him off-balance. He tried to steady himself, but the weight of his backpack betrayed him. He lost his footing and tumbled into a large hole, landing at the bottom against a damaged column sticking out of the ground.

"Are you all right?" she asked.

"Nary a scratch." He brushed dirt and leaves from his clothing. "I swear there was ground in front of me, and then there wasn't any."

"I'm coming down."

"Watch your footing. They must have had a lot of rain to create a sinkhole this deep." He glanced up. "Honey, bring my backpack, will you?"

She sidestepped her way down the steep slope. When she reached the bottom, Zack took the Swiss army knife out of his pack.

"I see you have your best friend," she teased.

"Leave my knife alone. It's very sensitive to criticism." He scraped around the edges of the column. "There's Greek writing chiseled into the marble."

"Hey, what makes you think it's okay to work on that?"

"This is incredible."

"Zack, it's wrong and someone could see us."

"Just relax."

He cleaned up the stone with a brush, and water from a bottle, until he could make out several words. He squinted while pondering the translation. "I think it says, 'Do not trespass in the temple of Apollo or you shall surely suffer disembodiment or the…the loss of your body'." He grinned at her, a boyish look on his face, clearly pleased with his discovery. "How about taking pictures?"

"You want proof you're a criminal?" She removed her hat and took out her cell phone. "Now, assume the position."

He stopped to search his backpack for a digging tool. He worked industriously, oblivious to the sweat streaking his face. "Honey, could you use the video camera? You can record longer and have no idea how important an artifact this may be."

"Zack, I want you to stop."

Ignoring her, he cleaned an area a foot around the wider base. Zack tried again to shift the column. It moved a few inches to one side. "I wonder if this is how my brother John feels when he's trying to pull a tooth in his office." He continued to manipulate the column in a circular motion. "Dang, this molar's got really long roots."

"Your brother wouldn't appreciate the humor."

Lauren tucked the cell phone into her backpack. Still standing on the rim of the hole, she withdrew the hand-held video camera. "I think we need dynamite," Zack said, putting his pack on.

"Yeah, to blow you out of jail when we get caught doing this."

Lauren focused the video camera on him, nervously chronicling his slow but steady progress. "You're going too far. Listen to me for once."

"Okay, just a little more."

As he pushed and pulled on the column, dirt started to disappear around the edges. He froze: the soil drained beneath his feet like grains of sand in an hourglass.

Then the sound of thunder. Lauren turned her attention towards the mountains. Clouds filtered over them.

She turned back. The earth moaned. The column disappeared below ground. "What the hell?" Zack shouted.

He fell through an opening, amid a rush of dirt, landing just above a stone stairway. Unable to stop himself, he followed the stone column until it made solid contact at the bottom. He rubbed his sore knees while staring into a darkened doorway, his observations interrupted by the sound of Lauren screaming his name – and a flash of lightning that illuminated the hole above him.

"Zack, where are you? Answer me!"

Fast-moving clouds exploded overhead, pelting the landscape with huge raindrops. Small puddles formed, along with ever-expanding streams of mud-filled water that sought out and found the least path of resistance.

Lauren leaned forward to peer into the hole. "I'm okay," Zack said.

Thunder snapped just above Lauren's head. She threw her arms up and struggled to keep her balance atop the ledge, but teetered and toppled into the hole. She grabbed at a tree root, slowing her descent. Landing on her feet, she fell against a dirt wall and then half-slid down a rough-hewn stone stairway.

She landed in front of Zack, who helped her up. "I took that last flight of stairs on my rump," she said.

"I heard you scream and then you were coming at me like a pearl diver off a boat." He gently massaged her lower back. "Better?"

She nodded. "Crap, I dropped the video camera. It's hanging off that root up there, and my backpack is still up on the landing." She took a calming breath. "At least you still have yours." Lauren paused again, her head tilting to one side. "Do you hear that rumbling noise? It sounds like a generator."

"Yeah, has kind of a high and a low pulse to it."

Lauren shivered. "I don't like it down here. Let's go back up and tell the museum about this."

"Come on, this could be a great discovery. You know, in for a penny, in for a pound. I heard something break loose when the column rolled down in front of me."

Zack illuminated the darkness with his cellphone. A wooden door lay on the floor next to the column. He raised the angle of the light beam.

"Lauren." He grabbed her arm. A cloud of what appeared to be molasses churned before their terrified eyes.

"Let's get out of here!" Lauren shrieked as the vibrations shook the walls of the corridor and the landing.

The cloud boiled, increasing speed as it moved toward them. A deluge of rainwater poured in. The sludge cascaded down the steps, and washed across the stairs to where they stood. Joining hands, they jumped on the door to avoid the rushing wave. Zack blocked the rainwater with his free hand, and peered up to ground level. The backlit figure of a man stood above the hole.

Lauren lifted her foot from the column, which glowed red, but oddly, sent icy shocks up her leg. She slipped and fell against Zack, her arm entangled in the strap of his backpack. He reached for her and dropped his phone. They fell backwards, throwing up their arms.

The cloud cleared briefly. They saw their own lightning-flashed images pelted by raindrops within the tight revolutions of the mud. Then the cloud leaped forward and engulfed them, sucking their bodies into the roiling mass, cutting Lauren's scream short.

Then, just as suddenly, the rain and thunder in the atmosphere stopped, as if it was a spigot being turned off.

Apollo withdrew one of his two bronze medallions from beneath his shirt and waved it over the tunnel opening. There was no need to watch the process. The gradual grinding of rock would follow and the hole would slowly close.

The wild weather and sound distortions dissipated. Later, he would make the journey himself, after allowing enough time for his prospects to adapt. He would observe their actions by following them inconspicuously, or in disguise. *They have so many struggles to overcome.*

He weighed the success of his manipulations. *The dream I sent you, Traveler, is more important than you know. I saw a photograph, showing the conspirator and your Professor together at the fundraiser within The Book of Histories. Archives led me to you, his students. I selected you for qualities I require: knowledge of the past, strong physical stature, childless, citizens of a powerful country; and a link to the evildoer, who if left to his designs, will change the course of history.*

The corners of his mouth turned downward as he contemplated the fated photograph. He and the other gods had discovered it in *The Book of Histories,* and now he was satisfied that the archive was accurate. How he wanted to destroy that infamous evildoer, Saabir, when he appeared with Traveler at the museum party! *It took all of my will not to cook the criminal's brain with a single pulse. But I will follow my plan. I need*

heroes to do my work. The lessons of history must be learned the hard way,
so they will stick. As much as I want to, I will not save your world for you.

All has gone well so far. Sowing the seeds of their departure to
Greece proceeded without incident. The young man in the classroom and
the others did my bidding. All served to destabilize Golden Hair. The
threats by the Savage brought no significant injuries, served as valuable
tests of their abilities, and surely provided enough of a menace to prod their
departure to Greece and on to Delphi.

Certainly, they enjoyed the transit essence mixed into the hummus
within that heavy bowl at the luncheon, and also the additional dose of
ambrosia dripped into the Traveler's brew. Oh, what a laugh inside the
taverna watching them rub their hot bellies. Only they do not know how
much they needed the essence. Perhaps I should be more patient and
compassionate with the unknowing. Only, this will not serve my purpose.

Time is a process that bears advantage for no one, maybe not even
for gods.

His thoughts wandered to more interesting ground. He drew in
through his nostrils, regenerating a fragrant memory of the Golden Hair.
After allowing her quintessence to linger a moment longer, he cast her
away, for it only brought to the surface a woeful yearning. *I cannot allow*
this distraction. Too much is at stake.

Alas, Golden Hair, how perfect you would be for me. I am sure of
you. Of the Traveler, I am not so sure. You, Golden Hair, will suffer for
him and you will certainly need all your good humor.

He laughed aloud, remembering the confusion on her face when he
said as much to her at the *taverna*.

I am in control. Chance, risk, the unknown: these are all Tyche's weapons. What an absurd process by which to influence events in the realm of mortals.

Assuming all was perfectly in order, Apollo left to attend to his own transformation. He didn't notice the nearly buried camera strap hanging on a root.

CHAPTER 7
DELPHI
JUNE 2011

CHANCE DISCOVERY

Demo would do just about anything to get away from the orphanage. With school out for the summer, he would run the kilometer from the orphanage's location just outside the village of Delphi to his job at the museum each morning. All he had to do was keep the grounds clean, stay out of trouble, and be friendly to tourists. That was easy, but it was far more difficult to stay away from the tempting aromas of *spanakopita* and cheesy *tiropita* at the snack bar.

He waved his curly locks out of his eyes while sipping on a soft drink, waiting for a sudden rainstorm to move on. Still early for the tourist buses making the long uphill trek from Athens, there would be little work to do at the refreshment stand, so he swept the walkways until a tall man walking down the Sacred Way approached him.

"Good day, young man," the tourist said. Demo liked being called a young man. Tourists should see that he was nearly a grown man.

"*Kalimera*," Demo said brightly, studying the dark-haired man who wore a black short-sleeved shirt and black slacks. His muscled arms extended from the sleeves. Maybe the man was a television wrestler, or a movie star with all the gold and leather chains around his neck and his slicked-back hair. The man bent over to talk to him. One part of his hair gave way from the holding gel, releasing a long lock of hair from the side of his ear. "An industrious lad up so early and attentive to his duties is a joy to behold," he said, holding Demo's attention with his eyes.

The tourist's stare felt like it reached inside him. His stomach fluttered. "A young man, when his efforts are turned to good endeavors, is an asset to his people. Do good, and it will come back to you in ways you cannot imagine."

"Are you a movie star?" Demo asked, embarrassed by the man's compliments and wanting to avert his eyes, but he couldn't look away.

The man looked at the sky, then back at him. He brushed back the long curl of hair. "I am just as much of the stars as I am of the ground you stand upon."

Demo looked at him queerly. "Huh?"

The man patted him on the shoulder and left for the museum. After watching the tourist slowly walk away, Demo ventured uphill along a ragged stone path, aimlessly walking and picking up errant soda cans.

Suddenly, he came upon the edge of the ditch. Only his splaying arms kept him from falling into the opening. He peered over the edge, eyeing a hole about a meter in diameter at the base, with a large root sticking out just before the bottom. He shimmied down the side. As he drew closer, he spotted what looked like a camera strap half-buried at the base of the root.

CHAPTER 8

DELPHI

TRANSITION

THE DISEMBODIMENT OF THE GODS

Torn apart…torn apart…torn apart.

Zack held no other thoughts in his scattered hold on consciousness. He tumbled, simultaneously pulled forward and then jerked backwards by Lauren's weight, her arm still entangled in his backpack straps. Through his closed eyelids, he sensed darkness. Heat pulsated in his stomach, contrasting with the unrelenting cold outside his body. The one time he opened his eyes, mud blinded him. Neither could he draw a breath. He clenched his jaws, held Lauren tightly, and absorbed a velocity he could never have imagined.

The gasp will come; the one I will have to take. The same one that will suffocate me; both of us will die. What have I done?

The tumult jarred them apart, as if they hit a bump, but the shoulder straps of the backpack held.

They managed to reach out and hold one another, despite spinning uncontrollably. The muddy mass propelled them into a surreal landscape he could not see or fathom. The mud was cold… so cold.

His heart pounded and lungs begged for air. Lauren tightened her grip on his wrists, the digging sensation of her fingernails a certain sign of her desperation.

I've failed you, sweetheart.

Mud broke the thin barrier of his lips. An overwhelming roar assaulted his ears. His joints ached. He felt himself stretching.

The end is here.

They ricocheted off the sides of what seemed like a tube. It narrowed, threatening to crush them. Just before he completely tore apart, they decelerated. A membrane seemed to burst. They tumbled through space in a splatter of tunnel material. They finally hit a solid surface, rolling until they slammed into a wall.

Zack opened his eyes, and saw only a dim red glow in one corner. He gasped for air. Lauren sprawled across his legs, not moving. He shook her shoulder. She drew a ragged breath, and then gagged.

"Honey, talk to me."

"Zack," Lauren coughed. She coughed some more, clearing her airway. "What... happened?"

"We got on the wrong roller coaster." Zack drew her into his arms and felt the shuddering of her body.

"Not funny." She hacked again.

"Sorry. I thought we were history too."

"Lucky we wound up together."

Zack rolled her off and hoisted himself onto his hands and knees. "I feel like I've been on one of those medieval torture racks."

"Be happy to be alive." Lauren rid her mouth of the last of the tunnel mud. "Where are we?"

Zack cleared the sludge from the zipper and opened his backpack. He flicked on the butane lighter. The flame outlined a small square room. The wall where they had emerged was now solid rock. Below it sat another pillar of dark marble, similar to the one Zack had previously dug out. Its glow subsided. The room remained cold.

On a wall to their right, dark clothing hung from wooden pegs pounded into the wall. Behind them, a large wooden door with metal panel reinforcements barred the exit. A sturdy plank slid through iron slats blocked entry from the other side.

"Why is it locked this way? Did we fall down a mine shaft or get caught in some kind of mudslide?" Zack asked.

Lauren sneezed, leading to a symphony of sneezes, each louder than the one before. Zack's lighter revealed a hazy distillate in the air, so fine he thought he could see the individual molecules. "It's getting hard to breathe in here. Let's open the door and try to figure out where we are and get some help," he said.

"I feel like I've been through a bunch of karate tournaments, and lost them all. What a headache."

"There's water in my canteen and pain medicine in my pack. I think I swallowed that mud, too."

He gave Lauren two tablets, and she gulped from the water bottle. After doing the same, he helped her to her feet and took his first look at her. "Crap, this lighter's burning my thumb."

She covered her nose. "Zack, why'd you have to mess with that column?"

"Nothing I can do about it now. Maybe there's a place out there where we can clean up. C'mon, between the two of us we should be able to lift this thing."

On the count of three, they shifted their full weight into the task. The bar budged.

"It's so damn heavy," Zack said.

Lauren jumped out of the way as he dropped it to the ground with a dusty thud. "After all that, I hope the door opens."

She sneezed again. Zack set his feet and pulled on an iron ring attached to the door. The door opened a crack.

"We need something to stick in the opening," Lauren said.

"I still have my best friend."

"If it helps us get out of here, I'll never complain about that knife again."

Zack stuck the knife in the crevice. He flicked the lighter back on.

"I smell incense, and I think I hear chanting, but it's faint," Lauren said.

Fresh air seeped in. "This must be what King Tut's tomb smelled like when it was first opened," Zack said. "You stay near this crack in the door until we get some decent air. Maybe we should both take antibiotics for a while, in case we're breathing in some kind of weird bug. I'm going to get one of those clothing pegs on the wall."

He knocked off one of the wooden pegs with his fist. He fingered the finely woven garments. "Hey, this is one of those short dresses, a chiton, like they used to wear in ancient Greece."

She shrugged. "Maybe the museum puts on plays and the actors use this as a changing room."

"Look at the embroidery on the hem."

She smiled. "Professor, let's deal with the door first. I'll get the chiton. At least we can wipe down with it later."

Zack braced the opening with one of the wall pegs. He forced his arm through the breech and grasped the door from the other side. "Lauren, pull."

The door hinge surrendered.

He found a wooden three-legged stool outside the door. Extending the lighter, he saw a few feet of hallway, and the faint outline of a torch-holding sconce mounted on the wall.

Lauren squeezed through the opening. After setting the stool to keep the door ajar, they crept tentatively down the corridor.

"Hello?" Lauren called out.

"Honey, watch your step. The floor's full of potholes."

"My knee is still a little sore from the chase and I don't need a sprained ankle to go with it."

Zack ran his fingers over the convexity of carved stone, the lighter held up close. "Look at the walls. Is that some kind of bas-relief on the surface? It has bumps in some kind of checkerboard pattern. It's undulating down the hallway wall, like a giant snake."

"Didn't the Greeks think Delphi was originally occupied by the Earth Goddess and a giant python? Maybe we're down inside the original temple."

"You mean we've discovered an unknown subterranean temple, say 1400 BCE Mycenaean or earlier?" He pumped his fist in a victory sign.

"This could be a great discovery," she agreed. "Do you see anything else?"

"Yeah, dirt, rocks and big roots. And I smell that incense again."

The narrow hallway curved to the right, dropped sharply as though the earth had shifted, and then rose again raggedly, straightening out at the end. They found steps cut into a rock wall, ladder-like, positioned beneath a small wooden door ten feet above their heads.

Lauren shook her head. "I don't like this. How far do you think we just walked?"

"Length of a football field, maybe. Seems a little odd though, with all the earthquakes through the centuries. You'd think the corridor would be more distorted than it is."

"Whatever happened, at least we can get out of here. Up you go."

Zack climbed the ladder, and put the palms of his hands on the door. "I'm going to lift it just enough to see where the heck we are."

He peered beyond the opening. The lighter illuminated a small room filled with antique furniture, along with wall murals depicting scenes of priests with bulls and sheep brought to sacrifice. Chairs and a chaise were on one side of the room, along with a large terra cotta basin supported by a wooden mount.

"This must be one of the exhibits," he said.

"Let me see."

"Hey, only one newly famous archaeologist allowed at a time."

Zack crawled onto the floor of the room and cleared away a woolen fleece rug that covered the hatchway.

"It's beautiful, at least what I can see of it," Lauren said, joining him. "There's so much more to this museum than I imagined. I don't remember ever seeing this exhibit."

He opened a creaky door. After a quick glance, he whispered, "There's a procession of priests walking down the corridor, and torches lining the hallways. Can you hear the chanting?"

"Yeah ... hey, that's not modern Greek—that's classical Greek. Let's keep a low profile and follow them."

A line of priests walked through a doorway in long white robes and disappeared.

They crept along the corridor, jumpy as thieves, closing the distance to the room the priests had entered. They peeped around the corner. A short stone stairway led into a small oval room, the *adyton*. The priests fixed their attention on a wild–haired, grotesque-looking older woman who sat atop a three-legged chair, just behind a diaphanous curtain, positioned over a chasm in the stone floor. With her chair set uncomfortably high, she had to bend her head down to avoid hitting the ceiling.

Lauren touched Zack's arm. "It smells sort of sweet in here. Don't archaeologists think that gases leaking from volcanic fissures beneath the temple caused the Pythia to hallucinate?"

"Probably true," he whispered. "Instead of the spirit of Apollo, they think it was ethylene and it's not exactly safe to be breathing it in. Isn't this risky for the actors?"

The woman rocked, ranting in an unintelligible language.

"Zack, this is an excellent rendition of the ancient ritual."

"The priests are going to have a hard time interpreting that blabbering as the word of Apollo," he said quietly. "Is this a rehearsal, maybe?"

One priest raised his hands, separating them as if in prayer, his voice echoing within the small enclosure. Another threw leaves on a brazier, filling the room with the aroma of laurel. Just inside the room, a warrior stood behind the priests, his feet set wide apart as if ready to receive a blow. He faced away from Zack and Lauren. Torchlight danced off the image of a lion on the back of his bronze breastplate, and shone from steel-gray hair groomed into long locks. A priest, standing aside from the others, bit on the end of a writing stylus, deep in thought. He finished writing on a papyrus scroll. Finally, he stood and read the words aloud in ancient Greek. "Hear the words of Apollo. Either Sparta will perish or she must mourn a Herakleid king." Gasps followed. Priests and officials present murmured to each other. The warrior didn't move.

"So cool, I've never seen a re-creation like this. They're portraying the prophecy of Leonidas's death at Thermopylae," Zack whispered, placing a finger to Lauren's lips. "Let's go to the museum and get cleaned up."

Just before ascending a long staircase, they found the statue of a tall, muscular god holding a lyre.

"That's Apol..." Zack said, until he stumbled in dimming torchlight and whacked his knee on an egg-shaped stone sitting on the floor. "Oww! I tripped over that rock."

Lauren ran her fingers over a woolen net that covered a carved relief on the stone. "That's not some rock; that's the Omphalos. The Greeks used it to mark the navel of the earth. It's supposed to be upstairs in the museum."

Zack massaged his knee. "I'm bleeding."

Lauren cupped his chin. "Oh, Mommy will get you a Band-Aid when we get upstairs," she said singsong.

"Oh, you're so comforting."

He limped while pushing Lauren up the staircase. Reaching the top, they entered the main temple to find another statue of Apollo and three women dressed in white, throwing pine branches on a hearth. The concentrated smoke and pine incense made Lauren cough. The women turned with horrified looks on their faces. They brandished the pine branches like fly swatters, and chased the couple towards a set of slightly open doors.

Lauren raised her arm over her face. "What are they doing? Don't they screen the employees here?" When they reached the doorway, the sunlight revealed just how disgusting they looked.

"We're going to scare the hell out of somebody," Zack said.

"They've been doing some remodeling since we were last here," Lauren observed. They emerged through a square doorway, hands in front of their eyes to lessen the light of day. "What on earth…"

Zack's confusion became shock when his eyes adjusted. He turned to Lauren. She blinked, moved her head forward and backwards, as if near-sighted. Then she faltered. Her shoulder hit a temple wall. He grabbed her arm. They took a few stiff steps, as if an imaginary string pulled them slowly forward. Above them, blue squares were inlaid into the stone portal above the doorway. They exited the temple between a pair of red-painted pillars onto the *pronaos*, the entry porch. Ancient Greek writing ran on one side of the stone portal, the finely chiseled words outlined in blue. He read the proverb: "Know Thyself".

"This can't be," he said.

"Zack."

He heard the question in her voice. "Lauren, stay next to me."

"The temple… the whole complex is… intact. It's as if it was erected and painted yesterday. What… in the world?" She tightened her grip on his hand. "Something is very wrong. Where are we?"

Zack followed her gaze. He, too, spotted distant guards dressed in the costumes of ancient warriors. Some stood as though on duty, while others in red capes patrolled in a square formation, like policemen on a beat. "Look around," he said, his voice more fearful. "In the distance; the museum should be here. It's like everything disappeared and an entirely new complex has been built."

Temples and stone buildings lined the Sacred Way, the curved roadway weaving down the hillside. They crept down a short ramp, both wide-eyed, until a loud voice from behind caused them to halt. They turned to face a man clad in a purple robe, shouting angry words, pointing his staff at them.

"He's saying something like... how filthy we are and how dare we desecrate the temple grounds," Lauren said with her head cocked. "He wants us to leave before he sets the guards on us."

The robed man gazed with a puzzled look upon her bare legs, muddy clothing and hair.

Zack managed to swallow a laugh. "You *do* look like a Rastafarian on a bad hair day."

"Stop it."

Other men came forward, shaking their fists at them.

"We're sorry, really," Zack said in English. "We don't have tickets. Where do we get them?"

The men tilted their heads as if trying to understand his words.

"Let's get out of here," Zack said.

They looked back. "I'd swear we just walked out of the Temple of Apollo, but it's the archaic temple, Zack." Lauren pointed toward the east pediment. "That's Apollo arriving at Delphi on a chariot. That's after 548 BCE. It's intact, and so are all the other buildings. This is the best reproduction I have ever seen. What happened to the museum complex?"

"This is exactly how the site must have looked in antiquity."

"I don't know, but I've got a very bad feeling, and it's getting worse. The clothing they're wearing is Classical Greece. The language they are speaking is authentic. The temples... look at the paint."

They walked down the Sacred Way, past statues of gods and goddesses lining the sides. "The statues look alive," she said as people hugged the feet of the statues or prayed to them with their palms held out.

Lauren braced a hand against her face to arrest the twitching of her jaw muscles. She muffled her voice. "Come on, before I faint."

Red-tiled roofs topped one-story stucco houses. A number of small rectangular buildings were the recipients of heavy foot traffic.

Two museum guards, dressed as ancient warriors, stood in the gateway at the end of the path. The men leaned on their spears, their helmets off and shields propped against a wall.

"Lauren, check out those guards. Talk about virtual reality. Maybe we should ask them what the heck is going on here."

"Forget it. Let's keep going." She tugged Zack forward.

They lowered their heads while making their way to the gate. A guard jumped into their path.

"By the gods, your filth is a disgrace," a second guard said, leveling his lance. "If the gods do not strike you down, I will."

Zack raised his hand to acknowledge the order, but the first guard pinned him against the gate with his forearm. Lauren screamed in English, "No, don't!" The other guard hurled her to the ground, drew his sword and pressed it to her neck. She froze. Her voice cracked. "What's going on?"

"Silence!" the guard demanded. Lauren dared not swallow with the naked blade drawing a tickle of blood from her.

"Who let you in here?" the guard asked, pulling her hair hard, drawing a cry. Zack replied in Modern Greek, "Look we're just..."

The guard rammed a forearm into his throat. "Speak not your foreign tongue or I will run you through." The guard was seething. "You offend the gods and I'm in a nasty mood this day with all these Spartans running around. Could you be Persian spies?"

A young female voice intervened. "Sir, I beg you, these are my slaves. What have they done?"

"What?" The guard cast a glance towards the girl, then increased his pressure on Zack's windpipe. Zack gurgled and flailed his arms. "These giant stinkers are yours?"

"My uncle will beat them severely for leaving the farm without permission. He's carving a good switch for them right now. May I take them home to him?"

The guards released their holds.

A teenaged girl stared at them. She had arranged most of her dark hair in a bun atop her head, while the rest cascaded down her back. She wore a linen knee-length *chiton* over skinny, fine-haired legs that showed an assortment of bruises and half-healed cuts. Zack coughed, rubbing his throat. The guard threw him outside the stone gateway. Lauren helped him up.

"Come with me," the girl said in ancient Ionian, motioning with her hand. They walked fast down the dirt road leading away from the complex towards the sacred Castalia Spring.

Zack held his throat. "Are you okay?" Lauren asked. "I'm scared shitless and trying very hard to persuade myself that we entered another area of the museum built since our last visit. How can they treat us like this?"

"What did that girl say to save us?" he asked in a ragged voice.

"I didn't understand it all. I think she said we belonged to her."

Zack scanned the scenery. "Are we on the right side of the mountain? Oh God. The mountains can't be altered…" His voice trailed off.

They turned around to be sure the complex still stood as before.

Pilgrims washed in the Castalia Spring. "I don't believe what I'm seeing," Lauren said, shaking her head. "Look at the sanctuary of Athena Pronaia down there. It should be in ruins. This temple is smaller and square. There's a farm beyond it."

A quarter-mile hike brought them to a single-story farmhouse, about fifty feet from a wheel-rutted road. It was set on a flattened area just above where the land sloped into a deep ravine. Goats and sheep nibbled on grass within a large pen next to a chicken coop, both made with rows of rickety sticks tied together with twine.

"I don't remember a farmhouse being here when we drove up," Zack said quietly.

The girl faced them. "What manner of strangers are you?" she asked. Her eyes and manner spoke of curiosity. She angled her head, squinting. "Can you not speak? What has happened to you? Have you been injured?"

They looked at each other, hesitating. "It's a little difficult to understand her," Lauren said.

She turned to the girl "Can you help us?" she asked in Modern Greek.

The girl raised a hand to her ear. She replied in Ionian that she did not understand.

Lauren asked for help again, this time slowly, in ancient Ionian.

The girl grinned, her expression bright but still concerned. "Your Ionian is rough." She gestured in the direction of the temple. "Many travel here from great distances and I have heard many tongues. Who are your people?"

"She's talking too fast. I think she asked where we are from. What do we tell her, Zack?"

"What tongue did you just speak? I've not heard it before," the girl said.

Zack set his hands on his hips. "Tell her we're Americans and we want to know what the heck is going on here."

Lauren elbowed Zack, hard. The girl leaped backwards, bringing her hands to her face, as if she had witnessed something shocking. Lauren put her hands out to calm the girl and spoke slowly, repeating each word, using gestures and changing pronunciation until the girl understood.

The girl asked, "Where is this land you speak of? Are all your people giants, and is it your custom to bathe in mud-holes?"

Lauren laughed. "No, we do not. Do you know of America, the United States?"

"What?" The girl's silky cheeks attracted the sun.

"What is your name?" Lauren noted how the girl's olive-shaded eyes had subtle gold-colored streaks radiating from the pupils.

"I am called Cassandra, after the Trojan princess, whose ears were licked by snakes so she could see the future."

"Cassandra, a beautiful name." Lauren's skill in ancient languages was being put to the test. 'My grandmother's name is Cassandra also."

"I live in that farmhouse with my family."

"Your eyes are very pretty. I've never seen golden specks in someone's eyes before."

"It is generous of you to say so. Priests at the temple have said my eyes also speak of prophecy, and that one day, I may be Pythia."

"Did she just say what I think she said?" Zack asked, scratching at his mud-caked cheek.

"Zack, don't interrupt, this is too incredible." Lauren waved her hand to shush him. "Thank you for saving us from the guards."

The girl smiled and bowed. "I have seen those guards rough-handle a lot of pilgrims, and someone told me not long ago that I must be kind to strangers."

"Do you think your family could help us?"

Cassandra folded her arms, weighing Lauren's request. "Remain here. My uncle may understand your words better than I. But I beg you; it is not wise to strike this man in his presence."

The girl skipped barefoot to the house. She entered a front door set between two wood-shuttered windows. She emerged a minute later in the company of an older man.

"What do we say to him?" Lauren asked, biting a nail.

"Hey, did I hear her say you can't hit me?"

"Zack, I may ask you to hit me back really hard if it would wake me up from … whatever the hell this is." She threw her arm in a sweeping motion.

"I'm as confused as you are. These people are either the best actors in the world, or we've managed to find our way to another galaxy."

Lauren studied his face. "I don't want to admit to the possibilities."

Zack nodded. "I can understand some of what they're saying, but I'm going to need a hell of a lot more practice to maintain this charade."

Cassandra escorted the older man, who walked with a limp. White hair ringed his nearly-bald head, but his beard and mustache retained some strands of the dark hair of his youth. His nose was bulbous and his lips thin, partially hidden by the untrimmed facial hair. With deeply tanned skin, and limbs that still held tone, he carried a farmer's musculature beneath his dirty *chiton.*

He looked them over with his soft blue eyes. "Ah, you are correct, honeybee. They do look atrocious. Cassandra tells me you need assistance."

"We beg you to help us. We would like to cleanse ourselves, and we need lodging, if you can direct us," Lauren said in measured Ionian.

The man sniffed. "By Zeus, you two certainly do need a bath. Come no closer to the pens; you will terrify the goats. Perhaps you should dive into the gulf beyond and remove the filth. It's a short walk. Now tell me, where is this land you are from?"

"Sir, what is your name?" Zack asked in Ionian.

"If I understand your words, I am called Nestor."

"I am Zack. This is my wife, Lauren."

Lauren smiled, still looking like the Medusa herself, with only her white teeth and eyes contrasting the swabs of dark mud that covered her. Nestor managed a weak smirk.

"Nestor, may I address you?" Lauren asked. "I speak your words better than my husband."

"Your Ionian is crude, but I understand you." Waving his hand in front of his nose, Nestor turned away from Zack and Lauren. Cassandra giggled.

"Sir, we want to go to *Atheni.*"

"To Athens, with the invasion so close?"

Lauren's knees buckled, as if an invisible fist struck her.

"What'd he say?" Zack asked, supporting her.

"He said invasion," she replied, her voice fast, frantic. She steadied herself. "Sir, what invasion do you speak of?" Her eyes darted between Zack and Nestor.

Nestor studied them gravely. "You do not know? By the gods, Xerxes is bringing an army of slaves here to slay us all."

Lauren's jaw sagged. She slumped against Zack. He tried to hide his own shock as the stark realization of their situation began to sink in.

"Forgive me. Do you mean the Persian King Xerxes?" Lauren's voice broke.

"I do. Swarms of his barbarian troops are heading through Macedonia. We are consulting the Oracle for guidance. I think the answer is clear. We must form a coalition to fight them."

Lauren's lips trembled. Zack felt her shock and devastation. He took her in his arms. "Honey, we'll be okay," he said softly. "Let's approach this situation with common sense. I'm sure we're smack in the middle of some kind of revival festival for tourists."

"What on earth is going on here, Zack?" She put her hand to the side of her jaw, taking long breaths and holding them. She turned to Nestor. "Is there a place nearby where we might rest and bathe?"

Nestor nodded. "There is a stream that is down the hill beyond our farmhouse. Maybe then we shall see what you really look like. Your attire is quite strange. How distant is this land you are from?"

"A long and difficult journey."

"If we survive the war, it may be wise to strike an alliance. Perhaps our heralds should journey to your country."

"We are here as envoys from our people," Lauren said, glancing at Zack. "Our ship was wrecked as we neared the coast, and we lost most of our possessions. We crossed a vast ocean in a vessel rigged for high seas."

"Have you a change of clothing?"

Lauren shook her head. "May we borrow robes? We would appreciate your kindness."

"Honeybee, gather two *himations* and lead our visitors to the stream."

"Follow me, Master Zack and Lauren." Cassandra opened a gate of bound sticks. They walked past a chicken coop to a backyard with a barn. She opened the dual doors, exposing two horses, oxen, and a large wagon. "Wait here."

She returned with the robes and led them through a small wheat field, then onto a downward slope past the sanctuary of Athena, back towards Delphi. They moved onto a tree-covered path that ended at a stream cascading from the mountain. "I will leave you. Return to the house when you are finished."

Lauren smelled the washed robes. "Did your uncle call you bee or honeybee?"

Cassandra smiled." He says I flutter and dart around the farm like a bee, and I'm sweet as honey."

She scampered back towards the farm. When she was out of sight, Lauren and Zack stripped off their sodden clothes, shielded from sight by dense shrubbery. They collapsed in the mountain stream, letting the cool water roll over their bodies.

Lauren shivered. "A cold bath is better than nothing. This has to be the water from the Castalia Spring. Is there a bar of soap in that backpack?"

"Wait, I kinda like your barbarian-woman look."

"Cut out the jokes. Have we traveled through time, or is this some kind of a hoax?"

Zack smirked as he handed her the soap. "Never bathed in sacred water before. Can you think of a rational explanation for what we went through?"

"This can't be happening. Time travel is impossible. We're university professors, for Christ's sake." She lathered herself, scrubbing off the last of the tunnel mud.

He rinsed his hair. "The people could be actors, but they can't change buildings, roads, and developments in the few minutes we were in that... whatever it was."

"If it's true, we're in Delphi in 480 BCE and the Persian Wars are coming."

"If we're somehow misplaced in time, we know what's going to happen here. Think of the opportunity for us. If we were layman, we wouldn't know what the hell to do. Consider it another externship."

"You're not recognizing the gravity of what we're up against."

"Don't worry, honey, we'll be okay." Zack hugged her. "You're shaking."

"I can't accept this. Are we dreaming?"

"As impossible as it seems, the evidence is overwhelming. You're really going to have to help me out with the language and dialects, though."

"If we're in ancient Greece, can we tell people about America? We could screw up history." Lauren squeezed water out of her hair. "We should change the name. How about Atlantis or Atlantea? It's only a legend, even to them."

"It works for me. The fewer explanations, the better." Zack wiped driblets of water from his legs.

Lauren steadied her breath. "This is just too crazy. We need to get back to that temple and see if we can find our way back home." Zack studied her with wanton eyes. She flipped her hand at him, signaling him to forget it. "I still can't believe this."

They slid into the ankle-length robes Cassandra had left and pinned them near the shoulder with broaches. After retracing the path through the woods, Zack knocked on the rear door.

"Enter," Nestor called out.

"May the gods bless this home," Lauren said, studying the home's interior, illuminated by bright sunshine pouring through open shutters.

Nestor directed them to benches next to a table. Off to the side were reclining red couches, with a rolled pillow on one end, easily the nicest pieces of furniture. Bronze tripods stood in each corner, along with mounted candles. Next to one of the tripods stood a waist-high altar containing a miniature reproduction of a Greek temple and the statuette of a female goddess.

"May the gods be with you." Zack winked to Lauren before studying the simple wooden table, its legs shaped like Doric columns.

"How much better you look," Nestor said. "Join us. We don't take our meals as they do in the city, reclining on the couches with the womenfolk in their own quarters. Here, we eat together, like a squad of Spartans."

Cassandra's giggle lit up the room. "My mother will join us later," she said, pouring from a clay pitcher into wooden cups. "She serves Athena at the temple."

Moments later, Cassandra set down a square relish tray of black olives, unleavened bread, crumbled goat cheese, and a small bowl of olive oil.

"Zack," Lauren whispered. "Watch what you say."

Nestor asked, "Is that your tongue?"

"It is impolite of us," she said. "With practice, we should be able to talk more easily in your language."

"Gods willing, first we must give them their due."

Nestor hobbled to the altar, broke off pieces of flatbread, and placed them at the feet of a stiff, Egyptian-style statue of a woman. He extended his palms and prayed quietly. Zack and Lauren heard "Hestia", and realized the statuette was the goddess of the hearth.

Their host tore the bread into four pieces. "Now, I beseech you to tell us of your land."

"Would you allow my wife to speak for us? She speaks your tongue better than I do," Zack said, noting their culture in which males dominated.

Nestor nodded.

"We come from a land far beyond the Pillars of Hercules," Lauren said, referring to the ancient name for the Straits of Gibraltar that led to the Atlantic Ocean. She held out an olive, recalling those she had eaten a day before at the *taverna*. Might as well have been an epoch. She shook her head to clear her mind.

"Zeus's thunderbolts," Nestor remarked. "I have heard there is nothing out there but sea monsters and the domain of Poseidon."

"To reach our land, one must travel many months by ship." She bit into the olive, savoring the brine.

Nestor leaned closer. "Why are you here?"

"Our leaders told us there would be much to learn from so noble a people as yours." Hoping to stop his questions, she asked, "How long have you lived in Delphi?"

"I resided in Athens for many years, but I decided to retire in these mountains. I grew tired of pestilence, politics and crowds. I moved here to live with my brother's widow, Persephone, and my niece, Cassandra. My family has owned this farm for many generations. Proud we are of its placement so close to Athena's sanctuary."

Nestor ripped at the bread with a half mouthful of teeth and talked with a swelling inside one cheek. "I am an architect by trade, but I've also been a warrior, as are most of us these days. I have never been a sailor, although we Athenians, by nature and commerce, are seafarers."

"Nestor," Lauren said, avoiding the issue of Cassandra's parents, "What kind of preparation is Athens making for the war?"

"Ah," he sighed. "Many flee to the mountains or the far reaches of our land. Others are willing to fight, and my friend meets with the leaders of these city-states this moment, to organize and debate our strategy."

Lauren cast a sideways glance at Zack. "May I ask the name of your friend?"

"Themistocles," Nestor said matter-of-factly, crumbling cheese on his bread.

Zack choked on his olive upon hearing the name of the famous Athenian politician and admiral. After coughing and spitting the pit into his hand, he settled down.

"It is well to have powerful friends in time of war." Lauren pitted the olives with her fingers and, along with the cheese, created her own pita pocket sandwich.

"This will be a fight to the death and a bad time to be an outlander. Soon, the barbarians will arrive in the northern city-states. The curse of war is that it always takes its worst fury upon women and children." Nestor's arched bushy eyebrows studied Lauren's pita technique. "Well, my friends, did you enjoy your meal?"

"We did, many thanks to you," Zack said, feeling better now that they were clean and fed. Lauren yawned.

Nestor dabbed bread into the last of the oil. "This land you are from, what is it called and how are you ruled?"

"It is called Atlantea, and we are ruled much like the Athenians. We have a government of the people, by the people, and for the people." Lauren's eyes met Nestor's curious gaze.

Zack glanced at Cassandra, wondering if she had noticed the name change from America to Atlantea. The girl seemed preoccupied with miniature clay figurines of adults and children arranged beneath the small altar.

Nestor paused, slid his jaw back and forth, and then looked up at the ceiling crossbeams before he stood. "We once had kings and tyrants. Athens eventually decided that the men who toil and fight should have a say in their lives. A system based on the logic and fairness of those men, rather than the extravagant desires of a despot, like Xerxes."

Lauren nodded. "Our nation is founded on one principle that we hold very dear. Our people must remain free."

Nestor raised his hands as if in prayer. "Even though you are from far away, you understand our way of life. I beg you to stay the night to dine and talk."

"We accept." Zack draped his arm over Lauren's shoulder.

"It is our custom to provide for strangers in need. There is a room in the barn where you may rest."

"That would be most welcome," Lauren said, returning Zack's squeeze.

"So be it. May the gods be with you."

Cassandra, clearly proud to bring her uncle such fascinating strangers, escorted them out the back door to the courtyard. They entered the barn-like enclosure, passing a mound of hay and several empty stalls before reaching a closed door, which Cassandra opened to reveal a small room containing a round lamb wool bed. The breeze blew through an open window. They took in the panoramic view of the mountainside and valley, both awash in sunshine.

"Visitors so enjoy the view of the lowlands," Cassandra said. "The last visitor was so tall he could barely stretch his legs out on that bed. He must have been a warrior. I'd wager he could slay twenty barbarians with one swipe of his sword. He kept twirling a long curl near his ear, but he talked and laughed with me until the sun fell and we had filled our bellies with all of his honeyed-drink and bread. Told me if I was kind to people, the gods would reward me in ways I could not imagine."

Lauren and Zack embraced, causing her to cover her eyes. "I will leave you now." Cassandra waved farewell and headed back to the house.

Lauren shook out the wool. Satisfied, she collapsed onto the bed. "I can't believe this. We begin our day in Athens in 2011, and now we're in Delphi in 480 B.C?" She edged closer to him, her voice turning more solemn. "What if we never make it home? What if we get hurt or sick?"

"Sick? Hurt? This is the opportunity of a lifetime!" Zack pressed a kiss to her forehead. "I don't know why we're here. Maybe it was some cosmic accident. Just for now, let's immerse ourselves in the majesty of ancient Greek culture. I'd like to see Athens before it was burned down in the war. This is my favorite period of history. I can't believe how lucky I am."

Lauren looked at him with disbelief. "I understand where you're coming from, I really do… but Zack, what's ahead of us has some very serious and complex implications," she said, massaging her temples. "We could get stuck here. There's a war coming and we're foreigners. You know strangers would be outcasts in ancient Greece. I want to go back to the Temple and see if we can figure out a way to get back home." She gripped his shoulders and fixed her eyes on his.

"Honey, listen… Let's just see Athens and then we'll figure out a way to get back home. I promise."

"Figure out a way back? We don't even know how we got here."

"Lauren… lifetime opportunity…"

"Okay, on one condition. You promise me, Zack… take a vow, right here and now that you won't leave me alone under any circumstances."

An array of emotions filled her eyes. "I'll never be far from your sight. I'll stick to you like a T-shirt in a Chicago summer."

Lauren flinched at his attempt at levity in this moment of truth. He realized his error and wrapped his arms around her. "I won't leave you. Don't worry."

She exhaled in a long sigh, slowly easing her grip. "I need a nap. My head is pounding, and that stuff I swallowed in the tunnel is still hot and churning in my stomach."

"Good idea. Maybe with a little rest we'll gain a better perspective on this situation."

They burrowed into the comfort of the wool.

A few hours later, Zack awoke and stretched. Lauren stirred beside him, opening her eyes. She smiled and snuggled into his welcoming embrace. "How was your first nap in antiquity?"

He grinned. "I was dreaming of the beach in San Diego. You were in a thong bikini holding a bagful of fish tacos."

She gave him a coy look. Before he could stop her, Lauren rolled off the pallet. "C'mon, let's get up. I want to practice my Ionian with Nestor again. Remember when the professor had us speak only in ancient Greek for an entire month during that dig near Tiryns?"

Zack rose, not questioning her change of mood. "Yeah, I remember, but you told me to stop when I used the old language to describe your legs and..."

She pressed her fingertips to his lips. "Right now, let's visit our new, twenty-five-hundred-year-old friends. I'm fascinated by how it sounds like they're singing when they speak."

Once outside, Zack hopped from one stone to another in the courtyard. "The gravel is still hot. I need my sandals."

He headed inside the barn, and noticed two sets of armor in a corner. Polished breastplates, sword and scabbard hung on the wall, near an eight-foot-long dory, a spear with an iron blade. He felt its weight and reflected on the remarkable balance gained by the sharp warhead and a butt spike on the other end. A polished Corinthian-style helmet was displayed in a cupboard, adorned with a black and white horsehair plume. Near the door, a blanket covered a large round object. Zack peeled back the cover to find an oval bronze shield with a frightening rendition of a blue-faced Medusa, her hair a menagerie of threatening red serpents.

Incredible. After retrieving his sandals and backpack, he rejoined Lauren at the back door.

Cassandra answered their knock. "Welcome. You appear rested."

"We feel much better," Lauren replied, recognizing Cassandra's impeccable manners. One day, their children would be just as courteous.

"Pray enter. My uncle is with my mother, and they await your arrival."

They found Nestor and Cassandra's mother seated at the table. "I am Persephone. Welcome to our home." She stood to greet them, her smile measured. She turned to Nestor. "This woman appears to have my same number of years."

Persephone wore a yellow formal gown of a woman of means. She had the same wide bright eyes as Cassandra, the obvious source of her daughter's beauty. Her dark hair was curlier and held in place by a golden ribbon. She was slightly built, but held her chin high and looked back at them with the same curiosity. When Lauren bowed before Persephone, her eyes fell to the woman's golden armband.

"I am Lauren, and I thank you for allowing us into your home. What a beautiful band. May I see it more closely?"

"Of course," Persephone answered, displaying slightly uneven teeth as she smiled. She held out her arm.

Lauren inspected the coiled band, shaped like a snake with a pair of purple gems serving as eyes. On the body of the snake, raised images of grain stalks alternated with pomegranates, torches, and crowns. Unpolished and granular, they added an elegance of contrast to the shiny gold of the snake's body. Lauren looked to Persephone's face and then at her wristband in wonder. She guessed the item was probably a representation of the goddess Persephone, whom her hostess must surely be named after. The important deity in Greek life was associated with rebirth and revival of growth in springtime. Lauren fawned over the ancient symbol of fertility.

"I have rarely seen anything so striking, and your earrings. How did you acquire them?"

Persephone brought a finger to one of the large gold loops. Three small balls of intricately woven gold wire wrapped each loop and hung freely at the bottom. Tiny grains of gold covered the loops in the manner of the bracelet and gave it a pebbly appearance.

"They are from Etruria, on the coast of Italia. I am pleased you favor them."

Lauren smiled broadly, silently registering the presence of the Etruscan civilization flourishing in Italy … now. *The new now.* If they were to remain stuck in the past, they would have to travel across the Adriatic Sea and study a people largely lost to subsequent history.

"Lauren, you are the living image of Aphrodite. Before, encrusted with all that mud, I could have mistaken you for the Medusa that adorns my shield," Nestor said, grinning.

She laughed, revealing her perfect white teeth. "Zack, I think he just made a joke about my hair."

She turned back to Nestor. "I'm sorry. I beg your tolerance. I am still learning your tongue."

"Come and sit." Nestor took his seat at the table head.

Cassandra placed skewers on the fireplace brazier just outside the doorway. Soon, the smell of roasting fish filled the room. Zack's stomach grumbled audibly. "I love it, barbeque in the 5th Century BCE." He touched Lauren's arm.

"Again, you speak in your tongue of Atlantea?" Nestor asked. "Could you teach me?" He drank the contents of his cup, after which he set it down for Persephone, who quickly refilled it.

"I would be happy to," Lauren said. "Perhaps you could show my husband how to wear the armor we saw in the barn. He said he saw two sets."

"Yes, the second was my brother's, Persephone's husband. He died in a great battle ten years past."

"Soon after Cassandra was born," Persephone said.

Zack and Lauren glanced at each other, realizing the implications of her statements. Lauren asked, "Do you mean the battle at Marathon?"

"I do. How do you know of this?" Persephone asked, surprised.

"The valor of the brave Athenians and Plataeans against the first invasion of the Persians is well-known, even in my land."

"The gods work in strange ways," Nestor said.

Lauren joined Persephone and Cassandra at the hearth. "I am sorry about the loss of your husband and Cassandra's father."

The anticipation of hearing firsthand about one of the most important battles in ancient times overcame Zack. "Nestor, did you fight in this battle?" he interrupted.

Nestor sipped watered wine from a drinking cup shaped like a horn. He let out a satisfying exclamation. "Good wine, last of an amphora from the islands I purchased down at the port. Wish I could grow grapes here properly."

"Nestor, Zack asked about Marathon," Persephone said, barely rolling her eyes.

"Oh, yes, yes, I did fight there, and a desperate contest it was. We stood for ten days in the hills above the beach, arguing as to how best to defeat the Persian horde camped below us. Leadership transferred to a different *Polemarch* commander every day. Finally, Miltiades formed us into a battle line, and all ten thousand of us attacked." Nestor pounded the table with his fist. "In heavy armor, running such a distance would cause a man to sink to his knees. We were possessed, singing to the gods and screeching like eagles, drunk with the promise of their blood and our survival. We were far outnumbered and our center buckled as planned, but we struck from our reinforced wings and they ran. Many times my shield and armor saved me from arrows and spear thrusts. After our meal, I will show you the dents from the axe blows."

Lauren assisted Zack with the translation. "I can't believe what I just heard," he said, leaning back in his chair. He considered the extraordinary physical condition of a man who could run any distance wearing a full *panoply* of arms and armor, some sixty or seventy pounds worth.

The aroma of the seafood signaled it was time to eat. Zack enthusiastically plunged into the meal. Through open windows, twilight cast long shadows across the mountainside.

"It is time to light the candles, honeybee."

Cassandra lit an end of a small stick in the brazier. She set candles aglow and tripod pots holding oil and wicks. The flickering light cast lively shadows on the room and its inhabitants. Persephone placed a steaming plate of filleted fish on the table before Zack. He juggled a hot morsel in his fingers before tossing it into his mouth and chewing vigorously. Everyone laughed.

"I ate with the same passion when I was young," Nestor said.

"Tell us more about your land, Lauren," Persephone urged, propping her chin in her hands, elbows on the table.

"Our country is many times the size of Greece. We have gone to war against large countries and, at times, with those who hold no regard for the lives of others. We have our share of troubles, and we make mistakes, too. We had a terrible civil war many years ago to stop slavery among our people."

"Slavery, did you say?" Nestor asked, arching his eyebrows. "We have many slaves in Greece. They are the spoils of war."

"Yes." Lauren silently cursed her lack of tact. "In our country, we had to look further into our hearts to decide if each man and woman deserves the dignity to be free and equal, no matter who they are or the color of their skin, how much wealth they possess, or how royal a family they were born into."

"If we fail and fall under the barbarian yoke, our women and children will become slaves. Free men fight to remain free. Slaves deserve to be slaves if they cannot free themselves," Nestor declared.

Lauren paused, wondering if she should continue the discussion. "Do you have slaves here to help you?"

Nestor widened his eyes. "I sent them to other family members when we moved here; too many mouths to feed. Slaves require oversight, although there are times I want them." He watched Zack clean his plate. "I fear that we may run out of mullet before your hunger is satisfied. We don't often eat the meat of beasts. We hold cattle and sheep for sacrifice to the gods. We much prefer fish from the gulf."

"Many thanks, Nestor, but I cannot eat anymore."

"Then we shall go to the barn and inspect my armor. Perhaps the bronze has stretched since I last wore it." He patted his girth.

"I'll be close by, Lauren," Zack reassured her.

After the men left, Persephone inspected Lauren from head to toe, specifically her austere *chiton*. She sighed. "We can do much better for you, Lauren. Accompany us to the *gynaeconitis*."

They walked into a separate section of the farmhouse where the women slept and worked. Persephone opened the doors of an armoire and took out a white gown similar to the one she wore.

"Your hair falls about your shoulders. Is this typical of your women?" Persephone asked while separating clumps of Lauren's hair with her fingers.

"For some. But it is up to each woman to choose how to wear her hair, paint her eyes and face, and express opinions as she desires."

"This pleases my heart. Nestor allows us so many more liberties here than in the city. I can plead my point to him and he has never once beaten me. In Athens, we do not eat with the men or join their symposiums. We stay in our quarters and attend to our duties."

Lauren nodded. "I am aware of your customs."

"Nestor treats Cassandra like a son. He has taught her numbers, to swing a sword, and she can recite long passages of Homer. This would never be so under the eyes of the family in Athens. In a few short years, she would be betrothed and appealing Artemis for the birth of a healthy little one. I survived childbirth, but so many young girls do not. I think Nestor fears tempting fate. He delays her marriage, and I am pleased that he does."

"He is a remarkable man."

Persephone smiled. "Do not listen to his babble about slaves and spoils of war. He objects to their ownership. Another reason he moved here was to be beyond the sight of those who would find fault with him. He will not talk of this, but I know he would free his slaves and announce it publicly on that long wall before the temple of Apollo."

"When we are together, let us speak of anything we wish."

"It is my hope." Persephone smiled and squeezed Lauren's hand.

"You know, I have face-paints from my country. Would you like to see how they would look on you?"

Persephone nodded and smiled again. Lauren produced her small makeup case, with its lipstick, blush, eyeliner, and mirror. Persephone asked to hold the eyelash brush in her hand, and then the brass lipstick container. When she looked in the mirror, her smile disappeared. "I have never seen myself so clearly."

"You have beauty a goddess would be jealous of."

The women set to work.

Lauren lifted her head upon hearing the ring of metal outside the house. "Do not be concerned. They play like boys," Persephone said as she held the mirror at different angles.

Lauren's pensive look subsided. She resumed applying eyeliner and lipstick to Persephone while Cassandra sat beside them, wiggling in her seat, waiting her turn.

Nestor helped Zack into the armor. Picking up the bronze breastplate, he placed the two halves over Zack's head, fitted the pieces, and tied them together with leather cord. "It's heavier than I thought," Zack said in English.

Nestor strapped bronze greaves over Zack's shins. Then, he reverently set his brother's helmet in the visitor's hands. "Place it on your head."

Zack found the fit too snug, and his front and peripheral vision hindered by the protective design of the eye-slits.

"Here, hold the shield and spear," Nestor said. "Accustom yourself to the weight. Thread your fingers around that leather grip on the spear. Now hold the shield before you and strike out with the spear."

Zack nodded. He slipped his forearm through a bronze sheath on the underside bowl of the shield, and then gripped a tight cord near the inside rim. "How do you hear with this on your head, Nestor? There are no ear holes. I feel like my head's stuck in a pail."

"Battle is a noisy affair; you can hear the flutes, drums, the screams, and little else except your own fast breathing. I'll retrieve my arms and give you someone to stick."

They alternated striking each other's shield with their spears, the clanging heard all the way to the house. After a few minutes of exertion, Zack was out of breath.

"Now, plant your back foot sideways… that's it. Stand your ground and thrust with your spear, like this." Nestor crouched, dug in his heel and pushed forward, spear raised over his shoulder. "We form a line, lock our shields and then give them the *othimos*, the push. When they stumble and we break their line, our spears do the work. This is how we vanquished the enemy at Marathon, although a huge savage with horns on his helmet killed my brother with an axe. I was lucky to get my shield in the way of his next swing. See the dent?"

Zack ran his fingers over the concavities. "I see a lot of dents."

"After I slashed the barbarian's face, I took a spear near my manhood. The wound healed, but it has plagued me ever since. Poor goddess of love, Aphrodite; she knows too well my inabilities…"

"I'm sorry."

"You never leave battle without a scar, be it inside or out. It's my right to take my brother's widow for a wife, but I thought better of it since I am useless in that way. I would not stand in her way if another wanted her." Nestor scrubbed the lance-head with the hem of his *chiton*. "Though lately, I think it may be best to secure the property to them by arranging marriage. Cassandra lights up my day. Did you see the cuts on her legs?"

"I did."

"She fought off two wild dogs seeking to make dinner out of our chickens. Stood there and beat them back with a long stick, like a hoplite. She's a girl of substance, that one."

Zack nodded while watching him protect the lance head with a leather sheath moistened with oil.

"Practice lifting the bags of sand I keep in the barn. I have swords twice as heavy as the one I carry in battle. It'll take a season or more to build your strength. Now let's join the women and partake of some wine."

Zack looked squarely at Nestor, and wondered why it never occurred to him than an ancient Greek man might have blue eyes.

PART TWO

CHAPTER 9
Lydian Coast (modern day Turkey)
June 480 BCE

Dark God's Servant

Bessus hungered for revenge.

He craved it more than the rich earth of his hard-won farmlands or the soothing thunder that assured him his ancestor's gods still dwelled in the mountains near home. He longed for it more than the final running of his hand over the head of his son.

Bessus pounded his temple with the flat of his palm. He would not allow these heart-felt memories to weaken his resolve. Hate would rule him.

Dragging blackened nails along a scar that ran a jagged course across his face, and remembering how the wound came to be with guts twisting and boiling, he braced his insides with his free hand, holding back a rage threatening to burst from within. He yearned for the day when his name would be long-feared in Greek lands and in the grand halls of the Persians—both had a debt to repay him.

His day of vengeance neared. He had waited long enough. Many must die.

Bessus gazed at the gathering army of Xerxes, the Persian king who decreed that all march with him to conquer the West. To refuse meant death. As he stood upon a knoll overlooking a broad plain crowded with warriors drawn from the four corners of the earth, Bessus saw no patch of ground escape the stamps of boots or the hooves of warhorses.

He led battle-hardened warriors, borne on the backs of their horses, from the black dust mountains of Bactria at the far eastern reaches of the empire. His grandfather and father, respected rulers of mountain tribes in the south, had taught him well the ways of war. He could not quench his desire for territory, horses, and cattle. All their holdings should have come to him; all should have then passed to his son, save for the Persians and the bad times. It was a wrong he could never release.

Bessus prayed aloud to Angra Mainyu, the dark god: "Lord Mainyu, guard my son and deliver my enemies to me."

He untied the rawhide laces of his trousers, loosened the codpiece underneath, and shot a stallion-strength stream into the scrub brush beyond his command tent. His petition and offering finished, he fumbled with the laces and, losing patience, tied them quickly into a knot. The evening breeze comforted him after a long day in the saddle. Having vowed he would not be late for the ceremonious river crossing into enemy lands, Bessus had driven his horsemen to the limits of their endurance. He hoped to reap a rich harvest of treasure on this campaign, then return home to take back what should be rightfully his, and more. While turning to watch the pitching of his tent, Bessus counted those who would soon know his wrath.

As darkness descended, a burly guard seized a tall, shapely girl from the camp followers. After escorting her to Bessus' tent, he held her before a wooden barrel. Another guard ripped the purple robe from her body. A massive warhorse tethered nearby snorted while watching the men dump buckets of seawater over the girl. They took their time wiping her down with coarse rags. Finally, a guard handed her a drab woolen robe to cover herself. He lifted the tent flap and threw her inside.

Shivering, she searched the dim confines of the tent as candles barely illuminated the interior. Smoke from a small corner brazier escaped through a hole where the poles met at the top. Sodden rugs and blankets lay in a heap, soaked by a leaking water bladder. The closed-up tent, a patchwork of rough-sewn cowhides dampened by a recent rain, smelled of beasts and unwashed bodies. It was as suffocating as a crypt. She wrapped her arms tightly around her chest and crouched to await her fate.

A warrior's helmet met her gaze. It lay atop a wooden chest banded with bronze straps. Along with curved horns fastened to its sides, a row of small hobnails ran from the slim nose guard up and over the top. The meager light from the candles revealed the helmet's dull sheen; patches of black stained its surface.

The girl raised her dark eyes to glance at the bearded guard. She looked past him, her eyes settling upon a long wooden handle with a leather grip stitched midway along its length. When she craned her neck to see to the other end, her curiosity turned to terror. Twisted scalp and clumps of tangled hair adorned the hub of a broad, double-bladed axe. She buried her face in her hands, conjuring up hideous visions of the warrior who owned it. Rocking on her knees, she began to pray.

From his perch several yards from the tent, Bessus heard rustling in the bushes, interrupting his meditations. An upstart wind blew his wild black hair as he peered into an encroaching darkness, the crackling twigs capturing his attention. He spit hair from his mouth. As he bent down to conceal his form against the light from a nearly full moon, he heard his men making fires for the evening meal. The outlines of his supply wagons were barely visible between his command tent on the edge of the camp and his horsemen. Bessus strained to hear the snap of twigs as he made a straight course to the wagons. Scooting behind the hull of a wagon, he pulled his dagger. Three warriors walked by; Bessus signaled them to be silent. He motioned for two to go around the wagons, and one to follow him.

Timing his surprise, Bessus leapt upon his prey: four boys dressed in tattered ram's wool. When they scrambled to escape, he seized two by their rags. His men captured the others. "Young thieves, poor ones at that," Bessus growled.

A guard kicked one boy in the back, sending him sprawling. The child wailed. His companions joined in. "Silence!" Bessus bellowed. Eyes hollowed by famine beheld him.

"On your knees, whelps," a guard demanded. "Shall I fetch your axe, Lord Bessus?"

"My knife will do the work as quickly."

The boys listened as their captors debated their fate. One wept, while another raised his arm to block his view of what was to be. The others watched the blade approach.

He grabbed one boy by his fleece tunic, hoisting him off the ground. "Come to steal my grain?" Bessus asked.

Other warriors heard the commotion and peered at the spectacle from their campfires.

Astonished faces watched Bessus sheath his knife. "No, they shall live."

"My Lord?" one of his captains bleated.

Bessus snatched the man by the collar of his robe, lifting him so the tips of his boots scraped the ground. "I said release them!" Bessus snarled.

He had seen the eyes of his young son in one of the boys. During earlier campaigns, no heir had caused him to cast his eyes back home. Now, all that he valued might be lost. He had never known fear of this kind, and it bit into him with teeth he could not shake away.

"If I grant this mercy, I pray my son will be spared in turn," Bessus declared to his men. "Not a word of this to the others. Tonight, I will regain the favor of the Mainyu."

He turned to the boys. "Come this way again and I will fill my bowl with your chopped up guts," Bessus barked.

They bolted.

"My Lord, the girl is ready," his trusted captain, Cyartes, said.

Bessus headed to his tent, but turned a last time to see if the demons that threaten by starlight followed him. He held forth a necklace of toe-bones from his line of ancestors, strong magic against spirits that would do him harm. "Guard me this night, fathers," he pled aloud.

He neared the sanctuary of his tent, his pace quickening as his codpiece crowded his pants, more with each step.

Bessus dismissed Cyartes and entered the tent, dropping the flap behind him. As he straightened to his full height, the girl beheld a monster. He halted, stroking his filthy beard, braided at the ends and tied with beads. The flickering candles revealed his face. A ragged scar, beginning at the left side of his chin, ran up his cheek and over the bridge of his nose. Deep, dark circles encased his eyes. His bushy eyebrows did a poor job of concealing the thick bony ridges beneath them.

The girl sucked in her breath.

Fully aware of the impact his size and looks made upon the women on whom he feasted, Bessus strode slowly and confidently to a clay pot, averting her terror-filled stare. When he brushed past her, she covered her nose with the back of her hand. He dipped a stone mug into a pot that held a newly pressed batch of milky soma, the favored drink of his homeland. She watched the rhythmic jump of his throat as he downed it in a few gulps. He glanced at the tent flap, then back to her face. He twitched his lips and sniffed the air as he positioned himself between her and the only way out.

The girl frantically sought another means of escape. Bessus put down his mug and pointed at her robe. She backed away and scrambled behind the wooden chest. With nowhere left to run, she grabbed the axe handle. Unable to lift it, she moved her hands closer to the dual blades. Her arms trembled as she hoisted his axe. Bessus unbuckled his bull-hide chest plate, threw his head back and barked loudly. The girl spread her feet to balance herself, holding the axe at shoulder height.

"Give me the axe," he said, holding out his hand.

The girl crouched and mouthed voiceless prayers in her own tongue. Her heart thundered.

"My axe will not be tarnished by a whore. Give it to me."

The girl raised the axe, warning him to stay away.

Bessus sprang.

The girl screamed, closed her eyes, and swung the axe with all her strength.

He caught it by the handle and it stopped suddenly, ringing in her hands. Bessus ripped the axe from the girl's grasp and delicately laid it aside while gripping her arm. She squirmed to free herself.

He raised his fist. "Defy me. You do not know how you will pay. Drop your robe."

She obeyed.

He studied her desirable curves, took a deep breath, and expelled a bear-like growl. She turned her face away from his breath. He unfastened his codpiece and watched her gaze descend to his manhood.

As she shrieked, he gathered her flailing arms and legs. Savoring a practiced ritual, he shoved her onto the pile of rugs. The girl squeezed her legs together. Unwilling to yield, she ripped at his eyes with her nails. He howled and restrained her arms in a vise-like grip.

He drew back to push into her with all the force he could gather. She bucked, bared her teeth and sank her canines into his wrist. He roared, and covered her mouth and nose until she relented.

Quickly satisfied, he rose, and motioned the girl to stand. She tried, but her knees buckled. Bessus hoisted her up against his chest, raising the blade he had concealed. He plunged it low into her back, muffling her screams with his meaty palm. Drinking in eyes that slowly lost their light, he held the dagger's handle tightly, so it pulled free when he let the body fall.

Bessus lifted her corpse beyond the rugs. He clapped his hands, beckoning trusted men who waited outside. They entered, but tensed when they saw the girl's lifeless form.

The warrior next to Cyartes spoke first. "What... she's slain?"

Cyartes took a step back.

Bessus whirled around and backhanded the warrior, propelling him through the tent flap. "I am Lord here," Bessus assured all within reach of his voice. "Take it away."

Cyartes grabbed the body by the feet and dragged it out of the tent.

"Open my tent flaps when you are done," Bessus said, kicking dirt over a puddle of red.

Cyartes and three others returned to reset the commander's tent. "I will not be crowded, even if the night sky downpours upon me. Now leave," Bessus ordered.

Unable to quell his anger, he took another long draft of the soma and then retired to his pallet. He nestled his mangled nose into the earthy aromas of horses, hides, and the coppery scent of the girl's lifeblood.

None had fought him like this one. Worse, she had soiled the sacred axe, one handed down by his grandfather and father. For that, she could not live. There might be a curse to torment him. He was in enough trouble with Mainyu, he feared, because of his choice to spare the boys.

Bessus fondled the toe-bone necklace, jogging the memory of his forebears. Bold warriors they were... until they stoked fires of rebellion against the Persian king. He remembered their painful betrayal to the Persian overlords, a betrayal the king could never forgive. They lost all the land and cattle gained by guile and the sweep of their swords. The Persians, with the help of traitors from the northern capital city of Bactra, hunted his father and grandfather down and sent them to their graves, disgraced.

Bessus took another drink, finishing the last of the batch, and settling his belly. He detested the bad times, his escape and the long years spent hiding in the wild, just a boy, moving within a network of caves and spider-holes known only to his family. Forgotten and finally old enough to wield a spear, Bessus joined the Persians, fought their battles and gained their trust—his lever for when the time was right.

The Greeks would not stop him, nor could the piss-ass Persian generals who crawled towards Greek lands at a turtle's pace. Even the great King Xerxes could not deny him his plans, no less a young girl. No one would dominate him again.

"Are you pleased with my sacrifice, Mainyu?" he murmured.

The strength of the soma overtook him. His head flew straight up to float among the stars.

Bessus awoke to the sounds of camp breaking. He surveyed the host of warriors who had arrived during the night. Tents crowded the landscape, and campfire smoke curled skyward. The early summer heat would make the march all the more grueling.

He finished his morning meal of roasted grain and dates. Swiping at his mouth with the back of his hand, he noticed the streaks of dried blood, a sweet reminder of a proper sacrifice the night before. The Mainyu might demand more girls, if his good fortune were to continue. He kicked at the campfire, sending plumes of smoke into the air.

Horns blared. The army moved north towards the Hellespont, where two pontoon bridges spanned a mile-wide stretch of water they would traverse into Greek lands.

Cyartes approached with a fresh mount, Bessus' favorite having succumbed to the hastened pace from the homeland. He strained to hold the horse that bucked to free itself. "Have there ever been such numbers of warriors?" he asked.

Bessus mounted the oversized stallion. "The sight pleases me," he said, sucking the vast army's aroma into the depths of his nostrils. "The Great King will have his empire from east to west, but the stink of so many warriors and beasts speaks to me only of spoils and victory."

Cyartes threw his commander a troubled look. "So many do not speak the king's tongue. Others wear the skin of cats and hold sticks tipped with horns. Will they run from the bronze men we will face, said to be the fiercest warriors of all?"

"Pile of dung. I care nothing for the king's men," Bessus bellowed. "They'll clear a path for me, and then I'll stomp my boot on the carcasses of the Greeks. Rid yourself of weakling thoughts and bring our horsemen to the crossing. If we're late, you'll bathe in that water for far longer than you wish."

CHAPTER 10
HELLESPONT EARLY SUMMER
480 BCE

THE CROSSING

Bessus reached into his saddlebag, only to withdraw a few stale crumbs of barley-bread. Disappointing. He popped them into his mouth and swallowed dry. He studied the distant hills and the supply depot that marked the location of the bridges. His eyes narrowed. "After I cross, there will be no mercy," he declared to his captains.

Representatives of the forty-odd nations in Xerxes' army stood in long lines waiting to place their orders for food, water, and equipment. "My Lord, how can such a large army be fed?" Cyartes asked, licking chapped lips.

"The ships bring supplies for the army. Fill our bags now, but later, we'll take what we need. Now get that limp worm you call your manhood out of your hand and get those ponies moving."

Near the depot, Bessus halted his horsemen. All heads turned towards the hills. No one spoke. Bessus stared at Cyartes, who returned his astonished gaze. Those distant hills they were seeing were not made of boulders and dirt. Instead, enormous mounds of salted beef rose before them. Workers shoveled the meat into barrels as the men exclaimed their wonder over the finding.

Bessus led his warriors to the water station first. "Our water bladders run dry too fast."

"We'll be old hags before they are filled," Cyartes said.

"Bessus will not be made to wait. Watch me."

He jerked on his horse's reins. He walked his mount past all others to a table where the king's quartermasters sat. Before he could speak, an official shouted at him to get back in line and wait his turn. Bessus thrust out his chest, his disdain apparent, but quelled his anger. He might loathe delays, but he and his troops could ill afford the enmity of the army's quartermasters if forage could not feed them. His troops hovered silently behind him.

While Bessus fumed, two camels crossed in front of him. He pulled his new mount away, but the animal panicked, unaccustomed to the stinking beasts. His horse reared and bucked, throwing him. Bessus slammed to the ground, his dagger scabbard stabbing his leg. Uproarious laughter erupted from the officials at the table and warriors in the lines.

Bessus unsheathed his dagger. He bolted to the nearest soldier, the one hooting louder than the others. He gripped the man by his beard and hurled him to the ground. When he pressed his dagger to the soldier's throat, the man gasped. Bessus leaned in close, his dagger drawing blood. The soldier's eyes bulged as the commander's hand gripped his throat. The soldier struggled to breathe. Bessus heightened the pressure.

"You son of a whore, you will live today only because there are too many eyes here. Don't cross me again."

Bessus flicked his dagger, slicing the man's lip. The man rolled over, groaning, and covering his bloody face with his hands.

Still raw with embarrassment, Bessus stormed to the table of officials. "Supply my troops now. I've a long ride ahead."

An official rose. "There will be no bullying here, Commander. You will receive your quota, but any more trouble, and water will become very scarce for you."

Bessus dismissed the threat with a wave of his hand. He motioned for Cyartes to oversee the loading of supplies. He cringed, recalling the last time his favorite mare threw him, when camel spiders the size of cats surrounded them in a gully back home. Finding himself upended, he had to bat them away and crush others. Fearsome devils they were, fast and ugly. He shivered at their memory.

After midday, Bessus and his men arrived at the dual bridge of boats stretched across the water. They rode past enormous tree trunks implanted in the earth, angled away from the shoreline to serve as anchors for the ropes securing the pontoon bridges. Cables made of papyrus, thick as a man's fist, lashed the boats in a line, securely tied to the hedgehog of tree trunks positioned on both sides of the mile-long expanse of water. Two side-by-side identical bridges were constructed of long planks of wood nailed in place to form sidewalls high enough to keep the horses from seeing the water. More than three hundred boats were lashed together to form each long bridge of wood and ships. Dirt covered the ground boards to provide the horses with a more natural setting for their hooves. The bridge swayed and shifted downstream as the strong current pressured the mid-point.

Bessus' horse stamped its hooves, hesitating at the breach. "Send me into the water and you will roast on a spit tonight," he warned. Three hard kicks later, the horse lurched forward.

Thousands of his kinsmen followed, as they had for the last two years since leaving their homeland. Reaching the opposite shore, his men cheered themselves hoarse. On the opposite bank, a raucous reply erupted from the King's infantry.

Bessus rode to where a man studied scrolls. "The bridge moves," he said bluntly to the engineer. "Tighten the ropes."

"This is one river the army could not drink dry for us," the engineer answered, scurrying back to the safety of his colleagues.

Bessus followed, wiping sweat from his brow. He peered through the gleaming sunshine at the twin bridges. "Will these bridges hold?" he asked, scratching his whiskers.

"A storm came up and destroyed the first set. The king ordered the engineers executed. We made these new ones to last."

Nearby, the king's white marble throne was being positioned to review the great crossing. The army would take many days to cross the bridges. Bessus wondered how many of the king's generals would die in battle, bringing him closer to the top of the steps. If he could maneuver himself to be the king's confidant, then he could learn their ways and strike when the time was right.

Oh, Mainyu. Guide me and I will sacrifice a city of women to you.

The engineer studied Bessus. "How were you wounded?"

"The battle on the beach, ten years past, with the Athenian swine. I will never forget the man who struck me. He had blue eyes behind his helmet and a witch with a head full of red snakes on his shield." Bessus patted his axe, secured in a brown leather sheath attached to his saddle. "If he still lives, I will cleave his skull."

The engineer looked at the enormous double-bladed axe. The handle, long as a man's leg, was covered with gouges that proved its use in battle. Dried blood and strands of hair clung to the blades, no doubt donated by vanquished foe. The sharpened edges reflected sunlight in his eyes.

"Now, make our efforts worthwhile and kill the whores' sons," the engineer said. He returned to his calculations.

"Make sure the bridges are here when I return," Bessus told the man and his fellow engineers, "or I'll make a new crossing out of your corpses."

The engineers held their tongues.

He galloped to the head of his men. He traced a finger along the scar, on his way to search for Greeks.

CHAPTER 11
DELPHI
SUMMER 480 BCE

THE TRIP OF THEIR DREAMS

Zack and Nestor burst into the house, laughing and slapping each other on the back.

"How many times now have you landed on your backside, Zack?"

"How many daughters does Zeus have?"

Nestor's laughter shook the walls. "Yes, yes, I've lost count, but you're improving. The armor is heavy. We have our youths train for many years in the gymnasiums, taught by *pedagogues,* slave instructors. The boys learn our system of justice and how to respond when the *salphinx* are raised to the lips of the trumpeters, summoning them to battle. Let's clean away the grime before we eat."

Zack followed Nestor's lead, brushing olive oil over his skin and scraping it away with a stridgel, an angle-shaped tool. Would he ever get used to always feeling so greasy?

"Having fun?" Lauren inquired.

"Absolutely, but I'm worn out. Nestor's only five-five, but he's kicking my butt and barely breathing hard. I've been on my back more than Michelangelo."

She laughed. "I'm appreciating their company, also. Life on a farm is so simple. This is how my grandmother Asimos lived. If we must adjust to this new life, we're lucky it's with Nestor and his family. Come with me to the barn before it gets too dark."

Zack pulled open the barn door. He reached under his *chiton* and into the pocket of his hiking shorts. He took out the lighter, flicked it on, and held it above his head.

"Zack, it might…"

"Great Zeus!" exclaimed Nestor, running up to them. "What?" His eyes widened with disbelief. "Are you a god in disguise? How did you bring fire from your fingers?"

"I am not a god, although Lauren might argue with you after last night," Zack said. Lauren kicked his shin. "This is a simple invention. I will show you how it works when we return to the house for supper."

"Supper…"

"The evening meal," Lauren said.

"By the gods, Atlantea must be a wondrous land." Nestor watched Zack rub his shin.

"It is… or is going to be," Lauren whispered, pangs of homesickness suddenly gripping her.

Zack lit a torch and handed it to Nestor, who grabbed a round of cheese from the storage chest. He and Lauren went to their room.

There, she whirled on him. "Nice going, Professor. How are you going to explain a lighter to a man who lived 2,500 years before it was invented? A simple mistake could unknowingly influence the natural flow of history as we know it."

"I agree with you, but not completely. A lighter will not change history."

Her tension eased. "Just don't go too far. There are many things that won't come across as one of our 'customs'."

Zack gathered his backpack and they returned to the house. The women stared at them with puzzled looks, making it apparent Nestor had already shared his news. "Sit, so we may eat," he said, extending his hand.

After Nestor finished praising the gods, Persephone served the usual appetizer plate overloaded with bread, olives, and eggs. Her gaze lingered on Lauren.

"Would you like to see the fire stick?" Zack said.

Cassandra jumped up, all bright-eyed eagerness. "Yes, I beg you, may we?"

"Try it." Zack extended the lighter in his open palm.

Nestor put up his hand. "When I know it's safe, I will let you handle it, honeybee."

"Yes, uncle," Cassandra said, bouncing her knees under the table.

Zack blew out a candle. He took out the lighter and summoned flame by flipping the wheel with his thumb. Persephone and Cassandra gasped. He placed the lighter in Nestor's hand and showed him how the mechanism worked.

"The iron is rough on my thumb, and what is the writing on the side?" Nestor asked.

"It spells my name."

After a few false starts and some coaching, Nestor successfully ignited the lighter. "By Zeus, it makes fire. But what is the source?"

"Vapor inside the container feeds the flame. The iron wheel turns against a special stone that makes a spark."

"You mean a flint?"

"Exactly, but don't leave it on for long, Nestor. There is only a small amount of vapor inside and we must not waste it. It will burn your finger if left on too long. Cassandra, you want to try it now?"

Cassandra flipped the wheel and it worked the first time. She lit and blew out the candle, and then did it a second time. "You must try it, mother."

Persephone worked the device with equal delight. Cassandra clapped her hands after receiving it back from her mother. Persephone went outside and returned with a steaming platter of roasted turbot. "The meal is ready."

His stint with the lighter past, Nestor untied a leather scroll. "I received this summons today. I will leave tomorrow to join the debate on our war strategy." He strained to read in the candlelight. "By Zeus, the scribes should make the letters bigger. I'm not a pup anymore." He held the scroll at arm's length.

"Just a moment." Zack took his reading glasses from the backpack and placed them over Nestor's eyes. Lauren bit her lip.

"Great Zeus. The words are big as a summer moon. What magic is this?"

"No magic. They're called glasses," Lauren replied.

"It has been many years since I've read with such clarity." Nestor tapped the lenses with his fingernail. "What am I looking through?"

"Highly fired particles of sand, polished in a special technique. We have many workshops that make them."

"Atlantea must truly be a wonderful place, by the gods, and you must come to Athens with me."

"We would be pleased to accompany you to Athens," Lauren said, gathering the plates. "In fact, we have waited a very long time to see it."

"Then you shall."

"Master Zack," Cassandra asked, her hands clasped in prayer-like fashion, "may I be the keeper of the fire stick? I vow to return it."

Zack glanced at Lauren. She agreed, albeit reluctantly. They watched Cassandra waltz off, clearly proud of her new possession.

"I pray that you both return to us." Persephone embraced Lauren. Into her ear, she whispered, "And I will teach Cassandra to speak her mind."

"And you too. We promise to return. I need help arranging my hair."

Persephone smiled. "I promise to cook the water for drinking and insist everyone wash their hands before eating."

"Gods on Olympus," Nestor added. "There will be no more wood in all of Greece if I have to keep up with your demands to keep the pots boiling."

Lauren laughed. Cassandra bounded into the open doorway, holding a thin linen shift, stretched over light wooden crossbeams and attached to a long tail of slender string, tied with tiny bows.

"Come now, Lady Lauren, before you go. Help me dash through the fields and hoist this high so it will dance in the realm of the gods."

"Wait for me, young lady." Lauren ran to catch up with her.

A lumbering cart drawn by two farm horses bounced along the dirt road from Delphi toward the lowlands. Nestor held the reins, gently guiding the horses around fallen boulders. Lauren and Zack sat comfortably atop straw pilings, aside trunks bearing clothing, bread, olives and boiled eggs in earthen jars, along with wine and water-filled amphora.

Zack grinned. "Do you think we should explain the merit of shock absorbers?"

"Zip your lip. You've given away too much already."

"Honey, we're revealing conveniences, nothing more. Eventually the lighter will run out of butane, and it'll be useless. I didn't give the glasses to Nestor 'cause I need them. So far, everything's gone okay."

"So far."

"Are you speaking your tongue again?" Nestor called out over his shoulder.

"Sorry," Zack said. "What if we teach you another song? It's about a lady traveling in the mountains. It goes like this: 'She'll be coming around the mountain when she comes...'"

Lauren joined in.

Nestor grinned. "By the gods, teach me. My voice is known all the way to Olympia and I am the proud winner of a wreath from the Pythian Games. The road goes by more quickly this way."

Dust clouds swirled toward them, funneled from winds held in by mountain ridges on both sides of the road. They covered their faces with *pestasos,* wide-brimmed straw hats.

"I want to sing the song again about the woman that chases the mice with a knife," Nestor said.

Another hour of songs passed. Then his look turned solemn. "We must leave Athens after our visit. The Acropolis will not stand a long siege. We cannot expect mercy from the barbarians."

"Will your city-states band together to fight?" Zack asked.

"It is our great hope. Each city, or *polis,* is truly a state unto itself. So many cities find argument with each other. If the gods could only bless us with unity, we might prevail."

"We had a wise man in our country long ago. He was our leader during a terrible war we had among ourselves. He said, a house divided, cannot stand."

"Wise words," Nestor replied. "Themistocles has been on many missions to persuade other leaders of this same wisdom. Nevertheless, there are many who wish to surrender. They mock him to gain political advantage and do not care that they weaken all of us and encourage our enemies."

"If you do unite, it will be the people of Hellas together for the first time," Lauren said.

Nestor pointed skyward. "We need a *daimonia,* a sign of divine intervention. Sparta and her allies want to defend the Isthmus, but it can be flanked by sea. I am meeting with my friend to help devise a strategy to persuade the Peloponnesians to defend us north of Athens." He winked. "I wonder if you have a bit of magic that will make the barbarians disappear?"

"No, but there may be magic in a free people fighting for their families and homes," Lauren remarked.

Nestor faced them, tears filling his eyes. "You sound like Themistocles. You will enjoy meeting him."

They gave each other high-fives behind Nestor's back. "We would be proud to meet such a man," Zack said.

"When we arrive in the city two days hence, we will tell him of your faraway land, and I will request that Lauren be allowed to join us. By Hephestion's singed tunic, it will be an enjoyable *symposium*, a welcome diversion for a friend who bears a Herculean burden."

"You know him well?" Zack asked.

"We're old friends, but I haven't seen him much since I left Athens. The mountains bring me peace; the excesses and confines of the cities can breed illness of the body and mind." Nestor sighed deeply, his baritone voice adding weight to his decision. "Here, I can separate myself from the greed and lust for power that is the ruin of all men. In the springtime, wildflowers blanket the hills with their beauty, and pine is in the air."

"Have you ever been inside the temples on the mountain?" Zack asked, glancing at Lauren. She glared at him.

"When I was a lad, I spent many a day there with my grandfather. My father was an architect also, but he was frequently drawn away to Neapolis in Italia, and I missed him greatly. My grandfather gave me a great love of building. As a known architect, he was commissioned by a wealthy Athenian family to renovate the temple of Apollo back up the hill after it burned down many years ago."

Nestor shook the reins of the horses. "I worshipped him and thought he was Zeus himself. He had a flowing white mane of hair, a grand moustache and beard. I could see the results of his labor when he finished his beautiful buildings. I used to run like Hermes himself to fetch chisels for the stonemasons. I learned how a sturdy back, strong arms, and determination could raise majesty from the earth."

Nestor pointed at a hawk flying overhead, alerting his companions to its graceful flight. "Many a day, my grandfather sat me on his knee. 'Lad,' he would say with his eyebrows curling over his eyes, 'the gods work in strange ways; it is not always easy to determine what plans they have for us. Worship them, but rely on your wits and your own resolve."

"He would point to his head as if telling me to use my own, his blue eyes piercing mine. 'Pave your own way; work honestly and the gods will look kindly upon you.' He would tousle my hair and then send me running for more buckets of water. That was over thirty-five years ago, during the reforms of Kleisthenes, who brought changes to our government. By the time my late brother was old enough to help, my grandfather had made the final boat trip to Hades."

Nestor cleared his throat. "On one hot day back up the hill, my grandfather fell over. His eyes were open, blue as the sky. He appeared to be in a deep conversation with the gods. That is a day I will never forget."

Nestor raised the goatskin and squirted diluted wine into his mouth. He passed the skin to Zack, who drank and turned to Lauren. "You want some?"

"Not now. I don't want to have to stop and pee all the time."

Nestor regained the reins. "Your original question was about the temples. My grandfather brought me to the temple of Apollo to see his architecture. It is said that two eagles were sent by Zeus to fly in opposite directions over Mother Earth. Where they met, he placed a sacred stone that marked the center of the earth. That stone, Omphalos, sits within the temple of Apollo. Gaia, the goddess Mother Earth, was placed in charge of the sacred site and attended to it, as well as to the prophecies it delivered, along with her serpent son, Python."

Nestor motioned to have the wineskin returned to him. "The infant god, Apollo, slew Python with arrows from his silver bow. He took command of the site, made the Oracle his own, and began delivering prophesies to the people through the priestess, Pythia. She is chosen from the chaste women of the area. Many come to hear the advice of Apollo – when to plant crops or start a colony, when to venture to war. Only the gods know what is to be."

"Did you ever ask for a prophecy?" Lauren asked.

"I have seldom asked the gods for favors." Sadness etched Nestor's voice. "I remember clearly the times that I have. Why does it seem that when your mortality is threatened, you beseech the gods on your knees? Then you wonder later, did I bring the proper offering? Will they answer quickly or deliver me from danger? The gods, of course, do not always answer."

He dragged a forearm over his cheek, swiping away beads of sweat. "I prayed to Apollo many times for guidance before I left Athens. Finally, I decided to move to our farmhouse, where my grandparents and parents spent their summers away from the heat of the city and where they worshipped Athena in the temple next to the farm. By the time I moved here, I had found deliverance from torments of the mind."

Nestor took another swig. A long silence followed. He cleared his throat. "I did consult the Oracle once long ago and the memory is as clear as the peaks of Parnassus. I was a young man. My wife and I were blessed with a son. The world is a fine place when an Athenian household has a male heir to carry forward the memory of his ancestors and the deeds to his property. I can still see him playing with his favorite toy, a red chariot pulled by two stallions with the proud figure of Achilles holding the reins. Such squeaky wheels it had."

He laughed aloud. "That boy delighted in dragging that chariot through piles of dirt while making war cries. A fine lad he was until a pestilence cast an ill wind over Athens, and our lad. It was a sickness of the bowels, and his head turned hotter than Hephestion's furnace. My wife, Thetis, attended to him night and day, but the boy shriveled and the light of life left him. My wife lost her smile that day and it never returned."

Lauren slumped against Zack as Nestor's shoulders heaved and then settled down. His wide-brimmed hat, angled down, made his face difficult to see, but his pain was all too clear. "I had my work to distract me. Many projects arrived at my door, and I commanded a fair sum for the expertise I learned from my forbearers."

He cleared his throat again. "One spring night in the month of Pyanepsion, before the first barbarian invasion, I sat on a bench in my garden courtyard in Athens, humming and tapping my heels on the stone. Then Thetis called me to the *gynaeconitis*. She lay on her couch and guided my fingers to a stone lying under the surface of her breast. I did not speak, for I did not know of such matters. But her eyes betrayed her despair; she fell into my arms, weeping."

Nestor twitched the reins and the horses halted. He faced Lauren and Zack. "It was then that I decided to consult the Oracle. What should we do? What treatment might save her? I left Athens in this wagon, bringing bundles of barley and silver as offerings, and traveled to Delphi. Oh, how the gods play with us."

He flung his fingers at the gods, in recognition of their power and the uselessness of deciphering their ways. "Alas, I left the farmhouse early in the morning and walked to the Temple of Apollo, but I paused near the entrance to read words etched into the marble: 'Know Thyself' and 'Nothing In Excess.' How much wisdom is found in these words? I only glanced at them, having seen them many times before. My mind was sick with worry as I placed the offering, my *pelanus*, at the feet of the bursar and whispered my request into his ear. I watched him scratch the request on papyrus. Since Pythia ranted only on the seventh day after a new moon, I had to wait for a day."

Nestor fed the horses grain from a leather sack while he talked. "The day before Pythia hears Apollo's prophecy, she fasts, and then cleanses herself in the sacred Castalia Spring. The next day she chews on leaves of laurel while perching on a three-legged stool, breathing in the god's spirit. I came back the next day, bathed in the cool waters of the same spring, waited for the lottery to give me a position in line, and presented myself at the entrance to the temple. I had my turn in front of Pythia, equally fearful and hopeful for the advice of the gods."

He climbed back aboard the wagon. The horses whinnied as he negotiated turns in the roadway. "An old *Prophetai*, bent at the waist and wearing a wrinkled white robe, peered at me with the penetrating eyes of a hawk, recognizing me from years and deeds past. He read the oracle to me, these words of Apollo that I will never forget: 'Fate can nay be altered once the three sisters measure the string and wield the shears. When adversity plants its banner at thy door, thou canst only strive to persevere. Revel in what is yours. Peace can only be found if your own thoughts will it.'

"I looked at him, at first confounded and then angry. Could not Apollo be a bit clearer as to my wife's fate?"

Nestor passed the wineskin back to Lauren as he spoke. "That priest replied in a crackling little voice, 'Apollo reveals to you what it is you need.'

"Despair held me in a tight grip. I knew then my wife would not survive. I sat on the stone bench underneath the statues of the gods along the Sacred Way. I looked at Apollo's stone likeness: a strong, handsome god, blue-eyed, a silver bow in his grasp. As I prayed to him, it occurred to me that the oracle was not for my wife, but for me. The three sisters of fate had long ago determined my wife's time. Atropos, the most terrible of the three, would soon cut her string."

He shook the reins, and looked at the position of the sun as if weighing the time. "Heya!" he shouted, spurring on the horses.

Wagon wheels creaked and crunched gravel. "Perhaps Apollo, in his wisdom, had seen that the loss of my son and wife would cast me upon the rocks of dejection and corrupt my mind, forever. Upon reflection, I decided his message was to find peace within myself. The words carved into the columns at the entrance, 'Know Thyself,' and his recommendation for me to be happy with what I have, struck me like a thunderbolt from Zeus. I returned to my wife, tended to her every need for two seasons… and reveled in what was mine. The oracle had said to enjoy her while she lived."

He stopped the wagon again. His shoulders heaved and then stiffened as he tried to control his emotions. "I am long-winded today. I have not spoken of these events for some time."

"We are happy to listen," Lauren said softly. "Please go on."

After a time, he smiled. "Her spirit left with a gentle puff, and Hermes accompanied her to the boatman with a coin on her body." He gave them a dubious look. "Perhaps you do not understand our beliefs. When one gives up his hold on this earth, his shade travels to the underworld. There, in Hades, one must endure a dour eternity. The messenger-god, Hermes, guides the spirit to the river that divides the land of the living from the land of shadows. The boatman rows the spirit across and receives the coin as payment for his labor.

"Thetis was cremated, northwest of Athens, as is the custom in our land, at dawn. As I watched the funeral pyre, I realized that I must hold my friends and family much more closely to me."

Nestor wiped his eyes. He halted the horses again. "This was well before I took the sacred rites in Eleusis, after I moved to these mountains. We have many gods and festivals in Hellas. We are a people of the earth as well as the sea. South of here, along the path we take to Athens, is a most holy place where each fall we give our thanks to the reborn reveler Dionysus, and the goddesses Demeter and Persephone, who are responsible for the harvest and the rebirth of life from the earth each spring."

He stopped for a moment to catch his breath, and then raised a finger. "But it is more than that. The rites and purifications, which are a secret no one who experiences them will reveal, constitute a different hope when we leave this world. For those who believe, death sends us to a more joyous place, an eternal life one can welcome … ah, I am sidetracked once more."

Nestor shook the reins and reached his hand inside a ceramic pot sitting beside him on the driver's bench. He withdrew an olive, chewed on it, worked the pit forward, and spit it onto the road. He reached for more. "My brother, Theseus, and his Persephone were blessed with Cassandra not long after Thetis died, and I decided that they would be my meaning and joy in life. Soon though, the Persians launched their first invasion. My brother and I joined the other members of our tribe, the Leontis, as is our duty. You know what occurred."

Zack rested a comforting hand on the older man's shoulder.

"Here, have an olive," Nestor said.

"My heart is in my throat," Lauren whispered.

Nestor dropped his head. "I beg your forgiveness. Life is filled with victories and defeats. It is a game the gods play with us. They wish us to struggle, rise up, work, fight, stand proud and defeat our enemies. But gather too much arrogance, greed, or pride, and they will quickly set us back on our heels."

Zack spat out his olive pit. He could not help but smile as Nestor had outlined all the basics of a perfect Greek tragedy, delivered to the ages by the Greek playwrights Aeschylus, Sophocles, and Euripides.

Nestor passed the pot to Zack. "But I see now, my friends," he said, "that enjoyment in life, like paradise in the great beyond, lies within your own thoughts and deeds. Hear me closely: You are together, and that is all that matters. Be more insistent than you have ever been in your desire for each other. Fate is rarely generous with time."

Nestor pursed his lips and launched another olive pit that hit a bush twenty feet away. Zack tried to match Nestor's marksmanship, but fell short and received a quick, derisive snort from him.

Lauren climbed onto the bench next to Nestor. "Thank you for sharing your life and wisdom with us."

Nestor smiled at her. "How is it with your gods?"

She paused thoughtfully and glanced at Zack. "That philosophy, the peace within that you speak of, is similar to the religion of a people far to the east, beyond the empire of Xerxes."

Nestor raised an eyebrow. "It is interesting that you say this. Not long ago, I spoke with a traveler from a faraway eastern place. A man with slanted eyes told me of lands, peoples, and gods beyond where the sun rises. Strange beasts, enormous long horns, like the bones of the Titans we have found. He revealed the same philosophies the Oracle posed to me those twelve years past."

"There are many ways to worship God," Lauren said. "And many ways of living your life, but it seems the same wishes are true wherever humans reside. We all desire safety, sustenance, the freedom to choose our destiny, and better lives for our children. This cannot be accomplished under servitude or with a whip at one's back."

Nestor nodded. "It is a philosophy to ponder, Lauren."

"Remember I told you about our wise man who said that governments should be by, for, and of the people?"

"Wiser words were never said."

"He also said that all men are created equal, and he meant it."

Nestor grew quiet. He stared into the distance, and then met Lauren's gaze with characteristic directness. "Are you making a case once again for Greeks to give up their slaves?"

"You may draw your own conclusion. We are discussing only what I feel is in every person's heart. Perhaps one day, it might be a question to ask the Oracle."

"There are many inscriptions on that long supporting wall back at the temples. You will see many refer to the emancipation of slaves. I do not think this is a common occurrence. It would take a change in the way men think."

"Given time, I think the Greeks will see the humanity in it."

Nestor raised an eyebrow. "You are clearly a woman of wisdom, Lauren. I can see why your country has given you the duties of an envoy." He chewed another olive and sent the pit flying.

She inclined her head in appreciation. "Thank you for your compliments, but it is we who appreciate you. Would you mind telling us how the Athenian democracy was founded?"

"Ha, ha," Nestor exclaimed. "You Atlanteans must truly crave torture. First we must stop at the Hermea monument and pay homage to the god of all travelers."

Just as Nestor finished, Zack spit an olive pit that hit one of the infrequent statues positioned aside the roads, that of the traveler's god, Hermes.

Nestor groaned and spun his head. "What have you done?" he cried out, a horrified look on his face. He leaped from the wagon, clasping a small clay bottle. He ran to the stone bust of a bearded older man set atop a mound of stones and dripped oil liberally over the head. "Fleet-footed Hermes, protect us as we make our way. Deliver us from robbers and mishaps. And forgive this foreigner. He knows not what he does." Nestor patted the statue's head as if to calm it down, then returned, scowling. "Behave," he warned Zack. "The gods are everywhere. Even if you don't see them."

CHAPTER 12
ATHENS, GREECE
SUMMER 480 BCE

"CITY OF GOD-LIKE MEN"

Two days later, at dusk, the rocky promontory of the Acropolis came into view. Zack and Lauren sat on the driver's bench with Nestor, their eyes riveted on the temples atop the heights.

Wagons hauling wares, furniture, and families clogged the main northwest road into the city. Hoplites manned intersections to keep the flow of refugees and commerce moving south. When all traffic halted, Nestor stood on the driver's bench.

A mule brayed and refused to move into the line of carts. The owner jerked at the bridle without success. Finally, a hoplite poked the butt spike of his spear into the animal's backside and sent it forward.

Dust obscured their view as they passed through the Thrasian gate into Athens. Poorly built stone and mortar tenement buildings lined the narrow roads. Naked children stood in doorways watching the vehicles passing. The beauty and wealth of the city was concentrated in the government buildings and temples near the Acropolis, and two other nearby heights.

Elsewhere, the appearance of Athens surprised them. "I feel like I'm in the hills of Tijuana," Lauren said. "I guess we shouldn't be surprised by the squalor. All of these people make the city, not just the aristocrats."

Sewage and water ran down muddy alleyways, and mothers scolded their children as they darted out of the way of oxen, horses, and handcarts. The pungent smells of manure and garbage assaulted them, intensified by the early evening summer sun. The inhabitants sought reprieve in the open air after spending the afternoon indoors, avoiding the heat.

A thought struck Lauren. "Wait, Zack. We left San Diego in mid-June. The action takes place up north at Thermopylae in late August. We haven't been here two months."

Nestor turned to them, clearly surprised by Lauren's mention of Thermopylae. "How did you know of the Hot Gates?"

"Anyone can look at a map of your land and see a natural chokepoint there," Zack said, hoping to deflect his suspicion.

"One could…" Nestor's tone grew darker, more serious. "Be careful what you say. Do not talk of such matters, even if you are my guests. Xerxes has spies everywhere."

Nestor halted the horses before a walled complex. Lauren climbed down from the cart, grimacing at the ache in her backside. "Zack," she whispered, "I think I'd rather walk in the future. My rump is killing me."

"Or ride a bike."

Lauren jabbed her elbow into his ribs.

Nestor grabbed the large iron ring and rapped three times. A young man, skinny- armed and legged, opened the massive oak door and bowed. "Greetings, who may I say is calling?"

"Tell the master that the incompetent nail-whacker who built this sorry house awaits him."

The slave bowed and left.

Nestor patted the thick walls. "It took over two years to build."

Moments later, a middle-aged man in a formal-looking toga appeared in the entranceway. He was stocky and bull-necked, with short wavy hair and beard. A long mustache drooped below his chin. He immediately smiled and embraced Nestor. The two men held each other by the shoulders.

"Ah, farmer, do you still know your way around the city? You have been away too long," Themistocles said.

"City people, living among the throngs, you should come visit with us where it is quiet."

"I may have to if our defenses do not hold. I shall be looking for a cave in those mountains."

"I know just the place for you, old friend. It comes complete with a goat to keep you warm at night."

Themistocles slapped Nestor on the back. "I thank the gods for your visit. I crave your counsel. They argue if we should defend Greece in the north or at the isthmus. Others demand outright surrender. Nestor, we can only prevail if we join our forces. Indecision and petty differences may be the ruin of us."

"I have confidence in you, old friend. If anyone can join these city-states together, it is you."

"I will beseech the gods for guidance, but now you must introduce your companions."

Nestor turned to Zack and Lauren, only to find them staring slack-jawed at Themistocles. Zack studied him, the Churchill of his time, seeking to grasp the indomitable character that dwelled in him. The man had almost single-handedly stood for unity when Greece threatened to fracture, its city-states both ancient allies and adversaries, continually at war with each other.

Man for man, the Greeks were superior soldiers, Zack recalled, but their meager numbers meant nothing in the face of such overwhelming odds. Their success hinged on the way they used the topography of the land against their enemies, striking with a deadly concentration of forces when the enemy was most vulnerable.

"These are my friends, Lauren and Zack," Nestor said. "They're envoys from a powerful distant land beyond the Pillars."

Themistocles arched an eyebrow. "Enter my home and tell me of your country. We may be sailing there with you soon enough." He smiled and wrapped his arm around Zack's shoulder. "Any friends of Nestor are welcome here."

"Our thanks," Zack said carefully, still struggling with the dialect despite repeated lessons on the trip from Delphi. "This is my wife, Lauren, and we gratefully accept your offer of hospitality."

Themistocles led them through an arched doorway into the *andron*, a central meeting room with five reclining couches encircling a gray stone table. On the opposite side, a doorway led to an enclosed open-air garden, a common feature in most Greek homes. Slaves lit candles and oil lamps that flickered and cast shadows on blue walls that grew gray as the evening settled in.

"Sicinnus, bring water bowls so our guests may cleanse their hands," Themistocles said to a silver-haired slave who bowed. "Afterwards, you may serve us watered wine and a meal." Sicinnus left the room.

Walking behind the two elder statesmen, Lauren and Zack listened to their animated discussion.

"How goes the training of the crews? They were all farm boys not long ago," Nestor said.

"We drill them harder each day," Themistocles replied. "The shakedown cruise last year to Italia was of great help. We were also able to scout out alternate sites for our citizens, should we lose the mainland."

"Oh, my friend, were it not for your golden tongue, the citizens would have found themselves ten drachmas richer but 100 triremes poorer." Nestor punctuated his words with his fist. "You were wise to convince them to use the silver from the Laurium mines to purchase timber from Italia and build a navy instead of disbursing it to spend on wine and the comfort of youth."

"Desperate times require desperate measures, Nestor, but we are finally seeing the seeds of unity now. The conference at Corinth has yielded some commitment to join and fight."

"I can't believe we're watching history unfold, honey," Zack whispered. "They don't know how this is all going to turn out. Themistocles jokes about disaster. He seems so confident, but underneath, he has to be terrified."

Sicinnus returned with wine as Themistocles reclined on a purple couch. Leaning on an elbow, he gestured towards the couches. "Please sit. And tell me of your people."

Lauren fidgeted. "My wife speaks your words better than I. May she speak for me?" Zack asked.

Themistocles signaled his approval by waving his hand. He sipped wine from his *kylix*, a shallow drinking bowl.

Lauren continued to stand, unsure about sitting with the men. "Our people live many months' journey from your land. We are here as envoys. Before our arrival, we learned of your struggle for freedom. We wish to bear witness to these events, return to our land and give testament to the bravery of the people of Hellas."

Themistocles thoughtfully fingered his whiskers. "Friends, we are a desperate people, but we shall prevail with the help of the gods."

"Our land has experienced many trials also, but freedom prevails for us as it will for you," Lauren said. "It lives in the hearts of any people willing to fight for it."

Themistocles smiled. "I sometimes feel I must fight both sides at once. Not long ago, my enemies tried to ostracize me from our fair city. I was able to generate enough support to remain and build the fleet."

He brought his hand to his forehead suddenly, a wave of pain contorting his face.

"What is it, my friend?" Nestor asked.

"At times, I feel that Zeus is throwing thunderbolts into my skull. I sacrifice to Apollo and the pain subsides, over time."

"You are bearing too much of the burden."

"Ah, pains come with age anyway. I received word today that the Spartan king will soon arrive in Thermopylae."

"This is wonderful news. Now the defense will be in the north," Nestor said.

"On the surface, but the Spartan king, Leonidas, can only bring his personal bodyguard of three hundred warriors. Even with allies, there may be only a force of six to seven thousand hoplites against the whole of Asia. Our navy will protect his back, but we are as dependent on him holding his line as he is upon us guarding his."

Themistocles again massaged his temples, the strain clear on his face. "Themistocles, in my country, we have special herbs and medicines for afflictions of the head brought on by times of trouble," Zack said.

"What the hell are you doing?" Lauren hissed.

He removed the large bottle of Ibuprofen from his backpack, placed two pills in his own mouth, and washed them down with watered-down wine. He then dropped two tablets in Themistocles' palm.

Forced to commit to Zack's scheme or have him appear untrustworthy, Lauren said, "This is strong medicine. Swallow them and rest. We will stay with Nestor and labor over the fate of your land."

"The tea of marjoram I have been drinking has not lessened the pain. Are you a physician in your country?" Themistocles asked, rotating the pills in his hand. He licked one, but scrunched his face, finding it distasteful.

"No, but our people are well-versed in medicine and herbs. Our children attend academies from a very young age, and we are well-educated in the sciences, mathematics, and rhetoric."

Themistocles looked to Nestor, his apprehension clear, wondering about the wisdom of accepting medicine from a stranger.

Nestor stood and placed a comforting hand on his friend's shoulder. "I trust them, and they have even greater marvels from their country."

Themistocles dropped one of the pills in Lauren's hand. "Take it. What man would poison a woman like you?"

Lauren swallowed it with a measure of wine. He followed. "It is rude not to entertain guests in my house, but I beg your forgiveness that I must rest."

She smiled. "We would be pleased. When we talk in the morning, your pain should be gone."

Themistocles managed a smile, grasped Nestor by the arms, and whispered a few words to him before departing for his private chambers.

Servants soon arrived with platters of food, and more wine. Zack ate with his usual enthusiasm.

Sicinnus arrived at the end of the meal. "When you are ready, masters, I will show you to your quarters," he said.

Nestor thanked him. "The strain on Themistocles is enormous," he said. "I will make an extra sacrifice to the gods. I hope your medicine will aid him. He has many more difficult days ahead."

"We are glad to be of service, Nestor," Zack said before he gulped the last of his wine.

"My friends, it has been a long day. Does your medicine cure the aches caused by travel as well?"

"It does. Here are a few more for both of you in case we don't see you tomorrow."

"I shall see you in the morning when Helios brightens the heavens. I will pray to the all-wise Zeus to bring comfort to you and wisdom to my troubled friend. Sleep well."

The head slave led Nestor to his quarters while another guided Zack and Lauren down long hallways.

Inside their room, Zack tossed his backpack on the floor mats and hard, sausage-shaped pillows that made up their bed. "Ibuprofen should help his headache."

Lauren bent down to smell the bed. "I guess a good night's sleep won't mess up history. Stress is etched on his face."

"Did you hear him? The Spartans have marched. The war is going to start within a week. Honey, you're going to think I'm nuts, but I want to see the battle of Thermopylae."

"What?" she gasped. "That battle was a slaughterhouse. I don't want us within a hundred miles of it. After a little sightseeing in Athens, we're going back to Delphi like you promised and do our best to get back to our own time." She rolled the linen into a makeshift pillow.

"Lauren, please. We don't know how to get back."

"I know, but that doesn't mean we stop trying."

Zack clenched his fists. "All my life, I've read about this war. I *have* to go. We know what's going to happen. We can leave a day or so early and head south."

"No. It's a huge risk." Lauren stood and folded her arms. "Zack, this is not up for debate."

"Honey," he persisted, "our risk is a hell of a lot less than what these people are facing. We can observe, and I won't interfere."

"You keep saying that but you keep interfering."

"Don't you understand? These people are the first freedom fighters. We'll watch the Spartan army in action in a most desperate battle. I need to see it."

"You're crazy, Zachary Fletcher. Aren't you the one telling me you're a pacifist, complaining about my father and his service in the military, the wars he fought in? I'll never forget you laughing at me every time I cried watching the Navy ships leaving San Diego on deployment. You know I felt for those families."

"They knew what they were getting into when they signed up, and I wasn't really laughing at you. I was just surprised at how emotional you were."

"You don't know crap about anything that's important. You sit in your professor's chair passing judgment on people doing all the sacrificing while you're having trouble deciding where to go for lunch." Lauren's face turned light red. "I know what *I'm* talking about. My mother told me what my father went through as commanding officer of his squadron. Every letter he wrote to the families of the people he lost in Vietnam tortured him a little more. Now you want to see butchery up close?"

"But this is our life's work…"

"No, Zack, listen to me. War is horrible. Here in ancient Greece. There in modern America. We're not taking any more risks, so drop it."

Moments later, the exhaustion of the long journey claimed her. As she slept, Zack used the flickering light of an oil lamp to stare at a mural of two hoplites struggling over the armor of a fallen warrior, while circling carrion waited to peck at the remains.

In the morning, Zack awoke to voices outside the door. Dim shafts of light, the day's first, moved through slits in the shutters, clamped shut to keep out insects. He walked to a terra cotta bowl, cupped his hands, and splashed his face with water. He brushed his teeth using a dwindling tube of toothpaste and ran his fingers through his hair before returning to check on Lauren.

"I'm sleeping a little more," She said, waving her hand for him to go.

"Okay. Get up when you're ready." Zack closed the door gently behind him.

Later, Lauren stepped out from their guest room and negotiated the hallways until she found herself in the *andron* where they dined the night before. She called for Zack, only to hear her voice echo off the sparsely decorated walls. Strong sunlight beat down on the central courtyard.

"Zack?" she repeated, more anxiously.

"Out here."

She walked barefoot toward his voice, leaving the smoothness of terra cotta flooring for the open-air garden. Zack sat on a stone bench, out of her sight, biting into a yellow pear, watching tiny birds chirping and darting among the fruit trees. "Would you mind letting me know where you are? I was worried."

"I've been up for hours, waiting on her majesty. Did you rest OK? Should I call your maids to dress your hair and pin that *chiton* properly?"

"I'm amazed by what these women can do with an oblong piece of wool. Where is everyone?"

"Busy moving furniture and supplies. I guess we wait until Nestor returns. I'm just sitting here; thinking, actually."

Lauren yawned. "Don't think. You'll weaken the war effort."

"Funny. No, really, I'm eating this pear which existed thousands of years ago, but it's providing nutrition to a body that didn't exist until the twentieth century."

"And it's all over your chin."

"I've always been intrigued with the past, but I never imagined that I'd experience history in present tense." Zack stretched out, his legs hanging over the edge of the bench. "I smell the lavender and the spices in those planters. I hear the noise from the street outside these walls and sense the tension as the people prepare to fight or flee with their families. I see the grapevines curled around those olive trees. We're beyond academic and theoretical postulations about how these people lived. We're *here*, with our five senses, experiencing a life that is long gone."

Lauren closed her eyes and shook her head. "It's too confusing to think about, and there's already too much stress being here without us arguing. Can we just have a good day together?"

"All right, we don't have to talk about it now…"

"I only want to concentrate on what is concrete…like this garden," Lauren said. "Look at those wildflowers. If we ever get back home, I'm doing this same thing in our backyard." She stuck her nose into a hyacinth planter.

Zack reached for a second pear that hung by its stem. "If you figure a way for us to get back eventually, I won't care if you plant the Garden of Eden in our backyard. By the way, we've lost all our keys to the house, but I'm pretty sure I put a spare one in an Altoids box underneath that big boulder in the backyard."

"Not something we have to worry about right now, Zack."

The garden was divided into four sections. Each contained fig and olive trees, shrubs, and square planters that held sage, chamomile, thyme, and parsley. A narrow dirt trail led to each section, making its way around the gnarled trunk of an olive tree before converging with the other trails at the center, where a white marble statue of a woman stood. Bent at the knees and holding a large bowl, she gracefully bathed, spilling imaginary water over her shoulders while watching for onlookers.

"Isn't she elegant?" Lauren smiled. "It's definitely not an archaic-period statue. Look at those flowing lines. She is not stiff like most of the statuary. Maybe the artistic transition to classical-style sculpture has already occurred. She's almost real."

He chuckled. "Don't say that. The way things have been going for us, she just might step off that pedestal and talk to us."

"Ahhh, there you are. A fine garden, is it not?" Nestor asked, joining them. "We Athenians do enjoy a little piece of countryside within our walls."

"You're a fine architect," Zack said as he ran his hand over the alabaster exterior of a column that supported wooden lattice and hanging ivy.

"The muses favor me. I am going to rest for a short while," Nestor replied. "This morning's meeting has given me thunderbolts in my head. There is still no decision on how to defend our cities. By the gods, I may need more of your medicine. Zack, would you care to visit the Agora later? I have shopping to do."

"When you get up from your nap, we will be happy to accompany you," Lauren said.

Her quick response surprised Nestor. "It may not be wise for you to accompany us. Our wives and daughters rarely venture from their homes. If they do, they are escorted by an army of trusted slaves."

"Nestor, for years I have sat by the fire and listened to tales of your city and the men who gave it greatness. It would take Hercules himself to keep me from seeing how the Athenians live and prosper."

"You do not understand, Fair One. You will be looked upon as a slave or a harlot."

"What they think will not change who I am. I will not be wounded by their stares."

"If that is all they do…"

Lauren beseeched him with an intent stare. "I beg you to allow me to come with you."

Nestor crinkled his brow and rubbed his forefinger under a baggy eyelid. "I'm weary of debate. If you desire to go, wrap a *himation* over your *chiton*. Arrange it so it covers you to your heels, though not tightly. Pin it on the inside and leave yourself a hood to cover your face. There will be no slaves to carry a peacock fan for you. It is against my counsel, yet I see the desire in your face, and I will not deny you."

"I will be a good little shopper and stick to you like pitch."

Nestor turned to Zack. "The gods will be sorely taxed to assist you with this one. She is headstrong."

He nodded his head in Lauren's direction and trudged off to his chamber.

They departed in late afternoon, wearing wide-brimmed straw hats and thin, ankle-length robes of white to reflect the sun's rays. Nestor tapped his walking stick and smiled at Lauren's apparel as he led them down the stone road toward central Athens. They entered narrow dirt roads with potholes, stones and litter. Along the way, a group of boys, escorted by their *pedagogue* teacher, poked at a dead goat that lay in an alleyway.

"It wouldn't be easy to find our way back if we lost you, Nestor. There are no road signs or numbers on the doors." Zack blocked the afternoon sun with his palm.

"Signs, numbers… who would be in need of this? Can you not see the Acropolis ahead to gain your bearing? Remember the small temple at the end of this road. It does no good to be lost after dark. The guards patrolling the city cannot be everywhere at once to protect you."

The road twisted past the small temple at the end of the road, alongside continuous walls of tenement houses with no windows and only occasional doorways, each with a small statue of Hermes in front to bless the residents.

"How do they ventilate houses without windows?" Lauren asked.

Nestor waved his hand toward the decaying gray stucco that covered the walls of the row houses. "See the patched-up holes in the walls? Those holes were dug by robbers trying to get inside. There are no windows facing the streets out of safety."

He motioned with his head for them to follow. "When it is hot, we wear our *chitons* for modesty, and when it is cold, we wrap our woolen *himations* about us. We are accustomed to heat and cold, and you must take into account the sea. Helios and the sea breeze are in an endless clash for dominance. The sea tempers all. We have no need for extravagant finery like the barbarians and their king. They desire luxury. We desire character. A man's task in life is to strive for excellence. Is there any other way?"

At a busy crossroads, Zack held Lauren's hand high as she hopped like a kindergartner over stones that led from one side of the road to the other. Each stone was a measured walking-pace to the next. Positioned higher than the road, they allowed pedestrians to avoid the water and mud that fouled the streets during rain.

They were two-thirds across when a chariot pulled by two chestnut mares thundered down a side street, wheels and hooves spitting stones. The driver stood with reins in hand, snapping them to inspire his steeds to move faster, but with a learned dexterity as he maneuvered the wheels between the stones. Pedestrians darted to the sides, and Lauren leapt into Zack's arms while Nestor shook his staff, vexed at the charioteer's arrogance.

"Come back here, I'll flog you myself and feed you to the strays." Nestor rushed over to them. "Are you hurt, Lauren?"

"My gallant knight saved me." She kissed Zack's cheek.

"Only too happy to assist you, my lady." Zack switched to a feigned British accent. "I say, did you get that chap's license plate?"

Nestor noticed others watching them. "Must you always speak in your tongue and carry on so?"

"Sorry, Nestor, we keep forgetting." Lauren became aware of the disapproving glances.

"And is it your custom to clasp hands with your wife in public?" Nestor asked.

"It is," Zack answered. "Our affections do not cease at the door to our home."

"I see, but you are not in Atlantea. Restrain yourselves when we enter the Agora. Ah, look, a bakery. Hungry?"

Zack smiled. "You don't have to ask me twice."

The aroma of freshly baked bread drifted from the ovens in the small stucco building and permeated the neighborhood. Rolls and long slender buns lay in rows on an outside counter, stacked precariously.

Nestor pointed to a large basket of flatbreads. "These are made of wheat from the lands beyond the beloved colony of Artemis at Byzantium, near the mouth of the Euxine Sea. Brushed with olive oil and herbs, perhaps I will eat them all myself," he said, grinning and patting his belly. "Or, you may try a bowl of their porridge; it is raw barley meal and will fill your stomach for the entire day." He inhaled deeply and looked upward, clasping his hands in prayer. "Demeter, goddess of the earth, you are truly a wonder. Say the words and I will be your servant for eternity."

He spit out miniature coins from his mouth. After calculating quickly, he handed a few to an elderly woman behind the counter.

"Yuck, did you see that?" Lauren whispered to Zack.

"There aren't any pockets sewn into his clothes, honey. This was the custom for small purchases. He's probably got a money belt underneath, just like we do."

Nestor bit into one of the rolls. Complete joy spread across his face. "Many subsist only on these breads, although it is the curse of our soil that we can't grow enough to feed our people," he pointed out. "We are dependent on our colonies in the Euxine Sea for grain. Our poor lack the means to purchase fresh fish and fowl. They live on beans, peas, figs, salted fish, or whatever they can catch. There now, let us wash it down with wine. You sir, serve my friends something to drink."

Zack and Lauren sipped cautiously from the mugs, wondering about the water that diluted the wine. "It's not very strong, Zack. At least you won't have to carry me home," Lauren said.

Zack reached for another long roll, but knocked its neighbors onto the dirt street like tumbling logs.

"Be gone!" the old woman erupted. "You have a handful of thumbs and the manners of a Thracian. Pick them up, or I will box your ears."

"Calm yourself, rattle-tongue," Nestor interrupted. "I will purchase them. You'll be no worse off."

The old woman smiled, her toothless grin revealing her satisfaction with the transaction. She turned to another customer.

"I have an idea." Zack picked up the loaves, dusted them off and delivered them to a woman sitting on a doorstop with a baby on her lap. Nearby, two young boys watched a worm slither among the garbage.

"It's a newborn. I wonder if it's a boy or a girl." Lauren smiled at the woman.

"A girl," Nestor said. "You can tell by the strings of wool hanging above the doorway. Were it a male, there would be an olive branch."

Zack handed the woman three loaves. She kissed his hand and called to her sons, who ripped off pieces ravenously.

"The gods appreciate your kindness, Zack," Nestor said. "Come, I want to reach the Agora before the merchantmen wheel away their wares."

The journey carried them through twisted alleyways barely wide enough for a cart. Foot traffic thickened as they emerged onto an open area in front of the Acropolis.

"There," Nestor cried out, index finger extended. "Our sanctuary, up on that mount. If the barbarians try to run to those gates in full battle dress, they will lose wind and their limbs will wilt. See the huge, rough-cut boulders supporting the walls? Cyclops, the one-eyed giants, set them in place before the time of heroes. My city…" He sighed, gazing at the heights of the Acropolis. "I worked on the Athena temple myself, a hundred steps long it is. We are not yet done. The new is built upon the old. It is the way of life."

He placed one hand over his heart. "You see my friends from across Poseidon's great wash; our city is not just stones, buildings, or a crowded marketplace. Long ago, one of our wise men, Solon, gave the *demos*, the people, a voice in our political process."

He squeezed his eyes shut. "All men must share the responsibility of government, just as we faced the Persians at Marathon. In battle, men of wealth are the same as those with less: the aristocrat, the wine mixer, and the pottery spinner. They rise before dawn to cast their votes in the assembly, just as they buckle on their bronze before the battle."

His voice cracked. "We are a city of ideas and of men who know in their hearts that there is no other way for us to exist. Our resolve is like the stone columns you see, but our ideas are fluid, like the streams that run from the heights of Parnassus. Our philosophies evolve, and our citizens are stronger for it." Nestor rapped his rod on the stones beneath his sandals.

Zack squeezed Lauren's hand.

"Look upon me and tell me if I speak foolishness." Nestor searched them for a response.

"No, Nestor, what you have spoken is for eternity, and your wise words should be carved in stone," Lauren said. She touched his forearm, but he withdrew it quickly.

"Only the gods know. Come now, the marketplace is just around the corner. Do not separate yourselves from me."

They walked from the dirty narrow alleyways to behold magnificence rendered in stone and marble. They plunged into the noisy flood of people entering the Agora, the center of Athenian life.

Nestor shouted over the noise of the crowds, "We place our collective wealth in the hands of the artisans and architects, and this is our creation. See that long promenade, and the pillars of the temples and the government buildings? By Hermes, the crowds have not abated, even at this late hour."

People swarmed the stalls, most dressed in white but others in multicolored *chitons* and cloaks. Sellers hawked oils, flowers, wines, pots, silver and gold jewelry. Tiny lanes wove between endless booths offering the same types of wares in each section of the market.

"Let's stop and look at the flowers," Lauren cried above the din. "It'll smell better over there anyway. I could make a fortune here selling deodorant."

Zack snickered, breathed in deep and patted his chest, teasing her.

"Myrtles are second in favor only to the fish," Nestor said. "We'll find them later, Lauren."

He guided them past pens of squealing pigs, donkeys chomping on hay, and shops with baskets of lentils, apples, peas, and barley. Aromatic smoke from roasting chickens and pigeons rose from braziers while vendors chopped the meat into chunks. Sweat-glistened male slaves, clad only in loincloths, hauled baskets and large clay pots onto carts. Off to the side, under a portico of columns with a round roof, clumps of men waved their arms in heated debate.

Nestor raised his walking staff to clear a path. "Let us move to the fishmongers. The crowd smells the afternoon catch. Stay close, Zack," he warned over the pandemonium. "Lauren, walk between us for safety. A horde of Athenians going after their fish dinner would frighten even the most savage barbarian. We shall be the owners of a nice turbot, or maybe a carp."

Slaves hauled five-gallon earthen jars filled with fish and squid. The fishmonger called out his prices, bringing fist shakes and angry words from the shoppers, who were separated only by a thin wooden rail.

"Give me that fat one there!" Nestor shouted. "Quickly now... and what's in that jar?"

"Eels from Boeotia, but they demand a rich fee," the man said.

The weight of the surging crowd pushed them against the wooden rail. "A delicacy I've craved for some time. What is your price?" Nestor scrunched his face.

"Five minea." The man looked away.

Nestor extracted the sum from a leather purse tied around his waist, handed the coins to the merchant, and asked him to wrap the purchases in beet leaves.

Zack turned to a sea of faces, all screaming like commodity traders for the attention of the fishmonger. "I haven't seen people this excited since our last U2 concert."

Hands found Lauren's backside. Someone pulled hard at her *himation*. "Get me out of here before they rip my gown off!" she screamed, setting the hood back over her face.

"Carry this bundle. I'll hold the other." Nestor held his staff like a spear, parting the crowd. "Great amusement, is it not?"

"Yeah, loved it, let's do it again tomorrow," Lauren replied.

"Follow me."

Nestor pointed his staff at a long overhang that covered rows of chariots for sale. A man announced from behind a counter, "Steeds ridden by the gods themselves. You sir, come over here."

"We have more need for a garland of myrtles than one of these overdressed and overpriced mares." Nestor glanced at Lauren and Zack. "Quickly, no good Athenian would be caught without garlands for his symposium. I think that roses or golden amarantos that match Lauren's hair would do well to honor Aphrodite."

Zack whispered in her ear, "It might be wiser to wear a garland of laurel and honor Apollo; it's his temple we came…"

"Zack… Oh my God, it's the slave market."

"This is no place for you, Lauren," Nestor said. "No good will come of it. These girls are probably from the northern lands, Scythia or beyond."

"Look at their faces, Nestor. Don't they have the same feelings as you and I?"

"Twenty minea is the bid," the auctioneer began. "A handsome flute player, skilled in sewing and cooking, a welcome addition to the staff of any lady of the house." As he held up the girl's chin. Lauren saw her vacant stare. The man unclasped her unadorned *chiton*, newly changed to improve her appearance and elevate her selling price. He jerked the *chiton* down to her waist, exposing her breasts. "She is no Amazon and will be obedient."

"Twenty-five minae," shouted a citizen with perfumed and oiled hair, a late arrival from the barber's booth. A tall, muscled onlooker squeezed in front of Nestor, separating him from Zack and Lauren. Bidders quickly filled the gap between them. With their attention focused on the auction, the onlooker turned to Nestor. He prepared to shove the man aside, but froze when the onlooker's eyes slowly changed from blue to black. Unable to draw his gaze away, Nestor dropped his staff and his package. Words lodged in his throat. Wearing an assortment of necklaces, rawhide strings and bronze jewels, the blonde-haired onlooker reached for Nestor, who could not move away.

"Venerable sir," Nestor coughed out weakly. "Who... are you? Wait, I know you. Did you not stay in our barn...?"

The onlooker grinned while pressing his finger to Nestor's lips. Nestor heard only the deeply resonant voice, as if all the market noise had grown muted, distant.

"Noble forebear," Apollo said. "You are the promise of what is to be. If only I could get them all to see in times to come how you are now. They have lost the way. They squander the sacrifice of generations, all that you have started here in these days of greatness. They know only greed and gluttony. It shames me, for only I know what will come and the deluge of misery that awaits them."

The man touched Nestor's shoulder with a long manicured fingertip. "Alas, I cannot leave you with too much memory of this meeting."

He filtered back into the crowd. Nestor brought his hand to his head as if dizzy. After recovering, he picked up his purchases and made his way to Lauren and Zack.

"Leave her alone," Lauren shouted, unable to restrain her outrage.

"Who speaks?" the auctioneer demanded, his irritation obvious.

Zack reached for her. Nestor hauled them both away, moaning his dismay. The crowd of astonished bidders turned towards them, scowling and pointing fingers.

"Are you mad?" Nestor cried out. "You're fortunate they didn't summon the guards for upsetting trade. Do you want a dart in your flanks? Hurry now, let's head to Themistocles's house before we are imprisoned and these fish rot."

"Your hands are shaking," Lauren said, feeling his tremors on her wrist.

Nestor withdrew his hand. "I've never before... thought that I'd encountered a god. Now I'm not so sure. He said something to me, alas I cannot recall it." He pointed his staff at the statue near the entrance of the Agora. "We must sprinkle oil on Hermes and beg for his forgiveness. He rules the marketplace. I don't know if it was him I met, but I will not incur his wrath."

"Where is this god?" Zack asked, surveying the crowd.

"Do you think the gods would allow you to see them if they did not wish it so? Don't you know they can disguise themselves?"

Nestor led them away, while craning his neck to see if he could spot the tall onlooker who had stunned him.

Lauren met the slave girl's eyes one last time before crowds of buyers surged forward to inspect the new prospects and block her view. She walked away, eyes downcast.

When they were clear of the crowd, Nestor stopped them, red-faced. "Is it your habit to walk up to a hornet's nest and poke it with a stick? You tempt the gods without regard. You ignore our customs, place yourselves in jeopardy and think that you will not pay? You're my friends, but this is folly." He frowned. "Stay with me and keep quiet. If there are gods nearby, they will hear you."

"If he only knew that we know everything that's going to happen." As Zack whispered, his face bore a smug grin.

"Not everything," Lauren replied. "Maybe we are tempting fate."

Nestor wagged his finger at a long set of tables with another large throng of shoppers. "Come with me. We must taste the wines."

He talked briefly to the man pouring the wine before smacking a coin on the table and receiving three clay mugs. "Try this red wine. The wine master says it is a superior vintage from Macedonia."

Before the others could sample it, Nestor's face contorted and spit out a mouthful, splashing Zack's *chiton*. "Blahhhh! Tastes like a dagger dragged across my tongue." He jabbed a finger in the seller's chest. "Thief, you insult us with the third press from a field of weeds. You must have better than this."

The man quickly dispensed from another jug. His cowering look assured Zack this batch might be better. Zack swirled the dark red wine in his cup and took a sip. He smiled at Lauren. "It's good. Go ahead."

She took a mouthful and swallowed. She laughed and took another sip. "Wine tasting in ancient Greece. Things are looking up. How do you think they make wine here?"

Zack stared at the sediment covering the bottom of his mug. "They stomp on the grapes, just like in Italy in the old days. Couldn't have been easy to predict how it would come out though. We control the yeast. They rely on natural yeast."

Lauren winked. "Maybe I should get you a job here pouring wine."

They heard a commotion across the road. A small crowd followed an exquisitely dressed woman, her dark curls tied atop her head with a purple ribbon interlaced through her hair. She wore a long white gown, the hem embroidered with birds in flight. Chin uplifted, she ignored the throngs following her.

Lauren inspected the woman's elegantly hooked and folded *himation*. "Who is she?"

"The most expensive *hetaera* in all of Athens. She fetches a fee few can afford. There are those who will squander their entire wealth for an evening with her. She is no mere harlot, either. She sings, has attended the academy, and can talk your ear off on mathematics." Nestor flicked his hand towards them. "Even with the barbarians at our gates, the men will not give up their courtesans."

They strained to see the woman, unaware that a few men broke off from the crowd and raced in their direction. They nearly knocked Nestor over, one wildly gesticulating, roaring in his face, and pointing his finger at Lauren. Nestor regained his balance, broke into a rage, and swung his leaf-wrapped fish at the men, whacking them on the head and shoulders. "Away with you. How dare you suggest such a thing?" He threw a stone at them as they fled.

"What did he say?"

"I tried to warn you, Lauren. A woman seen on the streets is assumed to be a slave for barter, or a courtesan. These men are like drunkards, swilling uncut wine, even more so since the great Antiope just graced our path. They offered a sizeable sum for you. I should not have brought you to the market."

"It was my choice."

Nestor ignored her. "Come now; let's get our dinner home. We'll have a feast fit for Agamemnon himself. And for the grace of the gods, no more mischief, I beg you."

Near dusk, Zack and Lauren stood atop the Acropolis, studying the ancient temples burned when Xerxes took the city. They had climbed the steep marble steps, passing through the wooden battlements, and walked slowly past painted statues of the gods, discovered in the modern era buried in caves below the Acropolis. After reaching the summit, they approached the large stone and timber temple of Athena. Inside, a painted wooden statue of the Goddess Athena, guardian of the city, stood vigilant, watching over throngs of people who brought gifts to her daily.

"Too bad we don't have our cameras," Zack said. "Can you imagine having photos of the pre-classical temples of Athena and Erechtheus? Look, there's the foundation of the temple they never completed. They built the Parthenon on top of it."

Lauren pointed to a tree separated from all the others. "Hey, is that the fabled olive tree? The gods planted it there." The tale came back to her. "The day after Athens burned, the Persians allowed some Athenians to make offerings to the gods. They looked at the olive tree and saw new shoots growing at the base of the burnt trunk. It helped them believe that they would see a new life, despite their desperate situation."

As the sun slipped down, Lauren's eyes glistened. They looked to the south, where the strategic island of Salamis awaited. A small strip of ground near the city-state of Corinth formed the only land bridge joining Northern Greece to the Peloponnesus. Fishing boats and military vessels inched their way between shores. The oars of three-banked *triremes* left wakes that made the vessels look like tiny bugs swimming on the surface.

"This will all be gone soon," she said. "How could we ever have imagined seeing the Acropolis before the Golden Age?"

"Athens is a living, breathing incubation of democracy," Zack continued. "One man with one vote, despite slavery, sexism, economic and military exploitation, shoddy housing, and sewage. That's why I want to watch how this plays out."

She reached up and wrapped her arms around him. "Look, sweetheart. I'm worried that we may never make it home." She choked back the emotions threatening to swamp her. "And... I don't think we should go to Thermopylae. It's too dangerous."

Zack backed out of her embrace. "Why didn't people who know nothing of this time end up back here? There may be a reason we're here. We'll be careful. I promise you. We'll never leave each other's sight."

"You're a risk junkie, and you're giving me a headache. I need your pills now."

"Will you come with me?"

Lauren paused. "No. I'm not going. Neither are you."

"You're telling me what I'm going to do and not do?"

"Zack, someone has to stop you. Something bad could happen. You should know from experience."

He turned his back and scanned the darkening skies. Mosquitoes began their evening feast of arms and legs. Zack smacked at one, then turned to face her. "All right, if that's how you feel, then maybe you should go back to Delphi with Nestor and I'll make a quick trip north by myself. We can meet up..."

Her jaw dropped. "You promised you wouldn't leave me, *ever*."

"You'll be safe in Delphi. The Persians never sacked it. You know that."

"I can't believe what I'm hearing. You'd actually leave me."

Lauren stormed away. He ran and reached for her hand, but she threw it off. "What kind of a husband are you?"

"Then come with me. We'll be okay. We're not tourists; we're explorers."

"I'm going back to Themistocles' house and right to bed. Don't talk to me till you're thinking clearly. You left your brain somewhere in that tunnel."

Zack heard a knock on their bedroom door at first light. "I bid you to awake," Sicinnus said. "My master wishes to address you before he departs."

"Give us a few minutes," Zack called out.

What a long night. Lauren had not said a single word, despite his attempts to make peace. "Why do you want to say goodbye to Themistocles?" he asked.

"I'll be there in a few minutes. Go yourself." She didn't look at him.

Zack followed Sicinnus through the zigzagging hallways until they reached the *andron,* where assistants wrapped a formal white *himation* around Themistocles.

"There you are, Zack." Themistocles dropped his arms so slaves could finish their tailor work. "I am so grateful. Two nights of your medicine and there is no pain in my joints, and my head is clear of torment. I could debate Zeus himself."

"I'm pleased. Still more meetings ahead?"

"The debate is nearly done. The rest of the *triremes* will rush north to join the fleet at Artemisium. It is time to trust the gods and fight these barbarians."

Zack shuffled his feet, wondering how he could broach the subject of joining them. He glanced quickly to the doorway. No Lauren.

"I regret that we were never able to sit and speak of your people," Themistocles said. "Before I leave, is there any deed I may do for you?"

Zack cleared his throat. "There is. I want to go to Thermopylae."

Nestor took a step back. "Madness. There will be a fight to the death on land and sea."

"I must see this Persian threat and report it to my countrymen."

Themistocles broke in. "We can offer no assurances that you will not be captured or slain. Do not tempt the gods so boldly. They will strike you down."

Zack folded his arms. "I must go. I'll walk if I have to."

"What of Lauren?" Nestor asked.

"I ask you to take her back to Delphi and keep her safe until I return."

"Persephone told me she never allows her eyes to leave you."

Lauren burst into the room with a leopard-like growl, ran to Zack and twirled him around to face her. "So, you've made your neat arrangements, no matter how I feel?"

Nestor recoiled, horror in his face. He threw his arms skyward. "Heavens! I will have to cover my eyes if you beat her in front of me."

"Beat me?"

"Do all Atlanteans act in such a manner?" Themistocles asked, calmly draping the last fold over his wrist.

"I'm going to Thermopylae." Zack's tone conveyed the finality of his decision.

Nestor pointed his finger at him. "Arrogance will be your undoing."

"In Atlantea, we do not believe in fate, Nestor, we believe in free will," Zack said. "A man charts his own course and is in control of…"

"Great Zeus," Nestor said. "I hope the Olympians have their ears covered. Send your houseboy for a goat, Themistocles. We must sacrifice to the gods immediately."

"Why did I open my mouth? It is the curse of all politicians," Themistocles complained. "I am going to honor your request, Zack, but not because your arguments have swayed me from good sense. The gods have preordained your fate, even if you do not believe it. I have ships heading north this morning to deliver messages to Leonidas. If you want to be on board, you must leave right now for the fleet docks at Piraeus."

Lauren stood with her hands on her hips, her head cocked to the side. Zack put his hands on her shoulders, gently. "I know you think I'm an idiot, but this is an opportunity impossible to turn down."

"You must decide quickly or walk to Thermopylae," Themistocles' voice boomed off the high ceilings.

"Lauren, I'm going to get my things," Zack stammered. "I'll be back in Delphi in a week. I promise."

She turned away. Rage and fear competed for dominance on her face.

"I have a team of horses and a chariot that Hermes himself would covet," Themistocles said.

"I will drive you, Zack," Nestor said. "You are a brave man, though a foolish one, I fear. Say goodbye to your wife while I gather supplies."

"He won't have to. I'm going too."

Zack spun around. Nestor slapped his forehead with both palms.

"The gods are having a good laugh today," Themistocles said. "I must go."

"I hope we meet again," Zack said, shifting focus from the storm of fury on Lauren's face. "I feel that the unity that you have worked to achieve will prevail. Victory will be yours."

"And will fate or free will be responsible for our victory?" Themistocles asked. "That will be a long debate for better days. For now, it is time for good men to act and trust in the gods."

He smiled, but could not mask the grave look on his face. He walked away briskly.

Zack reached for Lauren's hands. "Are you sure?"

Her arms remained folded, her eyes acidic. "You've left me no choice. When and if we ever get home, that's it. I'm done."

"What's that supposed to mean?"

"You figure it out."

The saffron streaks of light from the morning sun illuminated the fleet triremes at Piraeus, over eight kilometers south of Athens.

Nestor stepped from the chariot, rubbing his back. "Great Zeus' thunderbolts, I gave up riding these body-wreckers years ago." He pointed to the docks and a ship with a ram's head sewn on the main sail. "Follow me now, before they cast off. Don't forget your belongings."

He gathered several bundles and limped quickly while speaking over the noise of the shipyard. "The ships will sail around Cape Sounion to the southeast of Athens, and then up the narrow channel that divides the mainland from the island of Euboea; a long journey it is."

"It's like a hundred miles to Thermopylae by sea, isn't it?" Lauren asked, worry etching her voice and face.

"We've been out in that channel before," Zack said.

"Yeah, but not in a floating coffin. Those things don't look like they can stay afloat in a choppy bathtub."

"The inside passage offers the safest harbors and shelter from the winds," Nestor said. "Enough talk. Hurry."

They dashed past sailors pulling carts stacked with amphora while others carried long oars on their shoulders. When they reached the ship, Nestor turned to them, his face bearing the look of anguish. "I will stay in Athens to assist with the evacuation, and then I will return to Delphi. You know the location of our cave." He pulled them both to the side. "Call my name into the entrance. Make sure no one follows you but, if there is a battle before the wall at Corinth, you will find me there, with my spear."

"We understand," Zack said.

"Then, since I cannot stop you, by Athena and all the gods, I bid you farewell. Zack, I have a gift for you."

Nestor picked up a bundle at his feet, untied the cord, and revealed the sword his brother had carried at Marathon. "Keep it sharpened and oiled. Remember to stay low and turn your body to the side to give the enemy a smaller target. And keep lifting the bags of sand. You still lack the muscle to wield a shield and sword in battle." He handed Zack the sword.

"I am honored," Zack said.

"Many thanks." Lauren embraced him, ignoring custom.

This time, Nestor did not stiffen and push her away. Instead, he placed silver and gold coins in her hand. "Use these wisely. Now, may the Goddess Athena guide you safely back to us." He glanced at Zack. "Leave him if he will not listen to reason."

"I may have to."

Nestor handed Themistocles's hastily written letter of instruction to Poylas, the Athenian naval officer and liaison between the allies in the fleet and the land army that would hold the terrain at Thermopylae. The brawny sea captain read the note with a concerned look on his face. "You may ride near the stern, but fasten pull your himations on tight," he said. "The early morning breeze will be cool."

They walked along wooden planks that served as decking between the oarsmen. On their way to the stern, they passed twenty-five rowers on each side. The men set their fat-greased sheepskins on the benches under their flanks, lifted their oars and stroked in unison. Five Athenian marines occupied wooden benches inside the stern, wrapped in blue *chlamys*, woolen war cloaks.

The ship, a *penteconter*, was small and built for speed. It traveled among a contingent of *triremes*, the primary fighting ships of the Athenian navy, each manned by a hundred seventy rowers. Each *trireme* carried three banks of oars, two sails, and was armed with a bronze ram fastened to the bow. Ten marines and four archers were among the crew.

The strategy aboard a *trireme* was simple: They would ram the enemy boat and shatter its hull. Then, the marines would overpower the crew and capture their vessel. On each side of the bow, a wooden enclosure protected two archers. Zack could not take his eyes off the three banks of oarsman and the well-practiced and orchestrated precision with which they propelled the vessel.

While getting their sea legs, they anticipated a tour of the coastline no luxury cruise could offer them. They knew the position of Euboea in respect to the mainland would affect the outcome of the imminent clash. A bottleneck of land and sea presented itself at the northern tip, where the allied Greeks intended to mount their first defense.

The oars dipped and the ship lurched as its bronze bow split the current. The row master sat on a wooden bench, alternating the pounding of a drum with a hammer held tightly in each fist.

"You there, help our guests lay pitch under their sandals. I don't want them falling overboard," Poylas shouted to a marine from his captain's chair near the stern. "Aeolus sends a strong wind our way." He sniffed the air. "I smell a chill coming with it."

CHAPTER 13
AUGUST 480 BCE
LAMIA, SOUTHERN THESSALY

CONTACT

Bessus and his cavalrymen reached a cluster of abandoned farmhouses and burnt fields after several days of hard riding along dirt roads. Dead cattle lay bloated in the heat. Bessus saw smoke in the distance, halted his troops, and growled, "They deny us food."

"Soon it begins," Cyartes said, riding by his side.

Bessus squirmed in his saddle, plagued by sweat that streamed under his heavy clothing and leather armor. He scratched at sores along his thighs and groin. Up ahead, high mountains and a wide bay appeared to join together.

He stretched to gain a better view. "I want to know if the road stops at the water's edge. It's too steep to ride up those ridges ahead."

Twenty troopers carrying short spears and small round shields galloped away to scout the terrain.

After a time, the clang of weapons, horses screaming, and shouts of men echoed from a distance. He kicked the sides of his mount and led his horsemen forward.

Empty mounts ran towards them. The captain of the detachment rode double on the back of one of his men's horses. Only six riders returned. The horses stamped their hoofs in agitation. The captain fell from his horse, gripping a wound in his thigh.

"What happened?" Bessus demanded.

"The road is blocked by a wall where the mountains meet the sea. We saw Greeks wearing red cloaks sitting on the wall, combing their hair." The captain winced as a surgeon tightened a hemp rope around his thigh.

"Go on," Bessus said, irked by the delay.

The captain paused, gathering his courage. "We attacked. Most of my men were cut down."

Bessus clenched his fists. "Out of my sight!"

He jammed his horned helmet onto his head and led his horsemen to within a bowshot of where the Greeks stood atop the wall. "Come and fight me, if you have any eggs between your legs," he taunted, pumping a spear over his head. His troopers snickered.

The Greeks jeered and mimicked Bessus, enraging him "Whores' sons!"

A warrior with a crest built horizontally across his helmet emerged from behind the wall. He stood on its heights and barked out orders; immediate silence followed. A hundred hoplites marched through a reinforced gate and formed a tight defensive line, four men deep. Another shout, and the front line of Greeks braced their shields and lowered their lances into a fighting stance, making one loud snap of iron and bronze. Bessus saw only the helmets with wide cheek pieces and plunging nose-guards; the bearded warriors were faceless, demonic-looking. A trickle of sweat ran down his back.

"Gut them!" Bessus barked before the grind in his stomach got the better of him. He raised his spear. His troopers spurred their horses, and waved their swords and spears. "EEEAHHH! EEEAHHH!" they shouted, invoking the Bactrian battle cry.

Just before they reached the wall of shields, the second, third, and fourth Greek ranks lowered their spears into a porcupine of iron points. The horses and riders crashed into the sharp edges of the lances. Horses screamed, some riders were thrown, and others were impaled.

Bessus hurled his spear. It struck one of the bronze shields and glanced off. All around him, cavalrymen fell from their mounts. His bowels grumbled. He drew his sword, but realized more menace confronted him than he expected. He deflected a spear with his small shield, but his mount took a lance and sent him flying. He staggered to his feet, stunned, with empty hands. His warriors continued the assault in waves.

When his head cleared, Bessus turned to face the enemy. A lance tore into his shoulder, just beyond his leather armor. He squeezed his eyes shut and bellowed the cry of the wounded. Blood drenched his chest. His legs lost their strength.

Cyartes seized him by the helmet strap and dragged him away. Choking, Bessus flailed his arms until the strap broke and his horned helmet toppled free. Cyartes and two other troopers hoisted him onto a horse to flee the battle.

Without their commander, his troopers broke off the assault.

After reaching the safety of a distant hilltop, Bessus beheld the cost of his attack.

"Stinking Greeks!" He smashed a fist against his thigh. He had lost half of his men. Rider-less horses galloped towards him.

"Shall we attack again, my lord?" Cyartes asked.

"Not this day." Bessus averted his eyes. "Move the troops back to that second line of hills, post guards, and make camp. Summon the surgeon."

Bessus glanced back at the red soldiers who stood before the wall, banging their spears on their shields, resuming their taunting.

When the fire blazed, the surgeon took an iron prod from his instrument satchel. Bessus removed the bloody bandage that wrapped his shoulder. "Be quick about it," he said.

The surgeon held the wrapped end of a cauterizing iron, turning it in the fire. Two brawny troopers moved in quickly to hold Bessus down. Protha, his father's long-trusted surgeon, stuck the hot iron in the wound. As his flesh boiled and crackled, Bessus wrenched and hurled the troopers on their backs.

Afterwards, he staggered away, biting his cheeks to stem the throb in his shoulder. "Cyartes," he blared, "send a rider. Tell Xerxes the road south is blocked by Greeks."

CHAPTER 14
DELPHI, GREECE
JULY, 2011

BOY HAS A SECRET

"Demo, load these cases of soda in the cooler. It's going to be hot today, and we're expecting busloads of tourists from Athens," Maria said.

"Do you think we'll get a little rain to cool off the walkways?"

"Could be. We might get a *Meltemi*. My brother-in-law, who runs a shipping company out of Piraeus, says if the cold wind comes out of the north, it will slip under the warm air and send storms down the coastline like a hungry husband ready for his dinner."

Demo grinned while transferring the cans. "I heard about those storms in school."

"Well, he lost a freighter up the coast one year. He's very careful, because the storms are so unpredictable. Hey, after you're finished loading the cooler, could you post this notice on the front door? A couple of American tourists have disappeared. A professor down in Athens is looking for them."

Demo read the notice. "Sure. I'll tape it on the door."

"Thanks." Maria smiled at him and continued preparations for another day of hungry visitors.

After closing, Demo returned to the orphanage. While most of the children played outside, he sprinted up to the second floor to their sleeping quarters. Each child had a locked cabinet for their possessions. He opened his; the video camera hung inside. He wondered again why anyone would leave such a valuable item suspended from a tree stump. The camera wouldn't play, so he figured the battery was dead. Satisfied the camera was safe, Demo locked the cabinet and ran outside to kick soccer balls with the other kids.

CHAPTER 15
AUGUST 480 BCE
OPOEIS, EURIPUS CHANNEL

SEA LEGS

Gale-whipped waves slammed against the hull of the *penteconter*, pitching and rolling it. In the blinding rain, Lauren threw up on the deck. Seawater splashed up over the guardrail, washing the vomit away. Zack held her with one hand and a deck post with the other. The tempest blew the streamers horizontal on the mast.

"Row till your bones crack," Poylas shouted. He shook rain from his eyes. "Make it to shore, or spend your days with Poseidon. Now pull!"

Zack tucked in his chin. With both hands occupied, he couldn't protect his face from the storm. Lauren dry heaved.

The row master beat the drum harder and faster. "Row like we're going to ram the enemy," Poylas roared, spitting sea and rain from his mouth.

Zack opened his eyes. A strong gust broadsided the ship, sending the oarsmen on the opposite side underwater. Poylas pulled on the rudder. The *penteconter* righted itself. A white-capped wave caught the ship, helping to guide them towards a shore obscured by clouds and rain. After harder rowing, the keel scraped sand. *Land.* Escort ships beached themselves along the coast.

Crewmembers leaped from the rails and tied long ropes to boulders on the beach. The drenched rowers hoisted up their oars and set them on the deck.

Lauren stumbled along the rail towards the gangplank.

"Let me help you," he called out.

She headed straight to the gangway, pushed a sailor out of her way, reached the middle of the ship, and jumped off. She landed in thigh-deep water, waded ashore, and fell to her knees, gasping for breath.

Zack sloshed ashore, right behind her. "Honey, are you okay?"

She didn't answer.

"God, what a storm. Came down fast." Zack gently lifted her chin. "That was a bad one."

Lauren dug her fingers into the sand. "I've never been so happy to be on land."

Poylas walked by, carrying a bundle on each shoulder. "Arrogance in the face of the gods," he said, his face beaming despite the rain. "The Persian fleet will be shattered if they were caught out to sea. How dare they invade this land and insult the Olympians."

"Come on, Lauren. Let's head up to that farmhouse." Zack threw his arm over her shoulder, surprised she didn't shrug him off again. They negotiated an obstacle course of stones, following an uneven line of crewmembers dragging supplies to safety.

The squall assaulted them until they fell inside the doorway. Two sailors worked on a fire in the hearth. The men made room for Lauren. They bowed their heads and praised her as she passed, calling her a good-luck charm. They asked her to touch the miniature statues of Poseidon tied around their necks. Zack sat beside her. She blew out a breath from puffed cheeks. The crewmen laughed and poked each other like fraternity brothers, the life-and-death tension of a sea squall behind them.

"Do the gods only exist if you believe in them?" Lauren asked, not looking at Zack. "Or do the gods disappear once the people who believe in them no longer exist?"

"Let me see if there's any wine."

"When the storm was at its worst and I thought we might die, I kept wondering why we were here," she continued. "Do you remember the saying on the column about the disembodiment of the gods? That's what happened, if you think about it."

"If I think about it, I'd say this whole thing is impossible. There is no way you can travel in time, especially backwards. I took physics as an undergrad."

With that, Zack settled her under his arm, and they burrowed down together. The crewmen threw gutted fish into an iron cauldron.

"Are you hungry?" Zack asked.

"I just want to sleep. I'm happy to be on solid ground. I'm thankful for that."

"It's all going to start, any day now." He spoke quietly as if the Greeks could understand his English.

"This is crazy. What are we doing?"

"We'll be okay." He held Lauren tighter, sure of what he said.

Pretty sure, anyway.

After hours of intense rowing up the Euripus Channel, they reached the Malian Gulf. Their sails filled with wind, scores of allied *triremes* made their way towards the Bay of Artemisium and imminent battle with the Persian navy.

"I never dreamed I would see such a sight," Zack said, trying to get Lauren to talk. "There's so many differently colored sails. How does a battle fleet hold such close order in this wind?"

Lauren laid her arms over the side rail. Billowing clouds lay in the distance, but did not hold the peril of their last voyage. "From this distance, it reminds me of a regatta I went to in Newport, Rhode Island," he added.

The wind picked up. The planks groaned beneath their feet. Sailors yanked ropes through creaking pulleys and cleats. "Something bad is going to happen to us," she said.

Zack covered her hand. "Please don't think like that."

Strong north winds agitated the bay waters. Sails came down. The crew and marines looked port and starboard in search of the enemy. The beating of the cadence drums began.

"If they think they're going to fight, the *triremes* will strip the sails and drop them off on shore," Zack said. "Look how fast those ships are moving. They look like Harvard racing sculls flying down the Charles River."

She nodded. "Think of how much pressure they're under. They are clearly outnumbered and have no idea of the damage the storm has done to the Persian fleet. They don't even know that another two hundred ships have been sent by Xerxes to flank them and bottle up the channel we just came through."

Their *penteconter* left the fleet and sailed west towards Thermopylae. In the distance, a solid ring of majestic purple rose from the glistening sea, revealing the mountain chain that blocked the land route from northern to southern Greece.

Zack's eyes lit up. "This is just too unbelievable. We're going to meet Leonidas." He craned his neck to see if he could spot the famous pass in the distance.

As the ship passed an outcropping of tree-shrouded ground, the smoke of countless Persian campfires and thousands of multicolored tents blanketed the hillsides along the coastline. The sea breeze carried the clamor of a massive army camp and its stench that overwhelmed, even from a mile offshore.

"The whole of Asia seems camped in those purple hills," Zack said.

"A clash of cultures, religions, and governments; you can understand why most of the Greek states capitulated. Who could stand in the way of all that?"

Zack nodded soberly. "We're about to meet men who did. A society built on a few simple statutes: obey the law and make soldiers. The Spartans focused on only one trade: warriors. A true military state, by any era's standards."

"Such a paradox. The Spartans bred soldiers, but they also fostered a more lenient society for women. They ran their own households and enjoyed so many more freedoms than Athenian women."

Zack exhaled heavily.

"I wish we knew more about Spartan women and how they lived," Lauren added.

"There are only a few famous ones: King Leonidas's wife, Gorgo, and a few poets."

"'Come home with this shield or upon it.' Isn't that what Spartan mothers told their sons when they gave them those big bowl-shaped shields?" Lauren asked. "Can you imagine that being said in our era?"

"And here we are, about to witness what the ages have only heard or read about in books and movies."

"I don't share your enthusiasm."

Zack studied the expanding scenery as they neared the Hot Gates of Thermopylae.

"We're walking into the middle of a war," Lauren said, her voice rising. "Will you stop with the fantasizing? There's no guarantee we'll get out of this alive."

"We'll be okay, I promise."

"Stop saying that. You don't know the future... even if it's the past."

Sheer cliffs rose from the rocky shoreline to converge with a slightly sloping narrow path, bracketed on the landside by the sheer height of Mount Kallidromos. Midway through the pass, men were busily rebuilding a wall of stone. From this 'Middle Gate', the path descended into a narrower defile restricted by unassailable ridges on the left and a cliff extending over the water to the right. Thermopylae Pass, called the "Hot Gates," because of bubbling springs in the area, widened as it coursed north along the gulf toward the Trachis Plain and Persian army.

Zack marveled at the enormity of the moment. "Imagine seven thousand soldiers guarding a pass only fifty yards wide, against the power of Asia."

"You're in a trance again and beyond hope," she said, trying to quell her anxiety. "These men are facing a horrible battle, and everyone in it is going to be absolutely merciless. Spartans had to murder one of their slaves as a rite of manhood. You have no idea how they are going to receive us. We're outsiders. They're not going to like that."

"I can't stop thinking about the desperation these men must feel, and the strength of character necessary to stand up to a mission of certain death." Zack pointed at the narrow corridor the Greeks defended. "Man, this looks so different... the shoreline's so much farther out."

The rowers strained to slice through the still waters. As they neared the shore a quarter of a mile from the pass, Lauren and Zack noticed the distinctive red war cloaks of the Spartan hoplites. Contingents from other Greek cities stood guard also, some wearing black crests or alternating black and white-crested helmets.

The ship scraped the rocky bottom, jolting them out of their reverie. Zack gathered Nestor's bundle and felt the sword blade under the blanket.

An honor guard of five Spartans marched towards them while they disembarked. The sun reflected brilliantly off polished bronze shields and helmets; they covered their eyes. The effect reminded Zack of fighter pilots attacking their adversaries with the sun behind them, the rays piercing the eyes of their enemy. It was an effective tactic in any age. Red war cloaks, draped at the neckline and hanging loosely over their shoulders, cascaded like crimson waterfalls down the Spartans' backs. The Corinthian-style helmets, adorned with stiff stalks of horsehair, gave the hoplites a formidable appearance. Each man appeared taller than he was. Warriors held *aspis,* wide oval shields, painted with vibrant colors.

A Spartan officer, Dienekes, asked about their sea voyage. A horizontally positioned horsehair crest on his helmet identified him.

"A long lazy sail," Poylas answered. He grew serious. "The fleet is gathering nearby. We expect to wage battle soon."

The Spartan officer nodded, noticing Lauren and casting a disapproving glance at her.

"The wall looks stronger now," Poylas said, viewing the efforts of the allies upon the Middle Gate.

"The barbarians will soon know that the true barrier is the sting of our lances. Why bring a woman here?" Dienekes asked.

"They're envoys from a far-away country and guests of Themistocles. I will explain this to Leonidas."

"This will surely lighten the King's mood," the officer said sarcastically.

Zack looked past the wall to a gentle slope that led down to the more constricted area of the pass. Fully armored hoplites stood guard there, watching for movement in the Persian camp. The allies imbedded sharpened wooden stakes in a long ditch in front of the wall. Dust and flying insects tormented the workers.

As they followed the Spartan honor guard up the hill from the beach, Lauren listened to the men talk of battle strategies. "They expect an attack tomorrow," Lauren interpreted. "They're ready to take turns to relieve the front lines as the men tire. The Spartan says they are accustomed to the heat. Poylas is telling him that they hope to block the Persian navy at Artemisium, protecting the Spartans from the Persians landing behind them. Poylas says the recent storms must have dealt the Persian navy a serious blow."

Zack put his hand on her shoulder. "This is incredible. Thanks for letting me come here."

"*Letting* you come here? You really don't have a clue do you?" She shrugged his hand off.

He tried to brush off the icy chills of her rebuff as the Spartan commander led them past a small hill to the hoplite camp. The warriors camped between the rebuilt wall and the hill, aside a mountain spring. Darkly tanned officers sat on split logs surrounding a central fire pit.

In the middle, a lone warrior traced designs in the dirt with the tip of his *xiphos*, a Spartan short sword. His full beard, graying hair, and lined face reflected many years of duty. Dark penetrating eyes, heavily browed, shone above a flattened, off-center nose. He stood a head shorter than Zack, but his body appeared chiseled from stone, like the other Spartans. Zack gulped when he turned around. On the back of the warrior's breastplate was the picture of a roaring lion. He tugged on Lauren's hand. "That was him at Delphi."

Poylas smiled, revealing broken front teeth that complemented his rugged features. "Greetings, Poylas. See the proper reception we've prepared for our guests stacking up on those hills? They have walked a long distance to die at the point of our pikes."

Poylas chuckled. "King Leonidas, will you save a few of them for the Athenians after we sink their rowboats?"

"You know how greedy we Spartans are." The king looked as if he was going to say something else, but paused when he saw Lauren.

"My King, Poylas has brought two envoys at the favor of Themistocles," Dienekes said.

Leonidas fixed his eyes on Zack and Lauren, who froze before him. "Envoys, you say. What land is it that sends a woman to do such work in a place where no woman should be?" He was clearly displeased.

Poylas pointed toward the horizon. "A land far to the west, one never heard of."

Leonidas narrowed his eyes.

"They are here to witness the defense of the north and then report back to their countrymen," Poylas added.

"Is this so?" Leonidas' tone suggested distrust. He moved his hand over the hilt of his sword. "Are Athenians so gullible? Speak up and convince me you are not spies."

Leonidas drew his *xiphos*. Zack waited grimly, unable to breathe, wondering if one of the men he most admired in history would run him through. "Search them, Dienekes."

Spartan guards held them as Dienekes patted them down and rummaged through their belongings. "Just this *kopis*," he said.

Lauren straightened her tunic. "King Leonidas, may I speak in your presence?"

"I see the women of your country are well-mannered. The fortitude of your men, I am not so sure of." He inspected the *kopis*, a curved Athenian sword. "What land are you from?"

"Beyond the Pillars of Hercules, many months of travel by land and sea," Lauren said in her best Doric dialect.

Smoke spiraled upward from a cooking pot. Newly cut pinewood crackled, giving off a pungent odor as Leonidas set aside the *kopis*. "Give me your hands, foreigner."

The Spartan king squeezed Zack's hands hard. He gritted his teeth. "You are no warrior. Your grip is weak." He handed the sword back. "I doubt you could wield this well enough to cut through a crumble of cheese."

"He is a teacher of youths. Histories and cultures," Lauren said.

"A *pedagogue*? How learned. Spartans attend the school of survival instead."

She pressed on. "King Leonidas, even in our far-off land, we have heard of Spartan and Athenian courage."

Leonidas walked over to an iron pot suspended above a campfire. "A Spartan is not swayed with words from the honeyed tongue of a herald." The king stirred a thick concoction in the black pot. "Neither will it earn you a bowl of our soup."

The entire troop exploded in raucous laughter.

Lauren let the rumble die down. "If it's the legendary soup I've heard about, then I will cease the compliments now." The roaring and backslapping continued. "We are from a land called Atlantea, and we are here to witness the brave defense of Hellas. I am Lauren. This is my husband, Zack."

"Hellas, you say. The city-states have never united. That is a false dream. We can only work to join together the armed might of our warriors."

Leonidas snatched a spear and drove it into the ground. "Here we stay." The soldiers cheered and shouted until the king lifted his hand. Instant silence. "Join us in our noonday meal and we will see what Atlanteans are made of."

Leonidas knelt down, holding his ceramic campaign cup by a single finger hole. Its unique design included an inside lip to keep bugs, twigs, and other impurities from the warrior's mouth when he drank from less-desirable water sources. Leonidas dipped his cup into the thick black soup, a Spartan staple. Other Greeks found it foul-tasting, joking that now they knew why the Spartans did not mind fighting to the death. The soup bubbled and popped in the cauldron like lava. He filled a number of other cups with the stew, finally handing one each to Lauren and Zack. The warriors lifted their cups in prayer to Zeus and to the people of Sparta and Athens.

Zack brought the famous soup to his lips and took a small sip. It was much too hot on a humid day already surging into the nineties. The liquid held the texture of porridge and tasted like a nasty combination of meat, blood, onions, and vinegar. Which it was.

Leonidas tapped his cup against Lauren's and all the others within the circle.

"We eat the meat of cattle here, instead of swine, as we do at home. Sticks to your sides, does it not, Zack?"

Zack smiled. "It does, King Leonidas." He closed his eyes, savoring the moment and his intact hide.

"Vomit and I will force you to down another," Leonidas said. More hilarity followed. Then he addressed his commanders. "See that your men are fed. Finish your preparations."

The officers sipped their thick soup as Zack wondered if this day was the apex of his life as a scholar. He thought of Herodotus, who reported in one of his writings: "When the Spartans fight singly, they are as brave as any man, but when they fight together, they are supreme above all. Though they are free men, they are not free in all respects. Law is the only master whom they fear."

"Lady, how do you enjoy our soup?" Leonidas asked.

Lauren's eyes sparkled. "I would invite you to our land where I will serve you something equally as bad."

There were shouts and high spirits.

"Maybe if we serve our stew to Xerxes, he and his men will flee back to their rat holes," the king said, smirking. He waved his hand out toward the constricted pass. "No more talk."

The commanders took their soup with them, leaving only Lauren, Zack, and Poylas with the king.

"I warn you to stay well back from the fighting and far from the flight of missiles. Do not tempt Tyche to find you. Make your camp up on that small hillock there," Leonidas said, pointing to a hundred-foot rise set well back from the pass. "Violate my orders, and you will leave. Betray us, and I will spill your guts. Understood?"

"We will obey you," Zack assured him.

Leonidas turned to other duties as Lauren pulled Zack away. He saw the worry in her eyes. "Are you okay, sweetheart?"

"No. I'm nervous as hell."

As they made their way to the top, they both knew what significance this hillock would hold in the days ahead. .

Later, the constellations sparkled like diamonds on black velvet. "How appropriate," Lauren whispered. "The constellation Leo is high in the sky and here we are with Leonidas. It's hard not to tell him what we know will occur here."

Zack sighed loudly. "If we did, would it change anything? Bearing witness to this heroic stand has to suffice, and I'll keep my mouth shut, I promise."

A messenger came with an invitation for them to return to the command post. They dusted off their clothes. She pulled her hair back and fastened it with a broach that Cassandra had given her. Blazing torches set into prepared holes in the earth created a path through the camp. They passed hoplites sitting around the fires, eating their evening meal. Others hauled supplies of spears and arrows to the front.

Lauren and Zack followed the path of torches to where Leonidas and his command sat before a roaring fire.

"Sit at my side, Atlanteans," the king said. "Lady Lauren, you are a fair sight in the midst of these ugly faces. Join us for bread and figs."

They sat next to him on logs. "It is well for us to learn the ways of others," Leonidas began. "Tell us of your home."

"King Leonidas, we would be happy to tell you of our people," Lauren said. "My husband is less skilled with your tongue, so with your approval, I shall attempt to answer your questions."

The Spartan king nodded while drawing a sharpening stone over his sword. She stood. "We are also a people who have known much strife and warfare. Our leaders and armies follow the will of the people. We have no king. Instead, we choose a leader."

"Ah, like the Athenians," Leonidas remarked.

"Yes. We have a large country but, in our infancy, we were able to gain our freedom from a much stronger one."

The commanders murmured among themselves.

"Our leader, a man revered in our land, led a small army to victory many years in our past. After many difficult wars, our country is free and strong, and our people are numerous, wealthy, and generous."

"Tell me of your warriors. How do they arm themselves?"

"Very similar to your hoplites," Lauren said, choosing her words carefully. "The first Great War was for independence. In one of the first battles, our soldiers held a hill. The enemy charged, only to be turned back twice with heavy losses. The third time, our defenders were driven back, but they'd killed so many of the attackers, the enemy eventually left the city."

The Spartan commanders locked their eyes on the dancing fire. Leonidas broke the trance. "Tell us more."

"Soon after the war, our country expanded, eventually reaching the size of your enemy's empire. We came into conflict with another nation to our south. Our people defended a temple surrounded by high walls against an army perhaps twenty times larger, holding their position for twelve days before the final assault came. They fought bravely, but troops equally as brave overwhelmed them. Ultimately, their sacrifice inspired unity among my countrymen."

Animated conversation broke out among the commanders. Dienekes stood and proclaimed, "We understand these men. It is our code to fight to the death or to proclaim victory. You say that these actions brought iron to the people's hearts?"

Lauren nodded, satisfied with her descriptions of Bunker Hill and the Alamo.

"Few against many, as we are now," Leonidas said.

"Our next war was not with a foreign power..." Lauren broke off, drowned out by drums and music blasting from the Persian camp.

"They ready themselves for battle with drink and merriment," Leonidas said, smirking. "Continue with your tale."

"Our next war was within the borders of our nation, and it tore our people and our country apart. We decided that we didn't want our country to prosper through slavery."

Lauren wanted to kick herself. *Crap, why did I bring that up?* She was well aware that Spartans had subjugated *helots,* local populations, and forced them to toil in the fields. She felt sure that armed *helots* stood among the Spartans in her midst.

Leonidas searched the faces of his men, as if to determine their reaction. "This is not our way," he said. "We have conquered the Messenians, and they must submit to our rule. There are fifteen freemen and *helots* for every pureblood Spartan. Maybe you live in a world of order and safety. We do not."

"The bravery of your men will one day be sung in all of Hellas and even in our country as well," Lauren said, covering her error and hoping they wouldn't be tossed out of camp.

Leonidas rose. "It will be more pleasing to hear the Persians sing our praises. They will not forget us. Look upon the Spartan hoplites that guard these gates. They move to barracks at seven years of age and attend the *agoge,* our training school. They endure cold, starvation, and survival in the wild by their wits and skill. They've been born to fight, for Sparta."

The king held forth his *xiphos*, the muscles of his forearms rippling in the firelight. "You will see that each man is welded to another with ties stronger than bands of iron. They will destroy the barbarians for each other, to outshine the man next to him in valor."

Leonidas slashed the air with his sword. Zack ducked, even though the sword did not come close. Everyone noticed.

"My Spartiartes in the ranks, all pureblood peers, already exist in another realm," the king continued. "Their blood boils like the soup in that pot, and they will kill, and kill, and kill until I tell them to stop."

The night winds brought shouting and the screaming of women from the Persian camp.

"The Spartans will receive the enemy first, to be followed rapidly by the Thespians, and the other Peloponnesian contingents, by Arcadians, Mycenaean's; then the Thebans, and finally the Locrians." Leonidas pointed his sword at the wall. "We shall not yield this position. The Phocians have been sent to guard the mountain path."

Zack winced when he heard mention of the "secret" of Thermopylae: a long, winding, obscure goat path that ended behind their defenses. A path they hoped the Persians would not discover. He longed to interfere, to tell the king to dispatch Spartans to help defend the mountain track.

As Zack pondered Leonidas' instructions, he spied an odd-looking helmet abandoned near the fire pit. Made of beaten bronze with leather chin straps, a band of metal descended from the dome creating a nose guard. Two pointed horns fastened into its sides gave it the appearance of a Viking helmet. Zack waited until Leonidas had dismissed his commanders before inquiring about it.

"We took it from an oversized savage on horseback the other day. Sent him home, like a dog with his tail between his legs." Leonidas gave Zack both a wry smile and the helmet. "Even with your long limbs, you have never been a warrior?" Leonidas asked.

Zack looked away from the Spartan king. He took no pleasure in admitting to one of history's bravest men that he had never served.

"No, King Leonidas." He felt raw with embarrassment. "Our army is large and powerful, and not all men are summoned to be warriors."

Leonidas placed his hands on his hips just below the rolled edge of his bronze breastplate, shaped like the muscles of his abdomen. His eyes twitched and he clucked his tongue. "I see no iron in your eyes. A warrior has the eyes of a hawk. You gaze at me with eyes of a dove needing sleep." Leonidas moved directly in front of him. "You have just told us of wars in your kingdom, and yet all of your men are not trained to fight. Is your land so tame? I doubt you could stand in a line of shields. Maybe you are a *rhipsaspis,* a shield flinger, and would run like a dog, too."

Zack shifted uncomfortably, this gut-wrenching moment made even more acute by Leonidas' unrelenting stare. "I am now persuaded that it would be beneficial for me to learn how to fight," he said. He could not have felt more mortified.

"Our ways are not yours, but hear me well. You cannot learn the art of war or mold the heart of a warrior in a heartbeat. The gods change events at their whim, and enjoy toying with those most arrogant. Prepare, or you will give the gods a very hearty laugh."

Not the first time I have heard that, Zack thought.

"Strength brings safety, to this land or any other. Rub your eyes and remove the sleep from them, Atlantean, before it is too late."

Zack nodded, inclining his head in respect. "I hear and acknowledge your wisdom."

The king bid them goodnight and left the circle to supervise the final defensive preparations.

Zack and Lauren remained beside the roaring fire. "Crap, I thought he was going to beat the shit out of me," he said.

"Sometimes, I want to beat the shit out of you. This is a warrior culture, Zack. You think this is a playground for your academic curiosity?"

"What about you?" he shot back. "Every chance you get, you bring up the subject of slavery."

"So what?"

"So, you accuse me of trying to change history, but your telling them about ending slavery could also change history."

She knew he was right. Not that she was about to admit it. "We could easily advise Leonidas in ways that might change the outcome of the battle ahead. But we won't." She placed her hand on his forearm. "I may weep for the dead and maimed, but I won't reveal an outcome already recorded in the books. But telling him my point of view isn't going to hurt."

"You don't know that. Tomorrow the Athenians will attack the Persian fleet as they repair their storm-damaged ships, and Xerxes will mount an attack against Leonidas."

"Zack, I just want to go home. I mean it."

They fell silent.

The Persian army had reached a chokepoint. Their navy, blocked from further advance, had already suffered the wrath of the sea when the fast-moving storms slammed into them with little warning.

Many of the Greek city-states, especially the Peloponnesians, including Sparta, wanted to make a stand at the Isthmus of Corinth in the south. As a result, Leonidas was allowed by Sparta's council of elders to march north with only his personal bodyguard of three hundred knights and their *helots*. The Spartans all had living sons, insuring their individual bloodlines would continue if they fell in battle.

Lost in thought, Lauren and Zack returned to the hillock, passing rows of hoplites sleeping on the ground or under open–ended tents. She looked up at the stars. "Zack, I'm frightened. Tomorrow, it's going to be horrible, for both sides."

"We can't change that. I've been thinking about what Themistocles said about fate. Are we seeing this because we chose to, or because we're supposed to?"

CHAPTER 16
AUGUST 480 BCE
THERMOPYLAE PASS, GREECE

CLASH OF GIANTS

The beat of drums awakened everyone. The first glimmers of morning sun reflected off the still waters of the Malian Gulf.

They watched the warriors buckling on their bronze and laminar-linen breastplates. Below the breastplate, a girdle of leather straps reinforced with large bronze hobnails protected the groin and upper thighs. Each hoplite placed a leather cap on his head that absorbed sweat and acted as a buffer between scalp and bronze helmet. They carried wood-framed shields covered with sheets of beaten bronze.

As Zack watched, he recalled how the hoplites got their name: from *'hoplon'*, the bowl-shaped shields they carried. They decorated those shields with a variety of personal designs. Red snakes, black bulls, yellow griffins and other images might identify the city-state of the owner, but more importantly, might distract the enemy or strike fear within their ranks. As the sun rose, the shields blossomed. Along their lower rims, leather aprons were attached to deflect arrow and missile shots.

Many of the allied warriors armed themselves with straight and curved swords. Their eight-foot-long *dory* spears served as not only striking weapons, but when held in concert, formed an imposing wall difficult to overcome by frontal assault. Many hoplites rewrapped and glued the leather grips that secured their hold on the spears during battle.

Guards waited to relay enemy movement. Others made their way to the slit trench latrines dug into hard ground in the rear areas of the camp. The scrape of stone upon metal heralded their steps.

Zack reached for Lauren's hand. "All we can do is sit and wait," he said.

"A lot of these men are going to be dead soon. Maybe we can offer to carry water." She released Zack's sweaty hand and wiped hers on her gray chiton. "My heart is pounding."

"According to the history books, it will be late morning before the attack is launched."

She headed towards the medical bivouac. They spent the next hour carrying water to the troops and ripping linen into bandages.

Horns from the Persian lines broke the calm. Leonidas stood on the wall, watching his Spartan commanders give instructions, check equipment, and discuss tactics. The Spartan contingent filled the pass from the bay cliffs to the sheer mountain wall, six rows deep and forty men wide. More warriors lined up in square formations behind them, ready to move when summoned. The allies would take direction and derive strength from the Spartans. From a distance, drumming shattered the quiet lapping of waves against the shore.

Finally, dense rows of Persian infantrymen emerged from a line of trees half a mile away.

The *helots* removed the scarlet cloaks from their Spartan masters. With the freemen of Sparta, they took positions behind the solid wall of hoplites, stacking bundles of javelins and lances to hand forward.

The Spartan line stood motionless. Flute players blew shrill notes behind them, calling them to present shields and grip their lances. A stiff marching song followed, the. Ode to revered heroes Castor and Pollux, played before battle.

The Persians advanced in their dark embroidered jackets over thin fish-scale armor. They wore helmets of simple iron that offered no protection for their faces or necks and carried *sparabara*, light wicker shields, designed to catch a spear and entangle it. Their lances were much shorter than the Spartans.

"*Epi Dori!*" the Spartan officer barked.

"Hah!" The hoplites' response was guttural. The front line crouched and leveled their spears. The ranks behind them elevated their spears to deflect arrows. The men compacted themselves in a tight formation, shields pressed close to their bodies, singing the warrior's song.

"They look like a solid mass of bronze," Zack whispered, awe-struck. "History says the Medes are the first to attack. I wish I could make out the words of that song."

Lauren, riveted by the scene before her, could only nod.

Horns blasted out long notes. The Medes emerged en masse from the trees.

Zack swallowed. His throat was dry. He felt like an anvil was crushing his chest. He pointed. No words came.

Archers ran ahead of their ranks. Thousands of arrows split the air with a sound like ripping sheets, drowning the voices of the Spartans. The cane-shafted arrows peaked and fell on the Spartan formation. Bronze shields rang with the impact.

The missiles had little effect. The Medes attacked the Spartan shield wall. Cracking bones, snapping spears and the screams of dying men filled the air. A ceaseless cacophony of metal striking metal overwhelmed their cries. Oncoming rows of Medes trampled the wounded.

The front row of Spartan hoplites thrust underhand with their spears, catching and holding the thatched shields of the Medes while finding bellies, groins and legs. The second and third rows raised their spears and stabbed down at the enemy, skewering unprotected faces, necks and chests.

As the mid-day sun blazed, wave after wave of Medes shouted and strained to reach the shield wall, only to meet their deaths in a merciless slaughter.

After an hour of fighting, the Spartan front lines neared exhaustion. Pipes wailed and drums sounded from behind the allied line. A new, fresh battalion of hoplites marched forward, sifting through the ranks until they reached the front line. The new formation of Thespians attacked the Medes with a war cry and fervor that supported the Spartans. They pressed together in the Spartan fashion and pushed forward. The Medes, attacking in huge numbers but loosely organized, met with failure as spearheads penetrated flesh.

"My God, Lauren, they're tearing them to pieces," Zack said, his tone registering disenchantment with the scene before him.

"I can't watch this anymore." She covered her ears and dropped her head between her knees.

"Maybe we should move back."

"It won't matter. Let's see if we can help with the wounded."

They ran to the makeshift hospital closer to the wall, where *helots* removed blood-drenched armor from wounded Spartans.

The Medes turned to flee, slamming into the troops who arrived to reinforce them. Panic ensued.

Cheers erupted along the lines of hoplites. Lauren and Zack turned their heads, as did others around them when they heard the Greeks rap their spears against their shields.

The banging persisted, as if daring the Persians to come back for more. "Insult to injury," Zack said.

"There's so many wounded. How can we treat them all?" Lauren shouted above the pounding of drums, high–pitched flutes, cries of the injured, and sizzles of cauterizing irons.

Streams of injured hoplites at their feet, Zack and Lauren stood, dumbstruck. "This guy's been cleaved by an axe," Zack cried out.

They stared at the blood spurting from the wound. Lauren pressed her hand over a deep gash in the warrior's shoulder. Blood shot between her fingers with each beat of his heart. "We need something to choke off the flow!" she screamed.

Now frantic, Zack grabbed a linen bandage and pressed his weight onto the wound. The warrior groaned, looked up at Lauren and tried to speak, but blood poured from his mouth. He cleared his throat, and managed to say, "Goddess, my goddess."

His mouth filled again. Gagging, his eyes rolled back, and he took his final breath.

Lauren sagged to her knees while Zack stared at his stained hands. "Zack!" she shouted.

A hoplite staggered by as if drunk, holding his hand over one side of his head. He twirled and collapsed. The man's temple was a mass of smashed bone. "What do we do with this?" Lauren asked, horrified.

The warrior rolled onto the ground, moaning and rubbing his head wound with his fingers. Zack grabbed his hands, gripping hard as the warrior kicked his legs and struggled to free himself. Lauren squeezed a wine-soaked rag over the wound. The man bellowed, swung his fist and smacked Zack in the chest, sending him flying.

The warrior rose, took a few more steps and fell. Within moments, he lay still. Zack and Lauren stared wide-eyed at each other. Drums in the distance broke their trance. More wounded staggered from the fighting. Fast-moving *helots*, trained as medics, placed compresses, tied tourniquets, and soaked wounds with undiluted wine to halt bleeding. Hooked needle and twine served to stitch the wounds.

"What's that piece of wood tied to his left wrist?" Lauren asked, staring at the dead hoplite.

"He must be a Spartan. You've seen the first version of a dog tag."

"Come on, we need to move as fast as those guys."

"Split up, is that okay?" Zack asked.

Lauren didn't answer; she was already gone. Zack picked up a handful of leather straps and ropes. In the distance, Leonidas surveyed the defenses and shouted instructions. Lauren helped a *helot* pull on a warrior's leg to set his broken bone. He carried the wounded closer to the shore, where it was cooler.

From there, Zack saw what was happening in the pass. A fresh division of allied hoplites rested as they studied the pass like golfers waiting to tee off. Others sat cross-legged next to their shields, their spears stuck into the ground.

Marauding *helots* finished off the wounded Medes. They threw the bodies off the cliff into the bay, or carried them farther out into the pass to block the Persian troops when they advanced again. They gathered weapons and hauled them behind the wall.

Drums announced another attack. The hoplites rose and formed their lines. A Greek officer shouted, "Now make these jackals regret the day they dropped from their mothers' hind legs. Lances!"

The officer reinserted himself into the line of defenders. Persian infantry advanced. Behind Zack, warriors begged for water. He took a last glance at the developing battle and ran for more water and tourniquets.

Infantry from the Persian capital of Susa closed in. Carrion birds lifted off from the fresh corpses and flapped their way to the mountainside, a perfect perch for viewing their evening meals.

The barrier of corpses slowed the Persians' advance. Then Zack heard shouts from the front lines. Divisions of Persian archers stepped forward, drew arrows from bow cases slung at their hips, and fired from point-blank range. It sounded like a hailstorm pounding an aluminum shed. As before, the arrowheads failed to penetrate their Spartan targets, although many found purchase in the bodies of the dead.

The archers withdrew. In response, the entire formation of Greek hoplites attacked with a fury. Persian infantry toppled with gory predictability, finally fleeing the Greek spears, and colliding with waves of reinforcements moving up to attack. They appeared like conflicting tides.

The Greeks halted two attempts to secure the pass. The orderly replacement of fighting men provided time to rest, suture wounds, eat and drink, and prepare for their next shift.

Zack tried to swallow and found he had no spit. He had to sneak closer to the front because he knew what would happen next.

CHAPTER 17
AUGUST 480 BCE
THERMOPYLAE PASS

THE BEST OF ASIA

Xerxes sat in his marble throne chair atop a reviewing stand, ready to enjoy the destruction of the Greek army. A squad of the king's elite personal guard of Immortals, their spears decorated with a gold-painted apple, guarded the royalty that stood on the steps in the usual pecking order that culminated in Mardonius.

Standing to the king's right, his eyes mere pinpricks, arms folded across his chest, Mardonius watched his army march. He and other commanders had turned a deaf ear to the advice of a deposed Spartan king, who told them in conference that the Spartans and Greeks would fight to the death.

Even now, as they studied the topography of the area, the sheer arch of the mountains, the drop off from the cliffs to the sea, and the tiny pass ahead, all were confident the army could slay the small number of enemy troops.

Xerxes gripped the arms of his chair, scowling when the Meads retreated in disarray. Next, the infantry from Susa fared no better.

The king leaped to his feet. He glared at Mardonius as a courier sprinted up to the reviewing stand, out of breath. "My lord Mardonius, I have a message from the fleet admiral," he gasped.

"Report it then," Mardonius replied as his troops staggered back to their lines.

"Last night, the Greeks attacked," the courier said. "They captured thirty of our ships while we repaired storm damage. The admiral cannot deliver supplies of food until his ships breach the Greek lines. He will order a full-scale attack tomorrow."

"We must break through today," Mardonius said. "Food supplies dwindle as we pile up before this pass."

Hydarnes, commander of the Immortals, stood near the top of the line on the stairs, dressed like his warriors with a black robe fringed with gold tassels, his face covered by a diaphanous net hanging from a dark cap.

"Ready your division Hydarnes. The Greeks are exhausted," Mardonius said.

Hydarnes saluted, but held firm, since he took his orders directly from the king.

"Clear the pass," Xerxes told him.

Hydarnes bowed, and spun smartly on his doe-hide boots.

All eyes watched the king's crack unit march over the corpse and weapon-clogged ground toward the Greek lines.

From his perch, Bessus heard other generals appealing to Ahura Mazda to smite the Greeks. His stomach squirmed. His shoulder ached. *Mainyu, now these whores' sons rely on prayers to destroy the Greeks,* he thought.

CHAPTER 18

AUGUST 480 BCE

THERMOPYLAE

"RAZOR'S EDGE"

Using the excuse of bringing gourds of watered wine to the dense pack of troops beyond the wall, Zack moved towards the front lines as Leonidas addressed his men. "Defeat these barbarians now, and you will break their will. Favored kinsmen will be in the ranks. Let us give them a taste of Spartan superiority they'll never forget. Xerxes will feel a dagger in his heart for each of the men you kill. Does your lance head dream of sending one of Xerxes' brothers to lie in filth at your feet? We can destroy their resolve here and now. Show them you are Spartans!"

The hoplites growled. Zack left the gourds and ran back through the sally port in the wall. He dashed up the log steps to a vantage point on the top. Leonidas headed back towards him, but stopped before the wall, among his warriors, just as endless ranks of Immortals marched towards the narrow pass. They encountered the same difficulties as before, tripping and sidestepping over the corpses of two previous attacks. Finally, they advanced with their wall of wicker shields.

As they neared, Zack saw that each Immortal wore a thin black cloth that masked his face. Drum beats and the thunder of thousands of boots shook the ground as legions of faceless men, like ghosts from hell, approached the Spartan lines. Oppressive heat and humidity beat down relentlessly, as if a giant glass bowl hung over the pass, intensifying the sun.

The *helots* in the rear launched javelins and darts at the approaching lines. Immortals dropped, clutching at the missiles that pierced their thin armor.

Just before the fortitude of two worlds met, a moment of silence commenced. *So strange*, Zack thought, holding his breath. All waited, all watched. Hearts thumped.

The Immortals attacked with a fury, certain of victory. Their first two lines fell in unison as the Spartan lances tore into them. Their wicker shields shattered, some snagging on the Spartan spearheads. The Immortals were no less brave or determined to win. They cast themselves bodily at the Spartans, disregarding the danger, but fell in numbers never imagined by Xerxes.

A pipe bleated notes behind the Spartan lines. They heaved forward with measured steps, a single unit, beginning the *othimos*. Each man pressed his shoulder into his shield and pushed into the back of the soldier in front of him. The masterful tactic succeeded in knocking the unprepared Immortals off their feet. The Spartans stabbed the wounded with their butt spikes, killing them with ruthless efficiency.

Then, without warning, the Spartans turned and retreated. Surprised, the Immortals pursued them, confident again of victory. The "fleeing" Spartans reversed direction and faced the Immortals, which created a clean killing zone. Trained to strike the enemy to their right, the Greek warriors found it easier to pierce an enemy's body when he raised his right arm to swing a sword or thrust a spear.

The flower of Persian arms and nobility blanketed the pass. Zack could not remove his eyes from the battle scene.

Horns blared from behind him. A contingent of hoplites moved forward, filtered through the lines, dragged the battle-crazed Spartans from the fray, and replaced them. Zack leaped off the battlement and ran to help with the bleeding and smashed bodies carried through the sally port as the new division of hoplites compacted, lowered their spears and attacked. A furious battle ensued. Rear ranks handed spears to the front. The shield wall of the hoplites nearest the cliffs pushed Persian warriors off the edge. Scores plunged to their death on the rocks below.

Dusk approached. For over two hours, rotating Greek contingents butchered the Immortals. A scattering of clouds raced across the sky. The humiliated Immortals retreated amid rousing cheers from thousands of allied fighters. Hoplites fell to their knees, praising the gods. Leonidas and his hoplites had thwarted three separate attacks and vanquished the best that Asia could send against them.

Amidst the hoisted lances and mayhem of battered men celebrating their survival, Zack searched for Lauren. He had now seen it, this moment in history, when Leonidas's Greeks held the Pass and scattered Asia's most intimidating force. The cost of that victory lay all around him. *This is what you must be willing to sacrifice.*

The Greek warriors begged for water, praised the gods, but most shouted for aide from the goddess.

Zack guided a battle-worn warrior to the ground. "What goddess do you beseech?"

"There," the warrior implored, holding his gut wound, pointing to a sea of men with outstretched arms at Lauren's feet. "Bring me to her before I die. I can see she is god-favored. Look at her shine."

CHAPTER 19
480 BCE
THERMOPYLAE

ON THE JOB TRAINING

The hoplite writhed in pain as Lauren tugged on an arrow shaft embedded in his side. His eyes bore a heavy toll of agony and exhaustion. "Zack, get over here and help me," she cried out.

Zack grabbed the last of the linen bandages and sprinted to her side. He found her twisting an arrow shaft, but unable to draw out the triangular head.

"I think it's wedged under his ribs. I don't know how to do this. How do I get it out?" she cried frantically.

"Whatever you do, don't break the shaft."

Lauren shouted for an aide, but none were available. "Maybe we need to cut it out. Go get a knife from one of medics."

The wounded man prayed as Zack ran off. Lauren talked quietly to the warrior, comforting him, caressing his cheek.

Zack returned, steeping carefully over the wounded and heat-beaten Spartan. "That's not a scalpel," Lauren said.

"It's all I could get." Zack handed her an instrument with a rounded tip. "Use it to pull the skin back."

"Great. I have to do surgery with a butter knife. Hold him down."

Well beyond any thought of performing the surgery comfortably, Lauren dug the blunt instrument into the warrior's wound and pried the muscle and tissue apart. The warrior bit his lip bloody, holding back cries. Zack averted his eyes while putting his weight on the hoplite's uninjured shoulder. Lauren slid her fingers inside and felt the arrowhead, grasped the barbed edges, and twisted. The warrior coughed a spray of red. A medic, probably a helot, ran over and helped her hold onto the arrow. They twisted and pulled together. It came free in a deluge of dark blood.

Zack removed the warrior's leather skullcap and pressed it on the wound. Lauren wiped her forehead with a bloody hand.

"There are so many wounded," Zack said. "No end to them."

"Over here, lady, they ask for you," another medic called out.

Wounded men raised hands, begging her to come. Hoplites wrung out the sweat-soaked skullcaps they wore beneath their helmets. They massaged skin chafed by armor and heat. Others cared for their own wounds or those of their comrades.

As evening fell, a stiff breeze swirled through leaves and branches, an eerie scene backlit by the campfires. A rhythmic patter started before the sky opened up to deluge the pass with rain.

Lauren and Zack worked separately for hours. He found her tying a warrior's fractured arm to a stick. The surgeon had set the bone in place. He patted the wounded man on his good shoulder. The downpour soaked Lauren's hair and ran in red rivulets over the linen strap shielding her mouth and nose from the unrelenting stink of death. She rose to stir rags boiling in an iron pot.

"You haven't looked this alluring since we left the tunnel," he teased gently.

She pulled down her mask. "I must be scaring the hell out of these guys."

Zack wiped the pale crimson streaks from her face. "No, you're beautiful."

He embraced her as a huge crack of lightning flashed beyond the gulf. "Let's find a dry spot and get out of the worst of this storm," she said.

Zack took her hand and led her back to their hilltop campsite, only to find their blankets soaked. They gathered their belongings and scooted down the hill to a cliff overhang, where they cleared out a sanctuary. They squeezed the water from the blankets, wrapped themselves in them and munched on crusts of bread. Between darkness and the rain, the temperature had plunged.

"This is even more horrible than I'd imagined," Lauren said. "I've seen so many men die today, such painful deaths. My heart breaks for them."

"Both sides are giving their all. Even when I close my eyes, I see dead men."

"I'm exhausted and hungry." Shivering, she edged closer to him. "Hold me and don't let go."

They tuned out the chaos surrounding them. The wind surged and seized one of their blankets, which fluttered like a flag in a stiff breeze. Thunder crashed, and lightning illuminated the grim hoplites, wrapped in their cloaks, guarding the pass choked with rivers of water and corpses of the dead.

By early morning, the storm abated. First light sounded a blare of trumpets. After resting sporadically during the night, hoplites arose like zombies from the grave.

The clouds dissipated with the wind, and the sun's warmth strengthened. Zack woke first, cradling Lauren's head on his lap. He watched as campfires were started with difficulty. There was little movement in the Persian camp.

The second day in the pass loomed. His fascination with war and glorious battles had been dashed away by the slaughter and the despair in his wife's eyes.

A Spartan lurched towards them with the stiff, measured steps of a man favoring a wound. "The king will see you in the command pit," he said, stopping to rewrap a bandage around his thigh, securing it with the teeth of a small metal clasp.

Zack gently shook Lauren, who awakened with dark circles under her eyes and the clotted remains of yesterday's labors on her clothes. She looked like she had walked off a horror film set. "I need a few minutes." She turned away from the men.

"Let me help you, honey."

Zack dropped a rag into a bucket, squeezed out the excess water and carried it to her. He washed her face and arms while she tied back her hair. "I wish I could go to the bay and have a real bath," she said. "What I wouldn't give for soap."

"Hey, I might have a solution for that."

Zack gathered a handful of ashes from a campfire. He called to one of the *helots* dashing by for a cup of olive oil. Zack dumped the ashes in the cup and mixed it together. The Spartan warrior watched but said nothing.

Lauren watched as well. "What the hell are you doing, Zack? Leonidas is waiting."

Zack dipped his hand in the pot and pulled out dark ooze that he spread on Lauren's arm. She recoiled. The Spartan scrunched his nose.

"That's how we made soap in the Boy Scouts, honey. I'll have you cleaned up in no time flat."

"Yeah, but I'll smell worse than I do now."

"You couldn't possibly smell… never mind. Let me clean you just a little more." Lauren watched, aghast, as Zack painted her with the slippery soot. "Atlantean, you need lessons in keeping a woman," the warrior suggested.

Zack wiped her with rags dipped in seawater. "Hey, you don't look so bad after all."

Lauren tried to brush clean and smooth her stained *chiton* with her hands. "Oh, what's the use?"

Off she went. The hoplite and Zack exchanged grins before they could catch up. They entered the command ring where Leonidas instructed his men on the day's rotation of troops.

"We have lost three or four of each ten warriors," Diomedes, commander of the Mycenaeans, reported.

Leonidas glanced out at the Persian encampment and then down at the dirt. "We gave them a bloody nose yesterday. We can hold this pass, but we need reinforcements faster than Hermes can bugger a field full of wood nymphs."

Dienekes guffawed, as did the other commanders. All bore multiple lacerations, bound with reddened bandages.

"Ah, my envoys. Come here," Leonidas said, wiping grime from his eyes and nose.

Poylas stood to one side and waved as Lauren and Zack stood before the king. "We are grateful for your tending of the wounded. It is difficult to prepare for such a day as yesterday."

"A day I will never forget," Zack stated proudly.

"Nor I," Lauren added.

Leonidas turned away from Zack. "Lady, you may visit Sparta any time you wish… as a guest of our people."

"Thank you, King Leonidas. I saw what needed to be done."

The black soup boiled in the pot. "You've both earned a cupful." Leonidas said. "The troops will need to rotate more often today. I want the wine and food rations increased. Have the reserve troops rest in the shade. Have them repair their shields and sharpen their weapons."

The Spartan commanders filed out, leaving Leonidas, Poylas, Zack, and Lauren within the circle. "How go the sea battles?" Leonidas asked Poylas.

"We're avoiding what we cannot quickly withdraw from, and then positioning ourselves defensively, in a circle, and then attacking. We're ramming and boarding their vessels The Persians are no match for our armor. But I must return to Artemisium to consult with Themistocles and Admiral Eurybiades. Any messages for them?"

"Tell them we can hold as long as we have able men and unbroken weapons. I await word from Sparta regarding reinforcements. Another day of fighting will take more of our spearmen, and our situation will become desperate if they do not send help. If we can rip out their throats today, maybe the Persians may lack the will to attack."

"Then I shall depart, King Leonidas," Poylas said. "I'll return later today to escort the ambassadors south and deliver my messages to Athens."

Poylas turned to Zack and Lauren. "Be ready to depart well before sunset. We will need two or three hours of sunlight to make our way to the channel and head to Athens."

Leonidas looked out at the pass. Divisions of hoplites waited in their rotation positions. Helots walked among them, tightening leather straps, fetching spare lances, and passing out bread and water. Leonidas rubbed his neck as he studied the scene before him. "I can smell their fear." He sniffed and then hawked out black spit. "Their spears are short and do little damage, but the Persian battle-axes stave in our shields." He faced Zack and Lauren. "I will join my troops today. They will fight like madmen with me in the ranks. We must hold the pass, even if by sheer will."

A commander walked up to the king. "They're moving. Before long, the drums will begin." Then a squire arrived out of breath. "The scouts have returned from the Persian camp by half their number. They did not succeed last night."

Leonidas nodded, his face solemn. "So it's true they sent a secret mission to kill Xerxes," Zack whispered to Lauren.

Another squire handed Leonidas a cross-crested helmet and an *aspis*, a shield with red, blue and brown swirls. With an eight-foot lance in his grip, Leonidas strode to the wall at the head of his captains. He disappeared through the sally port.

"This is so damned frustrating," Zack complained.

"I know. Let's return to our camp. We'll be needed soon enough."

They returned to the hillock while listening to the drums. Zack rotated the horned helmet in his hands, and then lowered it onto his head. The helmet drooped over his eyes, blocking his vision. Its worn leather liner reeked of stale sweat. "Must have been a big bastard who owned this thing."

"It's ugly. Take it off," Lauren said, looking away.

Zack laid the helmet next to a pile of spare weapons, some Greek, others gathered from the Persian dead.

"I'm tired and so sick of this. Our families would never believe what's happened to us."

"They have to be worried."

"We've gone on digs and not communicated for months in the past, but eventually they'll know something's wrong. After all, we are their children."

"Children," Lauren said quietly. Then her face took on a look of horror.

Zack noticed. "What is it?"

Lauren collapsed backwards. She began to sob.

"What?"

"We can't have a child here, Zack. If we were stuck here, our child would change history. Don't you get it? If we have a child, it can't live."

"I'm sorry." There was little he could do to console her.

"I can't take it anymore. Nothing is right." Her voice grew shrill. "Why'd you take me here? How'd we end up in this nightmare?"

"I don't...know."

The look in Lauren's eyes suggested she could draw blood... from him.

CHAPTER 20
480 BCE
THERMOPYLAE PASS, PERSIAN CAMP

DAY TWO

Bodyguards dragged a woman's body from Bessus' tent. Her heels carved deep troughs in mud left over from the fierce overnight storm.

In the wake of the previous day's defeat and concerned over dwindling provisions, King Xerxes had ordered many camp followers to be sent away or slain. Bessus saw no reason to deny himself a proper sacrifice to the Mainyu. He probed the bandaged wound on his shoulder. Wincing, he muttered, "I will settle this score, and then taste the pleasures of the Greek women."

Drums and trumpets announced attack preparations. Behind each Persian contingent, Immortals waited with whips, ready to supply added incentive to their efforts. Bessus, bored by watching their slow progress in the mud, returned to his tent and sprawled across his rugs.

A short while later, Cyartes called out, "My Lord, the attack begins."

Bessus reached for his horned helmet, as he had done a thousand times before. Its absence reminded him of another score to settle.

They made their way quickly through the campsites, arriving at a sloping hillside where they could see the defenders. The red soldiers once again took positions in front of the wall in the narrowest area of the pass.

"Xerxes means to wear them down with conscripts," Cyartes said. "First in line are the Assyrians and their twisted metal helmets, followed by the Arabians with white gowns, bows and arrows, then the Ethiopians wearing leopard skins."

Bessus grunted, swatting at the gnats and flies tormenting his face. "I'm sick of those Spartan flutes. I will ram them down their throats when I..."

"And then we have the Libyans, Utians, and others from lands I have never heard of," Cyartes observed. "Maybe they can kill some of the Greeks. The Medes and Immortals will be licking their wounds after yesterday. We'll need them again when the Greeks are weakened."

Horns blared. The drums picked up their beat. Atop the observation deck, King Xerxes, Mardonius, Hydarnes, and a score of other generals analyzed the attack. Xerxes, wearing a purple robe, wielded a jeweled golden scepter with a red ruby the size of an apple on its tip.

"The King wears a new color today. Maybe it will bring him better luck," Bessus said sarcastically.

The troops marched onward. Thousands of arrows preceded the day's first assault, arching and falling on the enemy like hail pounding wheat. Shields rang with the insult.

Cyartes fell silent, watching again the slaughter of the king's men with horrified fascination. An hour passed. Heat tormented them. Footing grew untenable at the front line. Still, they attempted to cross the barrier of bodies in order to reach the Greeks. They attacked with courage equal to the men who opposed them. Bodies disappeared into the depth of the mud.

Fresh Greek warriors lurched forward and tore into the king's men, wiping out three more divisions.

Xerxes leapt to his feet, waving his arms and pointing at the battle. Within minutes, whips cracked. Draftees from conquered areas of the Empire stood between the wrath of their king and the deadly lances of the allied hoplites.

"How can we slay these men, my lord?" Cyartes asked.

"I know not," Bessus snarled, gingerly poking his shoulder wound.

Caspians, Arans, and Cappadocians marched forward, each unit eager to be the one that would breach the enemy line for their king.

Cyartes and Bessus stood for several more hours, watching the fruitless efforts of the king's army. Grime-laden sweat ran down Bessus' neck. He scratched furiously.

"These are the men we heard of on the march here," Cyartes said.

Bessus shot him a disdainful look. Again, fresh Greek troops entered with loud war cries and added to the mound of corpses that blocked Persian soldiers from penetrating the defense. Bessus set his eyes on Xerxes, who sat on his throne, his head resting in his hand. By late afternoon, the king signaled with a wave to stop the attack.

Three sharp bursts of horns followed. The Persian troops turned almost as one, weapons thrown and banners tossed. They ran, staggered or dragged themselves to safety.

Xerxes had lost control of the battle.

.

CHAPTER 21
480 BCE
THERMOPYLAE PASS

THE CRUCIBLE

The hoplites looked more like beasts from a depraved nether world than men. Their menacing Corinthian helmets, armor, and shields no longer had the color of bronze. Mud and the crimson remains of the enemy splattered armor, garments, and exposed flesh.

Defenders transported the wounded on makeshift stretchers made from two spear poles tied together with straps of leather. Others trudged to their camps for water, medical care, and a reprieve from the fighting.

This day was no different. When the fighting finally stopped, Zack found Lauren among the uneven rows of exhausted warriors. He watched her pull hair away from her face with black-stained hands, leaving behind dark swatches like war paint.

He turned to the sound of hoof beats. A rider with an extra mount galloped towards the command post. Was this the famed messenger of history carrying the news that there would be no reinforcements for the Spartans? The man jumped off his mount and sprinted to the command pit.

Zack walked over to watch Lauren finish up wrapping a warrior's head with a bloody rag. "Maybe we shouldn't have come here," he said, defeat in his voice. "There's just too much agony, too much death."

"Not now, Zack." Lauren shooed flies away from the wounded.

"Walk with me, please? I think the messenger from Sparta just arrived."

They hurried to the command pit. Leonidas stood in the middle, one stained bandage covering his bicep, another around his thigh. He wiped moist blood from his body with a rag. Grimly, he faced his men. "Our reinforcements have not been granted. The Spartan army will remain at home."

The commanders said nothing. Each stared straight ahead with exhausted, sightless eyes, knowing what the message meant.

Leonidas stabbed the dirt with his sword. "Allies, you have fought with valor," he said, raising his chin.

"Leonidas," the Thespian commander asked, "should we retreat from the pass?"

"We cannot. If our ships are triumphing at sea, then we will compromise that victory if we abandon this post. Our elders did not order us to leave. We stay. You go. Tell the allies to leave at once."

The commanders met each other's gaze. Lauren and Zack made eye contact, both acutely aware of what would soon occur. "The die is cast," she said quietly. After a lengthy pause, Zack whispered into her ear, "We leave tonight with Poylas. I swear to you, we'll be the first two people aboard that ship."

CHAPTER 22
480 BCE
THERMOPYLAE PASS

PERSIAN CAMP

Xerxes sat erect on his throne chair, separated from the earth by fine silk rugs. Slaves worked to reset purple drapes over the tent windows. Others dragged broken furniture away. Bessus, his arm in a sling stood at attention in a semicircle with the other generals.

"We did not lack preparation for this expedition." Xerxes punctuated each word. "Our heralds received the surrender of countless cities before our march here." Abruptly, he stood. "Now, the largest army on earth stands defeated before a few men in that pass. With the eclipse of the sun last year, the Magi informed me it was not an evil omen; the Persian moon would eclipse the Greek sun and victory would be ours." The king gestured wildly. "Tell me how a force such as ours fails, Mardonius? Explain this to me, now?"

Bessus wanted to say they were all worthless sacks of shit, that *he* could win this battle. The steep mountains above the pass were anthills compared with the 'black dust mountains' of his homeland. *Go around them.* The words bubbled in his throat.

Mardonius stepped tentatively forward. "I have no excuse, Your Majesty. We have thrown our full weight against them to no avail. The Magi have bellowed their curses. These cannot be normal men, but there cannot be so many of them that they can hold us back forever."

"And yet they still hold the pass while my army runs out of food," Xerxes countered. "The navy has taken losses in the storms, and we have not heard from the detachment we sent out to round the long island to block the retreat of their ships. Their fleet snaps at us like a Nile crocodile. Perhaps I need new generals and admirals. Are you so incompetent you cannot defeat a divided nation of Greeks?"

Then the king shouted at the top of his voice. "Last night, Spartans nearly killed me in this tent. Look at the bloodstains on the carpets! If I turn this expedition around, you will not leave this country alive. All of you... get out of my sight."

Bessus slid his arm out of the sling, freeing another hand in the event a fight broke out. It did not. The generals slowly filed out through the tent opening, dejected and immersed in thoughts of how to overcome the Greeks. The king's two assistants tried to fan away flies and the overpowering stench of death.

Holding a cloth over his nose, Bessus watched a stewing, sullen Xerxes retire to his bedroom chamber.

CHAPTER 23
480 BCE
THERMOPYLAE PASS

"THE DIE IS CAST"

Zack and Lauren descended the slope in silence. When they reached the makeshift pier, Zack anxiously looked out to sea for Poylas and his ship of deliverance. "If all goes according to the history books," he said, "a major fleet action should occur tomorrow. Tonight, a Greek traitor will tell Xerxes he can guide the Immortals through the mountains, cutting off any possibility of escape for the allies in the morning. Poylas must take us away… tonight. It has to be."

Lauren buried her nose in the hem of her *chiton*. A shoreline filled with stones and buffeted by surf bore the ugly debt of war. Water-soaked rags, broken shafts of arrows, shorn spears, and massive rolling clumps of the bloated dead clogged the coastline as far as they could see. She gave Zack a cold, hard look. He turned away, as if her eyes had cleaved him in two. He swatted flies away from his face. Hours passed. Night came, but the ship did not.

A Spartan hoplite hobbled over to them, using a broken spear shaft for a crutch. "The king asks to see you before you embark."

"We'll be able to see if our ship comes," Lauren said. "Let's hurry."

Leonidas watched them arrive. He stood. "You told me of a battle in your country. The defenders fought and died valiantly, their memories blessed with valor."

"That is so," Zack watched the moon rise. Torches flickered in the breeze. Leonidas wore bandages on his arms and thigh, along with multiple cut wounds and a foot missing toes. Nearby, a hoplite tried to hammer a shield together, but gave up and threw it aside, cursing.

Lauren trembled. Zack slipped his arm around her.

The king's face was a hideous collage of black and red contrasted with the white of his eyes. "I am grateful for your aid. You must know by now, we will not be reinforced."

Lauren ignored the gore on his breastplate and hugged Leonidas. She refused to let him go. "Do not be distressed, Lauren, our women understand war," Leonidas said, still in her embrace. "They know we are bred to stand and fight. In you, I see the same strength. You are stronger than you know. You have the courage of a Spartan."

Lauren lifted her head from his shoulder, engulfed by the dizzying smells of sweat, blood and death emanating from him. She met his eyes, astonished by his words. "My father said those words to me many times... I never really understood why he thought I was so strong."

"Let your fear fly away. We know we will be shadows when this battle is over. It does not trouble us. We have been moving towards this end since the day the elders decided our fitness to live after birth. We win or we die. When we are charred bones and dust, remember us. For all that will be left of us is our deeds, and what you have seen here. Live for us, since we cannot."

Lauren's shoulders shook in a losing effort to hold back her grief.

Zack choked on the boulder in his throat. "Be assured, King Leonidas," he said clearing his throat twice, "your actions will put iron in the resolve of all the Greek people."

"You speak again of all the Greeks, but I have more selfish goals. The Oracle at Delphi told us that either Sparta is defeated, or she must suffer the loss of one of her kings."

"I've heard of this oracle." Zack diverted his gaze. He remembered Delphi, how ignorant they had been that Leonidas had stood before them with his back turned.

The sky darkened further. No rescue ship in the bay. The Spartans oiled and combed their hair, by custom, preparing to die.

"Without more troops, the Pass will soon fall," Leonidas said. I choose this end so my people shall live. I am sure that when the moon rises again tomorrow, we will be dining on altogether different fare in the kingdom of Hades. I ask you to grant me a favor."

"Whatever it is." Zack straightened his posture. His throat constricted to this witnessing of living history. A swell of emotion threatened to overwhelm him.

Leonidas removed his bronze ring, twisting it past the crusted blood on his knuckle. He placed the ring in Lauren's hand and closed her fingers around it. "This was my father's, and his father's before him. Please return it to my wife, Gorgo."

Tears raced down Lauren's cheeks.

"Tell my wife and my son that they are so dear to me. Tell them we have kept the law, and that I expect them to be brave. She is still able to bear children, and I ask her to have more sons for Sparta."

Lauren saw the steely resolve in his eyes... and more. A single tear fell from one eye, but quickly dispersed into the muck beneath it. A drop of sweat maybe, or a real tear perhaps, borne from the realization that his valiant warriors would soon perish. The Spartan king was not made of stone, after all. He, like the others, would sacrifice themselves to save their homeland.

"I will do as you ask, King Leonidas." She struggled to speak firmly. "I want you to know that in my country, we also have seers of the future."

"Honey..." Caution rode Zack's voice.

"Your sacrifice will not be in vain." She stuttered with tears and sobs. "Inspired by your stand, the Greeks will be victorious. You will achieve here more than you know."

"I pray to the gods this is so. I have ordered most of the warriors to escape and kill Persians on another field of battle. Only the Thespians and Thebans remain with us. Now go and await your ship."

Zack clasped Leonidas' hand in a firm grip. "We shake hands in greeting and in farewell. I will take your advice, King Leonidas. I will learn to fight."

As the king squeezed his hand, Zack memorized every feature of his face: flattened nose and high cheekbones, graying beard, and bloodshot, weary eyes that demanded sleep.

Lauren spoke a final time to the king of Sparta. "I will deliver this ring to your wife. You have my promise."

Leonidas picked up a lance and began to rewrap the leather grip. "I am in your debt, and may the gods watch over you. Tell the people of Atlantea, I regret I will never see their lands."

Then they heard the hissing. Arrows flew out of the night. They struck along the hillside and into the command pit, hitting logs, dirt and men. A commander twisted and grabbed at a shaft in his back. Zack ducked as an arrow flew over Lauren's shoulder. Leonidas hobbled to Lauren and covered her with his body. The missiles zipped blindly past, ringing and ricocheting as they struck stone, breastplates, and raised shields. Hoplites moved forward to push back the Persian archers hiding in the dark.

Leonidas seized Zack by his chiton. "Get up and hold this shield," he snarled. "Take her away, dove-eyes."

Zack fumbled with the shield. More of the commanders leaped to protect Lauren. Finally, he raised the shield. Leonidas pushed them away from the paths of the missiles. They tripped over logs, recovered their feet, and escaped to the shore.

Lauren glanced back for one last look. The Spartan king stood with his back to them, hands on his hips, as if daring an arrow to find him.

"Get me the hell out of here." Desperation underscored Lauren's words. "We need light to sail through the bay. It's too dark now."

"Man that was close."

"Zack, you didn't even try to protect me back there."

"I'm sorry. I just didn't react fast enough."

"You'd better learn to."

Lauren stormed away, her fists clenched. Abruptly, she turned back to him, purple veins pounding thickly on her temples. "The Persians are coming through the goddamn mountains. Tomorrow, their fleet will attack the Greek navy too. We'll be cut off."

Zack grunted in acknowledgement. He kicked pebbles. "We can't be here in the morning. We've stayed too long," she said.

She gripped the ring the king had given her. It turned on her finger, far too loose. She tied it onto her finger with twine, feeling the sharp edges of the square-shaped ring as though it contained the magic that would liberate them from this predicament.

Zack peered out to sea. "Where the hell is our ship? We might not make it past the Immortals if we attempt a land escape tomorrow."

She searched his eyes. "Is our only real option to leave now?"

"Let's give it another half hour before we make a decision."

"Zack, we're in danger, and we have to go."

"I know. I know. I didn't think of it, but if we had left earlier we could have taken the mountain pass shortcut to Delphi. We've driven that road before. It's a rough trek, but it might have only taken us a few days. With the Immortals up there and the ship late, I'm not sure what to do now."

"Great. So says the man who knows all the history."

"Hey, give me a break. I was a little distracted here."

Lauren bared her teeth. The tip of her nose touched his. "What? This is all –your – fault! You've pushed me over the edge."

"Lauren, I'm trying…"

"You never wanted a child with me. You had to screw with that column and get us stuck here." She jabbed her finger in his chest. "Now the little boy who likes to watch history movies ends up in a scene he doesn't like. Our life is not cinema. You brought us here. I am sick of slaughtered men and stinking slit trenches. Screw you, Zack. Screw your selfishness. Ever since I've known you, it's always been about you."

Zack turned away. His shoulders slumped.

Lauren seized his arm. "No, you look at me." Whirling him around, she saw moisture around the creases of his eyes.

He wiped them quickly. "You're right. You never should have come here with me. I should have left you with Nestor. But I needed to see this for more than just historical curiosity."

"What the hell are you talking about?"

"I wanted to know what kind of men saved Western civilization; what hoplite warfare was really like. This is more horrible… than I ever thought."

"You're a Classics professor and now you figure that out. I already know about these kinds of men. My father and his friends are just like them."

"This is hardly the same…"

"It's exactly the same, but that's not the issue right now. You promised you wouldn't leave me alone. Then, you stuck me with a lousy decision. Some husband you are." Her hands whirled in front of his face. "Stay here and try to think straight for once. I'm going to round up transportation of some kind. We can't move fast enough if we're on foot."

Lauren jogged back to the pass. Zack clamped his temples with his fingers. He took a last look for their rescue ship. Light from a nearly full moon shimmered on the water, but it disappeared into the dark clumps lining the shore.

Zack let loose a primordial roll call of curses.

Lauren returned with a packhorse. "That's it," she said. "Let's mount up. We're riding south, and you're going to follow me for once."

CHAPTER 24

THERMOPYLAE PASS

THE BREACH

Bessus arose from a restless night. "Get everyone packed and ready to push south," he ordered Cyartes.

They hiked to the king's tent while warriors pulled up tents in the Bactrian camp. In the middle of a square ringed by guards, Xerxes turned to the east before the sacred fire and raised his golden goblet. He emptied the liquid onto the dirt as an offering. "Perhaps Ahura Mazda will listen today," Bessus said with contempt.

The army prepared for the morning assault with renewed energy, the panic of the previous day absent. The cavalry troops moved alongside the infantry, ready for a breakthrough. Horsemen would attempt to drive through the breech and strike at the hoplites if they tried to escape.

Bessus and Cyartes rode their horses on the side of the main attack force, viewing the remaining Greeks as they stood amid a sea of corpses. "I wonder if they realize a traitor is bringing our Immortals through the mountains," Cyartes said.

Bessus grunted. "They know they're surrounded, and yet they remain in the pass. These Greeks are light on brains. Who's that warrior that stands before them?"

Cyartes chuckled. "He urges them to make peace with their gods."

Bessus pondered his first battle with an enemy that had killed half his men and then laughed at him.

"My Lord, that warrior in front with a crosshair on his helmet and colored swirls on his shield, it is said he is their king. Is he willing to die here?"

"Bah, that is madness. A king would ensure his escape."

The leather straps and satchel attached to Bessus' saddle blanket squeaked when he adjusted his position. Ahead, the Greeks shouted and waved their arms in response to their red-dressed commander.

"Enjoy your morning, Greeks," Bessus muttered. "And if you are their king, bind your guts well."

Well before midday, drumbeats announced the army's readiness. Xerxes, standing in a gold-trimmed chariot drawn by four Arabian horses, raised his jeweled golden scepter. The army cheered.

The generals signaled with their swords to move forward. The Persian warriors hesitated at first, mindful of the past two days. Whips cracked them into place.

The Spartans moved forward into the pass, extending and thinning their lines to reach from bay cliff to mountainside.

The Persian troops reached the oval shields of the Spartans. They attacked with a fury, invigorated by the knowledge that it was only a matter of time before their army would prevail. They tried to pull down the Spartan shields. The defenders slaughtered their enemies with impunity, playing more of the tricks used in previous days. They advanced like a huge scythe, harvesting Xerxes' infantry.

"Look my Lord," Cyartes said, pointing. "The cross-crested warrior is in front."

Bessus watched Leonidas fight with his men. More Persian troops moved into the killing zone, whips snapping over their heads. "They have no reserves," Bessus said, nervously adjusting himself on his saddle.

"Still they slaughter us," Cyartes complained. He heard Bessus suck on the void in his front teeth.

Bodies piled up. Persian arrows rained upon the Greeks. The Spartans cut through the Persian lines, so close now that Bessus considered withdrawing his troopers. As he turned to give the order, a great howl rose from the attackers.

"What?" Bessus asked.

"Their king is down!" Cyartes yelled.

They watched as the red soldiers attacked with a maddened frenzy, killing scores of Persians to retrieve the body of their king. The Persians swarmed over the defenders, some of whom covered their fallen leader.

Finally, Persian warriors grabbed the fallen enemy king by his legs and pulled him toward their lines. The Greeks formed a wedge and struck at the Persians when they tried to escape with their trophy. Soon, the red soldiers seized the body of Leonidas, hoisting him onto their shoulders. They retreated to their lines and shifted his body within the ranks, moving backwards as a unit, leaving piles of Persian corpses in their wake.

The Persian infantry continued their assault. The Greeks, clutching broken spears and damaged shields, withdrew, only to turn and strike down more of the king's warriors.

Bessus's shoulder ached. He was secretly relieved that he did not have to face the Greeks in the desperate combat. "They're taking losses, too, commander," Cyartes said.

Both men watched the number of Greek spearmen grow smaller, their impact on the Persians steadily diminishing. The cracking of whips continued, along with the constant ringing of metal upon metal and crashes against breastplates and shields. Men died, replaced by others who suffered the same fate. The Spartan defenders retreated to their wall, their rear lines crossing over it while the front lines bought time with their lives.

Bessus could only watch as the body of Leonidas was carried over the wall. It almost appeared to float, hoisted high above the red soldiers.

The Persians attacked in droves, impaling their own soldiers on the sharpened stakes in front of the wall. Many tried to climb and cross the wall. Hoplites sent them spinning like tops. The Persian infantrymen used their axes on the sally port gate. There was no end to the mass of infantrymen coming forward, driven by the will of Xerxes.

"We can move forward now," Cyartes said.

Bessus, startled from his thoughts, replied. "What? Oh, then, move on." He could not take his eyes off the defenders, many of whom had no spears and hacked at his men with swords as they scaled the wall. Hundreds of men tore at the stones, flinging them aside, and creating large holes for troops to penetrate. No matter how many Persians cast themselves at the red soldiers, their lines wavered but did not break.

"Let's cross the wall," Bessus said.

They walked their horses slowly forward. The animals bucked, stepping over the multitude of bodies. Bessus whipped his reluctant mount.

No longer was it possible for the Greek warriors to rotate; too few remained. They slowly crept backwards, holding their moving circle formation, the body of their leader in the middle. They paused on a hillock a bowshot behind the wall. The Persian troops halted as the Greeks formed a tight circle, their shields creating a protective ring. Most sank to their knees, gasping.

Bessus directed his men to a position slightly behind a ring of Median spearmen.

Down the road beyond the hillock, war cries broke the silence. Hydarnes and the black-draped Immortals arrived, blocked the road south, and cut off the Spartans from escape.

Newly slain warriors clogged the pass, surrounding the wall on both sides, and marking the way up to the hillock.

"Will Xerxes offer them their lives if they surrender?" Cyartes asked. "They've fought a good battle."

Bessus grunted and spat on the ground. "The stink of this place is too much." He brought a cloth to his face.

Xerxes ordered spearmen forward. The Spartans fought on with swords, broken spears, daggers, and fists. They grabbed spears from fallen Medians and used them on their attackers. Once again, the red soldiers defeated any attempt to dislodge or annihilate them, and the Medes withdrew. The red soldiers closed ranks, their remaining shields packed together, domelike, as they awaited the next attack.

Fewer than a hundred Spartans and Greeks still stood. Others threw down their arms and ran to the Persian lines, begging for mercy. The Persians killed some and sent others behind their lines.

"They're finished," Bessus said with a satisfied grin.

Xerxes signaled the attack with a wave of his hand.

Bessus moved his cavalry troops closer to the action. "I want to see this," he said, harsh laughter escaping him.

The red soldiers stood resolute, the momentary rest enough for them to ready themselves. The Immortals marched forward in a half-moon formation. With no place to retreat, the Spartans managed to repel their attackers, who again fell in large numbers at their feet.

Bessus looked at Xerxes, who stood erect in his chariot, palm fans behind him deflecting droves of flies and shielding the sun. He pointed his enormous ruby-tipped scepter at the knot of men who would not yield. The king raised his arms, bellowing at the sun, invoking the Mazda. More Immortals advanced. Once again, the bodies stacked up and created a barrier between the adversaries. The red soldiers did not move from the hillock.

Xerxes smashed his fist on the rim of his chariot. "I'll waste no more of my infantry," he declared, the words hissing from his tightened lips. "Demaratus was right. These men have no equal in battle. I will no longer demoralize my troops. Let the bowmen slay them."

"As you wish, my king," Mardonius said, bowing. He signaled to Hydarnes to break off the attack. With three long horn blasts, the Immortals withdrew, dragging their wounded with them. Only the ring of red soldiers stood on the hill.

"Archers!" Mardonius yelled.

Immortals, along with other contingents, placed their bowmen in a circle facing the Spartans. Mardonius raised his sword. Bowstrings stretched.

He dropped his arm.

The air ripped with an uncountable number of missiles that hurtled toward the Spartan position. The sky darkened. Many arrows bounced off the shields, or struck dead or wounded bodies in front of the Spartans.

Some, however, found their marks. Holes in the ranks appeared as more men dropped their shields. The blizzard of arrows did not stop, nor did the javelins as infantry moved up to hurl their lean spears at the remaining hoplites. The volleys continued, endlessly, finding the remaining Spartans, who crouched together in the hope of deflecting airborne death.

The Spartans fell to the last man.

Afterwards, the victorious Persian warriors did not cheer. They stood quietly, watching the demise of the men who had fought them.

Neither Cyartes nor Bessus spoke. The battle delivered its sober realization of the cost of their triumph. Bessus and Cyartes dismounted, handing the reins to attendants.

Mardonius ordered the Immortals forward to make sure all the Spartans were dead. Bessus bowed before Mardonius, a man half his size. "My Lord, I want to study the weapons of the red soldiers."

"Proceed." Mardonius waved his sword in the direction of the Spartans.

Xerxes cast his eyes back towards the pass. His shoulders slumped. "Find the body of the Spartan king and bring it to me," he said, stone-faced.

Mardonius and Hydarnes, accompanied by several Immortals with Bessus and Cyartes following behind, ascended the hillock littered with Persian dead. "Clear a path for us," Mardonius told Bessus.

Bessus scowled at the order, but complied. He and Cyartes tossed bloodied bodies aside.

Mardonius called out to one of his commanders, "Send men to help us."

After nearly an hour, they reached the center where the last Spartans had died.

Cyartes dripped with sweat. "From a distance, they didn't even look like men with those helmets," he said to Bessus. "All you could see were these slits for their eyes."

Bessus picked up a staved-in Spartan shield before tossing it aside. "I don't want a broken one." He continued his search, and then ripped the spear from the hand of a dead Spartan. He resisted the urge to begin stabbing the dead hoplites, already mutilated by so many missiles.

"I have seen fewer needles in a seamstress' ball," Cyartes said.

The infantry cleared a wider path so others could help in the search. Since the Spartans had fallen atop each other, their bodies formed a tight, circular mound. Bessus' wound pulsated with each thudding beat of his heart. He weakened after lifting so many heavily armored bodies. Whenever they heard a moan, daggers finished the work. As the men neared the center of the pile, they received instructions to look for a helmet with a side-crossed crest.

The stacked bodies had huddled together, covering the corpse in the center. The Persians hauled the bodies away until the corpse of King Leonidas was revealed.

"We've found him!" a warrior called out.

Mardonius rushed forward, Hydarnes and Demaratus on his heels. Demaratus, a Spartan king exiled for being illegitimate, took no pleasure in identifying Leonidas. He had secretly warned the Spartans of the impending invasion, hoping that Sparta would survive and that he might be able to return. Now, he watched the removal of the helmet to reveal the face of a man he had known well. Leonidas' dark eyes stared at him. "It is Leonidas," Demaratus stated before turning away.

"Bring the corpse down the hill," Mardonius ordered.

Bessus and Cyartes pushed through the circle of warriors to raise the corpse. "Heavy bastard," Bessus grunted. As they lifted Leonidas, his sightless eyes surveyed the dead Spartans and Persians.

Mardonius directed the men to drop the corpse on the ground. "Your Majesty, this is the Spartan king."

Xerxes descended his chariot. Unlike the other dead Spartans who had been riddled with so many missiles, Leonidas's body bore only two arrows and a large ragged wound in the crook of his neck.

"Great numbers of my troops are slain because of this man… members of the royal family, even my own brothers. His murderers nearly killed me. How many of my subjects did we lose?" Xerxes asked, barely containing his rage.

"Over twenty thousand, Your Majesty," Mardonius whispered.

"It cannot be! Strike his head. Demonstrate the fate of those who oppose us. Hang the body from crossed timbers, and place his head atop it."

"Is it wise to desecrate the remains of a monarch, sire?"

Xerxes scowled at Mardonius. "Do it now and bury my slain quickly. Leave the Spartans for all to see."

"It will be as you wish, sire." Mardonius looked for a minion to do the dirty work.

"Marshal, allow me to carry out the king's wish," Bessus said, his huge biceps banded with bronze and his eyes sparkling with eagerness.

"You look like you can handle the task."

"Watch me." He sent Cyartes for his axe while standing over the body. "Set a rock beneath his neck. I want to swing only once."

Cyartes returned with a flat piece of shale. He tipped Leonidas' head backwards, exposing the king's neck. Bessus took two long deep breaths, enjoying the moment as he prepared to behead the enemy-king in front of his own king and the entire army. A broad smile cracked across his scarred face. He lifted his axe high, ignoring the pain of the wound on his shield arm.

Emitting an earsplitting war cry, he brought the weapon down with all his strength. It swished through the air and struck the dead king with a loud splat.

The Spartan king's head rolled to one side, connected to the torso by a thin strip of dark-stained skin.

Bessus took hold of the head and ripped it free of the body. He held it high, gripping it by the long hair. Cheers erupted up and down the ranks. Bessus roared while turning in slow circles to display the head.

Xerxes lifted his scepter. The cheering stopped. "We have met the bravest men of Greece and slain their king. Our forces will now proceed to the Athenian capital. We will fulfill our duty, by the Lord God Ahura Mazda, the wise and holy one. Mardonius, take the army south and burn Athens."

"I shall, your majesty."

Xerxes, a golden fluted royal crown atop his head, walked upon a white drape of cloth to keep his feet from touching unholy ground. His chariot took him back to his tent.

Four soldiers lifted the body of Leonidas and slammed it onto a large stake. They tied the waist and arms to the crossbeam to keep the torso from falling forward. Bessus grasped the severed head with both hands and jammed it onto the pointed end of the stake.

"Lord Bessus, they all know you now," Cyartes said.

Bessus emitted a battle cry known to the warriors of the Black Dust Mountains. His countrymen joined in the shrill, haunting screech. Then the whole army cheered as one. The deafening roar did not cease until horns and drums sounded, signaling the army contingents to move out.

Bessus strutted back to his horse. "Now we hunt down the Greeks who escaped."

PART THREE

CHAPTER 25
AUGUST 480 BCE
PHOCIS, SOUTH OF THERMOPYLAE

ESCAPE

Zack walked beside the horse while Lauren rode, her body swaying in rhythm to the beast's gait.

"I wonder how far we've gone. We've been traveling all night," Lauren said. "We'd make better time if this horse didn't take so many damn breaks. I wish it would go faster."

"I'm sure he's never run a day in his life."

Lauren slumped. "I'm tired. We haven't seen a soul since we left. Everyone must have evacuated."

"They're going to be overrun soon."

"I can't talk about it."

Zack focused on the trail ahead, canopied by long oak branches. "Maybe it's better not to. Hang on a while longer, sweetheart. There's got to be a village on this road somewhere."

The road followed the coastline. At a fork, they veered west, hoping to find a route less traversed and away from the coast, which would probably be crowded with Persian ships by afternoon.

Zack stopped the horse and handed the reins to Lauren. "Stay here while I scout ahead."

"Be careful."

He jogged to a line of shrubs. He peered around the foliage and spotted a cluster of farmhouses. He moved forward cautiously. "Anyone home?" he yelled in Greek.

No response. He crept toward some open shutters, calling out several times. No luck.

He jogged back to find Lauren slumped atop the horse. "Let's get you over to the farmhouse so I can search for food."

Too exhausted to respond, she simply nodded.

Zack tied the horse up at the well. He helped her down and they walked to the largest house. "I don't see anyone," Lauren said.

"Not a soul. No food either."

Her eyes narrowed. "I wonder if the water in that well is all right."

He lowered a wooden bucket and heard a splash. He pulled up the bucket, now full, and set it on the ground. "Let's see if the horse drinks it. I'll find a place where you can rest. Then, I'll start a fire and boil some water for us." He kicked open the door. "You can sleep on one of the pallets in here."

Lauren yawned deeply. "I don't care if there's an ant farm in those blankets, I'm putting a little perfume under my nose and crashing."

"Let's err on the cautious side." Zack snatched the top fur, carried it outside, and shook it out.

"Okay." He said, displaying the wool for Lauren. "You rest while I check out the village."

He quickly searched the remaining houses, finding a small knife, wooden bowls, and a little hay. Lauren was fast asleep in the main room when he returned. He started a fire in the hearth with matches from his backpack, reminding himself to conserve them. He remembered the butane lighter he gave Cassandra; a poor decision, in retrospect. He also needed a cooking pot.

He walked outside and noticed the horned helmet tied to the horse. He ripped out the leather lining held inside by small metal pins. Turning his nose from the rank odor, he washed out the inside with water.

The shiny top of the helmet turned black over the fire, as did the underside of the horns. After a half hour of boiling, he dumped the sterilized water into a clean bucket, filled the helmet again, and set it back over the flames.

He found a suitably straight stick in the brush, carved a point on the end with his Swiss Army knife, and practiced hurling the stick at a tree. After a series of pathetic tosses, he wiped his forehead. A rock felt better in his hand. He wound up and nailed the bull's-eye first time. *How am I going to defend her? I have to put more distance between them and us.*

He returned to check on the water, sipping gingerly from a wooden ladle. Lauren was still sleeping soundly.

An hour later, he shook her reluctantly. "We've got to get moving."

Lauren jerked awake. "I could sleep forever. Do you want to lie down for a while?"

Zack measured the sun's position through the window. "Midday's still a few hours away and I could use an hour of sleep, too. We'll have to push hard again. I've got some boiled water ready for you by the fireplace, and some roasted birdseed."

Lauren smiled for the first time in days. "Thank you."

"We'll find something else later."

She nodded. "We'll eat the rest of the bread and the gourmet birdseed. I'll wake you."

When Lauren roused Zack, he groaned, sat up and ran his fingers through his hair.

"Have some water. I've filled our jars and packed up the horse. We can leave as soon as you're ready."

They headed south from the village. "I wish I knew exactly where we are," Lauren said.

"Who knows which roads the Persians really take south," Zack said, still trying to shake exhaustion from his head. "Right now, they'll be swarming in Phocis, south of Thermopylae. I wouldn't want to be in one of those towns."

The corked clay water bottles clanked against each other as the horse stumbled over rocks, fallen branches, and potholes.

"Zack, do you remember that little fishing village we stopped at on the way north? Do you think it's far from here?"

"If we can find our way to the coast again, we should find it."

"But won't the Persian navy be coming down the channel?"

"You're right. Forget the coast. We'll stay on this road and make the best time we can. Ultimately, we have to head inland to get to Delphi. There's no way I'm walking to Athens."

"We're in good shape. No food, exhausted, lost… what could be next?"

"I've stopped making predictions. Teach me some more Persian. At least it will keep my mind off everything I've screwed up."

CHAPTER 26
AUGUST 480 BCE
PHOCIS

THE SEARCH

"Lord Bessus, these new riders don't look like they could tangle with a bunch of tent whores."

"If they argue or run, take their heads," Bessus said without hesitation.

With chest puffed out and chin pointed forward, Bessus rode past long lines of infantry on his way through the pass. "Find a good road south and take our revenge." He smiled at Cyartes. "I want scouts up ahead."

They rode past abandoned shacks set up to supply the Greek army. The trail showed signs of a quick retreat. Debris, garments, and weapons littered the dirt.

"Many escaped," Cyartes said.

Bessus grunted. "They scurry for cover like lizards." He drove his heels into the flanks of his mount. The troops followed at a steady gallop.

As evening drew near, Bessus swatted road dust from his leather armor. He untied the water bladder from his saddle horn and took a long drink.

"We have food and water for three days," Cyartes pointed out.

Bessus took another swig, gargled and spit it out at Cyartes' feet. "We camp here tonight," he said impassively, expecting no debate.

The next morning, Bessus and his men rode hard until they reached a fork in the road. "Send your men by the road that hugs the coast. If they find the Greek warriors, have them summon us with the horns or send a messenger."

He took the rest of his men farther west, along a trail shaded by overhanging branches. Finally, in bright sunlight, a set of tracks appeared. "Newly made," Cyartes remarked, "from a horse, maybe a couple of villagers… no warriors."

Bessus wiped away the sweat running down his face. To his left, he spotted a hill. "Send riders up there."

The troops passed a small empty village. When his scouts returned, Cyartes could tell from the grin on the leader's face they brought good news. The rider reined in his galloping horse. "There is a walled town not far off. The Greeks are fleeing."

Bessus grinned, revealing the blackened stumps of his front teeth. "Let us see who shall turn out to greet us."

CHAPTER 27
480 BCE
PHOCIS

The walled town lay on the eastern end of the Cephisus valley. The mayor had sent most of his people to hide in the mountains. A small number remained with him and his wife, awaiting news of the battle at the 'Hot Gates'.

When the guard announced the sighting of riders, reporting that they were not Greeks, the remaining people gathered to depart.

All eyes turned to the mayor. "It's too late to leave," he said. "Abandon the carts. Hurry inside."

They dropped the iron bar across the gates and ran to the parapets to view the oncoming barbarians.

"I've heard that many of the northern townspeople offered food and thus weren't slain. We shall do the same," the mayor announced, knowing well other towns in Phocis had refused earlier to come to terms with the Persian king. He would need a sizable bribe to compensate for their fatal mistakes.

Atop the parapet, the villagers watched the large force of approaching riders. "How many are there?" the mayor's wife asked.

"Too many. I will offer them wine and negotiate terms. Stay inside and keep our people calm."

Hundreds of the horsemen arranged themselves in a semi-circle before the walls. Their leader dismounted.

"He's enormous. Are all barbarians so big and ugly?" a townsman asked.

The mayor gnawed at his lip. "He's one huge son of a whore."

Bessus peered at the townspeople atop the walls. A gate opened, a Greek crept out, and the gate closed quickly behind him. He set a jug of wine and a basket of bread at Bessus's feet, and pressed his forehead to the earth.

Cyartes joined his commander in eyeing the groveling man. "We have no one who speaks their tongue."

"I don't care. I want to get through those gates."

Bessus returned the stares of the townspeople. He waved at them, grinning. "How many are you?" He turned to Cyartes. "We must lure them out."

He lifted the jug to his lips, drinking and then drenching his face with the wine. The townspeople laughed nervously as he poured the rest of it over his head.

Bessus handed the bread basket to Cyartes. "Give it to the men." He kept one loaf and offered it to the prostrate mayor. The mayor stood, accepted the bread, and then bowed.

"Do you have any more bread and wine for my troops?" Bessus asked.

The mayor raised a hand to his ear. Bessus pointed at the loaf of bread and then at his troops. He did the same with the jug.

"Ahhh…" The mayor clasped his hands together in prayer-like fashion. He nodded his head several times. Troopers inched closer in response to hand signals from Cyartes.

The mayor called out instructions to the people atop the wall.

"Prepare to rush the gates," Bessus said to Cyartes. He turned his smiling face, now streaked with wine, back to the people while rubbing his belly.

The massive door creaked open; the mayor walked toward it. When he reached the gate, Bessus sprinted forward, pushing the mayor aside.

He jammed his foot in the opening.

The townsmen rushed to close the gateway. Amid screams from inside, Cyartes and his soldiers jumped off their horses. Using their combined weight against the gate, they forced it open.

The townspeople ran. Cyartes caught the mayor, pinning him against a wall with a dagger to his throat. The troopers seized and corralled the people into the village square. Some of the townsmen swung swords to defend their women. A brief, pitched battle ensued; the troopers slaughtered the men.

The mayor groaned when he saw his wife hauled to the town center along with the other women. He voiced his outrage. Cyartes twisted the blade slightly into the mayor's neck, drawing blood, forcing him to silence.

"My Lord, we have slain all the men we could find," a captain reported.

"I expected more."

Bessus turned his attention to the women, who wept or were too stunned to cry out after witnessing the murders of their husbands. Bessus ripped away the remnants of a woman's garment. "Ah, you are of some importance here, are you?"

The woman squirmed when Bessus prodded her with his crop. "You I claim for myself," he snarled, pressing his nose to her shoulder, scenting her.

Bessus turned to the troopers. "Line them up. Bring the mayor."

When the mayor was brought over, Bessus kicked him hard in the ribs. Troopers jerked the mayor upright, intensifying his discomfort by hoisting him to his toes and wrenching his arm up tight behind his back.

Bessus drew his dagger. The women wailed in unison. "Now, I will show these Greeks the cost of defying the king."

He plunged the dagger between the mayor's ribs, turning the blade. The victim writhed as the dagger punctured his heart. He coughed blood, and life left his eyes.

Freeing his blade, Bessus displayed the slick dagger to the women. They cowered, their faces reflecting pure terror. He coated his hand with the mayor's blood, and marked the breasts of several women with the evidence of his ruthlessness. He pointed to a red–tiled apartment across the square. "Take mine over there. Let each man have his pleasure with the others."

The troops descended upon the women, ripping them from each other.

Bessus emerged from the hovel alone. He fastened the straps of his breastplate and looked around. Most of the townswomen lay dead upon the stones. The few remaining hostages endured unending rape as the line of soldiers dwindled.

He shifted his breastplate. "Fire the town!"

Soldiers seized firebrands. Bessus mounted his horse, gesturing Cyartes to approach. "There's still enough daylight for us to make some ground. Slay the women and take the troops back to that small village we passed earlier. Water the horses. In the morning, take the shoreline fork and head south."

Bessus emerged from the town. Clouds of black smoke ascended skyward behind him. He heard the ring of sword upon stone, silencing the screams of the women.

A small measure of revenge, he decided. The Greeks will pay far more dearly for the loss of my men, and for those stinking red soldiers who wounded me. Lastly, for the helmet I no longer wear.

His men streamed from the blazing town and returned to the small village. When they arrived, it was nearly dark. "Shall we spread out among the farm dwellings and the nearby fields?" Cyartes asked.

Bessus chewed on the inside of his bottom lip. "Send a squad to the crossroads to stand sentry."

"If that dwelling is suitable, I will have your pack brought in."

"It's better than stinking ants crawling up our asses."

Bessus wandered to the well. He pulled up a full bucket of water and took a long drink.

"Over here, my lord," Cyartes called out from a single-story farmhouse.

When Bessus entered, he raised his nose, turning to the stone hearth. "Used… recently," Cyartes said. "I have prepared your sleeping quarters."

Bessus entered a second room, where he found a pile of sheepskin mats arranged on the floor. He sniffed the air, a quizzical look on his face. "Have the food taken from the town dispersed among the men."

As Cyartes carried out the order, Bessus settled in. "A pox on all eight-leggers," he muttered while removing his armor, sword belt, and foul-smelling robe. Then he frowned. Lifting the top sheepskin, he held it to his face, inhaling deeply.

Bessus wondered what a highborn woman would find in this stinking hole of a village.

He collapsed atop the sheepskin rug, savoring its aroma and warmth. His mind wandered as he contemplated the kind of woman who might wear such a fragrance, one of flowers and more. Surely, a king's consort. Just as quickly, the sweet scent and his vision of the woman who wore it disappeared. Other memories, long buried memories, forced themselves into his thoughts. Memories he despised.

The flowers reeked, and brought visions of his mother. Sent to his father from Baktra, the capital of fertile lands to the north, she arrived with her dowry, a hundred head of cattle, in an effort to join the tribes together through marriage. Bessus was no more than nine years when his mother's people plotted rebellion against their Persian masters, convincing his father and grandfather to go along with the plan. Just before they were to act, his mother's people betrayed his family to the Persian satrap. Knowing death awaited her, she disappeared and returned to her family. His father, grandfather, and all his kin could not escape.

His grandfather gave him the horned helmet and double-bladed axe before being captured. They delayed the Persians until he could escape to spider holes and caves that only he knew of, hiding places up and down the 'black dust' mountain range. Later, he heard that the Persians tied his father and grandfather to rocks and had the great horned beasts from the east crush their heads with their giant feet.

His hatred for his mother festered over long years. Bessus beat his head on the pallet post until he shook her memory from his thoughts. He needed to sleep. The perfume tortured him. He threw the rug away and slept on the dirt.

CHAPTER 28
480 BCE
LOKRIS

LOST

Zack hurled a stone and ran into the brush. Lauren heard grunts and curses until he emerged from the shrubs holding a dead rabbit.

She eyed him curiously. There was a slight change within him, and she didn't know what to make of it. "The hunter extraordinaire has caught dinner?"

"Lucky throw, but I don't think we should stop yet," Zack said, tying the rabbit to the saddle blanket. Weighed down with its human cargo and their belongings, the packhorse trudged along the rock-strewn, potholed road with slow, even steps. A few minutes later, the animal came to a dead stop, forcing Zack and Lauren to dismount and walk alongside before it would continue.

Lauren's hand rested on Zack's ribs. The austere conditions and sparse diet of recent days had put another dent in his typically muscular physique. She ran her fingers through his hair. "Your hair's getting long enough for a ponytail. Scraggly beard, too. You'll resemble the locals in no time."

Zack rubbed the back of his neck. "I'd give my left arm for some serious rack-time."

"Hey, I'm thankful for my perfume. Whenever the stink got too bad in the pass, I'd dab a little under my nose."

"I think we should cut inland here pretty soon and head to Delphi. Play it safe."

"I'm a little surprised. Aren't you the one who always wants to roll the dice?"

Zack turned to scan the horizon for dust or any other sign of Persians. "Too often, I guess. Are we reversing roles here?"

Lauren pensively weighed her half of the decision. "Knowing the Persians never reach the Peloponnese, we'd be safe in Sparta, and I'll be able to keep my promise to Leonidas. If we can get around the mountains and get to Livadia, we can head for Delphi by the same road we drove down with Nestor, and then cross the canal to the Peloponnese."

She brushed aside overgrown branches that protruded onto the trail. "I keep seeing his face. All the faces of those men are going to haunt me forever. Have you ever wondered if Xerxes felt any remorse for desecrating Leonidas body? After all, Leonidas was a monarch in his own country, and he died bravely."

Zack nodded. "Whatever Xerxes felt was outweighed by his frustration and the need for propaganda. Leonidas caused him a lot of trouble. Xerxes doesn't want just Greece. His Carthaginian allies are attacking Sicily right now. He intends to take Italy and all of Europe. Not only is there the actual conquest of all of Western Europe, but Zoroastrianism would be the dominant religion in the west."

Tripping over an exposed rock, Zack fell across the trail. "Damn!"

"Nice pirouette," Lauren danced over other stones in their path.

Zack got to his feet, dusting himself off. "Hell, I'm happy I didn't sprain my ankle."

"Even though the Persian Empire didn't conquer Western Europe," Lauren continued, not skipping a beat, "Zoroastrianism lasted over a thousand years as their dominant religion until Mohammed and Islam took over around 600 A.D."

"I'm so freaking tired," Zack said.

"Five hundred years before Christianity, the Zoroastrians had as their main concepts heaven and hell, judgment for sins, god and evil god, prophecies of a coming Messiah, and angels and demons. Plus, we already know that the three wise men who allegedly followed the Bethlehem star were Zoroastrian priests."

"It's no secret that religions draw concepts from each other. Hey, you're preaching to the choir, and I'm just about comatose." Zack shook himself to stay awake. "Can we talk about something else? How about baseball?"

"What? Look out, Zack!" Lauren jerked him to the side of the trail.

The horse toppled over, pinning their backpack. "Is he okay?" Lauren stroked the horse's cheek.

Zack knelt down and placed his fingers over the horse's muzzle. "Slowpoke's gone. We walked him to death."

"We can't linger here, and we need our backpack," Lauren said somberly. They combined efforts to shift the carcass enough to free the backpack and the flattened rabbit.

She studied the dead horse. "He gave us his best, didn't he?"

She inspected the contents of the backpack. Zack's glasses were intact, as was her Jadour perfume, protected in a metal box. "Ah, rats, there's nail polish all over the place. Thank god, the rest of my perfume is okay."

"You have nail polish with you, too?" Zack asked, astounded.

"Shut up."

He held back laughter while looking at her in the moonlight. She had taken off her bloodied *chiton*. Her orange halter-top and khaki shorts were filthy with trail dust, and her hair and face still bore evidence of her nursing efforts. Despite the mess, her innate beauty remained undiminished. "I have a lot to make up for. I don't know how to explain it all to you," he said softly.

"Look Zack, you took me for granted. So moving forward, we really need to stick together and make decisions as one."

"You're right. I just have a feeling that we won't be returning to our time right away, and survival here is going to require big changes in the way we think and act, maybe for me more than you."

"I don't understand how you can be such a pacifist and yet watch all that slaughter. Did you find it exciting because you were not personally threatened, like a boy at a horror movie? Survival is a fulltime job here. I don't want to take any more chances. You understand?"

"I do, but… I learned something. Even when the odds are far against you, sometimes you have to dig in your heels and fight."

"God, you've led a protected life. No more buts or explanations. Finally, there's a little truth between us. I've coddled you long enough. What does happiness look like to you, anyway?"

Heavy thinking crumpled his brow. "Some author said wisdom comes in drips. I just had a bucket dumped on me."

"It took all this to bring on your epiphany?" Lauren asked.

"Yeah, I used to think that tenure and achievements were the most important goals in my life."

"I often wonder how on earth you became a professor." Lauren stared at Zack, daring him to argue.

"Look," Zack said in a downcast voice, riddled with guilt. "I've come to realize that happiness means I'm with you, safe and sound."

"We'll make camp when we find a safe spot." She rolled her eyes. "And hand over that little bag of toiletries. I'm going to tie it around my waist. All I've got of my past life is that perfume and my driver's license."

An hour later, they sifted through foliage alongside the road and made camp without a fire. They collapsed to the hard-packed earth, and slept.

Lauren woke early and walked further up the road. It widened to reveal a small village. Her heart thumped. She wondered if she should risk the foray.

It didn't take long. She ran directly for a grove of apple trees, ignoring farmhouses near the grove. The golden-colored fruit hung from the branches. She gathered an armful, raced back, and dropped an apple on Zack's chest.

He spluttered awake. "What? Is there trouble?"

"No. Look what I found down the trail."

Zack rubbed the apple against his filthy T-shirt and took an enormous bite.

"You're welcome," she said, grinning.

"Thanks. I'm beyond hungry."

"Maybe it's an omen of change for the better."

"Should we take the time to cook the rabbit?" Zack asked.

"It started to stink so I buried it, but let's check out the village and see if there's anything else to eat."

"Do you smell salt?"

She sniffed a few times. "The air does have a kind of briny scent to it. We're still close to the coast. We have to turn inland." Her stomach gurgled aloud. "I feel a little nauseous. Maybe I ate too many apples on the way back to feed you."

"Let's start walking. You'll feel better in no time. We need to find a road that will take us west and up to Delphi."

A few more hours of determined hiking brought them beneath a cathedral of tall pines. Zack carried the helmet under his arm, finding no comfortable way to tie it to his backpack. Lauren practiced swinging Nestor's sword. At the end of a tree line, a meadow came into view. The road continued beside a steep slope that descended to the Euripos channel. Tall grass waved in the late morning onshore breeze, diverting butterflies from their groundcover perches.

Zack paused uncertainly. "What's wrong?" Lauren asked.

"I don't know." He looked up and away. "Hear that?"

The line of small trees and intermittent bushes barely obscured a dark cloud formation in the distance. Standing atop a rise, he could see through the branches to the channel. "Looks and sounds like thunderclouds."

"We'll need shelter if a storm hits."

The thunder grew closer — and materialized into a mass of galloping horsemen.

"Oh my God, Lauren, hide!"

CHAPTER 29
480 BCE
NORTHERN BOEOTIA

HORSEMEN

Before dawn, Cyartes left the campsite with half of his men. He told one of his captains to have the rest of the men ready to march when the commander awoke.

Holding torches, they rode until scouts found newly made tracks on the road.

Cyartes smacked his pony with a riding stick, feverish for the opportunity to please Bessus.

Up ahead, the road looked blocked. As the riders closed in, they drew bows and spears, afraid of an ambush. They found only a dead horse. "Clear that rotting flesh from the road and move on," Cyartes ordered.

They stopped at a small village, disappointed to find only a well and apples from an orchard, hardly enough to feed them all.

Cyartes pushed his men to ride faster. Hours later, during a brief rest, he asked his captains, "Where did the Greek spearmen disappear to?"

"Did they take an inland road?" one asked.

"We must find them, or someone will taste the commander's axe."

They rode south under the shade from tall trees bracketing the road, finally turning a corner that opened onto a field of grass. Two peasants walked beside a line of trees. They saw his men, and ran.

"Seize them!" Cyartes yelled to his scouts.

The peasants scurried for cover. He kicked the sides of his horse, drawing his short sword. He swooped in low to swing his blade at the man, who had slowed to let his companion run ahead. The peasant ducked and rolled away. Cyartes heard a woman shriek, confusing him, since he thought both peasants were men. The peasant man used the distraction to escape.

The woman raised a sword, but a trooper struck it from her hand. She dashed for the bushes. The trooper dismounted, chased her down, but fell backwards when she struck him with her fist. Horsemen watching nearby burst out laughing.

Cyartes pulled on his reins, jerked his horse around and cornered the man. He swung his sword in a wide arc. The peasant quickly raised a helmet and blocked the blade, but the force of the blow sent him stumbling backwards. Cyartes turned his horse, but the peasant dodged him again.

Several others rode up. Cyartes closed in on the man, who now held the helmet by the horns. The realization of what the man used for his defense made him stop cold. "By the Mainyu, he shields himself with the commander's helmet!"

Cyartes' sword bounced off the helmet but sliced into the man's arm. The peasant cried out, fell backwards into a line of bushes, and disappeared over the edge of a ravine. The woman screamed. Cyartes jumped off his mount and ran to the rim in time to catch sight of his prey. The man rolled end-over-end down the rock-strewn decline.

"Ah, enough of him," Cyartes said.

Then he saw the damage to the helmet: blackened on the top, and worse, the charred horns. Cyartes heard the hysterical cries of the woman as four troopers held her down. Unable to tolerate the wailing, he stormed over to her. "Shut up, wench. You scream like a *daevas*." He struck her across the face.

The woman clamped her mouth shut.

"How did you get this helmet?" Cyartes demanded.

The woman glared back at him. She had fought his horsemen like a mountain cat. "Well, Bessus will get his helmet back and a surprise sweet cake for the evening."

Troopers gathered around the woman. She sat on the ground, her eyes darting from left to right when they encircled her. "Yes, whore, there are two hundred hungry men who will delight in your charms," Cyartes said, his blood-streaked sword in his hand. He motioned with his sword for her to stand up. She rose slowly.

Cyartes fixed his eyes on the woman, so muscled, like the acrobats in the caravans. A giant and a beauty, despite the grime, he thought. With hair the color of honey, Cyartes knew a rare prize when he saw one. He had heard women such as this lived in the north, another reason to conquer all the lands of the earth.

"Lash her to one of the horses. Have two riders escort her. If we don't find any Greeks, we'll make camp at the first sign of water. Ride!" Cyartes shouted.

Close to nightfall, they set up camp near a crossroads. A small pond drained into a stream that found a path to the channel. Cyartes instructed the men to pitch tents along the road. "Place the commander's tent near those woods at the end of the camp."

Campfires blazed. The horses drank from the pond. Soon thereafter, Bessus and the rest of the command rode into camp.

Cyartes waited with a number of his captains as Bessus climbed off his horse. He untied the side flaps of his cloth cap. Yanking it off, he wiped his eyes with it. "It is a suitable campsite, Cyartes. No contact?"

"No Greek soldiers."

Bessus swore under his breath. "When I find them, they will pay. That will be so, by the Mainyu."

"My Lord, we caught stragglers," Cyartes said, presenting the tarnished helmet to Bessus. "One of them had this."

Bessus reared his head back, emitting an ear-shattering war cry. His outburst faded when he noticed the seared bronze and horns.

"My helmet has been desecrated." He tried it on and found it misshapen and uncomfortable, the leather lining torn out. "Have it repaired," he barked.

"As you wish. There is one more prize for you."

"What?"

"We slew the man carrying the helmet; his companion, we captured."

The troopers parted their ranks to reveal the woman, now chained to a log and unconscious.

Bessus strutted towards her, whacking his barbed riding crop against his leather pants. He placed the crop under her chin, raising her face, then struck her across the face with the back of his gloved hand. "Wake up, sow."

The woman shrieked and fell onto the muddy sod, completely prone, sleep-consumed, with one cheek buried in the filth.

"Where'd you get my helmet?" he shouted in Bactrian. "Did those stinking red soldiers give it to you?"

Lauren didn't move.

"Filthy Greeks, they never understand civilized words, but there is another language I'll personally teach you." Bessus bent down. "You might be a fair maiden underneath the filth."

Bessus sniffed at her neck, a familiar scent teased his senses. "I do know you." He gave her a near-toothless grin. "Tonight will be better than I first imagined, king's whore." He rose. "You've done well, Cyartes. Feed the men. Let her sleep. Then have her prepared." Bessus walked away, scrubbing at the blackened streaks on his helmet.

"Right away," Cyartes said, pounding his chest with his fist, murmuring silent thanks to the Mainyu for his great fortune.

The troopers ate the dwindling measures of salted beef and the last of their stale bread. Cyartes set the night guards along the road while camp was set up.

A couple of hours later, satisfied with his preparations, he walked back to where the woman lay. "Ah, wench. I see you didn't make it to the bushes." Cyartes guffawed at his own joke. "We'll clean you up. Your master awaits you. Bad luck for me. I find you pleasing for my own tastes."

He unlocked her chains. "Bring her to the pond," he ordered the guards.

Awake now, Lauren didn't resist, or speak, but her eyes spoke loudly enough. Cyartes had seen the same terror gleam in the eyes of prey during hunts in the Bactrian mountains.

The men threw Lauren into the pond. She went under for a moment, and then stood in the shallow water. Wet hair obscured her face.

"Strip her," Cyartes said.

The woman struggled until one of the troopers hit her arm with the flat of his sword. The fight drained from her. She rubbed her arm. The guards ripped off her top, hoisting it to the hoots of fellow warriors on the shore. She covered her breasts. Guards pulled her hands away. They dragged her into the shallow water.

"Remove the rest. There is more to see," Cyartes ordered, nostrils flaring.

A soldier slid his dagger between the waistband of her shorts and her skin. She screamed. Freeing her arm, she broke the twine that tied a thin cloth purse around her waist, and the metal clasp that held the loincloth close to her. She strained to pull the wet loincloth past her hips.

The warriors froze. One of them emitted a low, guttural moan. Cyartes fixated his gaze on the short hairs at the apex of her thighs. A crowd of soldiers gathered at the shoreline, gawking and marveling at the exquisite form of the captive.

Cyartes passed a hand over her breasts. He pulled the hair away from her face. "You will not hide from me, wench," he said, his breathing quickening.

The woman raised her head. She looked Cyartes directly in the eyes as he groped her breasts and ran his hands along her hips and over her flanks.

"You are perfect. Are you a lord's whore, I wonder?" *I want this woman. She should be mine. I captured her.*

Cyartes gripped her chin with calloused fingers. "If the commander lets you live a second night, then maybe you will be mine once he's done."

The men shouted for her rape. Cyartes knew he would have to calm them down. This was Bessus' woman… for now.

"Guards!" Cyartes shouted himself back to his senses. "Gather her belongings, cover her with a blanket, and chain her to that log. She's the commander's, and will not be spoiled."

The disappointed soldiers turned away, mumbling and complaining, denied their entertainment.

When night descended, all of them waited for the screams they knew would come from their commander's tent.

CHAPTER 30
480 BCE
BOEOTIAN COASTLINE

PENANCE

Zack awoke, sprawled atop rocks at the bottom of the ravine. He heard the surf and breathed in the brine-laden air, which revived him like smelling salts, but without the noxious fumes. He drew his legs close to his stomach and stretched them slowly, testing for fractures. He licked his lips, tasting the copper tang of blood. Using an elbow as a brace, he struggled to his feet.

Then, he remembered: the charge of the horsemen... Lauren dropping her sword and running... the sword slicing through his shoulder... his fall down the hill. "My God, where are you, Lauren?" he cried aloud. "Please don't be dead."

Zack saw a thick flap of muscle and skin hanging from his left shoulder. Dried blood and dirt covered the wound.

He fell to his knees, head spinning. Now he knew how warriors felt: injured, thirsty, in pain and desperate.

After a minute, Zack rose and took tentative steps towards the surf. He knelt down and maneuvered the backpack free of his good arm. Pain lanced through him. He clamped his jaws together, grinding his teeth as he splashed water on the gaping wound, raw nerve endings making him cry out. When the ache subsided, his lesser injuries from rolling into the gorge surfaced for their share of attention.

Zack cursed himself for thinking they would survive this adventure unscathed. While lurching toward the sea, he recalled a tale about a wounded Marine in the South Pacific during World War II. Lacking the proper medical care, the Marine treated his wounds in the ocean. That gave Zack some energy. He dragged the backpack behind him until he reached the rocky shoreline. Spotting the Persian naval vessels in the channel, he kept his head down.

He dropped the backpack and searched Lauren's cosmetic case for the small sewing kit she always carried. He set it aside and then dug deeper for the plastic container of penicillin. The bacteria of ancient times would have little resistance to penicillin, which gave him some comfort. He popped four capsules in his mouth and swallowed them dry.

He waded into the water and dropped to his knees. "I can do it, I can do it," he said through clenched teeth, and then plunged his wounded arm into the sea. His shriek stood tall against any primordial outburst ever unleashed. He kept his arm submerged until the pain eased. As the afternoon sun beat down, Zack waded ashore, collected the backpack, sat on a driftwood stump, found the vial of Ibuprofen and took two pills.

The sewing kit loomed. He threaded a curved needle. Cringing in anticipation of the pain, he held the hook-shaped needle and drove it through a deep chunk of tissue, pulling through the severed flap of skin. Screeching, he did it again. And many more times. Anguish contorted his face.

Once he had closed the five-inch gash, he leaned back to face the sun. He tightened the top layer of sutures in an effort to close the ragged tear. He finished the job by looping the needle through the taut lines of thread and biting off the end.

Zack hoped he wouldn't need to redo the suturing. He recalled the injured hoplites at the pass, how they were seared with burning irons and then sewn up with heavy thread and sinew. They quietly prayed to the gods or cried out for Lauren to comfort them. Zack rinsed his shirt in the water, wrung it out, and wrapped it around the wound.

After an hour of crawling uphill, he reached the top of the gorge. *Thank God: Lauren's dead body isn't laying here.* Following the hoof marks, he stumbled over his sword, buried in the loose soil and overlooked by the riders. He wedged it between his body and the backpack. Between blood loss and dehydration, he needed to find water soon. More importantly, he needed to find Lauren before nightfall.

As he set out, he considered the physical pain insufficient penance for getting her into this mess.

CHAPTER 31

480 BCE

BOEOTIA

DESPERATION

Lauren convinced herself she could endure beatings and humiliation. Just not violation by these sick, infected… She shook her head violently to drive away the horror.

Cyartes and two soldiers marched towards her, holding torches. She stiffened. One of the guards unlocked her chains; the other yanked the blanket from her. The warriors licked their lips as they moved in for a better look. Her heart raced.

The soldiers pulled her roughly to the far end of camp. Warriors stared as she passed by them. Her knees wobbled. The soldiers led her to a large brown tent, patched and rough-sewn with animal skins. Outside, a horse buried its muzzle in a bucket.

Cyartes ducked inside, leaving her to the guards. She couldn't allow fear to cripple her. She felt the sharp edges of Leonidas's bronze ring tied around her finger. No one had seemed to notice it. It fed her with badly needed courage. She considered her options. Her very few options.

"My Lord," Cyartes announced, entering the tent, "I have the woman."

Bessus grunted as he reclined on layers of rugs. He idly inspected the repairs to his helmet, sliding blood-encrusted fingers over the charred ends of the horns. His breastplate and dagger lay to the side. A bronze goblet, adorned in relief with charging bulls, rested on a small table.

"We must break camp early to catch the Greeks," Bessus said.

"We will be ready."

"Where are they?"

"Maybe they used roads or passes like the Immortals took over the mountain."

"I've seen tracks. If we have to ride all the way to their dung-heap of a capital, I will catch them," Bessus declared.

"Do you want the woman now?"

"Get rid of the guards."

"My lord, I have a request."

Bessus studied Cyartes' face, clearly startled by his brazenness.

"I think there is more amusement in this woman than just one night." Cyartes paused. "Can I have her when you're done?"

"You have never asked such a favor before. I have feasted on many wenches since we left. What is so different about this one? So what if her hair is honey-colored?"

"She fires my loins. I would enjoy breaking her. I doubt she is a camp whore. The man she was with fought for her. She would tempt the Mainyu himself."

"She was filthy when I saw her, no better than a sow wallowing in the mud."

"No longer. She's a ripe pomegranate."

"We shall see, Cyartes."

Cyartes left the tent, boiling with envy. "Throw her into the tent," he ordered, kicking one of the guards in the leg. "Then go and feed your bellies."

The guards shoved Lauren inside. They tossed her clothing and belongings behind her. She staggered, but kept her feet. She stood naked before Bessus in the flickering lamps.

Lauren held her breath.

Cyartes stepped into the tent behind her. He clasped Lauren firmly by an arm and twisted it upwards, causing her to cry out and rise on her toes. His ragged breathing lifted the fine hair at her nape. Lauren tried to cover her breasts with her free arm, but Cyartes drew his knife. She dropped her arm.

Bessus stood. He strode towards Lauren. She could only see his eyes. They reflected a level of depravity she had seen only....

She sucked in a sharp breath. Oh my God! The man who chased us in San Diego and Athens! Does he know me now, like he did in my time? How can this be? If he calls me a witch now...

Her attempts to make sense of it all became moot. The bearded, scarred Bessus moved in, putrid odors emitting from him. He raked his fingers across her breasts. She recoiled and fell back against Cyartes, who ground his erection into her rump. Her eyes darted between the two men, her desperation growing as visions of gang rape ignited within her.

"Lords," she cried out in the language of the Persians, "I am not to be violated. I am a priestess."

Bessus paused, confused by her words. Cyartes tightened his grip on Lauren.

"You speak the king's tongue?" Bessus asked.

"Lords, I am not Greek. My kinsmen are allied with the Great King."

Bessus pursed his lips. Cyartes, deaf to her insistent words, ran his hands over her thighs and backside. She winced as Bessus exhaled forcefully into her face.

"Lords, I am an envoy and the priestess of a powerful god," Lauren continued, keeping her eyes on Bessus.

"You lie." He spat at her. "Your god is powerless in the face of the Mainyu."

Lauren could not easily interpret their words. She knew the Mainyu was the evil god of the Zoroastrian religion. *Are these animals devil-worshippers?* "What land are you from, my lords?" she asked, trembling, hoping to lessen their fixation on her body.

"The Satrap of Bactria. Silence your tongue." Bessus slapped her across the face.

The slap shook her, but she pressed on. "Lords, I am not to be violated, in the name of the Great King Xerxes."

Cyartes ignored her pleas, man-heat consuming him. He turned Lauren's face to his own hastened breathing. She squirmed unsuccessfully to free herself.

Bessus shook his head. "I don't care what god you serve. You're mine!"

He held up Lauren's cloth bag. Confounded by the strange fastening of the bag, he ripped it apart. Her driver's license fell out.

Cyartes bit her breast. Lauren cried out, pushing him away.

"Release her. She's mine to mount," Bessus said.

Cyartes did not hear, or chose not to. "I said *now*, Cyartes!"

Bessus threw the bag against the tent wall and tore her from Cyartes' grasp. Lauren screamed when she saw the anger inflaming Bessus' face.

Cyartes growled, reaching for Lauren. "I found her," Cyartes seethed, yanking her back.

Bessus pulled his dagger. "Defy me? You will pay."

He plunged the blade into Cyartes' chest. His grip on her loosened, released.

Lauren was free of one tormentor.

Not the other. Bessus crashed a fist on her shoulder. She fell to her knees. Confident his prize was too stunned to move, drove his dagger into Cyartes again.

Cyartes gagged and spewed blood before toppling over.

Lauren stood in shock, staring at Cyartes' twitching body. She drew back when Bessus turned to her. The eyes of a beast feasted on her. "You will feel my blade too, but first..."

Bessus lunged at her. She rolled aside, but not far or fast enough. He landed on her – hard. She cried out. He turned his rage onto her, his hands ravaging her body, his weight crushing her.

How can I fight him? He was too big and strong. Freeing his manhood, he straddled her, one knee wedged between her legs. Even in the poor lighting, she shuddered at the sight of his enormous length, marked with dark spots and warts. She screeched, and then kneed him in the groin with all the force she could muster.

Bessus sucked in a sharp breath and emitted a hideous groan. Still on his knees, he provided Lauren with an easy target. She swung, smacking him in the nose. Bessus dropped his dagger and clutched at his face. Lauren speared him in the larynx with her braced fingers. Gagging, eyes bulging, still he clambered to his feet.

She grabbed his dagger and swung it in a wide arc, catching his face, slicing his left cheek and nose. Blood spurted, splattering them both.

No sound came from his paralyzed vocal cords. Lauren only saw a black and red void that was his mouth, and desperate eyes that told her she was dead if he caught her.

Despite his agony, Bessus reached for the axe.

Lauren bolted to the rear of the tent. Bessus lunged towards her, digging into the flesh on the back of her thighs with his talon-like nails. She fell, held back a shriek, but managed to crawl away. She saw her cloth bag lying in the dirt next to the tent wall. Lauren stabbed the tent with the dagger, and then heard deep-throated rage behind her.

She turned. Bessus raised his axe overhead and swung it down in a direct path to her skull.

Lauren rolled. The axe ripped a hole in the tent, and a long flap fell away. She heard a guard calling. Bessus stabilized his stance and emitted a growl that announced no mercy. She kicked at his knee. He cursed, but readied his axe for another swing.

She widened the tent flap with the dagger. Bessus snatched a fistful of hair to rip from her scalp. Her screams spread throughout the camp. A guard struggled with the entry flap on the opposite end of the tent.

Lauren grabbed Bessus's hand as he yanked her hair. With her free hand, she cocked and swung her fist with all her might.

Leonidas's bronze ring made solid contact with Bessus's cheekbone, the same one ripped open by the knife. He shrieked in agony as never before. He swung his arms, but fell backwards, colliding with the guard entering the tent. They tumbled together.

Lauren seized the cloth bag and scampered through the hole in the tent. Bessus' face scrunched with rage. "Get her!"

She sprinted into the darkened woods, naked and barefoot. She heard the shouts and growls from the tent. Branch-whipped, little streams of blood trickled from her arms and face. She scampered over sticks and rock-strewn ground, wiping hair and sweat from her eyes.

The camp became a flurry of activity as men grabbed their weapons.

Lauren alternated sucking in air and gasping out the words, "Oh God... oh God... oh God." She finally broke through the trees at the edge of the Euripos Channel, which coursed north to south. She bolted south towards Athens, along the tree line, full of adrenalin. She lost all sense of the passage of time.

Finally, her lungs begging for reprieve, she stopped, sank onto her knees, and wiped the tears from her cheeks. Willing herself into calmness, she slowly rose. Her father's face popped into her mind. *You said I could be strong. So did Leonidas.*

She made steady progress away from the torch-wielding soldiers, who she knew were hunting for her in the distance. She soon found strips of sand to run on, parallel to the channel. After tripping over driftwood, she slowed her pace, and noticed a campfire in the distance. Fearing that other Persian troops had advanced down the coast, she crept forward slowly.

Lauren edged closer to the encampment under cover of darkness. She heard voices, but could not make out the language. She smacked into a shield, bounced off and collapsed.

Too drained to scream or fight, she waited for the final sword cut.

Nothing happened. She opened her eyes. A hoplite stood over her. He stepped back, shaken at the sight of a woman, bloodied and naked. Lauren deteriorated into a sobbing heap.

"Who are you? What are you doing here?" the hoplite demanded in Greek.

Lauren struggled to her feet with the aid of the confused guard. "I escaped the Persians."

The hoplite removed his cloak and draped it over her body. He and another guard escorted her to the campsite. Many men, already gathered around campfires, stood up when Lauren walked by. "I found this woman on the beach. She says she escaped from the barbarians," the hoplite said.

A young, dark-haired leader, bandaged on his head and arm, came closer. He brushed the dried strands of hair away from her face, took her chin in his hand, and raised her head. "By the Goddess Athena, this woman is our nurse from the pass. I last saw you treating the wounded the night before we evacuated. You put these bandages on me."

Lauren buckled against him, unable to speak. He held her in his arms, awkwardly patting her back. "Fetch water. Find her a chiton. Bring the rest of the bread," he ordered.

She alternately sipped water from a gourd and ate pieces of stale bread. She told the story of her escape and what happened to Zack. As she did, the vulnerability of the entire encampment registered. "We must head south right now. There's a large force of barbarian horsemen nearby."

"That's why we stay off the roads. By the Gods, break camp," the leader commanded.

CHAPTER 32
480 BCE
BOEOTIA

VOWS

Bessus pounded his fist on the small wooden table while a surgeon stitched the long gash that gouged the left side of his face. He slammed the table again, sending the surgeon's instruments flying.

"Sit still," Protha, the surgeon, barked. "You'll end up with stitches switching back and forth like the Oxus River."

"That sorceress!" Bessus coughed it out, his voice raspy and muffled. "Finish the job quick. Your needles are as dull as your handiwork."

The surgeon worked rapidly in the dim candlelight. He drove the curved needle through the flaps of skin and dug deep into the flesh, pulling the sides together. Jerking on the thread, he tied off the ends while thinking of the difficult task of sewing the thin tissue on the bridge of Bessus' nose.

"Stinking witch," Bessus bellowed, his knuckles turning white.

"Commander, all will be fine. This scar will match the one on the other side of your face. Then all will be terrified of you. Want more wine?"

Bessus grabbed the surgeon's shirt. "Finish!"

He rubbed his throat, still smarting from where the woman had struck him. "I will carve her into pieces. That sorceress cast a spell on us, killed Cyartes, cut me, and disappeared into the mist." He peered at the surgeon, weighing acceptance of his story. "By the Mainyu," he said, "she claimed she served a powerful god. I will find that sorceress, even if it takes me all of my days and some of yours."

"Stay still. I am almost finished. I can't see very well in this light." Having completed his work, the surgeon gathered his instruments and left the tent.

A pool of blood marked the spot where Cyartes had fallen. Bessus blinked, his vision wavering. "That bitch. That bitch!" He cursed her and his bad luck.

He smelled her clothing, burning the stench of her into his head. He picked up the small square of hard papyrus that beheld a likeness of the witch in yellow, crimson and blue. When he held it near the candle, the eyes of the witch stared back at him. "I will never forget your face. What was yours is now mine. It will be my magic against you."

He murmured additional vows to the Mainyu until the surgeon's potion, laced with the extract of poppy flowers, cast him toward a deep sleep.

"No matter where you go, witch, I will find you."

CHAPTER 33
LATE AUGUST 480 BCE
BOEOTIA

Zack followed the tree line while cavalry troops traveled the roads. After a few miles, he heard the same kind of music that came from the Persian camp at Thermopylae. The shrill flutes and drums grew loud, laced with boisterous laughter and shouts.

He threaded his way through the perimeter of the camp and found an empty tent. He lifted a dark gown, felt cap, and a leather belt from the interior. After returning to the shelter of trees, he dressed quickly and rubbed dirt on his face, stuffing the baseball cap and sunglasses in his backpack.

Zack penetrated the camp. Unable to find Lauren, he retreated to the trees and collected his belongings. He followed the road as it meandered south along the coast, then away from it.

After dark, Zack came upon another camp at a crossroads near a small pond. Guards ran around with torches, as if searching for something. Visions of Lauren's likely rape struck at his consciousness with unnerving repetition. *How could I put her in so much jeopardy?* Unforgivable.

He decided to wait until the camp calmed down. He laid down behind a tree and watched for his opportunity.

CHAPTER 34

480 BCE

ROAD TO ATHENS

DELIVERANCE

Lauren writhed in her sleep, battling a nightmare starring Bessus and his gang of henchmen atop motorcycles, cornering her, ripping her clothes off. She called for Zack, pleading with him to find her.

A hand jarred her awake. "Lady, awaken. The gods torture your rest."

She threw up a defensive forearm until she realized it was one of her protectors. "Sorry, don't know what millennia I want to be in," she said.

She sat up in a wagon, her bed since their hasty departure from camp. She had fallen asleep atop stacks of folded tents, spears, and shields. She could have slept on a bed of barbed wire. She looked out the back of the wagon. A long line of hoplites trudged behind her. *Finally, protection.* Streaks of crimson announced the break of dawn.

Lauren thought about Zack. *If he were alive, would he assume I'm trying to return the ring to Leonidas' wife and search for me in Sparta? If he's alive...* Dust billowed, disturbed by the stamping of sandaled feet. She coughed, settled back and slept.

Later in the day, the wagon jolted her awake again, along with a cacophony of voices, animals, and creaking wheels. She peered out to see desperate families fleeing south or west, their valuables loaded onto carts.

Feeling rested, though battered from her ordeal, Lauren climbed down from the wagon. A hoplite offered her diluted wine from a half-filled bladder and flatbread that she accepted with gratitude. She ate and drank while walking among the hoplites, bringing smiles to a sea of exhausted faces.

"Lady, are you well?" the leader inquired.

"Yes, I visited with the god of sleep for a few hours."

He laughed. "I can see he left dark circles under your eyes."

Lauren cringed. "What is your destination, sir?"

"Mycenae. We will march back to the wall at Corinth to make another stand. We expect the full Spartan army to join us there."

"May the gods grant you Victory."

"It will be that or death, Lady."

She nodded her understanding. "How can I arrange travel to Sparta?"

The warrior paused. "When we reach Corinth, make all haste to our detachment at the head of the column. I'll take you to Mycenae and arrange an escort for you."

"I thank the gods for your generosity."

"And your husband; what of him?"

Lauren bit her quivering lip. "If he's alive, he will find me, or I will find him."

"Perhaps you should make a sacrifice to Athena and trust in her blessings."

"I believe I will do that."

Lauren glanced backwards to the east, managing a last lingering view of the Acropolis and Athens. Within days, the greatest city in Europe would be in flames, its population facing slavery or death. What would become of them?

What will become of me?

CHAPTER 35
CORINTH, GREECE
AUGUST 480 BCE

MYCENAE AND FARTHER

The survivors of Thermopylae reached the next critical chokepoint in the defense of Greece, a wall erected near Corinth on a small strip of land joining Northern Greece and Attica to the Peloponnese. Thousands of hoplites massed near the wall.

Lauren's group passed beneath a gateway to the cheers and shouts of the warriors, who recognized them as veterans of the "Hot Gates." Her captain hopped upon a cart and shouted for silence.

"Hear me, men of Hellas," he began. "You already know that we met the enemy in the north. The Spartan king, Leonidas, stood with his men to the end, and he sacrificed himself to ensure our escape." He stabbed the air with his finger. "Know this. We can defeat them. Many a Mede fell, many ran from our spears, and our triremes sent their ships to the lair of Poseidon. Find strength in your hearts. The fight ahead will be difficult, but by Zeus, we can destroy them."

Cheering erupted. The lines of hoplites parted, and the veterans continued their march south. Lauren hurried to the front of the column; the captain smiled when he saw her.

"This way, lady," he said.

Lauren walked among the jubilant veterans, heartened by the unexpected reception they had received. "Sir, is there another name I may use to address you?"

"I am called Diomedes."

"Oh, you are named after one of the heroes of *The Iliad*."

"You know of Homer, even in your foreign land?"

She nodded. "Every young person learns of the feats of Achilles and Hector, Agamemnon and Menelaus, Paris, and Helen."

The man laughed. "Lady, the men compare your beauty to Helen herself."

"You must be kidding." Lauren tugged a piece of straw from her matted hair. "I fear that I resemble the Medusa." She laughed to hide her discomfort with the compliment.

"I hope Helen did as much for the wounded Trojans as you did for the men at the Pass, lady."

Lauren flushed at the compliment. Never in her wildest fantasies had she expected to witness the horror of hoplite warfare firsthand. She could not help but feel a certain pride in having participated to some small degree in their fight to preserve liberty in its infancy. She had given Zack hell for being there. Maybe she should not have done so.

"Thank you, Diomedes, you honor me," she replied. She looked around, and counted only fifteen or so returning warriors, nine walking, the wounded pulled along in carts.

Diomedes reminded Lauren of many U.S. Marines she had met in San Diego. She made a furtive attempt to untangle her hair, surprised by her subtle attraction to him. Guilt ran briskly up her back.

She excused herself and retreated into the ranks of the hoplites. The men brightened with her company as they continued to put miles on their sandals.

After making camp, they wolfed down whatever food they carried. Lauren assisted several men who needed the dressings on their wounds changed.

Later, Diomedes approached her as she sat on a blanket and stared into the fire. "Lady, how should I address you?"

"My name is Lauren."

"We are not far from Mycenae now. When we enter the city in the morning, the people will turn out to greet us."

"Their appreciation is well-deserved."

Looking pensive, he paused briefly. "We are not returning with victory, Lauren. We were defeated, and the enemy will invade the south."

"You did all that you could. Now, you have the experience and knowledge to direct the allies on how to defeat the Persians. They did not defeat you at Thermopylae. I saw them perish by the thousands. Your single disadvantage had to do with the size of your force. That is all."

He reflected on her comments. "You have the power to heal, Lauren."

"And you possess the power to inspire, Diomedes."

He peered into the fire and started to speak, but held his words. Silence lingered for a moment. Then, "Sleep well."

"And you."

Still restless from a long day of travel and her naps in the wagon, she looked up and marveled at the expanse of vivid constellations. Sirius, the brightest body in the heavens next to the nearly full moon, sparkled like a diamond. As the campfires dwindled, more stars appeared. Crickets chirped, the sound joining in the concert of snoring men.

Her thoughts returned to Zack. They had met on campus at Northwestern. She had seen him in the lecture halls and found herself attracted to his easygoing manner and engaging smile. They took a couple of classes together, but after she found out what gym he frequented, Lauren made sure she worked out at the same time. After graduate school and their internship together in Greece, they planned a wedding in Zack's hometown of Waukegan, Illinois. Her family did not object, having relocated so often during her father's military career.

Lauren said a last prayer for her husband. She curled up and gazed at the fire until she slept.

In what seemed like little more than a moment of rest, she felt a hand on her shoulder. "Lauren. We make ready to leave," Diomedes said, smiling down at her.

She jumped up, frowning at her filthy clothing. The hoplites had already packed their meager possessions. No meal was prepared; most simply took a quick drink of watered-down wine and got in line. Lauren swished around a mouthful and spit it out.

No time to freshen up. Just what a girl loves. She dabbed a bit of the *Jadour* behind her ears. It would have to do.

The troop headed towards the walled citadel of Mycenae, the fabled city of the Great King Agamemnon, who had led the Greeks when they sacked Troy. Mycenae gained prominence and wealth by commanding a major trade route between the Bay of Argolid and the cities of Corinth and Athens to the north.

Less than a mile from the city, riders greeted them with baskets of food and jugs of wine. Captains dispersed the provisions among the hoplites. Diomedes gave Lauren a sheaf of unleavened bread, goat cheese, and olives. She created a pita-style pocket, stuffing cheese and olives inside. Robbed of any restraint by her hunger, she launched into the sandwich. Glancing up, she saw the amused looks of a crowd of hoplites. Her face turned colors as they cackled.

Lauren accepted one of the bladders and drank some wine to wash down her meal. She swallowed wrong as she tried not to laugh at her own ill-mannered behavior. The hoplites laughed all the harder while she spit and choked.

Diomedes remarked, "Lady, you are more entertaining than a beginner bull jumper from Crete."

"Please, don't make me laugh. I'll start choking again."

The hoplites resumed their march. The massive walls of the city came into view, and cheering erupted from the parapets. The road led past farms, acres of olive groves, and the stone and brick huts of the general populace, who lived below the citadel. Farmers and olive-tree workers put down their pitchforks and sticks to cheer and run beside their warriors.

"Lauren, it is a long time since I have heard my men laugh so hard. May the gods bless you for easing their hearts so," Diomedes said.

She smiled, feeling intense gratitude to Diomedes and the others who had fought at Thermopylae and ultimately rescued her from the Persians. He represented safety and kindness in the face of crisis, and she cautioned herself to remember that she was not a woman of his era.

The colossal walls of Mycenae, fabled to have been built by the Cyclops, towered before her. She had visited as a student, inspecting the circle graves within the ruins that had offered up the bones and valuables excavated by the archaeologist Schliemann, late in the 19th century. *AD*. She recalled how she placed her hands on the stones and felt the pulse of time and humanity. Although a thriving fortress city, commanding a rich countryside of olive trees, Mycenae had lost much of its former power and influence as they arrived.

They reached the long ramp that led to the famed Lion's Gate. The walls were thirty feet high. Soldiers with spears and bows guarded the gates and parapets. It reminded her of Zack's comments about how difficult it would be to attack the citadel.

She wondered, as historians and engineers still do in the modern age, how they moved blocks of stone that weighed so many tons.

The cheers grew deafening as they neared the Lion's Gate. An architectural marvel, the gate consisted of three massive stone blocks, two vertical jambs and a twelve-ton lintel stone. The stone relief of two lions rested atop the stone, facing each other and standing beside a Minoan column. Symbols of Mycenaean power, the lions possessed full heads, not the damaged bas-relief Lauren had seen in her time. The relief also served to lighten the weight of stone that extended above the doorway. Stout bronze doors barred entry to the citadel unless invited.

Lauren walked with Diomedes, brushing garlands of roses and lilies from her hair and shoulders. Banners flew from the heights, while the crowd hung over the side of the battlements, waving their hands, shouting prayers, and singing paeans to the gods. Trumpets blared.

The massive gates began to open slowly, revealing what Lauren assumed were the king, queen and their reception committee. Diomedes approached the royal couple and saluted by pounding his chest. He bowed, and dropped to one knee. "I have returned with our countrymen, father."

Lauren sucked in a shocked breath as she silently translated his words. Diomedes was the prince and heir to Mycenae!

Diomedes rose and walked to his mother, a woman much younger than her husband. They embraced. She was richly dressed in a purple drape that covered a white gown. Large golden orbs hung from her ears.

"Welcome back, my son." She held him by his arms. "We praise the gods for restoring you and our warriors to us." She looked behind him. "So few have returned?"

King Andokides stood nearby, regally dressed, his beard manicured, a small golden crown on his head. "The battle was fierce, and we slew many, but alas, we retreated when ordered to by Leonidas," Diomedes said. "I will give you a full report when my men are bathed, oiled, and attended to."

"So be it, my son," the king replied.

Lauren thought of all her studies, the ancient texts, Linear B tablets, Mycenaean culture, and archaic and classical Greek works. The ultimate reward unfolded as she listened to their exchange.

"And this woman?" the queen inquired. "Is she a slave?" Fully aware of how she looked hellish, Lauren managed to utter no more than a short, embarrassing laugh. She'd worn the same gown for several days, and could not have felt filthier. What an entrance, she thought.

"I beg you, mother, give her leave. She is an envoy from a faraway land, and she cared for our wounded at the 'Hot Gates'. When all seemed lost and our hearts sank, she became our beacon of hope. Her name is Lauren."

The queen studied her. "Then, I will apologize for my comments. Does she speak our tongue?"

"Yes, mother, she does."

The queen smiled. "Then we thank the gods that you are with us. My attendants will see to you."

"I am grateful." Lauren knelt down, adhering to expected customs of respect.

"Please rise, lady envoy," the king said, "and accompany us through the streets. Our people await the prince and his warriors."

Diomedes extended his hand to Lauren. They walked together through the famous gate and upon the lanes of the city that led to the palace, passing circular graveyards surrounded by round walls. The people surged to touch the returning warriors while throwing red, yellow, and blue floral garlands upon them. The entourage turned and ascended a stone staircase. The wide steps transitioned at a higher level into carved and polished wood, eventually reaching a grass courtyard.

Citizens streamed up the stairs to follow, given this rare opportunity to see the higher levels of the citadel. Two large white columns supported the entrance that led to an ochre–colored palace. The royal party and hoplites halted the parade there.

King Andokides raised his hand to quiet the accolades of a grateful city. "Mycenaeans, long ago our citadels ruled all of Hellas. Brave warriors guarded our borders, brought us wealth from afar, and advanced the glory of our people. Today, our prince has returned with our warriors, bringing great honor to our people once again. In the time of heroes, we were many and strong. These few hoplites returning this day are all heroes, as are the ones who perished in the north. Many will be called upon to fight the barbarians and preserve the city of our ancestors. Show these warriors your appreciation."

The populace erupted into a sea of waving hands and garlands hurled toward a deep blue sky. Lauren put her hands over her ears. Zack would have loved to see this.

"This is a day few will forget," Diomedes said.

"You did not tell me you are the prince," Lauren replied.

He gripped her hand more firmly, but softly caressed her fingers with his own. "I did not see the need."

Lauren let her hand linger in his. "It is well for a king to be concerned with his soldiers and his people. If he is fair, and does not waste their wealth and their lives, he will be loved and considered a great leader."

A strong breeze blew from the Aegean Sea. It ruffled the flags and banners, sent papyrus confetti swirling, and the robes of the people fluttering. Lauren's untied hair blew across her face.

Andokides said to his son, "The hoplites will be reunited with their families. Now go to the royal apartments to bathe and rest. I will see you later at the banquet."

Diomedes grinned, bowed, and released Lauren to four young female attendants dressed in yellow chitons. They whisked her farther up the hill, to sun-bleached stone buildings set against the peaks of Mount Euboea.

The attendants opened the door to a chamber. Inside, servants filled a large marble bath with steaming water. She noticed a cot, blankets, and a three-legged table with a large polished bronze mirror. "Oh, I cannot wait to get in that water," Lauren said in their language.

The servants poured the last of the jugs of water into her bath. They bowed to her before closing the door behind them. Tapestries with scenes of birds, trees, and fruit decorated the walls of an otherwise simple but elegant suite.

Decorating one wall was the fresco of a woman dressed in a long blue gown, bare to the waist and holding two snakes. It seemed to Lauren further evidence of the historical and religious connections with Mycenae, the Minoans and ancient fertility goddess-religions that held power before

the northern thunder god religions swept down and conquered most of
Greece around 1200 BCE. The table held a number of small earthen jars.
Lauren opened them, elated to discover that they contained eye and lip
makeup.

She removed her robe and stepped into the warm, scented bath
water. Her bruises and scratches became more apparent, as did her weight
loss. Lauren lingered in the water, allowing the heat to soothe her aching
muscles. She scrubbed her hair, longing for real shampoo.

Towels and a robe hung on the wall next to the bath. They smelled
fresh and scented. *Ah, civilization.*

Lauren sat at the dressing table and assessed her appearance in the
large mirror of highly polished bronze. Finding a stiff horsehair toothbrush,
she brushed her teeth with a concoction of honey and mint. After applying
a bit of eyeliner and shadow, she dabbed red paste from a little pot to her
lips. She picked up another jar of a flower-scented salve, spreading it
liberally over her arms and legs, feeling more feminine than she had in a
long time. A couple dabs of *Jadour*, and she felt herself again.

Lauren walked to the window, dragging a wooden comb through
the snarls of her long hair. The breeze ruffled the tapestries behind her,
working like an electric dryer. Out the open window, she saw the Argolid
Plain below the citadel, along with distant farms and fields. Roads led from
the city in every direction. Olive groves and vineyards dotted the
landscape, the sparkling blue sea to her left.

She picked up a plate of red grapes. Yawning, she lay down on a
simple raised bed made up with brown linen covering a wooden frame. She
couldn't sleep. Too many fresh incidents competed for attention: her near
rape and escape from the barbarian, Diomedes and the journey south, the

entrance to a city only imagined by modern scholars, the bronze ring of Leonidas on her thumb … most of all, her missing husband.

If he were dead, could she forgive herself for giving him hell?

Maids knocked on the door and beckoned her to dress. She donned a bleached-white gown adorned with red and white trim shaped like little pyramids. White slippers completed her evening attire, and a golden diadem held her hair from her face. She walked to the partially open door to find the attendants waiting for her. They bowed and led her through stone corridors to an open walkway between buildings, decorated with potted plants and vines. Shale lined the waist-high barriers that ran the length of the walkway, with intermittent columns reaching the ceiling.

At the end of the walkway, she descended an enclosed stairway painted with scenes of hoplites with shields and spears. It led to an opulent banquet room, where the royalty of Mycenae awaited. Everyone stood when Lauren stepped into view, and she paused uncertainly. Gasps and cheers greeted her.

Not knowing the acceptable protocol, Lauren didn't move. Diomedes came to her, took her hand, and led her to a couch, passing four massive columns painted in blue, red, and yellow geometric patterns. A group of musicians, sitting quietly in the corner, began to strum their lyres and harps and tap lightly on drums. The attendants brought in large silver platters of food and ceremoniously delivered them to the several stone tables that surrounded a large fire pit in the center. Servants filled plates and offered them to guests. A plate of roasted fish, dates, olives, and bread was set before Lauren. The aroma caused her stomach to growl. She grimaced.

Diomedes smiled at her. "Oh," Lauren said as her stomach growled a second time.

His parents laughed quietly, sensing her uneasiness. "I take it the feast pleases you," Diomedes said.

"Me and my stomach." A servant handed her a shallow bowl of wine.

"Ambassador," the king asked. "May we call you Lauren?"

"Please." Lauren bowed her head.

"Queen Io and I agree that you truly are a woman of great beauty and grace. Please excuse our earlier ignorance of your trials. We now know of your escape and your separation from your husband."

Lauren's smile faded. "My husband is a resourceful man. I hope that he will meet me in Sparta. I have a special task to accomplish there, and I must see Queen Gorgo."

"I know the Spartan queen," Queen Io responded. "I will make arrangements for your safe travel there."

"I am in your debt." Lauren dipped her chin in deference to the queen. "I will make a sacrifice to Hermes, and I will pray that he will deliver my husband to me safely."

The faces of the king and queen told Lauren that her hope for Zack's survival was, in their opinion, remote. "The barbarians are devastating the countryside. Refugees are fleeing from Athens and the surrounding towns," the king said. He cringed and gripped his side for a moment.

"We went north to witness the valor of the Greeks. We hoped to be farther south when we were overtaken," Lauren said.

"Where is this land you are from?" the queen asked, reaching to comfort her husband. Andokides let out a short breath and smiled at his wife.

Lauren told her tale of Atlantea, leaving out technological advances and substituting the ancient equivalent for others. Cars became chariots, and lights became lamps. She shared the story about stormy seas and months of arduous travel that brought them to Greece.

After two hours of feasting and storytelling, Lauren felt her stamina ebbing. Too much wine again, she thought. She covered her mouth when she yawned.

Diomedes took note. He stood to address the gathering. "Father and Mother, noble families of Mycenae, respected elders and countrymen, the hoplites that Mycenae sent to Thermopylae fought well. We destroyed so many of the Medes."

He paused to acknowledge the raucous cheers of the audience. He held up his goblet, the torchlight reflecting off the polished silver. "We will send many more of them to their foreign gods—and very soon. Our gods have blessed us with this woman, an envoy from a strong country, far into the outer reaches of the world. She bandaged and treated me well, so say our surgeons. She bound the wounds of many of my men and our allies. When all our courage had drained away and our limbs had no strength, she gave us hope and comfort. Lady Lauren, I toast your kindness."

Everyone raised their bowls to Lauren, who stood to acknowledge them. "I believe that your beauty would surely have rivaled Helen of Troy," Diomedes said.

She gazed upon the aristocracy of a city long lost to history. Manicured aristocrats stared back at her, some robed, others in white leather armor worn for these functions. The women, in long gowns, richly accessorized with gold rings, bracelets and earrings, cheered her along with their husbands. Lauren wondered if, by the looks on their faces, they felt she was a threat.

She bowed and began to speak, but her knees buckled. She fainted into Diomedes' arms.

Lauren rubbed her temples, the throbbing a reminder of the evening before. She drank diluted wine and nibbled on grapes to settle her stomach. Then she slept for another few hours.

She awoke to gentle knocking, followed by servant girls entering her room to cork the tub drain and prepare a bath. They placed a cup of broth on the table and made it understood with gestures that she, in fact, had enjoyed too much wine the previous evening.

Lauren sat by the window, sipping the drink while the servants finished filling the tub. After a long bath and fresh clothes, she felt better. She nibbled on cakes and figs, while watching a sparrow dart along the wall outside the window.

Another knock at the door. She jumped, and quickly fastened her gown with a golden broach of intertwined snakes. "Please enter."

Queen Io walked in, wearing a flowing purple gown trimmed with gold thread. Lauren guessed her to be somewhere in her thirties. Her face, barely lined, reflected the pale complexion typical of an aristocrat, like a more pallid Sophia Loren, beautiful to the point of stunning.

"Lauren, I desire to speak with you before you depart." Her intent expression revealed that it would not be mere small talk.

"As you please." Lauren bowed.

"You have had a significant trial, yet survived by your own wits. I am queen of this proud city, but I am also the priestess of the earth goddess, she who gives life to us all."

Lauren wondered where the queen was going with this introduction. "We praise the Goddess Demeter and her daughter

Persephone too," Io said. "We nurture our homes and give confidence to our men. Is it so with the women of your land?"

"Yes."

The queen's gaze strayed to the ring Leonidas had given her. "Is it customary in your land for a woman to have such a ring? It reminds me..."

Lauren interrupted her. "It is the ring of Leonidas."

That stunned Queen Io for a moment. Then she embraced Lauren, who inhaled the extraordinary bouquet of the queen's perfume. "I know Gorgo," the queen said. "This Spartan queen will grieve in private. She would not expect such a treasure returned to her. You pique my interest, Lauren, and I have more questions to ask you. You are a woman of surprises; the gods only know the extent."

Lauren looked down at her feet, fighting the urge to be truthful with this endearing woman. "Please do not reveal to Queen Gorgo what I bear."

"I will only send her a note, recommending that she give you a private audience."

"I thank you, Queen Io."

"War is a curse. We all suffer in one way or another. Mothers nurture their boys into men until they become warriors; it is the will of the gods. The men must fight so the people can survive. Even if the barbarians were not descending upon us, our neighboring city-states threaten us. When my only son left at the head of our hoplites, I did not expect to see him again. It was his duty, and I accepted it."

The queen lifted her chin, but narrowed her eyes. "My husband harbors an illness within him and I don't know how long he will avoid the Boatman. I need my son's strength. Our very existence is in peril, yet since he has returned, I see that he is changed. He has slain our enemies and been bloodied. I also believe Aphrodite has pierced him with an arrow. His eyes are upon you."

I had a feeling. "I do not know what to say. I am a married woman. At least I hope I still am," Lauren said.

"If it is the will of the gods, Lauren, your husband will come back to you. If not, you will be welcome in my household as my son's wife. You could bear him many sons."

At the mention of children, Lauren paused. For a moment, she allowed her thoughts to wander to a picture of marriage to Diomedes, surrounded by a healthy brood. She tried to regain composure as she searched for the right words, not wanting to embarrass herself or the queen.

"You are generous beyond words, and I am very fond of your son. However, I must search for my husband, and I shall put all of my energy in that direction. I hope you understand."

Io did not release her gaze. "Make an offering to Hermes and to Athena, who is a treasured goddess in our lands also. As I look into your eyes, I see something behind them, but I know not what it is. There is a mystery about you. Will you confide in me, if not now, at another time perhaps?"

She knelt and kissed the queen's hand. "I am a simple woman who will not cower in the face of hardship. My father and mother taught me that," Lauren said.

"Women of our kind once ruled these lands and many others long ago when the goddess dominated the people of the earth. We still worship her. Her blessings are many. Return and be one of us, even if you are reunited with your husband."

"I would be pleased to do so, Queen Io."

"I want to ask you. The fragrance you wear is unknown in these lands. Did you get it in Aegyptos or some other flower-laden land?"

"No," Lauren replied, "It is from Atlantea." She placed the small bottle of *Jadour* in Io's hand. "If you have another carrier, I will give half to you."

As she awaited her transportation, Lauren pondered the ancient world—one filled with danger, wars, diseases, famines, and natural disasters. It was a wonder that anyone lived beyond thirty.

Within an hour, a servant guided her to a horse-drawn carriage, the luxury equivalent of a modern-day Cadillac. She said a tearful goodbye to Diomedes and his family. Queen Io made no more mention of their conversation. A squad of mounted hoplites surrounded her carriage and they began their southward journey.

After two days along a dirt road with deep wheel tracks, the carriage and escort arrived at Sparta, the city with no walls.

It was both everything and nothing like Lauren had imagined. History would conjure up a vision of a bleak city, stoic and plain, positioned in a valley between mountain ranges. She saw many unadorned buildings in the distance, but they were beautiful in their simple design, sturdy and constructed of painted wood and stone.

Yet, this was no city in the sense of Athens, Thebes, or Mycenae. No large palace or stone palisades enclosed the aristocrats and the royalty. Sparta looked more like a collection of villages dedicated to agriculture. Lauren saw red-cloaked soldiers, the Greek letter 'Lambda' on shields, and buildings with terra cotta tile roofs. On the outskirts, a dense pack of blacksmith shops bellowed smoke and rang with hammers upon bronze and iron.

Guarded by hoplites, farmers worked the fields and cared for pens full of pigs and goats. The Spartans, she knew, could field only ten thousand warriors. A large city-state, it encompassed several local populations that had been conquered and added to the Spartan holdings. A group of women carrying baskets of clothing stared at Lauren as she passed.

Spartan warriors halted the carriage when it reached a guard post. One of the guards said, "Greetings. State your business."

The Mycenaean captain handed the guard a tied scroll. The commander handed it to a soldier who ran with it toward a block stone building some distance away. Lauren surveyed the scenery while waiting for the soldier's return.

Sparta was the safest location for her in Greece. The people possessed an iron will, far stronger than any battlements. Warlike Dorians from the north conquered the Laconian plain around 1000 BCE. Subsequently, the Spartans descended from them, creating a military state under the reformer, Lycurgus.

When the guard returned, he summoned the group to follow. From a distance, she saw squads of men training, wrestling, and practicing with wooden swords. Then a deep-voiced male barked an order. The men dropped their weapons and sprinted as a group towards her. It wasn't until they all were nearly upon her that she realized half their numbers were nearly naked young women. They ran past her, each slapping a tall oak tree behind her, and then began the run back to their practice field. *Was this their version of sound mind in a sound body?* Nearby, she observed stoic squads of Spartiartes, the pureblood Spartan warriors, guarded groups of men tilling the fields or working on buildings—the *helots*, the conquered peoples of nearby Messenia. Behind a barn, she watched a Spartan beating a man to the ground.

She turned her face. History can be cruelly accurate.

The carriage stopped before a large stone building, whitewashed and adorned with red trim. Women led her inside and served watered-down wine, grapes, and olives. After a short time, the girls escorted her to a second chamber that served as the Spartan version of a powder room. Her escorts, two fit-looking young women clad in white chitons, were both gracious and happy to aid her.

Lauren freshened up, using the water in a bronze basin and linen hand towels. She reclined on a couch too short for her while the two girls waited nearby. Moments later, a more mature woman entered the chamber and led Lauren to an anteroom, where the light from torches danced and reflected off bronze shields adorning the walls. Simple but effective decorations for a military state, she thought.

Lauren heard soft footsteps. A woman walked in, her hair in a chignon and secured with a length of simple white lace. She wore a white gown drawn with a slim brown rope high on her waist and no jewelry.

As the woman drew closer, she smiled, paused and studied Lauren's face. Lauren squared her shoulders and raised her chin to meet the woman's inspection. With her hands clasped behind her back, she ratcheted the square ring around her finger.

"I am Queen Gorgo. I see by this letter from Queen Io that your name is Lauren. She also says that you deserve my respect and that you have something to tell me."

Lauren knelt on one knee. She reached for the queen's hand, secreting the ring behind her back. "Queen Gorgo, I am honored to be in your presence. I am an ambassador from a land far away to the west. I know that I arrive here at a difficult time for you." The queen nodded. "My husband and I came to Greece to act as heralds and unite our peoples. When we first arrived, we learned of the barbarian invasion. We traveled to witness the defense of the Hot Gates."

Lauren studied the queen's eyes, aware that the woman was intuitive enough to speculate on the direction of her words. The queen's lips quivered. Lauren struggled to contain her own emotions as memories of the pass flooded her mind. "We knew the king, your husband, and served him... we... witnessed the valor... of the Spartans." Lauren paused, trying not to choke.

The queen squeezed her hand. "Where is your husband?"

"He's lost in the north. We escaped... the end... but barbarians overtook us. I was able to flee, but I don't know what has become of my husband." Lauren wiped away her tears with her fingertips. She took a steadying breath. "We watched them fight; they... your husband... all of them, were so very brave. They destroyed many of the Persians. They needed reinforcements, but none arrived. The Persians found a traitor to lead them over the mountain and cut off the Spartan position. He... King Leonidas... gave me a message for you."

The queen moaned as tears slid from her eyes. The Spartan queen was not entirely made of stone, either.

"He told me to tell you that he would love you forever."

The queen fell into Lauren's arms, weeping. Lauren knew she was the final connection to Gorgo's husband. A Spartan wife, certainly a queen, understood her man was first a warrior, and would fight to the death or return victorious.

Lauren eased back and looked at the queen's face. "On the night we left the pass, your husband knew that he and his men should stay so that the others could escape." She continued to speak in what she hoped was passable Laconian. "He summoned us for a final meeting, taking me and my husband aside. He asked me to talk with you to express his love for you and your son—and also to give you this."

Lauren opened her closed fist. Shock and wonder blossomed on the queen's face. She took her husband's ring and clutched it to her breast. A mingled cry of anguish and happiness escaped her as she kissed the ring, rotating it against her lips, and then carefully placing it on her finger. Her voice trembled. "Truly, this is the work of the gods. I am in your debt, Lauren, and I understand now why Io wished for us to speak privately. Let us recline. We Spartan women bear our grief in private."

"I understand, Queen Gorgo. I wish to say that everything I have ever heard about the bravery of the Spartans is true. I want you to know that in my country, I am also a priestess of our gods."

"Queen Io wrote that you have a great mystery about you and that you may be a favored one of the Olympians."

"I don't know if that is true, your highness, but I do have great powers in seeing the future. The sacrifice that your husband and his men have just made will unite all of Greece. You will prevail against the Persian invaders. Believe me when I tell you this."

The queen looked at Lauren with large, piercing eyes. "You may, indeed, possess the favor of the gods. The fortunes of war are never easy to read, but I accept your prophecy, because I am confident in our men and in our laws."

"The barbarians will be in Athens soon. All will look desperate. But the Greeks all know that Sparta must lead if Greece is to survive."

"The elders have decided already. Sparta will lead."

"Then I will tell my countrymen when I return to my home that all Greece is filled with brave people, but that the Spartans are the most valiant of all."

Gorgo squeezed Lauren's hand. "What may I do for you? A favor must be returned."

"I must search for my husband, Zack. If by the gods' will, he arrives in Sparta, will you inform him that I will seek out our friend Nestor and stay with him in Delphi? Even if you simply receive news of him, would you dispatch a fast messenger to provide me with word of his well-being?"

"Lauren, the gods control the strings of life, but I will do as you ask. Do you wish an escort to Delphi?"

She nodded. "An escort would be a blessing. I hope to cross the Gulf of Corinth to the west, in Achaia. If you would not object, may I wait for a few more days in case he finds his way here?"

The queen smiled, again composed. "You will be our guest."

Lauren grinned. "May I make one more wish? Could I have some black soup? I have come to like it."

CHAPTER 36
LATE AUGUST 480 BCE
BOEOTIA

TRAVELER

Someone shook Zack's shoulder. Startled, he awakened, but found no one nearby. He looked at the camp. Persian troops gathered the last remnants of supplies and kicked dirt over campfires.

I cannot believe I fell asleep.

When the final troopers rode away, Zack ran to the pond that lay on the western end of the site. He cursed himself, not knowing if they had left with Lauren. His shoulder ached as he gingerly removed the shirt that had served as a bandage. Swelling had caused the sutures to stretch. The pond water looked too dirty to drink, but good enough to bathe in. He swallowed two penicillin tablets and waded in waist-deep. He needed to get back on the road, fast. As he waded near the water's edge, a floating rag wrapped itself around his leg. The orange-red color caught his eye.

He lifted the rag from the water. *Oh no*: it was Lauren's.

Zack ran wildly around the campsite until he saw a body sprawled on the ground. "Not Lauren. Please, God, not Lauren," he said. The mutilated corpse, laid face down on a tarp, had a mass of dark, tangled hair. Zack rolled the body over; it was the corpse of a man. He lifted his chin. "Thank you, God, thank you."

Glancing back at the body, Zack recognized the vents in the fabric for what they were: stab wounds. The face looked vaguely familiar, but he heard birds circling overhead and decided to leave him where he was. The Zoroastrians believed that a body should be left to nature as carrion. It made sense; earth and fire were sacred in their religion, and dead bodies must be separated from the earth. Thus, the tarp. Zack picked up his sword, positioned his backpack so that it was almost comfortable, and jogged in the direction of the cavalry unit.

Finally, near dark, unable to go any farther and seeing no lights in the distance, Zack left the road again, frustrated and spent. The combination of his wound, lack of food, water, and sleep forced him to be practical. He rested.

Chirping birds awoke him in the early morning. Almost immediately, he heard the thundering of hoof beats. He ran for cover, watching a cavalry unit galloping farther south.

By late afternoon, he could barely swallow. Nearly delirious from thirst, he left the road for the shade of the trees. His head throbbed. He swept aside branches, finally taking refuge under a tall oak tree. He listened to the pounding of blood in his ears.

My body is failing.

On the periphery of his consciousness, he heard a goat. He reached for his sword and staggered in the direction of the bleating. He would eat the thing raw.

Zack fought his way through the brush. He broke into the open and swayed, unable to hold his balance. A man dressed in farmer's clothing sat on a flat rock, a goat lying at his heels.

"Do you covet my goat, stranger?" the man asked, scratching behind the goat's ear.

Zack dropped his sword.

"It is easy to see that you are in need of refreshment. Speak up. Are you a barbarian? Your clothing is clearly not of these lands."

Zack croaked out, "I am… a friend of Greece."

The farmer motioned Zack closer, extending a metallic flask shaped like a canteen. "Satisfy your thirst so that we may talk."

Zack seized the container. The farmer let out a short laugh. With shaky hands, Zack poured a long draft into his mouth, the sweetness somehow familiar to him. He took another gulp. The liquid revived him. He sat down, the flask still at his lips. He drank once more, and then wiped his chin.

"You are a traveler, it is clear. Do you know where you are and what you seek?"

Both farmer and goat fixed their eyes on Zack. A round medallion tied to a leather cord hung from the animal's neck.

"I'm lost," Zack answered, returning the goat's stare.

Zack wondered if he was delirious. The goat did not appear to be whole. It looked almost transparent.

"Join me," the farmer said, ripping off a huge chunk from a loaf of bread. He handed it to Zack with an amused look. The drink went quickly to Zack's head. It quenched his thirst, but his shoulder also stopped throbbing. He had barely chewed the first piece of bread before he asked for a second, and then swallowed two more penicillin capsules.

"You have come a long way?"

Zack nodded and tipped the flask again.

"A journey of sea and land, or of the mind and body, Traveler? Which is it?"

Zack blinked. The mist thickened, the man and goat vibrating horizontally. Or so it seemed. "This drink is so strong... I feel… weird."

"It is a fair vintage, Traveler. Have you paid homage to the gods in these lands?"

"What?" Zack closed his eyes. He shook his head, trying to clear it.

An oversized *pestasos,* tied under his chin with a string, shielded the farmer's face. His arms and legs were deeply tanned and muscular, as would be most men of the earth toiling in the rocky Greek soil. The farmer wore no beard. Strange, Zack thought, since a full beard was a symbol of manliness in this time.

"The Olympians are to be respected, Traveler. The gods see all. Here, partake of more. Your body requires the sustenance."

Zack's feet and hands tingled. He drank again. This time, the wine tasted faintly of honey. The bread made his stomach hot and full.

"The gods can be sought for answers, for those who choose to open their ears," the farmer said.

Zack put his drink down. The farmer's voice confused him. Somewhere, someplace, he had heard it before.

When he looked up, the scene before him trembled like bad television reception.

"What is it you seek, Traveler?"

Zack rubbed his eyes. The farmer and the goat appeared to be in conversation. The goat's face transformed slowly between that of an animal and a man with a beard. Then the man-goat stood on his hind legs, and with both hoofs set firmly on the ground, raised a flute to his lips and played, twirling and dancing to his own music. The song seemed familiar, too. Tucked between a belt and the goat's body was a large conch shell.

The farmer spoke again. "I am Apollo Silver Bow, the Far-Shooter. You exist to serve me."

"An archer, did you say? A far-shooter?"

Mist swirled above the farmer's head, gathering density. Succumbing to fatigue and the drink, Zack wavered. The farmer steadied him, grasping his arm. Zack realized that the farmer was taller than he was.

He looked into the farmer's face, shaded by the hat. Blue eyes, deep blue, like the Aegean, captured his attention. He could not look away. "I know you…"

"It is I who know you, Traveler. The elixir and hot mud of the transit runs through your veins, as it does in your companion. Trust the gods and revel in their power, but know the road you shall travel is perilous. The ambrosia will restore you."

"My companion… do you mean Lauren?"

"The one with hair like molten sun."

"How do you even… know her?"

His stomach grumbled. Maybe it was the drink. Maybe something more troubling. He sat down. How to make sense of what he just heard? The drink tingled on his tongue. He liked it. He had tasted it before. "This drink, I know I've…"

"Ah, the fog clears between your ears," the farmer said, reaching for a lyre with silver strings. He plucked it, ringing out individual notes as he spoke. Zack closed his eyes, but flashes penetrated the thin barrier of his eyelids. He placed a hand over his eyes to halt the blinding strobes of light.

A low rumbling sound built in intensity, closing in and pulsating, as in the tunnel where they had barely survived. Together with the light flute music, the sounds served as a musical backdrop to the farmer's conversation. The goat played the same music, but more clearly now.

"Avail yourself of the gods' existence, Traveler, and the disembodiment may be reversed. Sacrifice to them. You may think our power fades in your time, but I am proof that it does not. We are woven into the fabric of this land, like the tapestry of Odysseus's long-suffering wife, Penelope. Here will always be our domain. Submit to our will now," the farmer shouted above the shrill flute, each word clear.

Zack turned his palm up. "Where is Lauren? Tell me."

"Receive this medallion and hold it dear. It will call forth the transit in my temple, and the way home. The journey ahead will test your resolve in the face of evil. Beware the Savage."

"Answer me, please."

"I have plans for you. Alas, there is much more for you to learn. You are not ready."

"Are you really Apollo?" Zack asked, not sure he wanted the answer and astounded to be asking the question at all.

The goat reappeared and just as quickly vanished, as if shut off by a remote control. Zack shifted from confusion to surprise, and then to naked terror. "My God, what the hell is going on?" He shuddered and braced himself against the rock behind him.

"Which god do you implore?" Apollo lanced him with a disproving look. "Are you worthy, Traveler? Can you survive? Save your family, your countrymen?"

The blackness closed in. "What do you want... with me?"

"Is it not your dream to be in this place? Did not your choices bring you here?" Apollo plucked the strings of the lyre. "There is a time to talk and a time to act. Heed my warnings. You will be humbled and you must labor, as did Heracles."

"What am I supposed to do?" Zack laid down, the last of his fortitude spent.

"Learn. Act. Where have you just been? What have you seen? You will understand when you are ready. You must learn from history and survive by your own guile and courage to be worthy. I need a hero who can persevere and carry out my plans."

"This is crazy. Where is Lauren?" Zack asked desperately, his voice just above a whisper.

"Know thyself, Traveler. Brandish a stout heart. I ask you now, what building do you hold dear over all others?"

"The Parthenon, but she won't be built till another forty years from now."

"I know. Will you fight for her, sacrifice yourself to save all she stands for?"

"I had a terrible dream about that."

Apollo flashed a grave look. "I sent you that dream. Do you recall the dealer, Saabir?"

"You mean that antiquities guy back at the museum?"

"Prepare yourself. Now sleep."

A single note sounded from the lyre. Just before Zack passed out, the song came to him "The Sun King," from the Beatles album, *Abbey Road*.

He awoke hours later, alone, and rose to his feet. "Farmer, I mean Apollo, where are you?"

The bronze medallion hung around his neck, with its bas-relief of a kneeling archer embossed on its surface. Rays of the sun extended outwards from the central figure to the edge of the medallion, where they joined and encircled the perimeter. He rubbed the medallion between his finger and thumb. It felt oddly comforting.

Night approached. Surprised at how well he felt, he credited the bread and wine given him by a *god*. The taste in his mouth was familiar… tunnel mud.

After finding his sword, Zack returned to the road, struggling to make sense of everything. He started to jog. His head cleared. *He said if I survive.* He reasoned that he and Lauren had already traveled through time. It was no less of a stretch to give credence to the possibility that he had actually conversed with Apollo, or that Apollo could appear in the future, or any other time he pleased. Apollo, a *god*. Unnerving. Belief in a pagan god shook every foundation of rational thought he possessed.

He walked in circles, absently fingering the medallion and seeking answers to impossible questions. His rambling thoughts passed through the meaning of the dream, then the cocktail party and the dealer Saabir. *Apollo gave me the medallion. That means we have a way home. He played the same tune as at the café. He set us up, from way back. Crap! That waiter was Apollo, too!*

"Christ almighty Lauren, where are you?" he shouted. "I've got to find you. I think I'm losing my damned mind. What just happened to me? What on earth has happened to us?"

Zack walked until the dim light of morning met the aroma of sea-suffused air. Needing a break, he wandered off the road through brush until he discovered wild blackberry bushes. He reached out to snag a handful, but drew back when a deer bolted out of the thicket.

Wrapping extra berries in an old T-shirt, he allowed himself a momentary chuckle, guessing that he had probably created the first tie-dyed shirt in history. "Thanks for leaving me some," he said.

Within an hour, he found another Persian encampment. Working his way around the perimeter, he spied a small knot of cavalrymen. One rider drew his attention. A huge warrior lumbered up to his horse, cursing and clutching at his groin. He failed twice to mount it until a soldier dropped to his knees to act as a stool. Zack watched the warrior struggle onto his mount, open a cloth sack and withdraw a horned helmet. *The same one I found at the pass!* The warrior stretched his neck to avoid pinching flesh as he fastened the helmet under his chin. It was difficult to see much more than the rear ends of trotting horses and their riders.

No sign of Lauren. She had to be connected to these horsemen. After all, the big bastard had the helmet.

CHAPTER 37

DELPHI

AUGUST 2011

PERMISSION

Demo stared at the hand-held movie camera in his locker. He couldn't stand the suspense any longer, but the battery was dead and the charger missing. He bit his lip while pondering the idea of taking the bus to Athens. Someone in the city would know what to do. He had seen many camera shops there on his last trip. The director of the orphanage would never permit him to go, and he didn't want to go to a shop nearby where everyone knew him. He decided the best course was to simply leave and apologize later for behaving badly.

While the others played outside, Demo dropped the camera into a pillowcase. He stuffed a wad of drachmas into the pocket of his shorts, thankful that Mr. Avtges allowed him to keep some of his work money. He snuck out of the orphanage and sprinted to the bus station.

Students with backpacks and work commuters filled the bus. The four-hour ride wound through slow-moving traffic. Finally, Demo stepped off the bus at the Terminal B station and headed to Omonia Square to find the camera store he remembered.

The bell jingled above his head when he entered. An elderly man with a bushy white mustache came out of a back room. "*Kalispera.* What can I do for you?"

Demo withdrew the video camera from his sack. "It doesn't work."

The owner clucked his tongue. "Where did you get such a camera? Did you steal it?" The man frowned. "Shall I report you to the authorities?"

"I'm not a thief." Demo raised his chin. "I found it and I want to see what's wrong with it."

The man easily determined the problem was a dead battery. "I'll charge it for you in the back."

"Can we watch what's on there?"

"Yes."

Demo followed the owner to the back office. As the tape rewound, a door jingle announced a customer. The man left, assuring Demo that he would return quickly.

After the snow on the screen disappeared, Demo saw a tall man with straight brown hair walking backwards, pointing, and talking in English. He recognized the location as the place where he found the camera. While the man dug around a rock, a woman began talking. The man worked the rock back and forth, trying to dislodge it. Suddenly, a hole opened up and swallowed the man. Demo's eyes burst wide open. The woman dropped the video camera. She picked it up and pointed it into the hole, illuminating the man, who looked dirty but unharmed. She put down the camera, which recorded her face...

The woman on the poster taped to the museum restaurant door for the last two months.

On the recording, the weather changed suddenly. The camera flew into the air as the woman screamed. When the camera came to rest, it pointed into the hole, displaying a cave and the two people. They struggled to keep their balance in the rain and mud. Suddenly, something dark appeared to suck them in. As Demo watched, slack-jawed, the couple disappeared into the hole. It closed itself, leaving only a tiny depression in the earth.

"Thank God tourist season is almost over," the man said when he returned, scanning the room to see if Demo had stolen anything. "What did it show?"

Demo averted his eyes. "A bunch of static… I'm going to take it with me."

"Young man, are you sure it's yours?" The man arched an eyebrow. "I'll give you fifty euros for it."

"A camera like this is worth much more. It's not for sale."

"I will give you a hundred, but not one euro more." The owner glanced at the door and moved to block it.

Demo ran around the counter, dodged the owner, and escaped out the door. He jogged to the National Museum, arriving near closing time. He walked straight to the receptionist. "Ma'am, I am looking for Professor Papandreou. May I speak with him?"

"You must be an important scholar, young man, to request such an audience," Mrs. Toyias answered.

Demo laughed nervously, showing the spaces between his front teeth. "I saw his name on a poster, and I have information for him."

"Oh, that's a different matter. I'll see if he's available." She picked up the telephone. "Professor, I have a young man here who says he has some information regarding the poster you put up... yes, sir."

Demo thought the woman had a kind face, like the women who brought cakes to the orphanage. "He will be here shortly. You are fortunate. The professor has just returned from Santorini. Please take a seat."

"May I look around?"

"Of course. Just stay nearby, please."

Demo studied the glass enclosures containing artifacts from ancient times, his imagination conjuring up warriors holding figure-eight shields and casting spears from speeding chariots. He turned when he heard footsteps on the polished marble.

"Is this the young man?" the professor asked.

Demo saw an older man in a coat and tie.

"I hear that you have some news for me regarding my poster. What's your name?"

"Demetrios, Sir."

"You may call me Professor," he said, a grin on his face.

Demo held up the camera. "Everyone calls me Demo, and I have something to show you."

"Okay, young man, follow me. We'll inspect what you've brought."

The professor pushed open the door, ushering Demo into his disorganized office. The professor rummaged through the lower drawers of a cabinet, and found a cord to attach the camera to his monitor. "Let's see what you have."

"I watched it only a few moments ago at a camera shop," Demo said excitedly. "I'm sure it shows the people you're looking for."

Professor Papandreou turned his head quickly. "I hope so. They have been missing since June. Where did you find this?"

"I live in an orphanage near Delphi and I work at the museum there. I found a video camera hanging on a root up on the mountain. Nobody reported one missing, and I didn't have any place to play it where I live."

The professor turned on the television. First, the screen filled with snow and static. Then, it showed Zack talking as he backed up.

"Yes, yes," the professor said, clapping his hands. "It's them. Wait a minute. They are up on the slope, but what have they discovered? It looks like a rock… wait, it's a piece of an ancient column. I have been all over that site; I don't remember seeing that column."

When Zack dropped into the hole, the professor sucked in a sharp breath. "Oh, my, he is okay. Lauren is showing us. What is happening with the weather? It's changing rapidly. Thunder… mud and rain! Lauren is down there now, too. She must have slipped." He fell silent.

The professor turned to Demo, his shock apparent. "It looks as though they were swallowed up in a mudslide. Did you ever see them again?"

"No, Professor. Like I said, I found the camera hanging from a root."

The professor leaned back in his chair, rubbing his chin. "This is remarkable. Are you hungry, lad?"

"You bet."

The professor called the museum's kitchen. "Yes, yes, I know you're getting ready to close, but I need some food brought to my office for a very important young man." He winked at Demo. "Yes… chicken kabob would be fine... yes, as soon as you can."

Demo smiled, pleased to be a "very important person."

"Just relax there in your chair. The meal will be here shortly."

As they waited, the professor played the recording repeatedly, speeding it up and slowing it down, taking copious notes, muttering "remarkable, totally remarkable," over and over.

After knocking, a man with a white apron wheeled in a cart with a large tray of skewered chicken, rice, tomatoes, and a large glass of milk with a straw.

Demo hopped out of his chair. "Is that all for me?"

"Take your time. Do you have to return to the orphanage this evening?"

"I've left without permission."

"Ah, I see... so you've risked disciplinary action?"

The boy nodded. "I'm probably in a lot of trouble."

"Don't worry. I'll call the orphanage and allay their fears."

Demo wolfed down the food while looking at the photos and posters taped to the walls. He listened to the professor talk to the orphanage director.

"Good, then. Yes, he is fine. No, I didn't realize he had Hepatitis-C." The professor paused, nodding thoughtfully. "I'll tell him the appointment has been rescheduled so that he can receive his interferon treatment, and I'll take full responsibility until I can deliver him back to you. Thank you, Mr. Avtges."

The professor hung up the phone. "Demo, how would you like to be my understudy for a day? You can stay with me at my home. Tomorrow, we'll drive to Delphi. Maybe you could show me where you found this camera."

Speechless at his good fortune, he stood like a soldier, nodding his head.

They arrived at the orphanage late the next morning. As professor remained inside the director's office behind closed doors, Demo waited outside, fidgeting. After half an hour, a smiling Professor Papandreou emerged and lightly patted Demo on the back. Mr. Avtges, a middle-aged orphanage director with a thinning comb-over and stooped shoulders, followed him, but did not look at all happy.

"I understand, Demo," Mr. Avtges said, "that you have greatly assisted the professor, but that does not make amends for not obtaining permission before you left the orphanage grounds. What kind of example are you setting for the rest of the children?"

Demo bowed his head. "I'm sorry, sir."

"Yes, I can see that you are. The professor, in his gratitude for your service, has donated to our facility. He has asked to have you delivered to the National Museum on a quarterly basis to advance your education in Hellenic Studies. Is this agreeable to you?"

Demo leaped to his feet, his face beaming. "*Ne, ne, yes, yes.*"

The professor asked, "Well, then, shall we take a walk together? Perhaps you'll give me a personal tour."

"Follow me, Professor." Demo pulled his hand. They strolled the kilometer from the orphanage to the museum.

"Son, I want to speak to you before we go any farther. I think it is best that we do not discuss this matter with others. I did not tell your headmaster exactly what it was that you delivered to me. I only said that it was something of historical significance, and you wished to discuss it with me. If others learn what has happened here, they might descend upon this site and damage whatever is there. We don't know what's happened to my friends. Until we do, I would like this to be our secret. Do you understand, young man?"

"I will keep it zipped shut," Demo traced his finger across his lips.

The professor laughed. He put his arm around Demo's shoulder and they walked through the museum grounds. "As you well know, son, this is a holy place, a place of pilgrimage and of immense influence in ancient times."

Demo led them up the Sacred Way, then uphill past terraces and undeveloped ground. "It's nearby, Professor. Over there." He stopped and pointed at a depression in the ground.

"It appears quite insignificant, does it not?" the professor said, catching his breath.

"I found the camera right there, hanging on that root."

The professor bent down and picked up a handful of dirt. "I would like you to be my watchman. Call my telephone number if you see anything unusual occur. Walk up here every day and check the site for me. That hole closed up for some reason. It may be telling us not to disturb it."

"How is this possible?"

"I don't know. The ancients had immense wisdom, most of which has been lost to the modern world." The professor continued to study the depression for several lingering minutes. "I want to keep the camera for now. I ask that you come to see me next month at the museum."

"Sure." Accepting a business card and happy to be the professor's eyes and ears, Demo squealed, "You can count on me."

CHAPTER 38
ATHENS
EARLY SEPTEMBER 480 BCE

DISASTER

Torches bobbed in the distance, lighting the escape routes of fleeing Athenians. Desperation knocked on the gates of the doomed city.

It took Zack all day and most of the night to catch up with the cavalry unit. Their encampment occupied a broad field on the outskirts of Athens. He probed the perimeter, identified the guard posts, and noted their location for the morning. He retired to the woods half a mile away and waited for the encampment to settle down for the night. He had no intention of sleeping. He had screwed up once, and that was enough. He suspected the group would muster early to try to seal off the city. Another cavalry unit had arrived; fast-moving scouts and infantry would be close behind.

He waited for an hour, asking himself the same puzzling questions that offered no answers: How did he draw the attention and wrath of an ancient god, one who played with their lives like some kind of Olympian board game? Could he admit to himself that other gods existed? Had Lauren survived? If so, could he find and rescue her? He did not want time to examine his faith. He dispatched the on-going argument from his head.

Agitated by his inability to make sense of any of the last month's events, he decided to check out the camp. With his dark robe as camouflage, he darted from tent to tent, listening for a female voice.

Without Lauren's linguistic expertise, he felt hamstrung. If he encountered Persians and had to speak, he planned to claim ignorance or explain that he was from a distant corner of the Empire. Scythia or Thrace, maybe.

Zack crept through the rows of sleeping men lying next to the dying campfire. The night breeze diluted the stench of sweat and horseflesh.

Still no sign of her. Too many ugly scenarios spun through his mind. Anything could have happened to her, and he had only himself to blame. He tried to take solace in Apollo's words; the god had plans for *both* of them.

Turning away, he crept back to his sanctuary in the woods.

The next morning, Zack awoke promptly. The Persian tents were still standing. Before the sun passed above the treetops, a large group of riders galloped into the camp. Commanders mustered and met in the center of the field near the cavalry mounts. The giant stood in the center of the men, wearing the great horned helmet.

"You know where she is, you bastard," Zack muttered as he made his way down the hillside. "Somehow, I'll make certain you tell me."

When the meeting concluded, the leaders dispersed to their columns of riders. The horses had been watered and fed, and the tents dismantled. Zack made his way into the camp. No sign of Lauren.

Someone grabbed his shoulder and wrenched him around. A warrior with a dust-laden black beard barked at him with all the subtlety of a drill sergeant, pointing his finger at the departing units. Zack shrugged, playing stupid. The warrior kicked him. Resisting the urge to strike back, he instead pointed at a fallen horse, implying he didn't have a mount. The man paused. The warrior brought his horse forward, gesturing for Zack to climb on behind him.

Zack took a step backward, but the man shouted at him again, reaching for the handle of his dagger. Zack pulled his robe from his shoulder, revealing his wound. The captain's face visibly softened as he took in the size of the slice and the clumsy stitching. He called his attendant to help Zack onto the horse. Adjusting his sword and backpack, he and the Persian soldier followed in the wake of the departing columns.

Using the Acropolis as a guide, the Persians cheered and waved their weapons as they rode towards Athens. Revenge was near at hand for the burning of Sardis over ten years earlier by the Ionian rebels and their Athenian allies.

The long cavalry column rode through once densely populated suburbs. Residences and warehouses, as well as stalls for food and other wares, lined the road, but the people had fled. Broken carts and discarded furniture littered the road. Public buildings stood empty, defiant and majestic in appearance. Stray dogs, abandoned by their owners, leapt out of doorways to bark furiously at the riders.

Zack endured the rough ride. Without stirrups, he dug his knees into the haunches of the horse and held on while his skin was rubbed raw.

When they reached the flat area below the rocky prominence of the Acropolis, the Persian column stopped. Riders stared up at an unmanned wooden palisade above stone battlements. A long set of stone steps led to a closed gateway. Wisps of smoke curled upward from behind the walls. Silence settled over the horde.

Without warning, archers jumped up from behind the walls and let fly a volley of arrows that tore into the massed cavalry units. They toppled from their mounts, clutching at the shafts. The Persian warrior pulled hard on the reins, causing his frightened mount to rear, tossing both him and Zack to the ground.

Zack landed on his injured side, screaming out curses. The Persian squirmed in the dirt, pulling vainly with both hands on the shaft of an arrow that had slammed into his chest. The horse, thrashing wildly to dislodge several arrows, narrowly missed kicking Zack in the head.

Panic gripped the Persians. Zack jumped up, his sword in his right hand, and moved away from the walls. Several more men fell from their mounts as arrows hit their marks. An arrow zipped over Zack's head, sticking into the back of a man in front of him. He bent low and moved quickly in his attempt to reach safety. Terrified horses and screaming men caused pandemonium.

Zack dropped to his knees. Crawling, he came face-to-face with a gasping soldier, eyes like a shot deer, unable to pull the arrow that transfixed his throat. Zack scuttled past the soldier, but found his progress blocked by a door. He shoved aside a body and kicked at the door with his feet.

It gave way. He rolled inside, escaping the arrows that continued to drop riders off their mounts. Wounded men cried for help, rolling in the dirt and crawling for cover.

Cheers erupted from behind the walls as the surviving horsemen galloped away. Arrows rained down on the wounded, pinning them to the ground.

Zack stood against the interior wall of the house, wincing as he removed his backpack. He peeled away his makeshift bandage; his wound had split open in two places. The lack of purplish color reassured him. At least the penicillin had done its job. He pressed the bandage against the seeping blood while considering his options.

He discarded the idea of joining the defenders. The Persians would slaughter them in a few days. He opted to stay put and remain quiet. The midday heat sizzled outside.

Thunder growled in the distance.

War cries announced a new attack. The area in front of the battlements quickly filled with fresh horsemen and infantry. Archers shot at the defenders while others carried hewn logs forward to the stone stairway. Defenders fell from the heights. In return, arrows flew from the battlements, felling more riders. In return, the Persian arrows overshot the tops of the wooden palisade or smacked into the stone and ricocheted.

Zack pulled on his Persian robe, slung the backpack into place, and picked up his sword. His tongue felt stuck to his palate. When the crowd of soldiers in front of the doorway provided enough cover, he entered the fray. The press of soldiers moving towards the battlements swept him along. They were lightly armored, wearing only leather jackets and carrying bows. The heavily armed troops must still be a significant distance from the capital, he thought.

Commanders shouted encouragement, smacking their men with the flats of their swords. The men in front of Zack held a battering ram. The soldiers maneuvered the ram up the steps, and then propelled it against the iron-reinforced wooden door.

Zack saw the defenders moving around on the battlements above. Arrows from Persian archers flew past the Athenians, who were lifting heavy stones to the top of the wall.

A round piece of column hung briefly on the edge before plummeting to the ground with a resounding crash. Screams of terror erupted from the Persians holding the battering ram. The stone column began to roll down the stairway, killing the few attackers who remained upright. It gathered momentum, smashing into a mass of charging soldiers and tossing them about like bowling pins.

The attackers hesitated after witnessing the devastation to their comrades, but several Persian commanders threatened them with swords and whips, forcing them forward.

Zack maneuvered away from the stairway. Since he was taller than most of the men, he could see their lines ended some twenty yards beyond. He pushed his way through the Persian ranks, thankful they did not keep a tight formation like the Greeks. He nearly reached an alley that would shield him from the missiles, but a Persian guard seized him, pointed a sword at his neck and tossed him into the mass of men. Movement became impossible. The dead and wounded became obstacles, causing men to trip and fall amidst the confusion, smoke, screams, and cursing.

Zack again found himself in the middle of the surge up towards the stairs, with the tip of a blade in the small of his back.

Arrows and smaller rocks pelted the Persians intent on breaking down the door. A few men fell to Zack's right, creating an opening big enough for him to slide toward one side. He reached the steps, tripping over the body of a half-crushed soldier, and fell sideways to the wall, in time to dodge another well-aimed, massive rock drum that crushed several men.

Zack flattened his body against the wall. It took an arrow slamming into the wall inches above his head for him to get moving. The column drum continued its destruction as it rolled down the stairway. Taking advantage of the chaos, Zack slid along the wall as the attack faltered. Warriors knocked over their commanders and ran. He moved with the fleeing men, dodging and jumping over the wounded. Stones and arrows flew past his head as he fled to the opposite end of the square. He weaved through the crowd, within yards of an alley...

A rock struck his thigh, staggering him. He raised his hand to cover his head, but not before a slinger's missile smacked him behind his ear, throwing him to the ground, landing him on his side. He noticed a bit of blood on the ground. His blood. He tried to lift himself, but a wave of dizziness knocked him onto his back. Terrified faces looked down on him. Once his head cleared, he rolled over and rose to his knees.

Another stone slammed into his back. He could barely see the medallion hanging from his neck, dragging in the dirt as he crawled towards the alleyway. Bactrian cavalrymen huddled in the doorway, motioning for him to head their way. Another man fell near him, writhing on the ground. A stone shot just missed his head and bounced off the wall. The soldiers held out their hands, but no one ventured into the line of fire to help him.

Zack crawled, maintaining a frail hold on consciousness. He made it to an outstretched hand, but another rock slammed into the back of his head and turned the world black.

CHAPTER 39

ATHENS

EARLY SEPTEMBER 480 BCE

A MISSION

"Miserable sons of whores," Bessus bellowed. "Do you have dung between your ears? I should cut out your gizzards, every one of you!"

He swung his fist, knocking over a full goblet of red wine and splashing it onto the officers who stood before him. "I told you to hold any attack until we had more engineers."

"Commander, we did not attack," insisted the more foolhardy among the assembled men. "The enemy surprised us as we rode through the city."

Bessus struck the warrior, sending him sprawling into the folds of the command tent. "You lie. One third of my men are dead in the streets, and another third require surgeons." Bessus looked apoplectic, his eyes bulging and his scars a mosaic of blue and black map lines on his face. "If you value your balls, do as I command."

His men took a step backward. Two collected the unconscious man and carried him out of the tent. The others milled around the entrance until Bessus booted the last man in line, sending him tumbling into the others.

"Am I surrounded by fools? By the Mainyu, Cyartes never would have..." His voice trailed off as he remembered what had brought his dagger to Cyartes' chest. "That bitch. That damned sorceress. Still she plagues me."

He ran his filth-encrusted fingernails along the stitches on the bridge of his nose and then over his cheek. Blood and pus seeped from the wounds.

A guard appeared at the tent. "Commander, more troops are arriving, and Mardonius demands a report."

"I will be there."

"He said, 'Now.'"

"Leave me!" Bessus shouted, red-faced.

He picked up the horned helmet, his most prized possession. Cyartes had returned it to him. He wondered now if she had cursed it. He stared at it for several seconds before placing it on his head. He belted on a sword and stormed out of the tent, in his thoughts blaming the sorceress for the loss of Cyartes.

"Commander Bessus, you made a hasty attack."

A long pause. Bessus watched Mardonius pace. "I have few experienced men. Most have not yet been bloodied."

"We will not embolden these Greeks any further, after what we experienced in the north."

Bessus spat on the ground. "My sword aches for the blood of these swine. I will lead the attacks from now on, especially if I can sever the heads of more of those red soldiers."

"Yes, yes," Mardonius agreed. "The red soldiers will surely flee at the sight of you."

Bessus cocked his head at the marshal's veiled insult.

"The army will be fully camped here in a couple of days," Mardonius continued. "Take your horsemen and one of my scouts and ride southwest. We have reports of a wall built by the Greeks across the isthmus. Secure any food you find and report back to me three days hence." He scanned Bessus' face. "I see you are wounded."

"I will have my revenge."

"I need more soldiers who hunger for blood, commander."

"Scores of my men are with the surgeon, and others litter the streets with their corpses."

"I will reinforce your unit when you return."

As soon as he reached the tent flaps, Bessus spat into the dirt, a clear display of his contempt for his superior. He pulled at a long leather cord around his neck and withdrew the strange likeness of the sorceress. He slid his fingers along the slippery covering, stared at her face, and then set it back under his leather cuirass.

"Where are you, whore? Know that the debt will be paid before long."

CHAPTER 40
SOUTH OF ATHENS
EARLY SEPTEMBER 480 BCE

AMBUSH

Bellies were empty and the men complained.

The retreating Athenians had taken everything. Bessus and his men rode their mounts past empty farms. They continued southwest until reaching a rise, where Bessus spotted scores of fighting ships anchored in the inlets. "Whose ships are those?" he asked one of his captains.

"Not the king's navy. There's Greek lettering on the sails."

"Count them and catch up with us."

The troops rode deeper into enemy territory until they saw the wall. Bessus dismounted within view of the Greeks. He defiantly surveyed masses of hoplites blocking a narrow strip of land, building a wall of stone more than twice his height. "Stinking Greeks!" He sucked on the empty spaces in his teeth, imagining the battle that would unfold. The fighting here would be more vicious than up north.

"No food or water," he complained to his captains. "No gold or silver in this cursed land. Why do we even want this worthless shit hole?"

"My Lord, I have heard talk of a great temple here," Mardonius' scout said. "It is said they reveal prophecies there, and store untold riches in their vaults."

Bessus peered at the scout through narrowed eyes. The man stood a bit taller than he did. His muscled limbs, long black hair with a strange curl on the side, confident eyes, and a silver-painted bow suggested he would be a formidable opponent in a scrape. The scout wore black fur over his shirt and his head to match the color of his fuzzy beard. "What more do you know?" Bessus asked gruffly.

"The temple is in the mountains, northwest of here." Apollo handed him a chunk of bread.

"Hounds' balls! Another Greek army will be guarding it. How long a ride is it?"

"With a reward of such value at the end, the distance is of no consequence. I have heard two suns will bring you to the mountaintop. With their armies behind that wall yonder, you will need only your horsemen and wagons to bring home the treasure housed there."

Bessus swallowed the bread and licked his lips. "Their seers can tell the future, can they? I see that wall before us overrun by the king's warriors. Their rotting Greek carcasses will be devoured by dogs and that sacred temple will entertain someone they do not expect."

Grinning sardonically, the scout turned his face.

"What are you called, scout?" Bessus asked.

"Cambyses, my Lord. My father named me after the Persian King."

"You should be a corpse with a name like that," Bessus sneered. He remembered hearing the Persian king, Cambyses II, had laid waste to his Bactrian homeland some forty years earlier, after his father, the Great King Cyartes, had been killed in a revolt. Many Bactrians were slain in the swath of revenge. His own grandfather hid in family caves to escape the slaughter.

It reminded Bessus of when he had been caught, hiding from the revenge taken upon his father's family after his mother's betrayal. The

Persians held a dagger to his throat, but the soldiers were unaware of his family connection and released him. Thereafter, he often hid in small caves dug into the rocks of the nearby mountains, not daring to tempt fate again. He despised the cramped hideouts swarming with bugs, and the lack of food and water for days on end. Enclosed places still turned his blood cold.

"What land are you from?" Bessus asked.

"I am Sogdinian."

Cambyses' words reminded Bessus that many of his replacement troops were also outlanders. He distrusted these men. "Then you must be a thief."

"Then I'm in good company." Cambyses smiled broadly, staring at Bessus straight on.

Bessus grasped his axe handle. "Be careful with your tongue or I will feed it to you." Normally, such a comment would have drawn blood, but Bessus was not certain he should pick a fight. This scout was far too confident. "How is it you've come to lick Mardonius's ass so cleanly?"

"Only because you were there first."

Bessus pulled hard on the reins. "Shithead, mock me and you will die."

Other troopers nearby drew their swords. Cambyses laughed aloud. "Oh, calm yourself, Bessus. You will have plenty of chances to direct your anger at those you really detest. Whom do you despise the most, the Greek warriors, women... or maybe others?"

"Shut that hole in your face. Push me no further, or I will forget that you are Mardonius's pretty boy," Bessus bellowed, unwilling to reveal to anyone, especially a scout working for Mardonius, that he harbored his most vile hatred for his Persian overlords.

Cambyses steered his horse closer and nudged both horses away from the other troopers. "Threaten me no longer, you big bag of trouser wind. Even if I am Mardonius's aide and enjoy his protection, your insults will compel me to challenge you. You may win, Bessus, but it is more likely you will not. If you lose face in front of your men, then say goodbye to your command and maybe much more."

Bessus bristled, huffed and puffed, speechless.

Cambyses leaned in. "You must think of who your true adversary is. Are you a warrior who values a say in his own affairs? Tell me now who the more bold warrior is: one who fights for himself and the freedom of his family? Or one who fights under the crack of whips as ordered by another? Think on it. Are you miserable because you are a slave and know your cache of warrior's pride and dignity is an empty shell?"

Bessus whirled, shaking his fist. "Enough of your fancy talk! I'm not a ship easily overturned by your bullshit. Leave me."

"I only try to penetrate that hardened plank of wood between your ears, Lord Bessus. Think wisely, we both have our goals and duties. I will not question your orders if you cease your insults and consider me your equal."

Bessus thought he saw the man's eyes actually change color. He blinked, and rubbed his own sockets. "Then halt that cursed tongue of yours and bring our riders to that hill over there. I want a better view of the countryside and the waterway."

Bessus galloped away, wondering if he could stand the scout's insults any longer.

The troops rode through fields of wheat waving in the stiff breeze. They arrived atop the hill to see a boat slowly nearing the shoreline. "They may have spoils and food," Bessus said to his captains. "Ride until we're closer to the shore. When they disembark, slay them."

The troopers galloped until leaving their cover, they emerged into the open and shot arrows at their surprised victims. Several passengers shrieked as arrows struck them. The survivors quickly turned back and attempted to reach the boat, their flight impaired by the knee-deep water. More passengers fell to arrows. Before long, all ten passengers floated in the water or sprawled on the beach.

Riders jumped off their mounts and pulled the boat onto the beach. Inside the vessel, they found chests filled with clothing, sealed earthen jugs, and weapons. Bessus moved among the dead bodies, hacking off arms, legs, and heads. Some of his horsemen turned their faces away, while others shot arrows at a second boat beating a fast pace away from the gruesome scene. "Don't let them get away!" Bessus ordered.

More horsemen drew their bows. Shields appeared on the boat, successfully protecting the oarsmen. The arrows struck the side of the boat, hit shields or fell short. Another volley followed, with even less success. Bessus pounded the sand with his fist. Some of the shields displayed the sign of the red soldiers.

Cambyses strolled down from the bluff. Viewing the butchered Greeks, his powerful muscles twitched, along with purple veins in his temples. The scout drew in a deep breath; his tight lips held back rage. A long dark curl fell across the side of his face. "Enjoy your little display of bloodlust?" he asked Bessus.

Pacing, Bessus shook his axe at the receding vessel. Cambyses studied him, an inquisitive expression concealing his outrage.

"I thirst for more than their guts," Bessus growled." I want their fear. I want them all to remember me. A warrior does not let a wound go unpunished."

"Shall I commandeer this vessel then? We can chase them. I can see those Spartan shields have you angry."

"You will never see me again on a ship. Give me earth and a wide stance to swing my blade."

"So you fear drowning? Is there anything else that sends your blood cold?" Cambyses asked, with the same deprecating look.

Bessus wiped bloody hands over his leather cuirass. He swiped sweat from his face. "I only fear that I must hear more of your wagging tongue. It's time to head back to their shithole of a city."

Bessus and his troops returned to the heights, leaving behind the smoking hull of a boat and the slaughtered Greeks bobbing in the surf. He headed north and then east, completing a wide circle. After assigning guards, they camped for the night.

The next morning, with little information gained and no provisions, Bessus led his men back to Athens, guided by the columns of black smoke billowing from the capital.

They reached the city in time to witness the storming of the citadel.

Bessus dismounted and pulled aside a warrior who was running towards the parapets. "What happened?" he demanded.

The man stepped back before talking. "Xerxes ordered an all-out assault, dispatching mountain scouts to climb the steep walls on one side with ropes and grappling hooks." He tried to shake away from Bessus. "Let me go. I want to kill a Greek before they're all dead."

The temples atop the walls were set ablaze. Bessus watched, angry that his men had earlier failed him in attacking too soon. Glory and reward could have been his.

"Is it wise to burn their temples, Bessus?" Cambyses asked.

Bessus shot him an angry glance. "What do we care what worthless gods they worship? If their temples go up, then their gods must hold little power. What kind of warrior are you anyway? You were cowering up on the ridge back at the beach."

"And deny you the pleasure of another satisfying kill?"

Bessus shook his head, perplexed by the scout's constant verbal dueling. He removed his helmet, savoring the screams of the last defenders suffering the fate of the vanquished. "What did these Greeks think would happen? Defy the Great King, bah." Flames licked at the tops of the walls and the temples. "Their armies cower in the south, their navy is cornered, and now their great city is torched. Ah, by the Mainyu, it is a great day."

Bessus swirled his arms above his head. He jabbed his fists into the air and began the nighttime fire dance of his homeland, contorting his face to ward off demons. He leapt into the air. The others followed, reveling in this supreme moment. Rousing cheers erupted among thousands.

Cambyses walked away, his face expressionless. "Come my way again and I'll chop off your eggs," Bessus yelled.

The scout moved on, gravely watching dead Greeks unceremoniously thrown from the battlements to the raucous soldiers below. Bessus ripped a wineskin from a warrior's hand and pulled the plug with his canines. He bathed his entire face with the juice and then filled his open mouth. The celebration spread, infecting units now infiltrating the city. There were no more Greeks to slay, only houses to set ablaze.

The warriors celebrated as conquering armies do.

CHAPTER 41
OUTSIDE ATHENS
EARLY SEPTEMBER 480 BCE

MUMBLER

Bessus staggered back to his campsite. The wine, along with the burning of the city, allayed his foul mood until a soldier told him his wounds were festering with pus and maybe he should see the surgeon. Bessus reached for his dagger, but the man ran.

He wiped the sweat from his neck. "This stinking land, the heat roars like a cave bear," he said to no one in particular. "I came to slaughter these rebels, seize my spoils, and return to my mountain fortress and my boy." He thought about the towns and cities he controlled as a lord, rich with property and cattle. His son would know wealth and power, and might one day throw off Persian rule.

Bessus took pride in his warrior pedigree. He loathed the Persian army, just as he hated following the orders of these generals – and now, the insolent tongue of their scout. He spat out his disgust with all things Persian. He heard talk of other campaigns ahead. Yet, these countries possessed little, if any, wealth. They had no cities like Persepolis or Susa, which brimmed with gold and other riches.

A land of goat turds, Bessus concluded, stepping over a pile of manure.

He wanted to see his son. He imagined him taller and stronger, a young mountain warrior. Even with his son protected by the boy's mother and her people from a neighboring mountain tribe, Bessus wondered how long he would live without his presence. His stomach grumbled. He swallowed back vomit.

Bessus arrived at the surgeon's station, surveying a staff overrun by scores of wounded. Many men lay on the dirt, groaning. Few were fortunate enough to languish in the shade provided by poles and a ship's sail. Some lay unattended, their wounds deemed fatal or requiring too much of the surgeon's time. Others, resting on an elbow or milling around, waited their turn for the hot iron and bandages. Every few moments, a man cried out as the surgeon extracted arrow tips or hacked off a limb. They suffered many crushing injuries, different from the usual puncture wounds and sicknesses.

He did not look at the wounded men. He focused instead on the surgeon, Protha, who prepared to use his enormous knife to sever a mangled limb crushed by one of the rocks thrown from the walls. He cleared his throat. "Surgeon, business is too good."

"That it is."

The surgeon brought his hatchet down, chopping through crushed bone and tissue. The wounded man screamed sharply and then passed out. "Bring in the next one," he said, blood-spattered, exhaustion straining his voice.

Bessus had witnessed the surgeon's work before. He'd also felt the probe of the surgeon's tools and the branding iron that sealed their wounds. He did not relish being sewn up again.

"You look like a child's nightmare."

"Your patients look worse, hack job," Bessus shot back. "And I tire of backtalk."

Protha laughed, pointing at a jug of wine. "I have saved you a slug of the local piss. Sit and I will attend you."

Bessus sat on a cut log, downed a swallow from Protha's personal jar, and watched the man work. The surgeon dug into flesh with a slim dagger, drawing out iron arrowheads. Bessus swished another gulp in his mouth, diluting the foul taste that permanently resided there.

"Let me have a look at you," Protha said. "Yes, you are only a bit less beautiful than you were earlier. Have you been scraping at my stitches with those ugly talons? Ah, I will have to redo my artistry."

"Cut the banter, surgeon, or you will do your work without your tongue."

"Wine on the wound might help the festering." Protha poured wine across the wound, cleansing it of dust and grime gathered while on horseback. "Attendant, bring my instruments."

The attendant stepped carefully over discarded limbs to reach the bag of stitching tools. The screams and groans had all but subsided, except for one man in the corner. He intermittently groaned and babbled.

Bessus glanced at the man. "You have a miserable habit of moving when I'm about to sew you up," Protha said. "Don't mind that one. He's been mumbling and moaning for a few days now."

The surgeon sewed while Bessus tightened his fist and grimaced. Through clenched teeth, Bessus inquired, "Do we know how many we lost or are now useless?"

"Easily half; most came in the first day, like the man over there in the corner. More were carried in the last two days. Not many defenders behind those walls, but they put up a good fight, those Greeks."

Bessus glared at the surgeon. "I hate this dung-hole already. Not a cursed thing to eat or drink, except what the king's commissaries dole out."

Protha continued his work on Bessus' face. His patient pounded on the wood armrests of the chair. "Quiet, or you'll set that idiot to mumbling again. He speaks a tongue I have never heard. When we finish here, I want you to listen to him."

The surgeon soon finished, dabbing at trickles of red running from the needle's puncture sites. "The men who dragged him in here said he suffered a blow to his head. The slingers marked his ribs and legs as well. He is as black and blue as your face."

"Be silent, or I will silence you."

"Ah, that would be a relief. This is only the beginning of the campaign and already I'm tired of this shit."

The wounded man began to mumble. Protha and Bessus walked over to him. "The clothing under his robe is unlike any I have ever seen, with strange symbols and letters," Protha said. "He's got a nasty sword cut on his arm that someone stitched up."

The man lay on the ground, his eyes closed, a bandage wound around the top of his head and under his jaw, obscuring his face that bore the beginnings of a beard.

Bessus frowned. "Could he be a spy?"

"I doubt it. Why would he have fought for us?"

"That is so. He is odd-looking, though. What's that medallion he wears?"

"Some bronze charm to an archer god."

Bessus twisted the medallion back and forth. "Not as good as our smiths make."

"Judging from his condition, it didn't bring him fortune, either."

Bessus grunted. The man opened his eyes briefly. His lids fluttered a few times, but closed again as he began to drawl.

Bessus leaned closer, his ear near the man's mouth. "What is he saying? It sounds like 'Low in'."

"I'm going to move him outside soon. He can talk to the crickets if he wants to. It's not likely that he'll regain his senses anyway."

"Whatever you dream, Mumbler, you will not need this when you wake."

Bessus drew his dagger, severed the rawhide string, pulled off the medallion, and held it up to the light. Though unimpressed by the artistry, the medallion's appearance still appealed to him. He closed it inside his fist. Maybe it would bring better luck.

CHAPTER 42

ATHENS

PROTHA

Protha cursed his own stupidity. Why didn't he keep the medallion for himself? At least he didn't tell Bessus about the sack that held so many other strange possessions. The evening before, the surgeon had examined the contents, marveling over the odd items and their possible uses.

"I have many questions for you," Protha said to an unconscious Zack. "By the Mazda, there is something strange about you."

The next day, Protha rested under the wide canopy of a shade tree, relaxing for the first time in several days. He studied one of the items in the mumbling man's sack: a little paper square with several red-tipped sticks. He scraped the end of one of the sticks with his fingernail, and then smoothed his thumb along the raspy bottom of the square.

His attendant approached. "The Mumbler is awake."

Protha walked to the tent, the flaps opened to ventilate the rank smell within. He found the Mumbler trying to drink, the bandages around his jaw and head loosened. The wounded man grimaced, set down the mug, and attempted to get up.

"Hold on!" Protha pushed the man down. "Your injuries are many and serious. Your tongue must be thick as the walls of Babylon, so drink and remain quiet, lest you harm yourself more."

The Mumbler fingered the bandage on his head, winced, and then looked at the bandage coiled around his ribs. He glanced at the surgeon.

"You took quite a few shots from the slingers. Do you understand what I am saying to you?"

The Mumbler shook his head.

Protha made a disgusted sound. The man shrugged at the surgeon before taking another long pull from a wineskin.

"Do you even speak the king's tongue? What's your name?" the surgeon asked in Persian.

The strange warrior cocked his head, motioning for the surgeon to speak the same words again.

"What is your name?" Protha pointed at him with his finger.

"Zack," the Mumbler croaked.

The surgeon saved his last stop of the day for Zack. He removed the bandage around his head, examining the slowly diminishing lump.

Zack flinched, working his jaw slowly from side to side. "Next time, get a helmet like Bessus has," Protha said. He probed at the bandages wrapped around Zack's rib cage and the stitched shoulder wound. "You will heal from these cuts. Whoever sewed you up was a clod, so I redid the wound while you slept."

Zack mimed sewing motions after tapping his own chest. "You did the work yourself? Thunder gods, I'm not sure I could stitch myself up. There is always pus in so great a tear."

Zack nodded.

Protha said, "Proud of your work, are you? Well, maybe I will put you to work here."

Zack searched his scrambled brains for any Persian words he had practiced with Lauren. "Where am I?" he asked, his lips barely open.

"Outside of the city burned to the ground by the king's army."

Zack pointed at the surgeon. "Your name?"

"Protha. We're from Bactria."

He churned the words in his mind, then repeated them aloud, "Bactria, Protha." He groaned when he tried to move, his broken ribs not lending well to torso rotation.

"Learned your lesson there, didn't you?"

Zack glanced around the tent several times.

"Looking for your sack?" asked the surgeon. "I'll get it for you."

He brought it to Zack. "Are you a magician?" The comment puzzled Zack. He put his hand on his ear again. "Or are you a priest?"

The surgeon held the small square of papers with the little sticks tipped in red. "What's this?"

Zack remained mute.

"Valuable, are they?"

He extended his hand, but the surgeon ignored him. Suddenly frantic, he searched for the medallion. *Gone.* "Are you looking for the medallion? Is it a part of your magic?"

Zack hyperventilated.

"I know where it is, but it will not be easy to reclaim it."

Zack extended his hand, palm up, his eyes filled with an obvious panic to retrieve the prized possession. "We'll have to trade, my young friend," Protha said. "Bessus will not give up your medallion easily."

"What?"

"He was in here to sew up his face. What a job that sorceress did on him. Cut him up like a festival hog, seven suns ago."

Zack choked and then coughed violently.

"Settle down."

"What... woman?"

"I said sorceress, and quite a fair one at that. She was full of tricks, that one. Do you understand?"

'Jadoogar'. Zack recognized the word. "Woman?"

"She cut Bessus, killed his best man, and then escaped in a mist."

Zack pointed to his neck and the missing medallion. "I want."

The surgeon shook his head. "You would not survive Bessus's rage if you challenge him. Show me what these strange items are. Maybe we can trade for the medallion."

The next day, Zack watched the tent slowly empty, leaving him and a few more seriously wounded warriors. He also saw the physical strain endured by the surgeon. After helping lift a dead man, the surgeon groaned and grabbed his shoulder. He sat down hard on a stool while one of his attendants tried to massage away the pain.

"Easy," the surgeon warned.

The attendant flushed and lightened his touch, searching for knots in the surgeon's shoulder.

"Protha," Zack said.

"Leave me alone," he barked.

"I... help."

"How?"

Zack pointed to his backpack. He opened it after several tries. He plunged in his hand, and came out with a number of small white pellets in his palm.

"What are they?" Protha asked.

Zack asked for something to drink. He popped two of the pellets and swallowed. When he opened his mouth, the pills were gone. "You hurt. Good, not hurt," he said.

He offered two pills to the surgeon and motioned for him to take them. "Me? What kind of magic is this?"

Zack waited.

The surgeon warily accepted the tablets. "If I get sick, I'll take your nose and ears before your head."

The surgeon placed the tablets carefully in his mouth, one at a time, and washed them down, swallowing with some difficulty. He coughed and took another drink, dribbling water down the front of his tunic.

"Rest now," Zack said. He gestured for the surgeon to sleep.

Protha stretched out on a cot, found a comfortable position, and fell asleep.

Later, when the campfires were being lit, the attendant returned to the surgeon's tent, carrying two water pots on opposite ends of a pole. "Master?"

The surgeon jerked awake. He pointed across the tent, near Zack. "Place the water jugs over there."

When Protha lifted one of the jugs, he stopped and rubbed his shoulder. A huge grin spread across his face. He rotated his arm, testing his new, pain-free mobility. "By the Mazda, you are a magician—or a healer. My shoulder no longer torments me."

"Help me," Zack said, pointing at his chest where the medallion had been.

Protha shook his head. "I wouldn't ask for it back if you plan to keep your head on your shoulders."

"I want," Zack insisted.

"Keep your mouth shut about the medallion. Get another. That one is gone."

The next morning, Bessus stormed into the medical tent, demanding relief from the stitches stretched tight over his swollen face. The surgeon hurriedly did his bidding by snipping away selectively at the sutures to loosen their hold.

Bessus noticed the man sitting on his cot. "The Mumbler has awakened. Where is he from?"

"I know not. He speaks little of the king's tongue."

"I can get it out of him."

"Try, if you must."

Bessus, helmet firmly under his arm and his head nearly scraping the top of the tent, walked over. Zack shivered at the sight of the blackened helmet.

"Where are you from?" Bessus said, sourly.

Zack swallowed hard when he spotted the medallion around Bessus' neck. *The madman from San Diego and Athens. Shit!*

"Speak up," Bessus bellowed.

"Land, Scythians," he said, realizing that only cleverness would enable him to live to see another day. The big bastard didn't seem to know who he was. Strange.

Bessus took in the words, but scrunched his nose as he deciphered this new version of the king's language. He inspected the man's wounds and bandages. "Well, you have the frame of a warrior." Bessus frowned. "Are you staring at my medallion?"

"I...I..." Zack stammered, not understanding the giant's words.

The surgeon cleared his throat. "Most of the wounded are back in their ranks or have been sent to the army surgeons."

Bessus noticed Zack still staring at his medallion. "Remove your eyes from my medallion, Mumbler. The magic inside heals me."

Zack closed his eyes, breathing heavily.

"Does it have magic powers, Mumbler? I dislike magicians and witches."

'*Jadoogar.*' That word again. He looked at Bessus.

Protha broke in. "Bessus, I must attend to your shoulder wound."

His gaze fixed on Zack, Bessus reached for his dagger. "I do not like his face."

Zack closed his eyes, grimly waiting. His chest rose and fell rapidly. He clenched his fist. *Leonidas told me to fight. If he draws his dagger, I won't make it easy for him.*

The sound of horse hooves drew everyone's attention. When the rider entered the tent, he saluted. "Commander Bessus, Lord Mardonius asks for you."

"Wait," Bessus spat out, displeased by the interruption.

"Commander, I'm to escort you back, without delay."

"My guts warn me that something rots in here."

"The marshal has called a meeting of army generals. They await your arrival."

Bessus flushed. He turned abruptly to follow the messenger, and stomped out of the tent.

"You are not long for this world, boy," Protha chided. "I don't know what angered him, but he will surely wet his blade with your blood. Speak to your god if you have one."

Zack breathed in and out to calm himself. "You are a strange one," the surgeon continued. "There is more to you than I can decipher. Alas, I'm late for a meeting myself. I wish you had not incurred the wrath of the commander."

Protha picked up a set of clay tablets marked with letters, along with several scrolls tied at the ends with twine. He looked at Zack, shook his head gravely, and left the tent.

Finally unattended, Zack tested the strength in his legs. He dismissed the notion of retrieving the medallion. Did Apollo already know he would lose it? He rubbed his stomach. It felt better than any other part of him. Maybe the food and drink Apollo gave him was keeping him together. He hadn't eaten anything in days, yet his stomach still felt unusually full.

Lauren had escaped. Had she been the *jadoogar*, the sorceress? That had to be it. And had the barbarian somehow connected him to her? This madman, the same they'd seen in San Diego and the Parthenon, did not appear to recognize him from those chases in the future. The same two characters kept showing up: this ugly bastard, and the waiter, rather, Apollo. Why? He considered his options while testing his balance. Either way, the Persian he'd practiced with Lauren when they escaped from Thermopylae just saved him. Sort of.

Persian troops controlled the area south to the Isthmus of Corinth. He needed to head west. In a few weeks, history told him, the sea battle would commence off Salamis. Chaos would reign in the region.

Zack made his decision. Even if Lauren escaped to Sparta, she would eventually make her way to Delphi. He would wait for her there.

He slung his backpack over his shoulder, stiffly working it around his bandaged ribs and over his left shoulder. He unwound the head bandage, gently put on his Cubs ball cap, and snapped a tent pole in half for a walking stick.

Outside, a forest led to rocky hills. Having lost his sword in Athens, he took a surgeon's knife, stuffed bread into his backpack, and limped to a dense cluster of elm and oak trees. The way north to Delphi would be a long, punishing trek. He would only find redemption if Lauren awaited him, safe and sound.

CHAPTER 43

480 BCE

ATHENS

SPECIAL MISSION

An annoyed Bessus tied his horse to a post. Why was he at the marshal's tent again?

He found Mardonius studying a large leather map. "My lord," Bessus said.

Mardonius turned. Bessus kissed the tips of his right-hand fingers and bowed. He would be happier to rip out the marshal's throat, but all these officers were kin to the king.

"Take five hundred horsemen and scout the area along the gulf where the Greeks have built a wall," Mardonius commanded.

"I've only just returned from there."

"Silence!" Mardonius barked. "You will speak when I allow it."

Bessus clenched his fists at his sides.

"Scout the shoreline, then turn north and west, sending me a messenger before you do so, outlining any troops or ships that you see," Mardonius said. "I'm giving you the same scout as before. He holds my confidence. Listen to him."

Cambyses appeared from behind a tent divider. He gave Bessus a smug look. "He will guide you to the Greek's mountain temple." Mardonius unrolled a map as he spoke. "Do not enter it. Simply seal the roads leading from it. We have already bribed them with gold, but I mistrust all these Greeks. After we slay their warriors, this shrine will come under our influence and the priests will say as we wish. Is that clear?"

"Why not simply put them all to the sword and move our own people into these lands?" Bessus asked.

"Under our control, they will help spread the Empire far to the west. They are sailors and settlers of some renown and we will use their talents to bring all lands under the reign of our king."

Bessus contemplated the image and ramifications of the Great King's domination over all lands. "How long should I remain at the temple?"

"I will send you a message if we need your troops elsewhere." Mardonius gave him a hard look. "Do not violate the temples. Am I understood?"

After bowing and kissing his fingers, Bessus hurried out of the tent, ignoring Cambyses. "He's made me an errand boy and sent a nursemaid to look after me." Still muttering, he mounted his horse. "Mardonius will grow flowers out of his ass before he denies me what I deserve."

He smacked the horse with his crop. "Ahura Mazda himself will not stop me from sacking those temples."

CHAPTER 44
ACHAIA, GULF OF CORINTH
EARLY SEPTEMBER 480 BCE

MOUNTAIN GOAT

"Lady, get down!"

The first volley pelted the wooden sides of their vessel like automatic gunfire. Many arrows fell short, overshot the boat, or hit the interior of the vessel. They slammed into crates, barrels and netting, wounding one of the oarsmen and hitting a goat. It bleated until one of the men slit its throat and threw it overboard. The men rowed furiously to turn the vessel and put more distance between the archers and themselves.

Despite the warning, Lauren peered over the railing. She saw the Persians raise their bows for another volley. "Watch out," she screamed. "Here it comes again!"

The men grabbed their shields and raised them at an angle to protect the oarsmen and Lauren. The shields rang with ricochets. She raised her head again, looked over the side, and saw something she had hoped never to witness again: the barbarian with the horned helmet, storming back and forth on the beach. After pointing his axe at their fleeing boat, he jumped from body to body, hacking off arms, heads, and legs, wildly tossing the severed limbs into the surf.

"Those poor people," Lauren whispered. She winced at each sickening splat as the corpses were hacked apart.

The oarsmen pulled with vigor, bringing them safely out of missile range. "If that 'horned one' gets in a boat and comes after us, I'll lizard-stick him myself," said Arimnestus, one of her escorts.

Lauren kept her eyes fixed on the shoreline. "I know him." The figures shrank in size as the boat drew farther away. "The barbarian with the helmet, he is unspeakably cruel. I don't want to face him again."

"You must be favored by the gods to have gotten away from him."

"He's a butcher."

"Who is the other, taller one standing on the bluff?"

Lauren squinted to make out the figure of an imposing warrior separated from the slaughter. His eyes seemed locked on hers. "He's too far away. I don't know."

"We are blessed by the gods to have been the second boat instead of the first," Posidonius, her other guard, said. "Merchantmen are always in a rush, and they didn't tell us they were going to make a stop just across the bay."

Lauren bowed her head, swiping tears from her cheek, remembering the cheery tradesman she had talked with on the dock. It had already been a long journey from Sparta by oxen cart. Her Spartan escorts, assigned by Queen Gorgo, walked until Lauren told them she was tired of riding and wanted to hike, too. They gave the team to a surprised farmer and made it to the Corinthian Bay in two days.

"We'll sail far to the west and disembark at night in a small cove. There are alternative routes to Delphi. They are arduous, but safe. Can you make such a climb?" Posidonius asked.

"I'm half mountain goat," Lauren said flatly.

The two Spartans fell backwards, roaring.

Lauren smiled, unsure which part of her comment was humorous. She regarded these two men sent to guard her. While neither of them was taller than five-foot-six, both were built like NFL linebackers. The long hair falling across their shoulders contrasted with their physiques and chiseled facial features. They were part of a race considered by history as stoic or "laconic", derived from Laconia, where the Spartans lived. Yet these two laughed easily, smiled often, and were exceedingly polite. Hardly laconic, in the way she would use the word. History would not remember them. Her protectors would probably die one day in defense of Sparta.

The vessel knifed through the Gulf of Corinth. The sun sank beyond the western hill that led to the Adriatic Sea. The scent of brine tinged her nostrils. Resting her arms on the rails, she thought about how only she and Zack knew the future.

Less than a hundred kilometers to the east, the fate of Western civilization hung in the balance. Themistocles would be weighing his options with his allies. While the Persian fleet had been much reduced, it still had the Greeks cornered and outnumbered. *Pray to the winds*, the Oracle of Delphi counseled.

The adversaries sat like boxers on opposite sides of the ring, studying each other. Each would wait for a mistake or a forced move. Commanders of each fleet would calculate the daunting issues of food, supplies, morale and, especially for the Greeks, unity. Divided nations do not win wars. Many Greek cities had submitted to or argued for surrender. Political adversaries campaigned behind the scenes to subvert their leaders.

All appeared lost.

The sun steadily dipped, creating a mural of orange and yellow in the horizontal lines of wispy clouds. With the light turning green and then purple, the darker clouds on the horizon formed a citadel, with fading rays of yellow light streaking out at a variety of angles. The clouds blazed. As light faded, tears crept from Lauren's eyes. The vision deteriorated and then disappeared completely. The apparition caused her to shiver because Athens, the city in the clouds was, in fact, burning.

The rowing stopped. All listened for the sound of men or horses, but silence dominated. They lowered an anchor. Posidonius slid into the sea. Lauren couldn't see him emerge from the blackened waters, but she already knew his destination. In a few moments, she heard his steady strokes as he worked his way to the shoreline. Afterwards, she heard nothing but the gentle beating of waves against the hull.

She thought of Zack. Had he survived? She said a quiet prayer for him, and vowed not to abandon hope of his ability to survive and find her.

Arimnestus crept over. "Lady," he whispered, "when the signal comes, we will move in and unload. The others are going farther west."

Posidonius was out there, she thought, checking the topography and scouting for cavalry. An owl hooted three times. After a short pause, there were two more calls.

"That is our signal, lady. When we near the shore, climb over the side, and keep your belongings above the water."

"I'm ready," she assured him.

They raised linen-wrapped oars and allowed the boat to coast in. The keel scraped bottom.

"Now, by Hermes, move quickly."

Lauren lowered herself over the side, holding her belongings above her head. She landed in the water, sandals on, and struggled to stand upright on the uneven surface of the rocky bottom. The water reached her thighs. She pumped her legs like a fullback, slogging her way to shore.

There, Posidonius met them while Arimnestus made another trip to retrieve gear. When he returned, they ran low and fast to nearby bushes. They helped each other secure sacks on their backs with leather straps that crisscrossed over their chests. The Spartans carried only spears, swords, and their prized shields, sacrificing heavy armor for speed.

"Lady," Arimnestus whispered, "we move to higher ground. Are your legs ready?"

"Lead the way."

They halted on a rock-strewn hill after navigating a mile-long obstacle course. Lauren dropped to her knees and looked up at her guards. Both breathed normally. *I need running shoes. These Spartans are kicking my ass.*

Undaunted by darkness, Posidonius scouted the terrain. Lauren's pulse pounded in her temples. She knew the Spartans trained from childhood to operate covertly, foraging for food or supplies. "Lady, we'll move higher still, and then camp. Shall I carry your sack?"

Thrusting out her chin, Lauren said sharply, "Hell, no, I will carry my own. Are your women not expected to do the same?"

"That is so. I was told that you are like our women."

Lauren hid her smile. "I am not their equal."

Arimnestus spoke next. "Sister, we move."

A mile further into the high country, they stopped on a hilltop, making a simple camp with no fire. With a hoplite to each side of her, Lauren settled into the shallow depression she had scooped out of the dirt, and immediately fell asleep.

A gentle nudge by Posidonius wakened her just past dawn. He munched on a handful of roasted barley and nuts. A squirrel crept up, hoping for fresh droppings. Arimnestus snatched a stone and hurled it at the squirrel. "We'll have fresh meat for breakfast!" he shouted.

The stone missed. The squirrel scampered away and stopped at a safe distance to nibble on its barley prize. "I'll not be beaten by a sliver of a beast."

Arimnestus launched another stone. It ricocheted off a rock and grazed the squirrel's leg. Though injured, the squirrel made its way to safety among boulders. Arimnestus pursued the furry creature, to no avail. He returned with a furrowed brow.

"Fear not, our barrack brothers will not hear of your defeat," Posidonius laughed.

Lauren scanned the ground leading to the gulf. "No sign of Persians."

"We're safe. If there had been barbarians in this area, I would have made certain they slept for all eternity," Posidonius smiled, the corners of his eyes crinkling.

Lauren returned his smile as she walked off to find a private spot. The dark figure of a hawk swept through the sky and screeched as it searched for breakfast. "I won't be long."

When she returned to the campsite, she tied her hair in a ponytail.

"Lady, we heard you were at the 'Hot Gates'. Could you tell us what happened?" Posidonius asked.

"I can tell you that the barbarians came on bravely and full of confidence. When they encountered your warriors, they fell in heaps, like wheat under the scythe. I tended the wounded for most of the battle, but I saw your king arrange his men into solid squares to repel the Persians as they came forward with their wicker shields."

"A tactic we practiced for many a day in the training fields, lady."

"Reinforcements did not arrive. Your king, once he knew he would be surrounded, chose to stay and fight so others might escape."

A long silence followed. Then Arimnestus said, "All who stayed in Sparta yearned to run like hounds to aid the king. We will avenge our fallen."

"I believe that you will—with the favor of the gods." Maybe I should sit on the three-legged chair above the fumes. I'd be a hell of a Pythia.

Spotting lights on the mountain, Posidonius estimated they would reach Delphi by midday. Lauren scanned the shoreline, noticing the tiny port of Kyrra nearby and making her own calculations about the ten-mile hike ahead.

After reaching their destination, Lauren took the lead, her long legs eating up the distance. Her companions gave each other surprised looks as she strolled past the temple entrance and started down the hill instead. "Lady, if you seek the barbarians, you will surely find them if you continue on this road," Posidonius cautioned her.

"Don't be alarmed. I am going to that farm you see just past the temple on the right. I have friends there." Lauren surged ahead, waving for them to follow.

Posidonius turned to Arimnestus. "She appears to know everyone in Hellas."

The Spartans escorted her along the final steps to the door of the farmhouse. Lauren set down her sack and brushed back her hair with both hands. She took a deep breath and rapped on the door.

"Yes, yes. By the gods, it's a little early for visitors," a familiar voice replied.

When the door opened, a very surprised Nestor peered out. "Blue thunder, Lauren! Where's Zack? Sit down. Persephone, Honeybee, come now."

He turned to Lauren. "Let me look at you. What's happened?" He glanced quickly at the door. "Spartans?"

Lauren tried to answer as Nestor buzzed around the room setting up chairs, but she could not get a word in. "Hurry, ladies. I have a surprise for you!"

Wiping flour on their aprons, Persephone and Cassandra burst into the room. "Lauren!"

Cassandra threw herself into Lauren's open arms, followed closely by Persephone. The three embraced each other.

"Ladies, let me look at Lauren," Nestor said, attempting to pry them apart.

The women stepped back. He held both of her hands. "You appear well, although somewhat dusty from your journey. Pray tell us, where is Zack?"

The Spartans quietly slipped out of the house.

Lauren's poise vanished in a flash. She crumpled into Nestor's arms, her sobs, so long held back, breaking free. The women looked at each other, their concerned expressions revealing their sudden anxiety over Zack's fate. Nestor awkwardly comforted Lauren, patting her on the shoulder as she slowly regained control.

She steadied her voice as she wiped her eyes. "I've not seen him in a couple of weeks. I don't know if he is alive or dead."

Her shoulders sagged and tears crept down her cheeks. Persephone and Cassandra each clasped one of her hands. They led her to a chair and eased her down. She told them everything. Afterwards, Nestor said, "We must sacrifice to Athena and beg for her assistance."

Posidonius announced his return. Nestor fell silent as both Spartans re-entered his home.

"Lady, we beg to interrupt. There is a small guard station down the road, and we saw no barbarians on the road."

"We should have a fair amount of warning if the barbarians decide to visit us here. We are prepared to evacuate quickly if the need arises," Nestor pointed out.

The Spartans glanced at each other, their concern for Lauren's welfare obvious. Arimnestus said, "There is much wealth here. Surely they will send their army this way."

"Perhaps Apollo casts a mist over their eyes, my friends." Nestor winked at them.

"We have great trust in the gods ourselves, sir," Arimnestus replied. "We must rejoin our kinsmen to prepare for battle. Do not linger here. The station is not well- guarded."

Nestor inclined his head in acknowledgement. "Many thanks for your concern, my Spartan friends. Your queen will be proud of the success of your mission. Please now, fill your sacks and bladders. You shall enjoy a hearty meal before you depart."

The Spartans ate with gusto, commenting on the flavors and variety of foods to which they were unaccustomed at home.

Before they left, Lauren knelt on one knee, kissed the hand of each man, and thanked him profusely for his protection. "Please give Queen Gorgo my humble thanks."

"We shall. May the gods bless you," Posidonius said. "If you need escorts to search for your husband after the barbarians are destroyed, send word to Queen Gorgo. We will request the honor of aiding you."

The Spartans stiffened as if they had jumped into ice water when Lauren hugged them. They said their final goodbyes and left.

Nestor shook his head. "Zack should never have hit the statue of Hermes with that olive pit." They sat again at the table. "We'll move supplies up to the cave. I fear that the gods may not grant us much more time."

CHAPTER 45

Outskirts of Athens

Early September 480 BCE

Road Warrior

Four to five days of misery: that's what it would take to reach Delphi, Zack thought. He struggled most of the first day to traverse mere miles. Sliding between groves of trees, staying away from roadways, he tripped on roots, slogged up and down ditches, and waded through streams. He fell too many times to count. He saw no one, except the enemy. He made it over the lowlands and rising hills, and then steeled himself for the agonizing climb up the long mountain road to Delphi. He stopped at every *Hermea* along the roads and begged for forgiveness.

Zack imagined the smiles on the faces of Nestor, Persephone, and little Cassandra. He hoped they would have news of Lauren, and focused on that to encourage him onward. If she were returned to him, he vowed he would move heaven and earth to give her the child she always wanted.

On the afternoon of the fourth day, Zack watched a cloud of thick dust rise from the valley floor and advance towards him on the road he had just climbed. He wondered if the history books were correct that the Persians had never sacked Delphi during their invasion.

After a couple hours, he heard hoof beats on the road behind. He scaled an embankment near a rest area for travelers, causing rocks and dirt to cascade onto the road. Reaching the crest, he hobbled between the trees, using them for cover. Pine needles littered the ground, each step resulting in a crunching sound that made him wince.

He took a short break to massage the black and blue bruise on his thigh and catch his breath. He sank to the ground beneath a cluster of trees, his position offering a clear but protected view of the road below. He mentally prepared himself for the final leg of the climb to Nestor's farm and the prospect of fighting his way there.

The rhythmic clatter of horses' hoofs shook him from his thoughts. Looking down, shock rippled through him: The warrior with the horned helmet rode ahead of two others. "God damn, it's that son of a bitch again," Zack whispered. They cantered quietly, pausing at each curve in the road to inspect the terrain. No other troops followed.

Zack watched their steady progress, barely able to hear their distant banter. He decided to head east along the crest to a point that allowed an unobstructed view of the rest stop he had passed earlier. Upon reaching it, he saw hundreds of cavalrymen erecting a campsite, blocking the road.

He maneuvered back to his original perch and then slipped down the hillside. He moved stealthily along the road until reaching the next bend. He peered around it. The Persians had moved farther up the hill, out of sight.

Zack weighed his options. Somehow, he had to get the medallion back. He thought of the lunatic in San Diego. *If he was there too...* Zack thought, trying to sleuth together all the loose ends.

He walked quietly along the edge of the road, the surgeon's blade gripped firmly in his hand. He heard horse hooves ahead, leaped into the bushes, and hid while a large warrior with a long, silver-colored bow steered his horse back towards the camp. Zack noted a strange grin on the warrior's face, despite the shroud of beard and a low-browed cap. The warrior lifted a metallic flask from his shoulder bag, took a quick drink, and tossed it in his direction. The flask bounced and clanged until it came to rest in front of Zack's camouflage. As the warrior rode away at a gallop, he left his cover, desperate for anything to quench his thirst. He tipped the flask and tasted the honey-flavored nectar.

His heart leaped. *Apollo...*

Zack dashed down the road. "Come back! Help me!"

He stopped suddenly, slipped on the gravel, and fell. He had to choose. Reversing direction, he ran toward Nestor's farmhouse.

Cambyses pulled on the horses' reins and turned uphill. Zack did not hear him say, "Traveler, maybe you are worth something."

Zack advanced until he found horses tethered to a tree trunk. He moved around a corner, recoiling as Bessus landed his axe with deadly strokes upon the guards.

Then Bessus ambled uphill, toward the temples. Zack approached the grisly scene, mindful of the proximity of Nestor's home and the jeopardy the older man and his family now faced. Then he found a third body, he quickly realized that an axe-strike killed the Persian, too. "Why would that sick bastard kill his own man?" he wondered, stooping to collect a broken lance.

Nestor and the girls. Only a dead sprint from Zack's injured body would prevent Bessus from reaching the farmhouse first.

CHAPTER 46
DELPHI, GREECE
EARLY SEPTEMBER 480 BCE

TREASURE

Bessus did not intend to share the wealth housed in the temples, hence his removal of his bodyguard from the world of the living. Convincing Cambyses to go back to his encampment proved far more difficult. He loathed the confounding talk this man spit out with his perfect teeth, and the irritating smile that rarely left his face. He dreamed of gutting him, smashing those teeth to pieces, and adding them to his necklace.

Torchlight illuminated the temple entrance. Bessus paused, listening for guards in the darkness, his axe ready. To bring him luck, he bit on the leather strings holding the Archer medal and his toe-bone necklace. Upon reaching flat ground, he noticed a dimly lit farmhouse close ahead.

He considered his next move while catching his wind. If he entered the farmhouse and ended up in a fight, it might ruin his plan to discover what riches lay in the temple. Still, he had to know who was inside.

Bessus took a path that led to the dwelling. Pausing at an open window, he heard the lilting voices of females. A smile appeared on his battered visage. His codpiece became crowded. Raising his axe, he clicked the latch and flung the door open.

Cassandra screamed as the barbarian burst in. Persephone immediately threw her daughter in the direction of the rear doorway. "Run! Find your uncle!"

Persephone followed and tried to slam the door behind her. Bessus kicked it aside.

Cassandra shrieked, "Uncle! Barbarian!"

Nestor and Lauren were loading provisions inside the bar when they heard Cassandra's cries. Nestor dropped a crate and grabbed a shield, the only thing within quick reach. He raced out of the barn, Lauren close behind.

Cassandra froze in the center of the courtyard as Persephone whirled to confront the barbarian. She leaped at Bessus before he could swing his axe. Her fingernails ripped at his face and eyes. Bessus slammed her to the ground before she could do more damage, and then raised his axe over her sprawled figure.

Nestor shouted, "Get away from her!" He lunged at Bessus with his shield.

Dear God, not him. Lauren grabbed a club-sized piece of firewood.

Persephone scrambled backwards, but could not evade the axe. Bessus put his weight behind the blow. High-pitched, agonizing screams came from her. She flailed her arms once as blood spewed from the cleaving wound that severed her spine.

Lauren gripped Cassandra by the shoulders as they watched the girl's mother vomit blood. Cassandra struggled to free herself from Lauren, screeching, "Mother! No!"

Bessus planted his foot on Persephone's twitching body and jerked his axe free just before Nestor slammed him with his shield.

Bessus spouted curses, falling against the doorway. He regained his balance and swung. Nestor ducked. The blade hissed past his head, imbedding itself in the doorframe. Nestor raised the shield over his head. "You ugly bastard!" He landed another blow. "It was you at the beach! You killed my brother, too!"

Nestor lifted the convex bowl of the shield above his head, cocking his arm. "You'll not leave my home with your head."

Bessus wrenched his axe free and drew back for another swing. Nestor smashed his shield against the horned helmet. The barbarian staggered but arched his axe towards Nestor's chest, connecting superficially. Nestor paused and doubled forward, losing his balance.

"Greek pig," Bessus spit out. "That shield, those eyes. Finally, I have revenge." Bessus raised his axe to administer a killing blow, but stopped short when a man in a Persian robe burst into the barn and hurled a spear with a broken shaft at him. It stuck in his bull-hide armor before falling away.

"Lauren!" Zack shouted. "Take Cassandra and run."

"My God, Zack!"

"Zack, watch out!" Nestor shouted.

Bessus swung at Zack, missing. Zack danced backwards, tripped and rammed into the wall of the house.

The barbarian, having compromised Zack's charge, turned his attention back to Nestor. Just as Nestor found his feet and readied his shield, Bessus drove his axe deep into the man's shoulder. Nestor groaned, grabbing at the axe head before toppling over. Bessus put his foot on Nestor's shoulder and yanked out the weapon.

He turned to Lauren, seething. "Now, more scores to settle."

Cassandra screamed incessantly at the horror unfolding before her. Lauren held the girl with one hand and the club with the other.

Nestor's legs scissor-kicked. He gagged and rolled over on his stomach. His tremors diminished. Life leaked away in silence. He reached his hand towards his niece.

"Cassandra," Lauren said sharply, "get behind me."

The women ran towards Zack as he tried to fend off Bessus. The blade of the barbarian's axe sliced through the front of Zack's robe and wedged into the house. While Bessus tried to wrench his axe from the wall, Zack caught him on the cheek with a roundhouse punch.

Bessus roared with the impact, his flesh already shredded by Persephone's fingernails. "The Mumbler," he cursed.

He seized the fabric of Zack's robe, raising his axe to finish him…

A loud shout. The snap of thunder.

Bessus turned his head. An overwhelming sound seemed to echo from everywhere at once. Lauren leapt at Bessus, clubbing him with her firewood hammer. He rocked backwards, stunned, and released Zack's robe. "Ahhh, *Jadogaaar*," he growled, staggering towards her.

Taking advantage of Bessus's momentary impairment, Zack pulled Lauren and Cassandra through the back door into the farmhouse. They sprinted to the front door, toppling chairs behind them.

"I can't leave my uncle!" Cassandra shouted.

Zack forced open the front door. "You can't help him. Run!"

They raced up the hill toward the temples.

Bessus kicked aside the obstacles. Hauling his enormous weapon of death, he barked, "I'll carve you up."

The road's incline steepened. Bessus strained to fill his lungs. When his shouting ceased, he heard only his own heaving breaths.

"Where were you?" Lauren asked Zack, gripping Cassandra's other hand.

"Athens," he wheezed. "You?"

"I escaped… from… him. Went to Mycenae and Sparta… God, I can't breathe. What the hell was that noise?"

He shook his head.

"Thank you…Zack."

He turned his head quickly towards her to acknowledge what she said. "Don't talk. Go faster." Adrenalin overwhelmed their fatigue.

However, Bessus gobbled the distance with his long strides, steadily gaining on them. Zack, Lauren, and Cassandra neared the temple entrance, which they identified by a torch and a lone guard at the post. "Help us!" Lauren shouted.

The startled hoplite readied his spear as he peered into the darkness. When the group ran into the torchlight, he held up his shield to block their entry. "A barbarian follows us," Lauren said quickly.

"What? Where?" The hoplite looked past them into the darkness.

"Out of the way!" Zack knocked the hoplite into the wall. Angry, the guard jumped up, searching for the spear he had dropped. Then, out of the darkness, the huge barbarian closed in, the axe raised above his head. The hoplite lifted his shield defensively, only to have it smacked aside. A second blow severed his head.

Cassandra shrieked, covering her eyes. Zack yanked her away. They ran into the complex, suddenly shrouded with mist, and up the stone-paved Sacred Way, lined with marble statues. When Cassandra tired along the steep switchbacks, Zack swung her onto his shoulder.

"Where can we go?" Lauren asked, desperate.

"To the rooms we came out of… trust me," Zack said.

"We need help. Where… is everyone?"

Zack glanced through the torch-lit mist and saw Bessus in steady pursuit, twenty yards behind. Lauren screamed for temple guards. They heard voices, but far off.

"Don't have the strength… can't stop him… wounded." Zack's face betrayed his agony. He pointed. "To the temple door… ahead of us."

Cassandra's extra weight sapped his strength. The pain made him want to lie down.

Inside the temple doors, Lauren ripped a torch from the wall. "Heeeeeeelp!"

Bessus lurched to the entrance, only to watch his quarry rush down a stairway. He ignored the priestesses cowering in the corner, and caressed the toe-bone totem to protect himself against the Greeks' evil gods. He hurtled down the stairs two or three at a time, dodging a statue at the bottom, only to smack his knee on a stone. He stopped abruptly, groaning, rubbing his leg, and loathing the shadows and nearness of walls that always panicked him. He closed his eyes, fell to his knees while holding the totem forward, and said a quick prayer to his grandfather's mountain thunder gods. His head cleared. Hearing voices down a corridor, his wind restored, he sprinted towards the torchlight.

"He's still behind us," Lauren coughed, black torch smoke in her face. They ran into the room toward the trap door. Zack shut the room door and put all his weight against it. Lauren pulled on the metal ring, opened the hatch and tossed the torch into the passageway below. She climbed halfway down the ladder and guided Cassandra towards her. Zack braced himself against the door.

Bessus slammed into it. The door held.

Once Cassandra was down the hatch, Zack timed Bessus' next charge. He swung off his backpack, threw it down the hole and followed it. Pausing on the wooden rungs of the ladder, he dropped the remaining eight feet.

The door exploded open. Bessus caught a glimpse of Zack's head before it disappeared into the darkness. He dropped his axe next to the trapdoor and laid his helmet aside before jumping inside. As he landed, he saw the group running to yet another door. Be bolted toward his enemies, cursing himself for leaving his axe above.

Zack and Lauren pushed on the door that had been left wedged open until all three squeezed through the narrow opening. "Shut the door. Quick!" Lauren yelled.

The hinges groaned, but Bessus shoved his boot between the door and the jamb.

"Can we call the tunnel we came through?" Lauren hollered, her feet fighting for purchase.

She glanced at Zack's face and gasped. He looked like he hadn't slept in a hundred years.

"God, what was that phrase?" The words came to her in a flood. "'Don't violate Apollo's temple or you will suffer the disembodiment of the gods.'" She clenched her teeth, waiting for the tunnel to take them away.

"Keep pushing, forget that damned phrase. The son of a bitch has the key."

"What?"

"The medallion!" Zack grimaced. "The medallion...with the archer... around his neck... it calls the tunnel."

At the other end of the room, Cassandra wept. "Help us, Athena. Help us, Athena," she prayed.

Bessus wedged his thigh and shoulder into the breach. Lauren stomped on his foot. "Ahhh, you will all die!" he screamed.

A humming sound drowned out his voice. Cassandra stopped her prayers. Terrified, she covered her ears when the walls began to vibrate around them.

"You need the medallion to travel between times," Zack explained. "Apollo gave it to me. Take Cassandra and go."

"What are you raving about? I won't leave you here because of some blasted archer's medal." They were slowly losing the battle.

"Apollo, the Greek god, he exists."

"What?'

"Trust me. I didn't believe it was possible, either."

Bessus worked his body into the door's opening. Lauren drove her heel into Bessus' knee. He growled and puffed his cheeks, but kept his hold.

"What the hell are you talking about?" Lauren screamed.

The room went cold.

With his eyes half shut, Zack said, "Apollo, we're... there's something planned for us, Lauren. Think about it."

"I have been. But how does this nightmare keep showing up?"

"This bastard stole the medallion from me. I couldn't kill him back there...so I had to lure him... here. I have so much to tell you... there's no time."

"Let's get rid of this guy first."

Lauren extended her arms, wedged her heels sideways, and pushed against the door.

"I realized that when you were gone… that I couldn't live without you."

"Zack… it's okay."

Bessus heaved.

"It's always been about me… but now it's going to be about you," Zack said, his cheek scrunched against the door. "It may take a lifetime, but will you find a way to forgive me?"

"I already have."

Bessus wrapped his arm around the inside edge of the door. "I'll kill you myself!" Lauren hollered, pounding on the barbarian's elbow with her fist.

"Take Cassandra and go. I'm sorry, for everything." His strength ebbed.

"No, sweetheart, I can't leave you." Her face bore the agony of a decision that she had to make, could not make… but must.

"I love you. Don't ever forget me, please." His face contorted. "I can't… hold him off… much longer."

Zack set his heels into a gap between stones. He summoned his last measure of strength to hold back the barbarian. "Go… before he gets in here."

"Oh, I love you." Lauren kissed his lips, hard. "Follow me right away, please."

"I am the instrument of your death, whore," Bessus hissed.

His blackened nails reached out for Lauren. She released her weight from the door, turned, and cried out as if leaving life itself.

The back wall of the room melted into a spinning centrifuge of dense black mud, emanating from the dark marble slab. It curled and spun, seeking them out. Cassandra stared at it, shivering. "Hold your breath and don't let go of me!" Lauren shouted over the din.

Zack's strength buckled, and Bessus forced open the door. Cassandra saw the monster behind her and screamed. She fought Lauren's guiding hands. Thunder shook dirt from the ceiling. The dark column in the corner glowed red.

Bessus powered into the room. Zack punched him squarely on his ripped nose. He howled, but recovered quickly when he saw the sorceress escaping with the girl. Bessus crashed his shoulder into Zack, cracking the Mumbler's teeth together and slamming him into the wall. Zack collapsed like a felled prizefighter.

"Witch, you will not evade me! I'm your destiny."

Bessus charged after his prize. He leapt, straining to grasp her garment. His long nails raked the fabric, but a brilliant flash of light snatched her and the girl away.

Enraged, Bessus muttered a fast prayer to the Mainyu while preparing to jump. The mud cleared briefly. Magically, he saw his own face and what he knew was behind him: the door and the 'Mumbler'. He cast away the confusing sights. He reset his haunches and leaped into the mud after the witch. "*Ja-doo-garrrrr…*"

They disappeared into the tunnel. Zack crawled toward the mud wall, digging his fingers into gaps in the stone floor, reaching and pulling, an all-out final effort. When he drew near, the mass thickened and the swirling slowed. "Laurennnn!" he screamed, a long, low moan of despair.

The tunnel transformed into an impenetrable wall of rock.

Zack felt entombed by the darkness and silence. The pain of his injuries confirmed he had not died, but he had failed the person he most loved in this world, or any other. Now he wished for death's deliverance.

CHAPTER 47
DELPHI, GREECE
TRANSITION

The vortex propelled their tumbling bodies. Cassandra gagged and thrashed, nearly separating herself from Lauren's determined grip when jolted by the same "bump" Zack and Lauren encountered when they were first swallowed up. For Lauren, it seemed like lifetimes ago.

Lightning flashes penetrated their closed eyes as the thunder roared to deafening heights. Cassandra dug her fingernails into Lauren's wrists. Her fingers went limp as the passage spit them onto a stone floor amidst a mess of transit afterbirth.

They both gasped for air. Cassandra's chest heaved. Lauren recovered more quickly, crawled over and shook her shoulders. "Cassandra, talk to me."

Cassandra swiped at the sludge in her eyes. "Freezing... hurts everywhere." Lauren caressed her gently, conscious of her pain. "We're in grave danger. Can you walk?"

She gave Lauren a helpless look. "Don't know."

"Try. That monster's right behind us."

Cassandra whimpered, but rose to her feet.

The chamber wall had not solidified. "The tunnel is still alive. We must leave."

She led Cassandra past the debris blocking the portal. As they approached the staircase, lightning illuminated the broken column canted against the rock wall, the same column with the carved warning against trespassing against the temple of Apollo.

"Oh thank God, we're back," Lauren said, sizing up the steep staircase. The rumbling continued. As she climbed the steps, she realized the hole had opened above them. Swift-moving clouds raced overhead. "Cassandra, you have to help me. I'm going to lift you up and then you have to pull yourself over the lip of the hole."

Cassandra dug her fingers into the hard soil above the rim. Lauren pushed her over the top, grabbed a long tree root, and pulled herself out. Behind her, the tunnel continued to roil.

In her haste to escape, Lauren didn't notice her own backpack squished into the corner of the landing. She began to panic. "Cassandra, you have to walk. Please."

They staggered arm-in-arm, gradually gaining balance, negotiating the steep terraces until they reached the temples. "It's unbelievable. These ruins were intact only a few minutes ago," Lauren said in English.

As Cassandra gave her a blank look, Lauren shook her head. *How am I ever going to explain this to her?*

They reached the glass doors of the museum, only to find them locked. A light bulb illuminated their images, frightening Cassandra. "Athena!" She pressed her cheek against Lauren's sodden chiton.

"Stay calm."

Cassandra nodded, but did not lift her head.

"We need to keep moving." Lauren guided her along the remains of the Sacred Way, over the gated entrance and down to the round temple of Athena.

"What's happened to the temples?" Cassandra asked. "The statues are gone."

Despite nightfall, they could easily see they were beneath the twin peaks of Delphi. Cassandra gripped Lauren's arm, her face a sea of confused expressions. "This is my mountain, but where is our farm? What is that building over there?" Her questions ran together, spoken so quickly, so desperately.

Lauren embraced the sobbing girl. "I've a lot to tell you, but this isn't the time or place. Everything around us will shock and surprise you, but don't worry. I'll always take care of you. Right now, we are in great danger if the barbarian made the transition with us into this… world. For now, I need you to trust me."

"Will Zack follow us?"

"God, I hope so." Lauren buried her face in Cassandra's matted hair. She surrendered briefly to her overwhelming anxiety, but then caught herself. She squared her shoulders. "We have to hide."

She peered into the darkness. A lone car whizzed past them and stopped next to the museum. She wondered if they could run to the car and escape with the driver. However, they were too far away to see who got out of the car, and doubted anyone could help them, unless they had a gun. Maybe they could make a dash to Delphi, a kilometer or two away, and find the police station. If Bessus was behind them, he might be exiting the tunnel this moment.

Cassandra swiped at her wet cheeks and straightened her slender shoulders, unconsciously imitating Lauren. "I know where we can hide."

CHAPTER 48
DELPHI, GREECE
OCTOBER 2011

DETECTIVE WORK

Professor Papandreou had not slept well for nearly a week. Perplexed by the video of Zack and Lauren, he theorized to distraction on what had happened to them, but could summon no logical solution for their mysterious disappearance. He decided he would explore the area around the temples, but under cover of night. Alone.

Now. He laced his tennis shoes, walked to his garage and located a flashlight and shovel, all the while speculating his prized students had discovered something significant. He threw a pair of thick garden gloves into the back seat with the other tools, and glanced at the clock. One a.m.

With no traffic in Athens to impede him, he drove his black Renault up the mountain pass and entered the museum parking lot at four a.m. He parked the car and gathered his equipment.

He climbed over the fence with some difficulty, ripping his shirt in the process. He walked between the buildings and up the Sacred Way, stopping to catch his breath, following the steeply graded path Demo had showed him earlier. He turned on his flashlight, working past the uneven ground. Raindrops splattered him.

The gods must be angry tonight. The TV said nothing about rain.

Thunder reverberated, punctuating his observation. He arrived at the depression in the ground and leaned over to catch his breath. He saw the same large hole as depicted on the video. Unbelievable. He shined his light into it, brightening the landing and stairway.

"Saint Stephen," he exclaimed, "There it is! What caused it to open up?"

Flashes from the cavern depths forced him to cover his eyes. Extending his flashlight, he carefully lowered himself onto the landing and descended the staircase. At the bottom, he saw a broken column with ancient Greek text carved into the stone. He rubbed his fingers over the dirt-encrusted letters: "Do not trespass the Temple of Apollo," he read aloud, "or you will suffer the disembodiment of the gods."

The professor studied the artifact from every angle, imagining how it looked in its original form.

Crashing rocks, diminishing thunder, and a gagging person caught his attention. He frowned, trying to discern the location and identity of the struggling tourist. Or... "Who's there? Zack, Lauren, is that you?"

Thunder overcame his call, bringing thick rainwater with it. A sudden sense of dread, *deisdaeomoneia,* swept over him. He ran up the stairs frantically, paused at the top, and turned the flashlight into the darkness.

He froze. A filth-encrusted maniac charged up the stairs.

"Who are you?" The professor dodged obstacles littering the floor of the landing while reaching for the rim of the hole. He pulled himself up by a tree root, a surge of adrenalin fueling his efforts. The maniac grabbed his ankle with a steely grip. The professor fell and lost his flashlight while clutching handfuls of dirt. "Release me!"

Bessus lifted himself out of the hole while holding the spindly professor's leg. He straddled him and wrapped his meaty hands around the man's throat. The professor fought back, punching Bessus' face. He flailed and gasped, jerking at the medallion's cord for advantage. Ignoring the weakling's desperate attempts to get away, Bessus squeezed, twisted, and snapped his neck.

He failed to notice the medallion within the man's grip.

Bessus rose from the slain man to search for the witch. The night sky cleared, thunder and lightning halted, and stars appeared overhead. Light from an iron cylinder the old man had carried sent a beam of light into the night. He poked at it with a stick, causing it to roll slightly. Then he touched it with his finger. There was no burning. The casing felt cool.

He picked it up. "What sorcery? Where's the bitch?" He held the flashlight. "By the Mainyu, what place is this?"

He shined the light on a building, a long stone's throw away. His gaze followed the beam over steep ground until it rested on the ruins of a temple. Unsure of his location, and wondering if he suffered from a spell, he walked back to the corpse. He stopped suddenly, watching the hole slowly shrink before his eyes.

Bessus stumbled in circles, his hands extended before him to repel phantoms. He was without his axe. And his toe-bones charm. Defenseless. "You witch!" he screamed.

He headed to the distant temples, shivering under the onslaught of the wind and a growing sense of dread. He passed empty pedestals and broken walls.

Finally, he reached the end of the path and turned to look behind him. "Mainyu, I'm cursed. This sorceress has powers I've not seen before."

Bessus stood at the entrance to a large building made of rock and timber. He jumped backwards when he saw a warrior coming towards him, copying his movements.

"You mock me?" he shouted at the warrior. Then he realized he saw an image of himself, cast back by a pool of water. The light bulb above his head gave off meager light. He turned his attention to it. "What manner of sorcery is this, a torch that lives within a ball?"

He rapped the bulb with the flashlight. It shattered, spilling hot shards of glass upon his head and shoulders. He fled down the hill.

She's set a spell upon me. My mother, this witch, all women are a plague. How did she defeat me?

Bessus found a hiding place in the wooded area around the temple. He sat on his haunches, fearing the malice of unseen enemies, humbled and angry by turns. He cursed the witch who had banished him from his world and replaced it with her own. *If this is her realm, how will I return home?*

"Mainyu," he begged aloud. "Deliver me. Send me back. My son needs me."

He withdrew the small square full of colors and Greek lettering from his waist-pouch, seeking its protection somehow from the evil the witch had sent his way. Her dirty smile on the square mocked him, even in the dim light. "This is your doing, witch. I have only to find you."

As the stars crept across the sky, he vowed to render unto her the most painful of deaths.

CHAPTER 49
DELPHI, GREECE
SEPTEMBER 2011

CAVE DWELLERS

Overgrown brush obstructed the moonlight and heightened the difficulty of remaining on the trail. Lauren followed Cassandra through the foliage. Pausing often, Cassandra complained, "These trees shouldn't be here. Athena's temple is in ruins. The trail's blocked, but we must go this way, I know it."

Lauren had been along the trail a few times, most recently on an oxen-driven wagon, circa 480 BCE, half a day ago. "Cassandra, this is futile."

"The entrance is somewhere in there."

After nearly an hour in the dark, they reached a spot far from the main road along the steep ridge, almost directly across and down from the museum. Cassandra dropped to her knees, sifting through the low foliage under the trees. She reached out to the face of the rock wall, moving her hands along it finding a small hollow. "I found it!"

Cassandra's family had constructed a blind to cover the entrance. It appeared to be a continuation of the dense surrounding of shrubs, built of four solid lengths of timber, reinforced with thin iron planks nailed into a square five feet long and four feet high. Lightly thatched branches and sticks created a screen, housing embedded leaves and clumps of moss. The structure she knew had long since deteriorated, but overgrowth on the hill and in front offered sufficient camouflage.

Cassandra chewed on her finger. "There are rocks in front of the entrance," she said.

Lauren helped pull away branches and sticks, and then worked on what appeared to be carefully set rocks. Together, they shifted the heavier stones until they revealed the cave's entrance.

Lauren entered first. She swiped at cobwebs, real and imagined. She recalled that the ceiling clearance was only five feet high; she couldn't stand. "I really hate places like this," she said. "How are we ever going to be able to see anything?"

"Don't worry, I can find my way."

When they reached the end of the portal, Lauren stopped. "We've reached the cave."

Cassandra crept past her, into the pitch black ahead. "What are you doing?" Lauren asked.

She heard rustling sounds. Suddenly, their immediate surroundings were illuminated. "My God," Lauren gasped.

Cassandra grinned broadly as she held aloft Zack's lighter. "I am the keeper of the light, am I not? I sewed it into a pocket in my clothing."

"Oh, sweetheart, you are something special." She put her arm around Cassandra, laughing at the relief from the simple gift of light. "Quickly, we need to light a torch or something."

"I know where one is."

Cassandra walked carefully to the opposite side and lifted the clay cover from a four-foot tall terra cotta jar. She dug her fingers into a layer of hardened wax. Scraping it aside, she withdrew a wooden handle with wrapped bristles, the tops covered in a black pitch. Cassandra held the lighter to the torch; slowly, it caught fire.

She handed it to Lauren. The light illuminated bigger jars set to the side. Thick cobwebs obstructed their view of the rest of the cave. Lauren held the torch to a small copse of webs, which promptly crackled and smoked into flames. They dove to the floor.

"Crap, I won't do that again," she said.

Cassandra ignited another torch and carefully set it into a sconce on the cave wall.

"How many torches do we have, Cassandra?"

She pointed. "That pot holds many."

"They won't last long, and we can only use a few. We might be here awhile."

"The rams' wool for the beds will be in those covered *pithos*." Cassandra pointed to enormous clay pots set into a corner near the entrance. "Those others will hold water and wine."

"Well, we can't drink it, probably can't even wash with it. If there was a cave bear in here, we'd scare the hell out of him the way we look."

"What is 'the hell', Lauren?"

"A place like Hades."

"Oh, the cave bear would be so badly frightened by us, it would die?"

"Yes."

Cassandra giggled. "Then we must cleanse ourselves."

"Are there any clothes for us to change into?"

"My mother always kept clothing in one of these. My mother..." Her voice trailed off. She began to whimper.

"Sweetheart, I understand. There will be time for mourning. Here, hold onto me." Lauren embraced the girl, wondering how she would be able to cope with the violent death of her family, no less the time change. "Let's get cleaned up. Then we can talk."

Lauren opened the first jar. Despite the wax seal, the clothing fell apart in dusty shreds. They scrubbed away the tunnel mud from their bodies with their hands as best they could. "I wish we had some soap."

"Are you speaking Atlantean again?"

"Yes. Sorry. We'll have to sleep on the floor." Lauren noticed that the smoke exited through an escape route. "There must be vents up there, or this cave would be full of smoke."

"This is so," Cassandra replied. "We have cooked in here before, and we once stayed for seven nights. There are holes above us to vent the vapors. Farther in, there are pathways and a small stream. The water tastes of metal; my uncle warned us against drinking it. There is also an odd smell deep within Mother Earth, the decaying fumes of the Python Apollo killed when he came to this place. We were told not to venture there for fear of madness or death."

"Even though we've had a difficult night, there's something you need to know."

"I am not so tired now, only hungry and thirsty."

"We'll have to wait for food and water until tomorrow. Tonight we must talk." Lauren moistened her lips, and pressed her palms together. "What I am going to tell you will be difficult to believe, but it's the truth. I cannot explain everything, because some things I don't understand myself."

Cassandra looked at her. The torchlight flickered off her large, intelligent eyes.

"Do you remember when you first saw Zack and me?"

"Yes, you were all covered in mud. You had just been through what we have just left." Her face grew ashen, as her sudden realization of what was now real was far different from anything she had imagined. "Then, you are not from Atlantea?"

Lauren said, "Yes we are, but it's not… Look, what you experienced with me in the tunnel was a journey. Not quite like going from here to Athens, but a journey through time."

Cassandra's face displayed her confusion.

"Remember when we ran through the temple area before we went on the journey, the buildings were intact and painted? You saw the condition of the temples, even though it was dark. The next time we made our way through the same area, everything looked quite different, didn't it?"

Cassandra nodded. "Temples were broken, and some strange buildings were present. And I could see into them."

"How high can you count?"

"Nestor taught me to count to one thousand. He was a builder, so he believed that one should be very exact when using numbers."

"Sweetheart, think of the tunnel as a chariot that takes you from your days to days far ahead, days that have yet to occur. We are now over two times your thousand years into the future."

"Athena!" she exclaimed in wonderment. Her mouth fell open. The realization of Lauren's words began to sink in. "If this is true, it is the work of the gods. Are my parents dead? Can they be brought back from Hades?"

"No, I'm sorry. In this time, they are long dead. The barbarian killed them, and he pursues us as well. I also don't know if there is a large difference in the time in which he or Zack might appear, even if they departed shortly after us." She raked clumps of mud from Cassandra's hair. "The barbarian is evil. Your family and Zack fought to save us. We owe them our lives."

They wept for the loss of the three people they held most dear, consolation that held the promise of appeasing their shared anguish.

After a long while, they dried their eyes. "So, we are agreed…we must be brave."

"Why did the gods send us here?" Cassandra asked. "To be punished? Did we not sacrifice properly?"

"Cassandra, you'll soon learn that this time is both as wondrous and terrible as your own. We have inventions that will astound you, like the fire stick. While there are countless spectacular inventions, some aspects of life never change. Even now, in my time, we have killing and wars, starvation and illness."

"I'm glad I'm with you, lady. What will we do?"

"I need to think. We are safe here. For now." *But for how long without food and water?*

Lauren explored the corners and extensions of their new home, the lighter revealing more hidden *pithos* in veins that branched from the main cabin. In a larger antechamber, she found a small temple with a miniature replica of Athena sitting on the Acropolis, rusted bronze candle stands on each side. Cassandra dashed to the statue and knelt before it. "Lady, I implore you, assist us in our hour of need. Deliver us from the rage of the barbarian."

Lauren searched the rest of the cave. She let out a distressed gasp. Her hand covered her mouth.

Cassandra ran to her. "What torments you so?"

Lauren stood transfixed as she stared at a flattened outcropping of rock. Holding her breath, she crept forward. The object of her terror: an earthen pot with her name carved into the surface in big letters, outlined with faded red paint, and set into a recess. She trembled violently from her core, through her arms, into her hands. With the pot shaking in her hands, she struggled to loosen the tight-fitting cover. She struck the cap with a rock, shattering the hardened clay seal, and dug her nails into a deep layer of wax. She withdrew a thick plastic freezer bag. Within, its ghostly contents: Zack's ball cap, folded papyrus, and a yellowed small spiral notebook encased in more plastic and wrapped in leather. The bag tumbled from her nerveless fingers, falling slowly to the cave floor. She dropped to her knees, lost her balance, and fell backwards. She drove herself further back in an attempt to escape from the contents… and a realization. She covered her face, sobbing in despair. "Oh…God…no…no…no! He didn't make it!"

She split into two separate selves. One, inconsolable, was embraced by a child; the other, detached, listening to a woman wailing hideously within the cave.

Something shifted painfully within her body; her heart was shattering.

She tentatively approached the package and fumbled with the zip lock. Frustrated, she tore at it with her teeth until the contents fell out. She separated the notebook from a wad of folded papyrus that bore more of his writing: "My Journeys in the Ancient World".

"Oh my god!" she cried. "I can't believe what I'm reading!"

Finally, she flipped open the cover.

Dear Lauren,

If you have found this package then I am overjoyed that you are safe. My celebration is tempered with the realization that we have no idea when we will be reunited. I can only hope that Cassandra is with you as well.

Lauren paused. "It's from Zack, sweetheart. He writes to us from the past, from your time." Hungry for him, she savored each line.

My whole being aches at the prospect of a life without you. I only survive with the knowledge that my heart still rests in your hands. Not knowing how you fare haunts my days and nights to the point of delirium. The frustration of it all has me hammering walls and crying out your name. If I could be with you, I would tell you over and over again that I love you.

I took too many chances with our life together and for that, I might be eternally sorry.

We had so little time to tell each other what had happened. I realize you must have overcome a great deal to survive the barbarian's attacks. You are not a woman to be underestimated. I have always admired that about you.

There is something very important I must tell you. I pray it will lead to our reunion. When I regained consciousness at the bottom of that ravine, I sewed my shoulder back together. The antibiotics, needle and thread saved me from amputation. I will never make fun of your packing routine again.

She half-choked and laughed simultaneously.

I followed Persian cavalry, sinking to despair when I discovered your orange top floating in a pond, but I continued to search for you. Desperately in need of water and rest, I finally collapsed in the heat.

I met a farmer, who gave me something to eat and drink, but this wasn't cookies and lemonade. The drink made me dizzy, and I felt as if I were levitating out of my body, but later I realized I had tasted this drink before. It was that honey taste, I now recall back at our house and at that café in Athens. The farmer said he was Apollo, Lauren. He knew we had gone through his temple, and he called me a traveler. I think we know what that means. He said if I desired to return to you, I must earn the right by overcoming trials.

She gasped, covering her mouth with her hand while reading on.

At first, I was not certain that what had happened was real. When I came to my senses, that bronze medallion you saw on that barbarian was hanging from my neck. The barbarian stole that medallion from me, as I lay wounded after the attack on Athens. I had hoped the guards at Delphi would kill him while he chased us, and then we would be free to leave together. When that failed, I figured it was best to get to the room and take our chances. He followed you into the tunnel wearing the medallion. His name is Bessus. Stay away from him, Lauren. He is more than dangerous; he is evil. I will deal with him, in my own way. I will make him pay for what he did to us.

I know I am to blame for much of what happened, but Apollo is responsible, too. He knew about you. He set us up, as early as San Diego. He was the waiter in the Plaka café. He has some plan in mind for us.

"This can't be possible," Lauren said grimly.

"What? I beg you," Cassandra pled.

"Zack says Apollo is responsible for our troubles."

"Of course he is. Is this not his temple? My uncle said never to offend the gods."

The letter shook in her hands.

Despite the chasm of time separating us, you are still with me. I see your face in all my waking moments. The scent of your perfume stills lingers in my senses, and it simultaneously comforts me and drives me crazy. I told you when I proposed to you that my love for you would be timeless. I never imagined that our lives would play out this way. The paradox of our situation has me humbled and on my knees wishing it were not so. I do not know what fate or the future holds for either of us, but I will spend the rest of my life trying to return to you. If Cassandra is with you, then she is ours. It has taken all of this to make me understand what it means to want and love a child.

Her tears splashed onto the page, the ink smudged and dried long ago with Zack's own tears. The two tears blended, as though to symbolize a treasured connection between their hearts. The man she thought would be by her side forever existed now in an ancient realm beyond her reach.

It has been a week, and I'm leaving for Salamis. It's mid-September, and the battle is imminent. You know I have to see it.

She paused, tears blurring her vision once more. "Please, don't go near the fighting."

Now I have a surprise for both of you. Ask Cassandra to take you to her favorite spot in the cave, and dig there in the center. Only she will know the location. There are treasures there you will not believe. If she is not with you, then we have no claim on what is there anyway.

I am ready to embrace my long appointment with solitude and regret. Never forget, Lauren, that I love you and I always will. I will not stop until I can find a way back to you.

Love,

Your husband forever,

Zack

"What does Master Zack write?" Cassandra finally asked.

Lauren took a deep breath, struggling to regain her composure. "He says he misses you and that I am to follow you to your favorite place in the cave. There is a surprise for us there."

"Athena!" Cassandra leaped to her feet. She ignited a new torch with her fire stick. "We must go." She pulled Lauren her to her feet. "Now, I beg you."

Lauren carefully resealed the notebook and clasped it to her chest, feeling her heart beat against it. "We'll fight to get back to you too, Zack."

Cassandra dropped to her knees and scooted through a hole in the cave wall, holding the torch in front of her. The glow of her torch quickly receded into the darkness beyond the opening. Lauren placed the packet into the jar, and pushed it deeper into the rock shelf.

Careful not to bang her head on the jagged opening, she crawled after Cassandra. "Wait for me, young lady!"

With one foot in the hole, she heard rustling in the bushes outside the cave. Terror carved through her guts.

CHAPTER 50
DELPHI, GREECE
SEPTEMBER 480 BCE

ZACK

Would death bring forgiveness? Could it erase the memory of the mistakes he had made? In the end, it wasn't fate or choice that drove him to this final disaster. He had been manipulated, big time.

He wanted to die, just let go, right here and now. A bitter chill below the stone floor suggested death would come quickly. Everything hurt. What he yearned for, more than deliverance from pain, was to return to the infinite calm of unconsciousness. There would be no self-assessment of his blunders there, or any more guilt to endure.

The nightmarish events replayed in his mind: the desperate farmhouse fight, and their escape up the hill with Bessus in pursuit, hauling his axe. Then, his own unbearable fatigue that hindered their escape and Cassandra's weight on his back, draining the last of his resolve.

Lauren and Cassandra were gone, separated from him by a chasm of over a hundred generations. The wall had solidified. He could only hope they'd escaped Bessus by a variance in the time or place of their transfer through the "passage." Where were they? How did they fare? He had no idea.

Their faces came to him. He cried out at deaf walls.

The bronze medallion hung around the neck of the barbarian, who probably had no idea of the power it held. He could still smell the dank ozone vapor remaining from the transit. There was no light, dripping water, or faraway voices. Only the wheezing of his breath, struggling through his beaten ribs.

Then he remembered Nestor and Persephone, slaughtered at the farmhouse. He heard again the horrible swish and smack of Bessus' double-bladed axe.

That was reason enough to get up. He would not go to his grave until Bessus paid for the ruin he set upon all of them.

His blood-crusted cheek stuck to the cold, subterranean stone floor. He tore his cheek open rising to his knees. He crawled in complete darkness to wooden clothing pegs set into a wall. Grasping them, he pulled himself up, but teetered when his legs couldn't hold him. His backpack felt like it had boulders inside. He braced himself against the wall until his head cleared. Opening the massive bronze and wood door, built to shut by its own weight, would take his last measure of energy.

He found the pocketknife in his backpack, stepped over the thick plank that braced the door from the inside, and set to work. When he tried to wedge the blade in the crack, the door moved towards him, by itself. He fell, swearing aloud, then backed away. There was no mechanism; the door opened from brute strength alone.

Nowhere to run. He waited.

With his back against a wall, he could swing blindly at whatever came through the doorway. At least he would go down fighting.

Golden lights appeared, set apart like eyeballs. They approached him, increasing in brightness. Zack put his hands up.

The searchlights abruptly shut off. Quiet ensued until he heard a guitar, or something like it, playing random chords that coalesced into a song. One he had heard before.

Here Comes the Sun King. Again. "Is it you, Apollo?" Zack asked.

"You're quite the paradox," the baritone voice answered.

Zack registered the precisely delivered syntax. The accent wasn't European. He waited in the dark, tense and confounded. "Apollo?"

"You have faced the realization of your own mortality. How did it feel to resign yourself to death?"

"What do you want from me?"

"Easily asked, but more difficult to answer you in one long breath of words."

"Stop talking in circles!" Zack grimaced, his rising voice bringing agony from his damaged rib cage.

"I ask you to put aside your discomfort, forget your troubles for the moment and listen."

Zack rolled on his side, gripping his ribs. "Lauren's in danger. That freaking monster has your medallion. He's after her."

"Listen, pedagogue. Leave your self-awarded pedestal and absorb what I'm about to tell you."

Golden beacons shot out from Apollo's eyes. The room lit up. Calchas, the muscular waiter from the café with the slicked-back dark hair, gold chains and leather straps hanging from his neck, stood before him.

"But…"

"You continue to underestimate me."

He walked towards Zack, sporting a smug grin. He rolled a bronze flask toward Zack. "Took a drink from it on the road just beneath the farm, didn't you?"

"I knew it was you."

Apollo pulled a small lyre from a leather satchel. He sat on the floor. A strange, subdued glow emanated from him. "I take it you enjoyed the beer while languishing in your home?"

"Why you lousy…"

Zack leaped at Apollo, fingers claw-like, bloodlust in his eyes. Apollo plucked a single high note, and Zack struck a pulsating field that surrounded the god, its sharp current burning and repulsing him violently. He collapsed on the stone floor before Apollo, groaning.

"You never used to lose your temper. What's changed you?"

Zack scrunched into a fetal position, eyes squeezed shut and teeth clenched, unable to utter a word.

"Will you react with such discomfort when I tell what will be, Traveler? Will you roll and wail when you find that your world is coming to an end?"

Zack drew shallow breaths, almost panting. *What did he just say?*

Apollo raised his voice. "You heard me. Yes, I can read your thoughts as well. I could form your thoughts if I wanted to. Waste no more of my precious time." He withdrew another flask from the satchel. "Partake. You will be restored, just as the hole in your mouth closed quickly at home and your vitality was enhanced on the road to Athens."

Zack drank from the flask. He felt rejuvenated from the moment it passed his lips. He sat up. "What do you want from me?"

"Are all mortals from your time so daft? I have told you before that you will assist me in my endeavors or I will leave you to perish right here and employ another. You must save your own world. I will not do it all for you."

He said he had a plan for me on that road.

"Behold!"

From Apollo's medallion, a moving picture of blackened corpses and burning cities in ruin appeared on the wall of the room. *Cinema?* The newsroom images flashed before him: warnings, financial collapse, electronic warfare, meetings between dignitaries, riots, attacks on embassies and military bases.

"Christ," Zack said, aghast. He looked at Apollo; tears streamed down his face.

My nightmare.

"Those are your people, your countrymen. Have you ever been frightened to speak your mind? Have you ever had a boot at your neck with the order to submit?" Apollo pointed his manicured index finger at him. "Will you fight for this fragile concept of free citizens brought back to Western culture from the time of the Athenians?"

"I want to fight back," Zack said with renewed vigor.

"Finally." Apollo strode over to Zack, seized his tunic violently, and drew his face close. "You must release your fear of death, just as Leonidas and his Spartans did. Did you think I sent you there for academic curiosity?"

"What do I have to do?"

"You'll not have a university chair to pontificate from. You'll live and breathe misery. You will struggle and you will most likely die trying, Traveler, but you will save others. Mortals do not learn lessons easily. They must struggle and suffer to understand."

"If I can save Lauren and see her again, I'll do whatever you want."

"Serve me, and you will serve them and yourself. You alone have the ability to stop an attack, Traveler, one that will shake the foundations of the West. Seek out the antiques dealer you met at the museum fundraiser."

He had a business. "Cyprus," the card said. Limassol Antiquities…
Saabir something was his name.

"You must stop him, and I will consider your reunion."

Zack looked in Apollo's eyes. "You mean, kill him?"

Apollo nodded. "Do what is necessary." He laughed heartily. "You
are amusing, Traveler. Just do not disappoint me."

Apollo removed the bronze medallion from his neck and held it up.
Zack heard rumbling. He knew what the sound meant. "Why rely on me?"
he asked. "Kill him yourself, and be assured your plan will succeed."

Behind Zack, the wall liquefied. The mud churned, reaching for
them.

"Heroes do the work of the gods," Apollo said. "Solve it
yourselves. or you will not learn and will sadly repeat your ignorant,
arrogant ways."

Almost effortlessly, he lifted Zack up and carried him towards the
swirling transit.

"I almost died in that thing last time," Zack protested.

"Simpleton, that's why I fed you the hummus at the café, and the
bread on the road – to keep you alive."

Instantaneously, a bluish dome bathed them in a charge of light.
"Enjoy the protections I provide for you."

Incredulous, Zack mumbled, "I don't believe it."

Apollo leaped into the swirling mud with Zack under his arm like a
babe. Only Zack did not feel like a hero. He felt like crying.

CHAPTER 51
DELPHI, GREECE
SEPTEMBER 2011

BLOOD HOUND

Bessus reached a road. Even in the darkness, he could see that the mountains, the swing of the land, and the curve of the road were the same as when he had chased his prey into the temples. He looked down at the road's hard surface and wondered what had happened to the sand and gravel. "More tricks," he muttered.

He sniffed the air. Her flowery scent was on the wind. She must be hiding nearby. Off to the right, he saw a glow of lights. Maybe she sought aid in a village.

He rounded a corner to find buildings, and more enclosed fireballs, but these stood on tall poles, like beacons. He decided to slip into the town and find the witch while everyone slept. Closing in, he saw no sentries on duty and a two-story dwelling in his path. Might she go there?

His stomach rumbled.

Bessus wrapped his sausage-sized fingers around the doorknob and pulled hard. It didn't budge. He scratched his head and stepped back. He tried again and felt a give when he twisted the knob. He gazed through the clear glass, down a long hallway, lit with more of the orbs. As the doorknob turned, it clicked. Bessus pulled the door open. A metallic popping was followed by a lazy creak. He smiled, pleased with his cleverness in deciphering the puzzle of the entranceway.

He moved inside but ducked and turned at the hiss of a serpent behind him. He relaxed when he found no snake at his feet—only the sound of the shutting door. He walked silently down the hallway, noticing open doorways with chairs and tabletops, strewn with errant sheets of papyrus. He exhaled forcefully through his nose. Earlier, when he had chased the Mumbler and the Sorceress into the temples, he saw the treasure he had longed for: statuary covered in gold, lining a long uphill path. All of it had disappeared from his grasp when the tunnel of cold mud swallowed him and swept him into this place of endless confusions.

"Curses, not as much as a whore's hairpin to take," he whispered. "Has the sorceress hidden the gold, too?"

He thought of how it would feel to finally plunder the sorceress' fruits and slowly choke the life from her. It brought a bulge to his trousers, but hunger spasms interrupted his fantasy.

He reached a large room with evenly spaced long tables, lit by more of the now-familiar bulbs. He discovered a side room stacked with pots and cooking irons, and found bread on a bench. The clear covering resisted his attempts to tear off a huge chunk with his teeth. He gagged on the slimy covering and spit it out, stuffed the flashlight in a pocket of his trousers, and widened the hole in the covering. Bessus drew out a large plug of bread. He chewed furiously with his few teeth for just a moment before swallowing like a starved dog.

He turned his attention to a large white box and pulled on its handle. The door easily opened with a pop. He cocked his head as he reached for a line of containers with drawings of cattle on the outside. Fed up with tricks and strange objects, he ripped open one of the containers. Milk spilled on his arms and chest. Grinning, he held the container aloft and filled his mouth. Underestimating the pour, he drenched his beard and black bull leather cuirass.

The raucous laughter of a child erupted behind him. Bessus twirled around, dropping the container and spraying the contents on the floor. A boy stood before him with a hand over his mouth. He gasped, and then giggled, pointing at the mess.

Bessus reached for his dagger.

A dark mess of hair hung from the child's forehead. Spindly arms and legs reached out from his pajamas. Without warning, the child ran up to Bessus and began jumping and splashing in the puddle of milk. The boy threw his head back and emitted a continuous stream of squeals.

Bessus smashed his fist on the counter. The boy froze, wide-eyed. Bessus brought his fingers to his lips and made a shushing sound. The child backed up. Bessus hid the dagger behind his back. The boy laughed aloud, and rushed forward, wrapping his arms around the huge man's knees. Surprised, almost horrified, Bessus recoiled and shook his leg to get free. The child looked up and smiled, displaying his miniature square teeth. His dark eyes reflected the sparse light of the room.

Bessus curled his fingers over the hilt of the blade, imagining the colorful contrast when the child's blood mixed with the milk on the floorboards.

The child released Bessus suddenly and dashed around the room with his arms outstretched, making a buzzing and blubbering sound with his lips. The boy ran among the tables, swooping around them, each pass just beyond Bessus's grasp. Above him, on a higher floor, Bessus heard scraping and a door creak open. On the next pass, tiring of the boy's antics and wondering if others might come see what the noise was about, Bessus timed his move, and seized the boy.

The child screamed and wrenched to free himself. The boy's eyes instantaneously switched from delight to terror when he realized this was no game. Bessus gripped the boy by the tunic, lifting the child off his feet. He rotated the knife in his hand. A door slammed. Feet stomped. Distracted by the potential threat, Bessus looked up and away from the boy.

The rascal twisted and latched onto the skin between his thumb and forefinger with his little teeth and chomped down. Bessus yelped and shook the little demon away from him. The boy bolted for the doorway and disappeared. Bessus followed, but seeing no one to confront him, he thought better of chasing his prey up a stairway and sprinted out the door.

Quickly reaching the cover of the trees and brush beyond the building, he halted and sat roughly on the ground, his chin on his knees, his breath coming in loud rasps. He didn't know what to do. The world of the sorceress made his head hurt. He kept glancing around the tree to see if he was followed.

Bessus sucked at the bite wound. It would have been so easy to dispatch the boy when he had the chance. He remembered how, as a boy, he had been in the same position and been spared. Too many tortured thoughts. He couldn't reckon with all of them at once. He feared for his son. How could he return to him when he was assaulted by the black magic of the sorceress, in a land of her making?

Evil lived here.

He laid his head back against a tree trunk and felt an overwhelming weariness. *Why did I leave my axe inside that temple? Curse that Mumbler.*

The door to the building opened slightly, and then shut. No one emerged, but what he saw drained the last of his courage. Along a paved road, lined by more buildings leading into a small town, a monster headed directly for him. It coughed and sputtered, with two large yellow eyes, and moved quickly, faster than a chariot. Bessus dove to the ground and reached for his dagger with trembling fingers. The racket from the beast grew louder.

It knows where I am. The witch sends her allies to slay me.

He panted, awaiting the attack.

The bright-eyed monster sped past him and raced towards the temples. Bessus released his breath and then held his next inhalation to slow his heart down. The drone from the monster gradually disappeared.

I will not survive this world. I will not be able to return to my son unless I can find and kill her.

Bessus ran from the town. He caught his breath, pulled the still-lit flashlight from his pocket, and surveyed his surroundings. Wind whistled through the trees.

He caught a scent. He drew breath again, lifting his nose higher, expanding his nostrils to capture what lay on the air so subtlety. He dashed past the temples, stopped again, and tested the air. He saw broken-down temples and heard the gurgle of a stream. Following the run of water below the road, he halted to wash away the sticky grime that coated his body and tormented the sores under his tunic. He removed one of the bronze armbands from his biceps, only to drop it into the stream. He set aside his bull-hide cuirass and leather satchel.

Then Bessus smelled smoke. It came from the downslope of a ridge, just a stone-throw away. He ran towards the smoke aroma, leaving his possessions behind.

He heard a muffled scream, as if it came from underground. He threw aside overgrown brush that narrowed a small path and found broken branch ends. The flashlight revealed newly made footsteps in the dirt.

A hunter's grin crossed his face.

CHAPTER 52
OMONIA SQUARE, ATHENS
JULY 2016

SAABIR

Zack blinked. He felt groggy, like he did after waking up from sedation at the oral surgeon's office. Shards of electrical pulse shot from him, but he saw no light, nor sensed any heat. The last thing he remembered was Apollo pulling him to his side and a blue envelope surrounding them; not just a barrier, but like a bath. An electrically charged bath. The landscape flew by him at unbelievable speeds before he fell asleep.

He stood in a city square with a gunnysack slung over his shoulder. The extra weight made him wobble until his head cleared. Across the street, a large black-lettered sign: Limassol Imports. A quick scan of the surroundings… familiar Omonia Square, just down the street from the National Archaeological Museum.

Apollo's directive rang loud and clear: He must devise a plan to stop a devastating terrorist attack on Athens. *How can I stop terrorists? Am I supposed to call the police? Or confront them? I'm not equipped for this.*

Then he remembered. Apollo said that I couldn't see Lauren unless I succeeded.

He laid the gunnysack down and opened the flap. "You're blocking the sidewalk!" a pedestrian complained. Another kicked the sack, hit something hard with his shoe and walked away, cursing illegal immigrants. Zack dragged the sack to the side and stuffed his hand inside. He withdrew a roll of paper money and clothing, and then reached the hard object.

He pulled it out, just far enough to see what it was. He smiled.

The darkened windows of Limassol Imports prevented a look inside. Zack crossed the street, dodging car traffic, and positioned himself twenty yards to one side of the front door.

The door swung open. Two men with dark, slicked-back hair and clipped beards walked briskly away, putting on sunglasses. One threw a cigarette butt into the street. Zack watched them stride away and hop into a taxi. His heart thundered. Apollo never told him how long he had until the attack.

He opened the door to find stacks of oriental rugs in rows. A bronze statue of centaurs, dragging women away to rape, rested on a tabletop. An attractive, brown-haired woman sat behind a desk, tapping on a miniature phone. Zack cleared his throat while picking up a business card.

The woman peered up through overextended eyelashes. The beauty of her eyes stunned him. "There are no appointments today," she said indifferently, returning to the phone, her thumbs texting rapidly.

"Saabir asked me to contact him," Zack said, watching the woman concentrate on her task and ignoring him.

"Your name?"

"Professor Zack Fletcher. Tell him I have something quite valuable for him."

"Wait here. He's very busy. I doubt he'll see you today."

She walked towards a keypad beside a door. Using her body to block Zack's view, she punched in numbers carefully. She opened the door with a click, slipped inside, and closed it. Zack wandered around the meagerly stocked showroom, noting the lack of presentation for tourists, and the nearly empty glass cases and foot-high statues of Pallas Athena leaning on her spear. They were of poor quality.

A brochure on the counter described Limassol Antiquities as a source for the discriminating buyer. But with no picture of Saabir on the pamphlet, printed on cheap paper, and badly folded at that, it didn't appear that they cared to impress anyone.

The young woman returned. She stared at Zack and bit her nail before pronouncing, "It's time for you to leave."

Something in her eyes. He didn't like it. "Why?"

"Because he says Professor Fletcher is dead," she said, with the same indifference.

"You tell him the last time he saw me, he knocked over a glass of wine and nearly broke a statue of the Parthenon."

He leaned over the front of the desk and studied the girl's dark eyes. They reflected a man who had not shaved in months. His hair hung like a dirty mop. The jeans and tee shirt Apollo had given him could not mask his lack of bathing. The girl twitched nervously.

Just then, Saabir emerged, his graying hair combed over a balding head. Heavier than when Zack had last seen him, he stayed behind the desk, arms folded, surveying the unkempt man before him.

"Why are you here? I have no time for nonsense." He looked at his watch.

"I have a piece you will certainly be interested in."

"I'm closing my business. The economy has not been advantageous for some time. And you, Professor Fletcher, are presumed dead."

"Can we talk in private?"

"Fatima, could you do some inventory in the back?"

The girl left. "How long have you been gone? Over five years?"

What? Did he say five years? Has Lauren been alone for that long? "I was… away."

"I have a piece… of incredible value… perfectly preserved. I discovered it on my 'sabbatical.' Dating will prove it to be around 500 BCE, Persian Wars period."

Saabir pursed his lips. "Very interesting. Who knows about this piece?"

"Only I do."

"What is it?"

"I'll bring it here tomorrow."

Gruffly, Saabir responded, "Tell me now."

"I guarantee you will be impressed."

Saabir turned to leave, but then stopped. "No one knows you're alive. Why hide?"

"Better this way. I've had… difficulties."

"Are you a criminal, Dr. Fletcher?"

Zack shook his head. "I will show you this one piece, and if you're interested, maybe others. I'll be back tomorrow morning. What time?"

"8 a.m."

Zack threw the gunnysack over his shoulder and walked out the door.

When Fatima returned, Saabir said, "The authorities made tremendous efforts to find him and his wife. I wonder if he killed her and went into hiding." He chuckled, reaching for a cold cup of tea. "When he returns in the morning, have Zagred and Abdullah stay in the back office. After we determine the value of whatever he has, tell them to kill him."

The girl returned Saabir's smirk. "Yes, father, but will we have enough time to leave unnoticed?"

"If Dr. Fletcher has anything of value, I know someone who will buy it sight unseen with a wire transfer. The extra money will help, especially since airports will be in lockdown afterwards. We can easily cross the border by car into Turkey and make our way east. Come here, child."

Fatima embraced her father. "I can't wait to see their suffering on the news. There will be celebrations, like none before," she whispered.

"We will bring the West to their knees. The Americans will soon be finished."

"You are a great man." A look of worship crossed Fatima's face. "Someone who will be remembered for his brilliance, and his service."

Saabir nodded, but then cast his glance away, far away. "Brilliant? Only God knows."

She released him. "What do you mean, Father?"

"Our plans have not been sanctioned by those who support us financially. We developed them in secret, and are executing our own timetable."

"What if our financiers find out?"

"They will bluster and complain, but in the end, they will thank us. Maybe we do their dirty work for them. In time, it could be that we will be swallowed by the dragons and bears from the East as well. They have no problem shooting tens of thousands in the streets."

"We will embrace one enemy at a time. You know whom you serve." Fatima raised her chin off his chest.

"When the news programs show the Parthenon exploding, it will be signal for us to begin our attacks. They will bleed from a thousand cuts."

Fatima lowered her eyes. "I will obey you."

Saabir checked his watch. "Cyberattacks from Fung's hackers will cripple their technological infrastructure. Their defense systems will be shut down. All commerce will cease. Then, the West will fall under weight of their debts. They have left themselves opened for domination from the East. They will finally know... submission and unrelenting fear."

Zack turned frequently while walking away from Saabir's office. He headed towards The National Archaeological Museum, wondering if Professor Papandreou would help him figure out what to do. However, Apollo warned him not to involve anyone else; it was his task alone to accomplish.

At the steps he paused, then turned around to make the long walk back to Monastiriki Square. *I cannot risk it. I'm obeying a pagan god. Five years I've been gone?*

Both he and Lauren's families would be distraught over their disappearances. What would happen to their house? Then, it hit him. *I've lost my position at State. Both of us have. Everything, our lives, careers, in shambles.*

He searched for the wad of bills in his pockets. The aromas of lamb and beef gyros emanating from the Souvlaki Row restaurants tormented his stomach. He had not eaten in days. People moved out of his way on the tightly packed sidewalk, pinching their noses. He paid for three gyros and French fries at the closest storefront and sat on the sidewalk. He wolfed them down. A street dog with matted gray fur halted a few steps

away, swallowing and licking his chops. It looked at him with intense eyes.
He dipped the fries in Tzatziki sauce and stuffed a handful in his mouth.
He motioned the dog over. After a few cautious steps, the dog was close
enough for Zack to throw him some meat.

"We look about the same, don't we?" he said.

"Don't feed the strays," a thickset man shouted. "We'll never get
rid of them."

"Live and let live," Zack replied in Greek.

The look on the man's face spelled trouble.

Others stopped and told him to leave Zack and the dog alone. An
argument broke out about illegal immigrants coming to Greece from
Africa, the Middle East, and the Balkans. From the back-and-forth
shouting, he learned that Greece was broke, many had lost their jobs, and
their pensions had been cut. The European Union and United States were
to blame, they said.

Zack gathered his food and gunnysack and slipped away
unnoticed, the debate continuing with fingers pointed and frustrations
unleashed. Once clear of the commotion, he sat on plastic roofing that
shielded the stairs to the underground trains. The same dog followed him
and waited for more meat. Other dogs, sensing a meal, walked towards
him, sat on their haunches, and gave him desperate stares. "You can all eat,
if one of you can tell me what to do," Zack said, returning the same doleful
look. He threw meat to each dog.

"Where's my wife?" Zack asked his canine audience. Tilted heads
and weak barks answered. "I have a god, did you hear me, a freaking pagan
god telling me I've got to save the world. Do I look like some kind of hero
to you guys?" He let out a deep breath. "He sent me all the way to ancient

Greece to learn… that it took sacrifice for freedom to survive and I still don't know if I'm good enough to do what he wants."

Zack put his sandwich down. "He asked me what kind of man I am. Was I all for myself?" The dogs neared him, sniffing. He ripped off pieces of pita bread and fed each of his listeners. "The thing is… he never said any of this to me. It's like I was asleep and he planted these thoughts in my head."

Teenagers ran up the train stairs. Rounding the corner, they noticed the lineup of dogs in front of Zack. One came over and kicked the weakest-looking stray. The animal transformed and drew its lips back, canines bared, its tail stiffened. A deep growl burst from its throat. The dog lunged at the boy and sent him and the others running. Afterwards, it limped back to Zack and reclaimed its position in line. *Sometimes you have to rear back and fight like a dog.* "Thanks, mutts." Zack threw them the rest of his food.

Without a passport or ID, he couldn't check into a hotel. He needed to clean up and get his head straight, get some sleep. The port of Piraeus would do, a half-hour away by train. Arriving near dusk, Zack walked past the massive commercial ships, ferry stations and fast hydrofoils ready for transport to the myriad Greek islands. He stopped at a store to buy supplies with the money Apollo left. He walked towards Paleo Falirou until he found a park and shoreline away from the ships, stripped down to his underwear, and waded into the Saronic Gulf past a statue of St. Paul, commemorating the apostle's arrival at that spot in 40 A.D. The statue stared at him with a betrayed, accusing look.

Zack walked, his shoulders hunched, past stone blocks from the ancient port. So long ago, he left with Lauren from here on a trireme. She endured a miserable journey to Thermopylae. He had failed her so many times. The seas could only do so much for him. He really needed a catharsis of his soul.

Emerging from the sea, the evening onshore breeze chilled him. He dried off with a beach towel he bought at a store. He uncapped a small bottle of olive oil, dribbled some onto his hands, raked it into his scalp with his fingers, and combed and dressed his shoulder-length hair, preparing himself to die.

Just like the Spartans at Thermopylae.

At 7:30 the next morning, Zack took the train back to Omonia Square. With shaking hands, he rang the doorbell and walked into Limassol Antiquities. Inside, Saabir hurriedly filled boxes with merchandise. He lifted his head when Zack walked in, his torso partially hidden by the glass case and row of statuettes.

"Show me what you have quickly," Saabir blurted out. "Is it in that silly sack of yours?" He slid unsealed boxes towards the back office door.

"It's one of a kind and in pristine condition," Zack replied, slinging the sack off his shoulder.

Saabir halted his packing. "Don't expect much for a fast deal, Dr. Fletcher. Do you expect me to sell it on the black market for you?"

"I was digging in the mountains near Marathon Bay, searching caves; you know, undiscovered shrines to the demigod, Pan. I found one with a number of sealed *pithos.*" Zack opened the brass bolt fastener. Saabir intently watched as he unloaded wrinkled clothing and a newspaper. "Did you ever wonder how history would have been changed if the Persians had won the Battle of Marathon?"

Perspiration ran down Saabir's forehead. He licked the salt from his lips.

"Think of the symbolism," Zack continued. "The Athenians attack from the heights and trap the Persians on the beach, saving Western culture from a first invasion from the Middle East. A critical turning point, and together with the other battles of the Persian Wars, they allow the concept of free societies to be born."

Saabir flipped his hand and returned to his packing. "Enough. Your history is not mine."

Zack paused, then: "How important would an artifact from that battle be? East and West have been in conflict since then." He needed to find out what kind of an attack Saabir had in mind. Quickly. And when it would happen. "I didn't tell you why I couldn't go back to the U.S."

He wiped oil from his earlobe as Saabir's balding head peeked up from behind the counter. He did not like the sticky, greasy feel, but it gave him strength. He tried to picture Leonidas' penetrating stare, the way the king looked into his soul, called him a coward. "I got involved with a group of, let's say, foreigners, who didn't take kindly to the imperialistic actions of the U.S.," Zack said. "I think they are looking for me. The CIA, I mean."

Saabir pushed the last of the boxes in front of the door. "The great Satan will learn humility in very good time," he said, grunting. "Now show me what you have."

"America has more lessons to learn, hard lessons."

Zack was treading carefully, hoping his ploy would work. He withdrew a long leather skin from the sack, unwound the tie, and unfolded the layers reverently until a long sword appeared. "A *kopis*, how marvelous," Saabir said. The joy drained from his face suddenly. "How could this be in such good condition? The iron blade barely has any pitting.

Look at the wood on the grip. Cheat me with a reproduction, and you'll be sorry."

"It will check out as 5th century BCE, guaranteed. I already ran the tests. Take a closer look?"

Zack held the still wrapped, curved blade towards Saabir, but did not let go of it. Saabir leaned in. "There's writing inscribed near the hilt," he pointed out. "It says, 'I gave Theseus just service and laid low many a Mede at Marathon.'"

A sneer flashed across Saabir's face.

"Imagine, a sword used in the battle of Marathon…" How could he get Saabir to talk about his plans? "Wouldn't the Greek museums love to have this, or a private collector? To me, it could be equally valuable for a Saudi prince, or others, not just historically, but something to cart out at the right moment, to disparage the West and its ideals."

"You talk treason to your own people, Dr. Fletcher. Why should such a man be trusted?"

Zack puffed out his chest. "Do you really care about that? How much can you sell it for?"

"A sizable sum." Saabir reached for a button on the side of the receptionist desk. "The metalwork looks authentic to blacksmithing techniques of the period. Should it prove to be so, I'll realize a healthy profit. Thank you for your donation."

A curious mix of surprise and confusion crossed Zack's face. "What do you mean?"

The lock of the front door clicked. So did the door to the back office. Two men in black clothing burst through, handguns extended.

Saabir reached to pull the sword from Zack's hands.

"You're not stealing this…"

Zack yanked it back. The oilskin wrap fell. Saabir latched his hands onto the cutting edge, screeched and grabbed his bleeding hand, bracing it between his knees. "Take him down!" he hissed.

The muzzles aimed at Zack's face. He heard pops, not the report of gunshots as he expected. Unable to escape, he crashed against the counters from the impact of the silenced 9mm slugs. Glass shattered as the assailants kept shooting. He groaned as more shots slammed into him. The floor beneath him turned burgundy and slick.

That's my blood.

He fell on his face as the sword dropped from his hands. He scrunched his legs, vainly trying to constrict the bullet holes, but found himself losing breath and strength. He heard laughing while spitting frothy blood. Zagred, one of the gunmen, strutted over and kicked him in the face. Starbursts exploded in his head.

Saabir wrapped his hand in a towel. "Filthy American, you're as stupid as you are corrupt. Did you really think we'd let you leave here alive?"

"A hostage might be valuable… for afterwards?" the other gunman, Abdullah, suggested, removing his sunglasses.

Zack looked out to the street. "Dream away, Dr. Fletcher. We only have a few moments more before we must go. You will watch your life leak onto the floor." Saabir squeezed the towel and turned to Zagred. "Take your position near the police headquarters. Did Fung's agent wire the money through Pakistan and Iran as arranged?"

Zagred nodded his head, but with a displeased look.

Zack flinched at the mention of a Chinese/Pakistani/Iranian connection. *What the hell is going on?*

"On my text-signal, set off the first bombs," Saabir continued. "Cripple police headquarters and the U.S. Embassy. Fatima has set the timers on the other vans for an hour after your attack, just enough time for fire and ambulance crews to arrive and for us to escape north."

"Silence, Saabir," protested Zagred.

Saabir snorted and waved his hand dismissively. "Far bigger bombs, planted within the reconstruction of that abomination on the Acropolis, will turn the Parthenon into a symbolic pile of little rocks; a poignant exclamation point for our attack."

Zack gagged and spit out bright red blood. Vision blurring, he watched Zagred leave for the street.

Saabir chortled. "We have waited so very long to begin."

Zack could not get enough air. Weakly, he managed to say, "Who are you?"

"We are everyone, and no one. Limassol Exports is just a front. We cannot be connected to any country, not even any organization."

Saabir waved his hand at Abdullah. "Enough talk. Now that he knows, get the sword and take his head with it." Saabir stuffed papers delicately in a manila folder with his injured hand. "This is such a fitting use for a sword of Marathon, might increase its value, too. I should record the execution on my cell."

Abdullah smirked as he sauntered over to Zack with his Glock 17 handgun. He drew his foot back. Grimacing, Zack summoned his remaining strength to roll away. Abdullah's foot missed his head and hit the glass case, sending more shards of glass flying. He cursed the glass stuck in his leg and hopped on one foot.

Zack grabbed the handle of the sword and swung it at the pant leg in front of him.

Abdullah screamed, peering down as the blade bit into the bone above his ankle. His blood seeped and mixed on the floor with Zack's. The gunman fell, grasping the wound, dropping the Glock.

Zack scrambled for it.

"Infidel!" Saabir bellowed as Zack pointed the gun at him. He reached for the door keypad to escape. Zack couldn't hold the gun steady, but pulled the trigger anyway.

The first shot blasted a hole in the wall, three feet off target. Saabir furiously punched keys. The second shot ripped the little phone out of the terrorist's hand. Abdullah groaned, reaching for Zack's wrist. The next shot hit Saabir in the back of the head just as the door opened. His face exploded outwards. He shook violently on the floor and then lay still.

Abdullah reached for the gun, but couldn't prevent Zack from aiming the muzzle at him. For a split second, Zack saw the gunman's clipped beard, the hatred in his eyes, and spit from his lips. He pulled the trigger. That same face disintegrated into a collage of blood-splattered tissue and bone.

Zack wiped blood spatter from his blurry eyes. He couldn't breathe anymore.

I am a warrior, Leonidas.

He passed out.

The shaking ground brought him back to consciousness. Then sirens, lots of sirens, in the distance. Then a ring tone. Abdullah's phone. Abdullah, who lay on his back, eyes vacant, mangled mouth open.

Zack reached for the cell phone. The caller hung up. He had to reach authorities, anyone. He hit buttons until numbers appeared. He started to call '911', but remembered he was in Greece, not San Diego. It was something else, but still three numbers. He punched in '100.'

After a delay, a female voice answered.

"*Voithya,* help," Zack whispered. "There's a terrorist plot..." Waves of pain lanced through him. "Vans parked near the Acrop..."

He could not catch his breath. Louder, he said, "U.S. Embassy, police stations... inside the Parthenon. Please, quickly, evacuate. They're set to go off within the hour." Zack held his chest.

The police officer asked, "Who are you?"

"I've been shot. Help me. I got two of 'em. I'm using their phone." More blood spurted from his mouth. Gasping, he muttered, "Limassol Imports, Onomia."

The ground shook again. He heard screams in the streets.

The bastards won. There wasn't enough time.

All went black.

CHAPTER 53

DELPHI

JULY 2016

SLAVE

Strong hands shook him awake to a view of stars. A cool wind grazed his arms, laden with the smell of the sea. Apollo's face filled his view. A gentle, reassuring grin graced the god's lips.

Zack took painful, shallow breaths. "Am I... alive?"

"You are on your own odyssey, Traveler."

Zack strained to rise from the hard earth. He looked down to see a number of white bandages over his chest, arms and legs.

"You still don't comprehend all that has transpired," Apollo said.

Moonlight glowed eerily on the god's clean-shaven face and golden hair. His single lock hung from the right side of his face. Always the right side.

Zack had no spit to swallow. His tongue stuck to his palate. Wind whistled through the trees surrounding their makeshift camp, beneath the peaks of Parnassus, on the downward slope, near the entrance to the tunnel.

Apollo lifted a small lyre to his lap. "You have never been too far from my sight. You are like a grasshopper that I hold in my hands. I peer at you through fingers that are separated just enough so you don't fly away."

The bronze medallion hung from his neck. He plucked on his six-string lyre, singing in the high-toned voice of the waiter at the Plaka taverna, "*I really want to see you lord, but it takes so long my lord.*"

Apollo halted for a moment to watch for the effect on Zack's face. He smiled and continued, "*I really want to know you lord, but it takes so long my lord.*" He grinned gratuitously at Zack, as if tolerating the antics of a child. "What have you learned, Traveler?"

Zack took a shallow breath. "I've learned how quickly I can ruin my life."

Apollo put down the lyre. "Arrogance, Traveler. You wallow in pity for your predicament. You're an interesting study in human frailty." He looked away. "Having done what men could, they suffered what men must."

"Thucydides. Peloponnesian War."

"Well, you are a *pedagogue* and should know those words. With your knowledge of historical events, you assumed you knew all that would transpire. Arrogance overcame your judgment and you had to suffer like the Athenians who attacked Sicily in the Peloponnesian Wars and failed. They labored and died in those miserable mines."

"That would be true if it was just my arrogance. Wasn't it you that manipulated us?"

"Marvelous, you choose to debate me instead of asking the most obvious of questions."

"What do you mean?"

"Why are you still alive, Traveler? How is it that you survived so many bullet wounds? Crude weapon, though very effective."

Zack ran his hands over the bandages. It still hurt, but not so much as when he fought the terrorist. "I guess the police took me to the hospital. How'd you get me here?"

"So naïve." Apollo twirled the long curl in his fingers. "The nectar you've ingested over time has saved your life, a few times now, by my count. It is a struggle to keep you alive. I collected you before the police arrived."

"Did I prevent the attack? Where's my wife? Is she safe?" Frantically, Zack attempted to rise, but fell back, holding his chest.

"A magnificent female she is, with the heart of a warrior. Tell me: you had hunger for knowledge, but did you weigh the risk to her when you journeyed to the Hot Gates? The answer again is arrogance, blind ambition. The woe of many a mortal."

Zack shook his head, tiring of all that had happened, all they had endured. "No, tell me, please. Did she and the girl escape the barbarian? You keep talking in circles and won't answer me."

"Rest your mind, Traveler. They are well, for now. However, Bessus still pursues them. And I reveal this to you not out of mercy, but so you can concentrate on the work I have ahead for you."

"They're alive." Zack collapsed backwards. After a moment to catch his breath, he asked, "Bessus invaded our home in San Diego, and chased us in Athens. Wait, he didn't know us back in ancient Greece, nor that he'd end up in the future. However, in the future, he knew us. This is so screwed up."

"Defeat him and you may be ready to face the far worse that awaits you. Bessus has his own path in all this. I will not restrain him."

"My god!"

"Which god do you invoke now? Is it I? Or some other?"

To Zack, both question and answer could not have been more loaded with danger and consequences. He swallowed, buying time.

"Your silence reveals all that I need to know. Then let us examine your thoughts, Traveler, for your introspection is muddy as a puddle is after a wagon wheel has run through it. In your desire to logically place reality, is all that you experienced the work of a mortal?"

"I guess… it isn't."

"Has any other god placed so much before you so? Can your mind grasp what has occurred right before your eyes?"

"It's hard to believe, but I can't deny it."

"Then forsake your God, Traveler, and declare me your one true god."

Zack dug his nails into his temples. He wished he could rip out his brain, twirl it in his hand and squeeze out a measure of understanding.

"I can't. You can't ask me to do that."

Apollo hovered over him. "The gods are gone forever. Was that not your bold statement at the Plaka tavern? How smug and confident of your intellect you were then, professor." He raised a finger to his lips. "But for what purpose did you gain all your knowledge? So you could divulge past lessons to students and enjoy a life of safety and luxury? Now, you're the student. Knowledge must be utilized to decide a course of action, or to save the lives of others. You were much too preoccupied with your own selfish desires, mortal. Otherwise, why would you have led your woman into a battle for the destiny of nations?"

That knife nicked his rib bones on the way in.

"Yet, you have merits. Each episode of your survival gained more of my attention. You finally decided to fight. You interest me, Traveler. You may be worthy yet."

Zack braced himself on an elbow. "What happened in Athens?"

"Only two of the bombs could not be defused in time, at the police station and U.S. Embassy. I left the corpses of Saabir and his conspirator where they dropped. Even though the others used throwaway phones, most will be captured and punished. The Chinese man escaped to his homeland, but you saved many from death and thwarted this first attack."

A futuristic image of an intact and rebuilt Parthenon projected from Apollo's medallion. Apollo sighed, pursed his lips and nodded. "The sacred Parthenon, sanctuary of my sister, Athena, is intact. You did well, but there is more danger ahead."

Zack laid his head back, exhaling a long breath of relief. "I have so many questions."

"I have questions also. How did it feel to slay a man?"

Zack stared at his hands. "I… felt out of my body, possessed, like I was overruled by a spasm of rage. Now, I only feel… guilt."

"Do you not think that every warrior has not endured the same introspection?"

Apollo inspected his fingernails from different angles as if deciding how he might better manicure them. "What is the best way for a man to live, Traveler? How can a mortal live happily if there is chaos all about him?"

"Where did the gods come from, Apollo?"

"Can a mortal ignore the chaos and maintain a bastion of safety for him and his? Can he remain an island and not join in the struggle?"

Zack sat up fast, feeling less pain this time. *Miraculous.* "Where did the gods go? If you were here… once… why did you leave?"

Apollo flung his hand dismissively. "If you do not understand the past and cannot see the *now,* how can you set a proper course for what is to come?"

Anguish contorted Zack's face. "I want to know. I am begging you to tell me. What is a god? Is there only one god?"

"First, you must know what it is to be a man. The answers to that are as complicated and as simple as the question you just asked of me." Apollo's eyes narrowed.

"It is not enough to postulate and play at words, Professor. That does not buy a man virtue. Performance and deeds earn you virtue. Live your philosophy, rather than just talk about it. Search for the truth, for that which never changes, that which is irrefutable, that which upon all things are built, and you will know god."

Zack buried his head in his hands. "Can't you just give me a simple answer?"

"A man will dig in his heels and fight when he needs to. Did not Leonidas and his brave warriors do just that?"

"Are you a god? Are you a god? Are you a god?' Zack repeated his question until all he heard was his own voice, dying in amplitude until no more than a whisper.

"Whatever you see that is indestructible and dependable reflects the mind of god, Traveler."

"Where did you come from?"

"I will help you to answer all your questions, but in time. You can feel yourself healing, can't you?"

"I want to see Lauren. I've earned the right to be with her."

Crickets sang in the dark. Below their perch, the modern town of Delphi lit up. The drone of cars and laughter radiated from restaurants. The Delphi temple site lay in darkness, except for the museum's outdoor lights.

"No," Apollo stated flatly.

Zack balled his fists.

"Approach me again uninvited, and you will suffer for it."

Zack hung his head, feeling defeated on so many levels. "Give us hope."

"By now, you should realize there are other means of connection."

"No. You promised me that I would see her."

"I said I might allow it, but you may weaken when you meet. There is still no time to waste. You are in no position to make demands. You exist at my pleasure, my call, and my mercy. You're being deployed, again."

Apollo lifted Zack to his feet. He placed the Marathon sword into the mortal's hand, and harnessed the backpack onto his shoulders. "The sword bears the legacy of liberty within it. Go now, Traveler. You're going back to the Persian Wars and continue your training," he said, pointing down the stairwell. "You'll awaken on the other side, and not remember what transpired in Athens, or even just now. That is important. You must be raw, desperate, and not softened by memories of the ladies' safety."

A golden sleeve of energy extended from Apollo's medallion and enveloped Zack. He fell asleep within its warm borders.

"Be on guard." Apollo thought back on the projection of thunder that he manifested to distract the barbarian during the farmhouse fight. "I cannot be everywhere at once. I will not guarantee that you will survive, but you *can* create your own new destiny."

Apollo held the remaining archer's medallion in his palm. "But know this: you are history to me. You have no idea of the sacrifices necessary to find the hidden histories; no idea of the miracles that had to occur for me to be standing before you, no idea of what will be necessary to change what history has recorded."

As the golden charge bearing Zack passed the portal, Apollo said in a booming voice: "Know Thyself, Traveler! Live by moderation and rescue the future. You will learn that one man, or any man or woman, suitably motivated and suitably trained, can make a difference."

The deep rumble began.

"The danger of Saabir, and others like him, is nothing compared to the treason that threatens you from within. Attacks from abroad are but a symptom; the real disease is the arrogance, greed, and corruption of your own. Only the strong and just will survive. You have been lied to and betrayed, and your eyes are closed to it. Wake up!"

The rock liquefied.

"Now go. I will only guarantee that you will learn from history in ways you could not have imagined. Like the Spartans, come home with your shield, or on it."

Zack could not answer, but Apollo's meaning penetrated his veil of sleep. He was a doomed man unless he could survive this odyssey of trials…

And no odyssey is over until you make it back home.

CHAPTER 54

DELPHI

OCTOBER 2011

TIES

I didn't close the entryway.

Light entered the cave. Lauren squeezed past the cave hole leading to the passageways and hid on the other side, holding the torch lower to lessen the glow. She didn't dare shout to Cassandra as the girl's torch-glow receded deeper into the mountain.

"Cassandra," she whispered down the passageway. "Hide! The monster's here."

She searched the cave floor for rocks. Her fingers swiped the rubble, but she felt only stones. Then she heard a thump near the entrance followed by muted, deep-throated swearing.

Lauren clicked the nails of her thumb and index finger, untended for a couple of months. She had been biting the ends off. *I'll rip your eyes out. That's what Persephone tried to do for Cassandra.*

A few rock volleys might halt the barbarian. Then she would get him while he was stunned and kick him in the balls again. Except this time, she would smash his head to pieces. She whipped her arm around a few times to loosen it up, holding the stone between her fingers and thumb, like a baseball, a grip her brothers taught her.

The light looked different from what a torch would give out. It was a straight beam, like a flashlight. How would the barbarian have one?

Zack. It had to be Zack… in the cave. Tears of relief burst forth. "Oh my god, Zack, I'm so happy you made it. We're both here."

Lauren dropped the stones and held the torch out to watch him enter. "Cassandra's down in the cave, going to the room you told her about in the letters."

Lauren tilted her head. The flashlight beam illuminated the cave, and blinded her temporarily. "But how could you write the letters if you're not stuck in the past. That's just too weird. Zack, answer me…"

She heard another smack and more cursing.

It wasn't Zack's voice. Lauren shielded her eyes from the flashlight beam.

"Ja-dooo-gar!"

She let loose a scream of abject terror.

Bessus crawled inside.

Lauren shook her head violently, in stark denial. She turned quickly to see if Cassandra had come back into the cave, but she wasn't there. Her arms felt suddenly devoid of strength. She took a step back, then forward, as Bessus got to his knees. "Hide, Cassandra," she tried to shout, but her voice failed.

She held the torch straight out towards Bessus, like a spear. "Stay away," she said, feebly.

"I smelled you, witch. I could smell your loins on the wind."

Lauren gulped. Bessus drew his knife and came at her.

She quickly bent to pick up the stones she had dropped. "Take this!"

The first rock whizzed by Bessus's head. The second stone cut a true path and struck him in the forehead.

Grunting, he dropped the flashlight, but it didn't impede his charge. He crashed into Lauren just as she thrust the torch into his face and set his nest of hair on fire. The torch spun end-over-end upwards, setting the dense layers of cobwebs above them ablaze.

Bessus dropped his knife and tried to put out the flames on his head. Panicked, he ripped Lauren's chiton from her body and beat it on his crackling hair. The burning stopped. A wreath of smoke rose from his head. Lauren tried to get up. Bessus yanked her by one leg away from the cave hole that led to the interior. Clumps of burning cobwebs fell from the ceiling behind him. He drew his fist back. *Thwack!* He clubbed her cheek. The sound resonated inside the cave.

She cried out and threw her hands out to protect her face. Bessus batted them down. "You will not kick me like you did before," Bessus said, throwing Lauren's smoldering chiton aside. "I know you speak my tongue. I'm going to tell you how you will die."

He squeezed her throat until she weakened. Then he straddled her and opened her legs with his own. "First you will know my Bactrian spear, witch."

With her head facing the cave hole, she strained to see if Cassandra heard her warning and had stayed away, but Bessus blocked her view. Lauren gagged when he released the pressure on her windpipe. She could barely raise her arms to stop what she knew would happen.

"And you will take a flood of my seed."

"No, no," Lauren whispered.

Hide, sweetheart.

"Shall I let you live and bear my child?" Bessus threw his head back and laughed. The fire spread along the ceiling and filled the cave with more smoke.

I won't be able to bear it. I'd rather die.

"That would be too merciful, and you deserve none of that."
Bessus pulled back his hips to thrust into her. "You took me away from
my son. You took me to this... nightmare."

Lauren twisted, just enough, and Bessus missed his mark. Rage
possessed him, and he squeezed her throat, harder. Lauren's eyes bulged.
She squeaked in protest. She strained her eyes towards the cave entryway,
hoping Zack would somehow save her, as he did at Nestor's farm.

Bessus held her in place this time. She couldn't scream. She could
only gurgle and endure the agony. Her arms dropped. She tried to buck but
had no strength left.

I tried, Cassandra. I'm not good enough to protect you.

The beam of the flashlight revealed an apocalyptic scene of flame
and smoke. Burning cobwebs set the dry contents of the large pithos pots
on fire.

Bessus positioned himself for another attempt. "I've decided you
will not live."

Lauren shut her eyes. His face was inches from hers. "I will cut the
womb from you after you take my seed. Receive me, witch!"

Bessus scrunched his shoulders. He groaned hideously. Then he
lurched again, reaching over his shoulders, backwards.

Cassandra drove Bessus' knife into his back a second time, then a
third, each stab deeper. She twisted the knife and left it in. "Get off her!"

Bessus fell to the side. He couldn't reach the blade. Cassandra
shook Lauren's shoulders. She gagged and coughed. "Please, lady. Get
up."

Cassandra pulled her by the arm. She watched the wall of flame on the ceiling. She put her hands under Lauren's armpits and hauled her towards the entryway. "Use your feet to help me. I beg you."

Bessus squirmed on the cave floor, moaning. Blood poured down his back. "Not a girl," he coughed out. He struggled to his knees, enabling him to reach the knife between his shoulder blades. He pulled the dagger out and stared at it.

Cassandra shrieked and pulled Lauren harder, past the burning pithos. She reached the entryway just as Bessus dug in his elbows and started to crawl towards them. "No escape! You'll be next, girl," he seethed through his few gritted teeth.

Grunting, squeezing his eyes to endure the pain, he passed the first pithoi as Cassandra hauled Lauren into the entryway. Smoke coursed past her, seeking an exit. Cassandra coughed. Lauren drooled out black spit. The enormous pithoi hissed.

"I am your destiny, whore." Bessus pointed the blade at them.

Cassandra doubled her efforts. "He won't die!" she shrieked.

A mass of burning cobwebs fell from the ceiling. Digging his nails into the cave floor for traction, Bessus inched towards them.

"You have to help me, lady," Cassandra pleaded.

"I will feed on you myself and throw what's left to the swine."

Lauren pushed with her foot against the passageway wall. "Good, lady. Do it again. Hurry! He's coming."

Bessus reached for his prey, his eyes glassy. He set a foot down and tried to get up, just as the second pithos cracked open and collapsed. Great shards of burning terra cotta smacked his head and fell atop him. His clothing erupted in flames.

"*Jadoogar*, come back," he said, barely above a whisper. "My son is alone. Don't leave me here."

Bessus reached out, but his fingers slowly curled together and surrendered. "*Jado—*"
The last word bubbled out of his mouth.

Black smoke billowed from the cave opening like a foul indigestion belched from the depths of the earth. Cassandra dragged Lauren from the entrance and laid her to the side. Both cleared their lungs of the detritus of the cave and breathed in fresh air. Cassandra collapsed.

After a few deep breaths, Cassandra said, "He has to be dead. I heard the pithoi fall on him."

The uncertain look in Lauren's eyes gave her no comfort. After a pause, Cassandra said, "We can't wait here. Why would the gods allow such a man to live?" She helped Lauren to her feet. "I'll hold you up. Just walk, I beg you."

Lauren found her balance with Cassandra as a crutch. They struggled back to the trail. Cassandra checked to see if Bessus followed and saw that the smoke coming from the cave had subsided. Her lip trembled.

Lauren made a motion with her eyes to press on. Still in the dark, they made it to the highway and hid behind bushes. The smoke from the cave dissipated from a breeze riding off the Corinthian Gulf.

"Where do we go now?" Cassandra asked, frightened. Her half-closed eyes betrayed her exhaustion.

Lauren could see that the girl's unbelievable display of courage had waned. She pointed her finger past the archeological site to the town's glow. She rubbed her throat. "There, men who can slay Bessus."

"If he doesn't die, then he must be a god."

Lauren felt her guts squirm. Her groin ached. She forced the horror out of her mind. "Feeling better, go faster." She picked up the pace.

They passed the museum to find a lone car in the parking lot. *The owner must have walked away.* She looked through the window, but there were no keys in the ignition. She turned; no sign of Bessus, either. She held Cassandra's hand. "Let's run."

Cassandra looked back at the car. "Wait. What is that?"

"Later."

The first building they reached had two–stories and a sign announcing an orphanage. Its lights were on. Lauren chewed her lip while calculating that anyone inside would be unlikely to stop Bessus. Kids would be living there. She was not about to lead the monster to them. She hustled Cassandra past the orphanage, but the young girl stopped suddenly. Her eyes absorbed a line of cars parked on the road. She slid behind Lauren. "Are they giant bugs? Are they alive?"

"They're like... chariots, just without horses."

Cassandra tilted her head, confused.

Lauren scanned the scene. None of the businesses were open. No one walked the streets. She remembered how Bessus chased them from the farmhouse, carrying his axe. Her heart beat fast. She thought about what just happened in the cave and sensed a ghostly jab between her legs.

Where's the police station?

"Come this way." Lauren pulled Cassandra away from the cars. The young girl's eyes drifted to the streetlights overhead. Her mouthed dropped open and she mouthed a silent "Athena." Dogs barked in the distance. Lauren directed them uphill from the main road. "I think it's up there."

"You mean the chariots move by themselves?"

Lauren felt the strain in her thighs. Sweat beaded her forehead. They passed the corner of a tourist shop and saw her reflection in the window. She halted. "Crap, I'm completely naked."

She turned in circles, suddenly cold. *What am I going to do? Break into one of these stores?*

Lauren ran to a set of trashcans on the sidewalk. She rummaged through the contents until she found newspapers. She saw the month printed on the front page: *October 2011. Back in my own time; just off by a few months.*

She dumped garbage from a few plastic trash bags and made a tunic out of them. Cassandra crinkled her nose.

Two dogs sprinted toward them, barking. Cassandra picked up a trashcan cover, and set it before her and Lauren, like a hoplite with a shield. "We need sticks," she said, setting her back foot to make a stand, as her uncle had taught her.

Lauren slid around the shield and walked up to the dogs with her hand out, palm down. The dogs ran up, sniffed her, and wagged their tails.

"What kind of food do you have here... in this...?" Cassandra asked.

Lauren flashed a smile. "You won't believe how good it is."

"Does it smell like that garbage?"

Laughter escaped from her. "No, no. Wait until you try pizza. It's made with bread, tomatoes and cheese and..."

"Goat cheese?"

"Well, sometimes. And we have ice cream. It's cold and made from sweetened milk and you bite into it on a hot summer day."

"From goat's milk?"

Lauren managed another chuckle. "Not ice cream and enough about the goats. We have to get away from here."

The dogs stayed with the trashcans. As they hiked into streets higher on the hill, Lauren saw a police car in front of a small building. She checked for Bessus, and then led Cassandra to the front door of the station. "Here, they have weapons that even Bessus cannot survive." *We beat you, you bastard.*

"Do you believe he's dead?"

Lauren bent down and held Cassandra by the shoulders. "Look, we're going to be safe now. The men in this building will help us, but I do not want you to say anything. Do you understand? Say nothing. They will ask many questions of you, but just look away. They wouldn't understand you, anyway."

"What if they ask me if I'm hungry?"

Lauren grinned. "You're a very special girl, Cassandra. Thank you for saving my life back in that cave."

Cassandra squared her shoulders and lifted her chin. "I am my mother's daughter."

Her stomach gurgled. "Come with me," Lauren said, now laughing. "I'm starved, too. Let's go be rescued."

CHAPTER 55
DELPHI, GREECE
OCTOBER 2011

THE BEST LAID PLANS

Apollo watched the two women trudge towards the town. A silvery shadow in the moonlight, he ascended the mountainside towards the tunnel entryway, rubbing his fingers over his chin, ruminating in silence. Beneath his feet lay the body of the professor. He took a knee beside the dead man and pounded his fist on the ground, seething. "Tyche! Now what will I have to do to correct this?"

Apollo removed a grasp of dirt and the second medallion from the late professor's hand. He glared at the medallion. "See what happens when I let you out of my sight?"

He tied the bronze plug to the rawhide string hanging from his neck. "I am sorry, Professor, that you're an unwelcome casualty. I regret that Tyche continues to wreak havoc with my plans. Know, however, that you had a role in saving the lives of others."

A glimmer of dawn showed in the east. "Do not play with me, Tyche," he shouted to the absent goddess, just as a rooster announced dawn. "I can afford no more of your unpredictable tricks. There is too much to manage."

In two bounds down the stairway, Apollo arrived at the portal. "Another deed I must perform."

He leapt into the churning mud.

CHAPTER 56
DELPHI
OCTOBER 2011

SHATTERED DREAMS

Demo ate lunch with the other orphans. As he carried his tray to the kitchen counter, the high-pitched chatter around him halted suddenly, replaced by the blare of sirens. Everyone ran to the windows. Police vehicles surged by the orphanage towards the museum.

"Something has to be terribly amiss to demand such a response," Mr. Avtges said, craning his neck to see the last of the cruisers whiz past.

"Maybe there's been a robbery," Demo said.

"We shall see. By the way, where is Stephan?" Mr. Avtges said, turning towards his office.

"He won't come out of his room. He said he had a bad nightmare about a monster, a big monster with wild hair and a face full of scars."

"Maybe I should go see him. Head to the museum, Demo, and see what's happened."

Demo bolted.

Buses idled in the parking lot, unable to offload tourists. A police officer guarded the gate to prevent entry. He held his hand up as Demo approached.

"Was something stolen?" Demo asked.

"Far worse than that. A professor, the director of the museum in Athens, has been murdered. His body is up there, beyond the grounds."

Demo froze. Wide-eyed, he stared in the direction of the police officer's index finger. He knew what – and who – was up there. "What's the professor's name?" he asked.

"Papandreou."

"He was my friend." Demo choked back tears, struggling for something resembling manly control. A tear slid down his cheek. He swiped at it with his fist.

A young woman walked over. "I'm so sorry. Come with me."

Maria led him into the museum. A tall, dark-haired man in a brown suit paced the floor smoking a cigarette while museum employees stood quietly by, waiting to be questioned. They listened to the click-click-click of the police inspector's heels.

"Mr. Pappas," Inspector Trokalitis asked. "You found the professor's body."

An older man stood, clutching a crumpled hat in both hands. "I didn't know it was a body at first. I heard a crash, as if a rock had fallen off the mountain. I went to see what damage it did to the upper walls."

"I see. Report to my staff when I am finished here." The Inspector twisted his salt and pepper moustache while scanning the faces of those assembled before him. "Is there anyone else who might have information to assist us?"

Confused and scared, Demo fidgeted in his seat. His thoughts shifted to meeting the professor at the museum and their drive back to the orphanage.

The Inspector coughed a few times before continuing. "Did anyone here know Professor Papandreou?"

Demo raised his hand.

"Son, do you have something to tell me?"

Demo felt transparent and vulnerable under the hard gaze of the Inspector. "Sir, I met him at the museum in Athens a few weeks ago. He gave me a ride home. He was interested in the ruins here, said it was an important site."

"Yes, of course. Anyone else have information?"

When no one volunteered, he instructed everyone to remain in the area and be available for additional questioning.

Demo followed his fellow employees out of the museum. He wondered why the professor had died, just as he was still confused as to what had happened to the professor's American friends on the video.

"Here's my card," the Inspector said. "Call me if you think of any detail that will help us find the killer of your friend." He tousled Demo's hair. Tossing away his barely drawn cigarette, the inspector left to follow a gurney that had arrived on the scene.

Demo lingered for a moment, reading the business card of Inspector Detective Alexander Trokalitis from Livadia. He didn't know what to do, worrying that he would get in trouble if he revealed what he knew. He had lost a good friend. Now he probably wouldn't be able to go to the National Museum to learn history. All the hope, the promises of a new life, popped like a busted balloon. He swabbed back tears as he sprinted back to the orphanage.

After Demo ran off, Inspector Trokalitis followed the ambulance attendants to remove the professor's body. He took a plastic bag from his inside coat pocket. Earlier, he had donned rubber gloves to examine the body and secure a number of coarse black hairs.

He mulled over the facts, lighting a cigarette while making his way up the hillside. A famous professor from the Archeological Museum digs in a remote area outside the museum in the middle of the night. The murderer strangles the professor, leaving boot prints, without heels, in ground softened by rain. That piqued his curiosity, for it reminded him of similar evidence, found at murder scenes near Turkey almost a year earlier. Additionally, there was blood and other tissue lodged under the professor's fingernails. Could it be matched by a technician? He could only hope. Aside from a shallow depression in the ground nearby, he had seen little else of note other than a broken light bulb.

He stamped out his cigarette. Rain began to fall. He looked up, breathing hard, but saw no clouds. He hurried to the professor's body, now covered in plastic.

Inspector Trokalitis recalled the last time he had seen Professor Popandreou, at the cocktail party fundraiser at the National Museum, a month before. He'd been terribly distracted by the presence of a stunning American woman. He couldn't take his eyes off her. The woman's husband didn't seem to be the kind of man that could command her. Trokalitis ruminated that only a real man, a real Greek man, could please such a woman. Then the married couple disappeared from the face of the earth. From his district. He worked many extra hours following leads. The woman's beauty tortured him. He could not imagine her dead.

The rain fell harder. Trokalitis grabbed the police photographer and led him towards the boot print. After only one picture, the evidence began to vanish as the boot prints deteriorated into muddy holes. Within the imprint of the murderer's foot, an island of mud took the shape of an eye: the evil eye.

Inspector Trokalitis took a step back. "How will I ever solve this one? Get that body out of here," he yelled at the ambulance crew. "We're already cursed with bad luck."

CHAPTER 57
DELPHI
OCTOBER 2011

OTHER MEANS OF COMMUNICATION

Lauren slipped in and out of sleep. She didn't have to feign exhaustion or hysterics.

She answered as few of the inspector's questions as possible. Then, after a light breakfast of bread and jam, the officer let them sleep in the station's duty bedroom. With the bed too small, Lauren took her pillow and blanket and slept on the floor. She had just drifted to sleep when she heard a phone ring and a one-sided conversation outside her door about a break-in at the orphanage and talk of a murder victim on the mountain. Lauren fell asleep again but awoke to the wail of an ambulance.

Cassandra opened an eye, but quickly fell back asleep. Unable to muster the energy to find out what had happened, Lauren joined her.

She was late for a lunch appointment. She tried to run, but her legs wouldn't obey. She rose a few feet off the ground and floated over the side streets of Athens. People looked up and pointed at her in wonderment. "Don't worry," she called out to them. "I really can't fly. It's just that I'm in a hurry."

She wondered if she should flap her arms like wings as she sailed into the Plaka, landing softly in front of the taverna where they had lunched with Professor P. She looked for him at his customary table and found it empty. In fact, there were no customers at all.

Lauren took a seat and unconsciously reached for her purse to see if she had any money. No purse. She searched under the table to see if she had dropped it. From under the edge of the white tablecloth, she saw shoes and pant legs, but had never heard anyone approach.

She lifted her head and bumped it on the table edge. "Zack, is that you?"

The waiter stood before her, grinning. Lauren breathed in his lemon-scented aftershave. "Oh, it's you. Calchas, wasn't it?"

Calchas smiled with his same perfect teeth and placed the heavy bronze bowl in front of her. "Try the hummus."

Lauren shivered. "Why is it freezing in here? I haven't been this cold since I went through that tunnel with Zack and we ended up…"

"Allow me to feed you. It will warm you, Golden Hair." He spoon-fed her and offered her drink from a silvery flask.

"I'm so hungry. Thanks…Wait. *Golden Hair?*"

Lauren looked into the waiter's deep blue eyes, the golden streaks emanating from the center of his pupils. She couldn't remove her gaze from them. Some recognition entered her thoughts, but she couldn't concentrate. The hummus warmed her.

"That is my name for you," Calchas said. "Now that you are satiated, perhaps we should talk."

"Aren't you going to sing a song?"

"I will tell you a story instead."

"Where's Professor Popandreou? Isn't he meeting us?"

Calchas sighed. "He will be unable to."

"That's too bad. Delayed at the museum?"

"He had an unfortunate appointment with eternity," Calchas said.

"What?" Lauren sat for a moment, shocked. "Wait, where's Zack? He wrote to me that he'd do whatever he could…" Her stomach suddenly felt heavy. Sweat broke out on her forehead. "What's happening to me?"

"Not long ago, I told you that you would need all your good humor."

The room started to spin slowly. She stood abruptly, confused and scared, but the dizziness brought her back down to the chair.

"Listen to me, Golden Hair. First, you must know that you are asleep. You are dreaming, but I will tell you the truth because you deserve it."

"Thank you. I was starting to worry I'd lost my mind."

"Dreams can be reality, or maybe what will come to be. I am sending this dream to you as a favor. Your Professor is dead. The beast, Bessus, killed him."

Lauren slumped in her chair. Her voice cracked. "Tell me it isn't true."

Mist began to rotate over Calchas's head as his features changed. His hair transformed from black to blond, and a long curl fell from the right side of his head. The gold chains and rawhide cord decorated his shirt, and twin bronze medallions gave off a blinking shine. She averted her eyes.

Then she fell out of her chair. "I saw one of those on the barbarian… Professor P. is dead?" She frantically crawled towards the door. "I can't stand any more of this."

"Wait, Golden Hair," Apollo commanded. "I know what it is you yearn for."

Lauren halted.

"And it is not just your husband. A child is what you truly seek. And it is a girl- child I have given you."

Lauren returned to the table. "Then you are Apollo. Zack told me about you, whatever you are. It's been you all along, messing up our lives." Her lip quivered. She set herself in the chair again.

"Did you know that what I've given you to drink and eat allows all of you to heal and survive the transit, too?" Apollo drew the hummus bowl back. "I choose to communicate in this way because I have more for you to do. You will be my warriors. You will save the future. Do not think you are alone, so we must save some of the hummus for another."

Apollo pointed at the bathroom door. When it opened, Zack emerged, bandages around his chest and legs. He took a few steps toward Lauren, but fell to one knee.

"Oh my god!" Lauren shrieked.

She dashed to Zack and ran her fingers over his face. "Are you real?"

He wrapped his arms around her and squeezed. "Oh Lauren…" Their lips met, assuring each other that this union was indeed happening.

"I never thought I'd see you again."

"Honey," he said, drawing back to look at her.

"You've been hurt?"

'I've been in the future, in 2016." He grimaced when Lauren helped him up. "The West is in trouble. Everything is going to be wiped out. I've seen it."

"Seen it, how?"

"Apollo showed me. I believe him. I believe in him. I stopped an initial attack in the future. That's how I got wounded, how I earned the chance to… see you, even for a short time."

"This is preposterous, Zack."

"Is it almost as preposterous as coming to you in a dream?"

"How can you believe in two Gods?"

"Maybe I can."

"What's he done to you?" She focused on Apollo, watching the reunion with his arms folded. "What kind of god would force you to worship him?"

Apollo said nothing.

"All I can tell you for sure is that we're under his control, as long as we live," Zack said.

Lauren drew back her lips. "Screw him, I've had enough."

She charged Apollo, but met a sponge-like wall of yellow light. It swallowed her, lifted her up, and laid her gently on the restaurant floor. She scrambled back to Zack, her voice trembling. "We're going back to San Diego with Cassandra, now… Oh no. Where is she?"

Zack whirled Lauren around and kissed her again, holding her lips to his. When he finally released her, he wore an anguished look. "You don't know. There's a major catastrophe coming."

"The young girl you speak of is asleep. I did not bring her to this dream," Apollo said. "But she has a destiny in this plan, too. You will not understand until later, but you must do everything in your power to ensure her safety."

Lauren shook her head. "I'm here. But I'm not?"

"Look, please," Zack interrupted her. "I have to tell you quickly." He read the confusion and the fear in her face and took a deep breath. "I can't stay with you, as much as I want to."

"This is nuts. We're not the property of some pagan god."

"I've work to do, maybe the most important work I'll ever do. I have been called to serve. So have you."

"He's my husband. He's not going!" Lauren blurted out, her voice shrill and nasty.

Zack wrapped his arms around her. "Honey, if we don't somehow alter the future, there may not be much to live for."

Lauren buried her head in his shoulder. "I saw your letter in the cave and I knew you were stuck in the past. You had journeys, many of them. I thought that maybe I would never see you again. Even now, if this *is* a dream, maybe that's still true."

"I never wrote letters to you."

"You did, and if you don't remember them, that means you must have stayed in the past and haven't written them yet." Lauren hung her head.

"You must all fight," Apollo said. "Gather those with the will to survive. I am telling you now a new Dark Age approaches. Its deadly embrace will destroy all you hold dear. That is your mission. Come, Traveler."

Lauren latched herself onto Zack. "Why do you want us?"

"I saw your professor with the villain, Saabir, in a photograph from your time. You are the Professor's students. You have the knowledge, the physical means and the presence of mind to do my work. And you are from the country that must be saved."

Apollo motioned for Zack to join him. "Dreams cannot be held forever in place. We must go."

"You know everything that's going to happen? And what exactly is this Book of Histories?" Lauren asked.

"I have come to you because I know what will occur. The Histories record the acts of man from the first settlements. The time is now to change the course of the future. Your nation cannot be allowed to fail. Those far less tolerant will fill the power vacuum. The suffering will go on for centuries. I have witnessed the suffering."

"So you mean the gods came back... to life?" Zack asked with a confused look, holding Lauren tightly.

Apollo exhaled, condescendingly. "Your husband succeeded in stopping the attack on Athens. The powder keg event is avoided, but the same forces that caused it remain. Traveler is to be congratulated. The future after 2016 is now alterable... though uncertain."

Zack broke in. "Lauren, you will not believe what's going to happen," he said, his words racing together. "You're still in 2011, but there's trouble coming and watch out for ..."

"Silence!" Apollo blared. "Reveal the future against my will and neither of you will live."

Lauren moved in front of Zack. "Wait, I'm sorry. I still don't understand. When did the gods ever care so much about mortals?"

"The hidden Book of Histories revealed to us how the free of spirit can thrive," Apollo said, raising his hands as if in prayer. "I yearn for the muses to brighten the lives of mortals once more, for the arts to flourish."

The god closed the door with a wave of his hand. "I want to return to when men had free thoughts, when each had the choice to control his own destiny. The young must work to insure their futures. It does no good to save virtual and fantasy worlds. You must save the *real* world."

He played the same moving picture on the wall that he did for Zack in the transit room. Lauren screamed and threw her hands over her face.

"I will not see darkness fall upon the enlightened as it did," Apollo said, his voice rising. "I will not allow long centuries to pass in a mournful wake of misery." He stabbed the air with his finger. "You must train harder. That is why you, Traveler, will live the glory and disaster that is ancient Greece and bring those lessons to your own time. I saw you give bread to the poor in Athens. I know you have compassion for the less fortunate. You just need tempering."

Apollo turned his steely gaze on Lauren. "That's why you, Golden Hair, must survive your own battles."

"But Bessus is dead," Lauren said to Zack. "We killed him in the cave, just before we were going to see what you left for us. He was on fire."

"Dead, finally," Zack said, his expression brightening. "Then you'll be safe, but I still don't understand how he can be in all these different times?"

Gravely, Lauren said, "Professor P. is dead too."

"No!" Zack staggered backwards, like he'd been socked in the jaw.

Apollo interrupted. "You'll have to mourn later and waste not your thoughts on the mysteries of the transit or of the sacred book. Concentrate instead on surviving, and know this: if you perish, I cannot bring back the dead." Apollo gestured with his hand. "Come with me now, Traveler."

Lauren grasped Zack's shirt with a death-like grip. "Let Cassandra and me go with him," she pleaded to Apollo. "We'll do this together. Be merciful."

"No," Apollo said with finality. "I will not have him distracted. He is returning to the Persian Wars. But, in time, you will see I am a benevolent god."

"Benevolent?" Lauren shot back. "You're forcing us to follow orders, and this is somehow benevolence? This is grudging obedience. This is slavery."

An irritated look crossed Apollo's face. "Come now. Have I not given both of you what you most desired?"

They looked at each other, surprised.

"It is a pity that neither of you have the same goals. Have I not sent you to dwell among the ancients, Traveler?" Apollo then turned to Lauren. "Do you not have the girl?"

This time, they regarded one another with equal measures of guilt.

"You cannot hide your innermost thoughts from me." Apollo said, moving towards the door. "Then, if you must be asked, I petition you to do my work willingly. Answer me now. The dream will not hold."

"We have to accept this. I'll find a way back to you, somehow," Zack said with a determined look.

"I'll be okay. Just hold me, sweetheart, one last time before you go." She gave him a long, luxurious kiss. *This is how Mom felt. She never knew if Dad would return to her.*

Apollo declared, "You, Golden One, will remember everything that transpired here. As I told you before, Traveler, you will remember none of this."

Lauren gave Apollo a dumbfounded look.

"It is not over for you either, Golden Hair. Did you mother suffer much less? Do any of your warrior's families suffer less? Hurry now."

He absolutely can read my thoughts. "I'll wait... I will," she told Zack, as if to burn the certainty of her commitment into him

She never knew if he heard her. His form disintegrated into a million particles of light, and he vanished, beyond her touch.

CHAPTER 58
DELPHI
OCTOBER 2011

REALITY

Lauren awoke on the floor, lying directly in the path of an overzealous air conditioner vent. She found the blanket off to her side, twisted and bunched up. She shivered and reached for it. Cassandra sighed, opened her eyes and searched for Lauren. Re-assured, the girl smiled and fell asleep again.

Lauren untangled the blanket and draped it over her.

That wasn't just a dream. My husband really is gone. All this is…real.

She glanced at Cassandra. This young girl has no idea of the challenges facing us. But, she has me.

Lauren lay on her back and stared at the ceiling. I have to get back into the cave and see what Zack left us. Maybe it will help me to get him back. Until then, if you can be strong, Zack… if my mother could, then so can I.

If I have to, I'll bring this girl up by myself.

CHAPTER 59

DELPHI

OCTOBER 2011

THE DOUR LADY

Apollo made his way slowly up the long stone stairway. He leapt to ground level at the spot where Beast squeezed the life from the museum professor, where Demo found the primitive recorder. *An event I did not foresee. This is your doing, Tyche.*

A shiver of vulnerability lanced through him. How much should I interfere? When shall I reveal the whole truth to them? When shall I tell them all that the Book of Histories holds?

Apollo scanned the topography of the mountains he loved so well, the gold flecks in his eyes expanding. The Traveler had come through. *You did save the Athens and the Parthenon. You preserved the greatest icon of Western culture. The Ionic columns will rise once again. There will be sculptured gods and giants painted with vivid colors on the metopes and pediments. Oh, what a glorious sight it will be! I vow I will never let the Parthenon suffer harm again.*

Now, Traveler, can you save your countrymen from self-destruction?

Aloud, he declared, "You, Tyche. I know you are near."

The wind howled its answer. His robe fluttered. The image of Tyche appeared from his medallions as the bells of a small herd of goats jingled during their morning walk.

"I love this life. I love Greece. It must be saved too," he cried out, watching the still-twinkling stars and the blossoming eastern horizon. "I want to be allies, dear lady. Would not the lives of men be blessed if fortune could be counted on to always be good? I urge you to bring a halt to uncertainty."

The wind blew harder and Tyche's image wobbled. "I know you will not agree to it," Apollo said, his voice somber. "You will confound me with events I cannot foresee. You will crack open the earth when it will hurt the most, or send a tempest to wash away a city. Parch the land when all are starved. Send men into an irrationality that will destroy them."

He exhaled a breath of total exasperation. "Maybe I look too unkindly upon your work, but it is your nature, and there is nothing I can do to change that. I crave order and you do not. You are the antithesis of me."

Apollo twirled his long curl. After a time, he secured it behind his ear. "Hear me well. I will teach the Greeks and the Western nations to govern themselves with the proper proportions of empathy and logic. I will safeguard civilization."

One of the goats hobbled over to him, favoring a bad leg. The goat stared at him and the image of the goddess. Apollo gave it a small piece of his bread. "The lovers of freedom will be preserved as the leaders of nations, because I have seen from far ahead of now, that there is no alternative to it," he said.

The goat munched on the lucky meal. Apollo manipulated the injured leg and cleaned a festering wound with dribbles from his flask. "I know, little one. Now rejoin your friends."

The goat stretched its bad leg and shook it. After locking eyes with Apollo, as if to thank him, he pranced away on four good legs.

Apollo grinned, toggling his medallion, but the image of Tyche stubbornly remained. "How can this be? Leave me, Tyche," he blurted out, staring at her likeness. Then as if listening to her, he cried out, "You say that the westerners brought this upon themselves and I want too much power over their fate?"

His voice took on a menacing tone. "All is in order now. You'll ruin everything I've accomplished?"

Tyche maintained an emotionless countenance. Apollo's face bore the ugly expression of angst. Finally, he declared, "I see. The nature of life itself will be altered if I am allowed full control. Order and disorder are what keep existence in balance."

His eyes widened and he brought his hand to his mouth. He shook his fist at her. "What have you done? You've distracted me!"

Her image disappeared from his medallion. He let out a long, agonizing cry. "Now I must hurry, or all may be lost."

CHAPTER 60
DELPHI
OCTOBER 2011

RESCUE

Apollo emerged from the cave, holding a smoldering Bessus in his arms. He laid him aside and reset the entrance with stones, though none so heavy or set so tightly that a deserved re-entry could not be made. While carrying Bessus away, he stopped at the stream and regained the warrior's armor and satchel, not noticing the bronze armband lying amid rocks within the stream.

From the medallions, the dome regenerated. Apollo filled it with nurturing emulsions. Once they were inside, the dome left a yellow trail as it streaked towards the secret entryway below the twin peaks.

"You may need more than one dose of the ambrosia, Stink-Pile, to restore you to serviceable form," he said to Bessus. "Not that you deserve it, but I need you. Fortunately for you, I arrived in time, for Tyche plotted to let you expire and ruin all I have accomplished."

Arriving above the steps, the dome dissipated. Apollo eyed the unconscious warrior at his feet. Already, Bessus' burnt tissue and charred bone had begun to heal. Singed hair fell from him in clumps. His dagger wounds closed from the inside out. Only a few burn marks and the crisscrossed facial scars remained.

"I cannot make you too beautiful, Bessus, and ruin what you are. Only I have come to understand that your simple mind is predictably cruel for reasons of your own."

Satisfied with his "surgery", Apollo dressed him in the bull-hide armor. He opened the warrior's leather satchel and withdrew Lauren's California driver's license. "You will need this to perform an important errand for me." He returned the license to the satchel and slung it over Bessus's shoulder. "You must live… for now." *Was it not he who set much of this in motion for me in America?*

Apollo reformed the dome around Bessus and pointed at the stairway. He smirked. "How confused you must be by all the twists that have come your way." The dome floated down the stairwell. "You are still my servant, and yet, you have your own destiny. I will not deny you that right."

The dome entered the portal. A deafening cyclone of motion and mud commenced. With a flash, the active transit swallowed Bessus.

A last glance at Parnassus' commanding twin peaks and the sacred ruins of Delphi brought Apollo a satisfied devotion. He descended the stairway. "I'm warning you, Tyche; I will fight in a way you're not prepared for." The earth shook as the portal opened. "I have discovered that order is not enough to counter your disorder. I need stronger virtues to continue the fight."

He thought back on the final moments between Traveler and Golden Hair. "Only compassion and love are powerful enough to see through disaster. I will come back at you armed with them, too, because it is not over for me, it's not over for you, it's not over for anyone."

The spinning mud reached out to him. He could go back to save Rome, or even Periclean Athens. *No. The time to act is the present time. The West must be secured.*

A thin spindle of tunnel matter curled itself around the bluish dome. Cold and dense, the roar of eons embedded in its swirls, Apollo was swallowed willingly into the transit.

Victory will be mine. I plan and am committed to this sacred mission. You, Tyche, on the other hand, will not best me because you cannot deny your true nature and must leave everything ultimately to a throw of the dice... to chance.

Together, those with the will to fight will change the course of history for the better. It is your dual fates, Traveler and Golden Hair, to suffer and struggle until you can serve. Destiny or free will – argue it either way. Nevertheless, we will make that stand together.

THE END OF BOOK ONE

GLOSSARY

GREEKS

Achaia	Northern district of the Peloponnesus, next to Gulf of Corinth
Acropolis	Rocky prominence in central Athens, citadel containing the Parthenon
Apollo	God of sun, light, music, medicine, and archery
Artemisium	Bay near Thermopylae, site of important sea battle
Athena	Goddess of wisdom, armed protector of city-states
Athens	Capital city-state of the Athenians
Calchas	A prophet of the past, present and future. Apollo in disguise.
Cassandra	Daughter of Persephone, niece of Nestor
Cerberus	Fierce dog that guards the entrance to Hades
Chiton	Ankle or knee-length garment made of linen or wool
Delphi	Site of ancient temples, 100 miles northwest Athens
Demeter	Goddess of the earth, agriculture
Euboea	Long island that shields the eastern coast of Greece
Hades	Where the dead dwell in Greek mythology
Harpies	Winged feminine creatures with sharp claws and beaks
King Leonidas	One of two kings of the Spartans
Marathon	Site of battle between Persia and Athenians in 490 BCE

Mt. Athos	Site of canal constructed by Persians in Chalcidice, Thrace
Nestor	Architect, brother-in-law of Persephone
Parthenon	Ancient temple built on the Acropolis, dedicated to Athena
Peloponnese	Large peninsula of Southern Greece, connected to mainland by a strip of land near Corinth.
Penteconter	Smaller naval vessel
Persephone	Mother of Cassandra, wife of deceased Theseus
Phocis	District of Greece, near Thermopylae
Poylas	Athenian naval liaison to the Spartans
Salamis	A small island near Athens. Site of important sea battle in 480 BCE
Sparta	Militaristic city–state, situated in Peloponnese
Themistocles	Leader of the Athenians
Trireme	Three-banked fighting naval vessel
Thermopylae	The "Hot Gates", strategic pass in northern Greece
Theseus	Nestor's brother, late husband of Persephone, died in battle at Marathon
Thessaly	Northern Greece, north of Thermopylae
Zeus	Father of the Greek gods

PERSIANS

Angra-Mainyu	Evil spirit, opposes Ahura Mazda
Ahura Mazda	The good and wise god of the Zoroastrian religion
Bactria	Far eastern province of Persian Empire, includes modern day Afghanistan

Bessus	Prince from Bactria
Cambyses	Cyartes' replacement, Apollo in disguise
Cyartes	Bessus' second in command
Daevas	Evil agents or "devils" of Angra Mainyu
Hydarnes	General of the Immortals
Mardonius	Marshal of the Persian invasion force
King Cambyses II	Persian King from 528-521 BCE, son of Cyrus the Great
King Cyrus	Persian King from 559-529 BCE, founder of the Empire
King Darius	Persian King from 521-485 BCE
King Xerxes	Persian King from 485-465 B.C.E., Son of Darius
Zoroaster	Prophet of Mazda religion, one true God, good spirit
Zoroastrianism	Dualist religion of the ancient Persians

Made in the USA
San Bernardino, CA
30 November 2013